TOWER ABBEY

TOWER ABBEY

A NOVEL OF SUSPENSE
BY

Isabelle Holland

Rawson Associates Publishers, Inc.
New York

Library of Congress Cataloging in Publication Data
Holland, Isabelle.
Tower Abbey.
I. Title.
PZ4.H735To   [PS3558.03485]   813'.5'4   77–77889
ISBN: 0–89256–028–2

Rawson Associates Publishers, Inc.
630 Third Avenue
New York, New York 10017

For the memory of my mother, Corabelle Anderson Holland,
who once lived in a house called Tower Abbey,
and for the little boy, my brother, Philip, who invented
the land and people of Bulzartgay

TOWER ABBEY

1

I thought at the time it was one of those unexplained and un-explainable coincidences that change lives.

I was coming out of Saks Fifth Avenue, where I had bought what had been advertised as a "simple little all-purpose dress" that had cost the earth and taken an ominously large chunk out of my associate editor's salary. But the dress had done worlds for my figure—which needed all the help it could get—so I decided to ignore the parsimonious nag who lived inside me. My morale, I told myself, needed the boost. The promotion I had expected had not come through. Neither had the raise. Not, I was assured, through any fault of my own, but for reasons stemming from corporate decisions about departmental expenses. I was not the only one. The same corporate decisions had blighted the ambitions of everyone in the same department. As my boss, himself disappointed, said gloomily, this is what happened when a large corporation bought a small publishing house.

But a job was a job. Rent was rent. I still had to live and

provide for Seth and Susan, my Siamese cats; Pandora, a stray mutt I had recently acquired; Archie and Alix, a pair of gerbils; and Wisteria, a black and white rabbit. There were also Nicholas and Alexandra, who lived in an aquarium, and the tortoises, Anthony and Cleopatra, who had their terrarium.

Which probably explained why I was finding my studio apartment a little crowded. To make matters worse, my lease was running out, and when I signed a new one, if I signed a new one, the rent would automatically go up twelve and a half percent. The raise I had been promised was—when I was feeling optimistic—going to provide for a move to a one-bedroom apartment in another apartment building, my current dream. When my optimism was more modest, I was willing simply to settle for a larger studio. But the move, an expense in itself regardless of what accommodation I could find, had gone abruptly from a dream to an immediate probability, pushed by the growing warfare between the owners of the apartment house and the tenants. The lives of the latter were being made increasingly uncomfortable for reasons that had not yet become clear—an unhappy state common enough in New York City.

So the dress was a budgetary calamity I was still trying to find an acceptable excuse for when, as I maneuvered my package through the door to the street, I cannoned into someone trying to come in and nearly dropped the box.

"Sorry," I said automatically, my mind on the precious box and therefore not paying attention.

"Candida," a voice said. "Candida Brown."

I felt, rather than saw, several heads glance towards me. It was that kind of a name, the result of a mother who had nurtured a strong admiration for the plays of George Bernard Shaw. Then I turned and saw the person who had spoken.

"Diana!" I said.

There was no reason why there should have been such a surprise in my voice. The Diana Egremonts of this world shopped as easily at Saks as I did at the dime store.

Her next words really did stop me in my tracks.

"It was meant," she said.

4

"Meant what?"

She put her hand on my arm. "Come out where people won't fall over us."

Diana was taller than I, and though very slender, quite strong. I found myself outside Saks and backed up against one of their plate-glass windows.

I disliked being handled. My natural orneriness asserted itself. I stepped a few feet from the window. "I have to get back," I said, wondering if Diana knew if such a thing as a lunch hour existed.

"Of course. I didn't mean to push you around like this, only you seemed the answer to a prayer."

"Oh." A light dawned. "You meant 'meant' in that sense."

"Yes." She stared at me. The way we were standing, her back was to the sunlight and her face in shadow. Then she said, "Do you really have to get back this minute? Could you stretch the time to a drink or coffee or something? Please?"

I suppose it was the tone in her voice that carried such a sense of urgency. I hesitated. It was true I hadn't eaten. Snatching a sandwich and coffee had been included in my statement about having to get back.

"Well," I temporized, "I was going to get a fast sandwich in the coffee shop over there."

"Come to the Silver Spoon instead. It's right down the street."

Dim memories of ancient wrongs wafted through my mind. Diana always did like being general in charge of telling people what to do.

"I'd rather not, Diana. For one thing it's too expensive. And for another, restaurants like that take too long."

"The lunch is on me. And I promise you they have cold buffet there. You can go up and serve yourself and be gone as fast as you could at the counter. Or almost. And what I want to talk to you about needs to be said privately."

When I still hesitated, she said that magic word again, "Please."

I suppose it was the sheer incongruity of having Diana Egremont plead for anything that got to me.

5

"All right," I said. And then, because it sounded ungracious, "Thanks. But," I finished firmly, "I really can't stay too long."

For all the exotically dim lighting in the quiet plushness of one of Manhattan's better restaurants, I saw Diana's face clearly for the first time, and I got a shock.

Like her wealth and blue-blooded family background, Diana's extraordinary beauty had been part of the immense distance that I always saw as lying between her life and mine, even though we were brought up within a few miles of each other. There was also, of course, the difference in age, some twelve years, which made her now thirty-eight to my twenty-six.

But thirty-eight, for a woman nowadays, was the prime of life—in many ways, the peak of her attractiveness. And Diana had the kind of bones and body that would improve with age, rather than diminish. But something, I thought, staring at the fine features, was missing.

"Yes," she said, as though reading my mind. "I'm not looking my best. I know."

"I'm sorry," I mumbled, embarrassed. And then, deciding I might as well be honest, "You couldn't look anything but beautiful, Diana. You don't need me to tell you that. But you don't look..." I groped around for the right word and, to my surprise, found it. "You don't look happy."

She stared at me and then laughed. "You always did have the facility of putting your finger on the nub of things. It hasn't made you noted for your tact, of course...." Her voice trailed off. She looked down for a minute at the huge menu the waiter had put in front of her. "Do you remember that collie?" she said.

"Yes." I remembered the gold and white coat, and the look of uncomprehending pain in the brown eyes. "Yes," I said, reacting to an old anger. "I do."

"Your father said he was dying of an advanced case of several polysyllabic diseases. You were helping Dr. Brown, then, in his surgery, after school. Do you remember what you said?"

6

She looked up at me questioningly.

"Yes, I do. I said he'd been neglected to death."

"Since I rather fancied myself as an animal lover in those days, I wasn't at all pleased with your comment."

"I remember that, too."

I had good reason to. My father, gentle and unaggressive, had come home later that same evening with a look on his tired face that made me ask, "What did she do?"

He had looked at me. "Do? Nothing really."

"Then what did she say?"

When my father still didn't answer I remember stamping my foot. "What did she say? She must have said something. I know it, because of the way you're looking."

He picked up the evening paper. "She just pointed out that if the Egremonts withdrew their patronage, and let it be known among their friends that they had done so, then what was left of a practice among the villagers with their dogs and cats would hardly keep a veterinarian in drugs, let alone supply a living." My father lowered his paper. "And I told her that I would be sorry to lose her patronage, and that of her friends. But that there was always room somewhere for a vet, and that everything you'd said was one hundred percent true."

I hugged him after that, worried as I was. "You have the courage of lions," I said.

My father hugged me back. "Much as I hate it," he remarked dryly, "I have to give the devil her due. Diana paused long enough after I'd said that to make me wonder which city I'd better try first. Then she said, 'You're absolutely right. And so was Candida.' And she turned on her heel and left."

Not as tolerant as my father, I had not been that eager to give the devil her due. And it took me a while to admit that, along with her arrogance and the kind of looks that made any female of any age who was around her feel outclassed, Diana Egremont also had her own sort of courage, the kind that looked an unpleasant fact in the face and accepted it.

That had been eleven years before, when I was fifteen. My father was now dead. The plans that we—he and I—had made for my going to veterinary school after college and eventually helping him in his practice suffered a total setback, because the money that he had always said had been set aside for my medical training turned out, when his will was probated, not to be there. It was only with the aid of scholarships offered me by my father's old college on the West Coast that I was able to take my undergraduate degree out there. After graduating, I stayed in the West and found a job with the press division of the local wildlife service.

And Diana? Eleven years before, she had just ended her brief second marriage. Four years after that my father succumbed to a heart attack and I left the district. In between those two milestones there had been, for Diana, a third marriage, a wedding I had every reason to remember. . . .

"You were right about my poor collie," Diana said now.

I put down the menu. When one's accustomed lunch is tuna fish on rye, being confronted by a list of six kinds of sole, all in French, can erode the powers of decision.

"What do you want me to be tactless about now?" I asked.

She glanced up to see the waiter, pad in hand, hovering. "What do you want to eat, Candida? Do you want to go to the buffet?"

I don't know really what made me say it. But I heard the astonishing words come out of my mouth. "A tuna fish sandwich on rye."

"But . . . mademoiselle," the waiter said.

Diana looked up at him. "Well, you heard her. A tuna fish sandwich on rye." She glanced back at me. "With coffee?"

"Yes," I said, fighting an overwhelming desire to giggle. "Thank you."

"And I'll have a Scotch and water," Diana said.

Probably, I thought, feeling almost sorry for the waiter, the Silver Spoon would accept her gross insult to its *haute cuisine*, whereas if I had been alone, someone would have sent for the bouncer, if there was one.

"Yes, it's all right. I know the owner," Diana said.

"I thought you probably did."

We paused as the waiter came back with her drink. Then I reworded my question. "What do you want me to do, Diana?"

8

She took a deep breath. "I was going to lead up to this, making it so irresistible you couldn't possibly say no." She looked down at her glass, moving it in slow circles around the white damask tablecloth. Then the magnificent eyes came up. "What I want, Candida, is for you to give up your present job for another—to come and live with me for a while at Tower Abbey."

I was so stunned, I could think of nothing to say, and simply stared back at her. It was at this point that the waiter placed in front of me a dish bearing the *haute cuisine*'s version of the lowly tuna on rye.

"Is that all right, mademoiselle?"

He sounded so anxious that it broke my trance. I glanced down at the towering mound of tuna inside the dark bread. "Fine," I said, anxious for him to stop worrying. "Thanks a lot."

But after he left I forgot about my sandwich and went on staring at Diana. Finally, I could think of no way to answer her except with my usual lack of finesse.

"No," I said. "I won't. But I will admit I'm curious. Why do you want me? Me, of all people?"

"Why you of all people? Because you're not family, or old family friend or a hanger-on. . . . Because around me and people like me you've always been honest—many people I know call it rude. And because I trust you."

"You mean to say that out of all that staggering number of people you know, from the studbooks here and abroad, I'm the only one you trust? I must say, that's some kind of social comment with a message." Deciding that the sandwich would be best consumed in small pieces, I cut off one end.

"It isn't that I don't know anyone else who is trustworthy in a general sort of way. It's just that . . ." She took a breath. "It's just that in a specific way . . . you would be the most help."

"Well, I'm sorry, I can't," I said, not sorry at all. "I have a perfectly good, if underpaid, job at the moment, in a field I like, and I'm not about to give it up for something that is obviously temporary. Besides, I have dependents."

She frowned. "Oh—I'm sorry. I should have asked, of course. Somehow I didn't think you'd married, let alone had children."

That comment didn't help my morale either. People always assume I'm not married. And while nowadays that doesn't carry quite the blight that I gather it used to, still, it says something about the way I look that I've always deplored.

"I'm not married," I said. "But I still have dependents."

"I see."

I could almost see visions of illegitimate offspring parading through her head, and waited, taking a certain malicious pleasure in not enlightening her.

But what she said was, "I thought you were going to be a vet."

"That didn't work out."

There was another pause. I finished one half of my expensive sandwich and said, "You still haven't told me why you want me to come and live with you."

"Since you have flatly refused, I see no reason to bother you further."

That was much more like the old Diana and, because arrogant, made me feel better about my terse refusal. Then I looked at her. The shadows under her famous aqua eyes were like carriage sweeps. Even to me, with the envy of the sturdily built for those of willowy frame, she was too thin. There were lines around her mouth. She looked tired, middle-aged, defeated—and frightened. I found myself, surprised, adding the last word. But I knew it was true.

At that inconvenient moment another scene from our common past came to my mind: Diana driving me to a neighboring vet's in defiance of all speed limits, the still body of my cat, Moo, in my lap. Father was away at a vets' conference. Moo didn't make it, but Diana had done her best.

"What's the matter, Diana?" I asked more gently.

And there, in that fashionable restaurant, with the soft lighting and hovering waiters, she started to cry. She was quiet about it, her slender hands up over her face, wiping away the tears. And in a minute or two she had herself back together.

"I'm sorry." The long hands that I had always admired and envied shook a little as she lit a cigarette. "I've given these up," she said dryly. "In case you hadn't noticed. But lately . . . I've started carrying them again."

I sat there, unable to think of anything to say, more shocked than I would have believed possible by Diana's breaking down. Her careless strength and fortitude had always been so much a part of the patrician grace that I had looked up to and resented.

"I think," Diana said, "I'll have a refill." And she turned and made a sign to the waiter, who hurried over. "Another of these," she said crisply. "A double this time."

We sat there in an uncomfortable silence until it arrived. I could still think of nothing to say, and Diana was staring down at her empty glass. Irritation that I was going to be late returning to the office fought in me with compassion. Her tears had gone, but the bleak look on her face made it impossible for me to abandon her.

After the waiter had brought her double, she picked up the glass and took a swallow. "Don't worry," she said suddenly. "I'm not about to get drunk and embarrass you."

"It wouldn't embarrass me," I said. And it wouldn't. What other people did had never been a great problem for me. One of my teachers at school had said it was because I was insensitive. Another said it was because I had an unusual degree of psychological independence. You could take your choice.

"If you hate being there so much," I said, "why are you going back to Tower Abbey?"

"For three reasons, I guess," Diana answered. "Because it's cheaper living there than paying a hotel or renting an apartment, and because I think that if I am, so to speak, in residence, it's easier to deal with offers. I've had two," Diana added. "Low ones, to be sure. But what else could you expect in today's market? Who wants a thirty-room mansion when servants are practically unobtainable? I had hoped . . ." Her voice trailed off.

"Hoped what?" I inquired after a minute.

11

"Oh, that a foundation of some kind, with lots of money, would buy it for a think tank, or something."

"Don't you have a lot of money anyway?" I asked with my usual delicacy and tact.

She looked at me and smiled then. "Much less than you'd think, Candida. I'm not welfare poor. But I'm far from rich right now. And I'm in debt."

Another silence. Finally I asked, "What's the third reason?"

She took a deep breath. "Because I think I'm going out of my mind—either that or I've got to find proof of something that happened that nobody told me about." She paused and shook her head. "I don't even know how to say this without sounding insane, a candidate for the funny farm." She stopped again, then went on in a flat voice. "There's something going on there. Either the house, or I, or both is being . . . haunted —for want of a better word. And I can't bear to be alone."

Diana was right about my thinking she'd taken leave of her senses. If she had not been so plainly distressed it would have been ludicrous. But as the word "haunted" echoed and re-echoed in my mind, it gradually became less bizarre and more aptly descriptive of something I saw in her eyes.

"Haunted by what?" I asked finally.

"Sometimes I think . . . I don't really know." Then, after a pause, "Did you ever hear at any time that I had a twin sister?"

"No. Did you?"

"That's what I don't know."

"What a strange thing not to know."

"Yes. Isn't it!" Diana agreed bleakly.

I stared at her, groping back in my mind for anything I'd heard about the Egremonts. In a sense, villagers like ourselves knew a great deal about the Egremonts, as we did about other great families of the upper Westchester area, such as the Barringtons or the Grants. That is, we knew the scandals, marriages, births, divorces and any other tidbits, disreputable and otherwise, that filtered down to our level through the servant and shopkeeper route, through the local and metropolitan newspapers, and through what could only be called the village tom-toms. Somehow when an Egremont, or a Barrington or a Grant, ended up in a divorce court or a drunk tank or with his hand in some corporate till, everybody in the village knew about it before it hit the papers or television. Surely, I thought now, if Diana, an adored only child, had had a twin sister, I would have known.

"And you think it's a possible twin sister who's haunting you?" I asked, playing along for the moment.

Diana took another swallow of her drink. "I told you it sounded crazy."

"Well, if you did have one—a twin sister—what happened to her?"

"I don't know. Obviously whatever happened to her happened before I could remember."

"What is it that makes you think she existed?"

"That's . . . that's what all of this, everything I've tried to explain, is about. Aside from the pleasure of your company— and it would be more than a pleasure, it would save my sanity—I'd like an outside objective opinion."

I shook my head. "I'm sorry," I said, and was.

I could almost see her withdraw. She stared down at her glass, which, I noted, was once again empty. And I became aware of a long-forgotten dread. My father, whom I loved very much, had had serious trouble with alcohol towards the end of his life. In a minute, I thought, she'd order another drink.

"I have to get back," I said. "I'm terribly late, and we have a new broom at the office who sits around with a stopwatch." Which, I thought grimly, was all too true. Our new office manager, who came with the compliments of the multinational corporation that had acquired us, took a poor view of the more relaxed attitudes towards time customary in most publishing houses.

"I'll pay you if you'll come to the Abbey with me," Diana said again. "And," she continued, as I opened my mouth, "before you get on your high, independent horse, please remember that this is neither patronage nor a bribe. It's a salary."

"Diana," I said pleasantly, because, after all, she had no

13

power over me and I had no intention of acceding to her request, "at the moment I'm an associate editor in a publishing house that is fairly small and has not been too successful lately, but has recently been bought and may pick up with some new money behind it." Then I took a breath and went on. "It may not seem much to you, and the pay would probably not keep you for a day. Still, I'm quite good at it. So I'm sure you can see why I wouldn't even consider a job as somebody's companion. Thank you anyway."

"What kind of editor?" Diana asked, ignoring the last part of what I said.

"I'm a project editor on a natural-life series. As a pre-vet student I majored in biology, and when I couldn't go on to veterinary school I took a job with the press division of the local wildlife service out there on the Coast and later up in Alaska."

"I remember hearing you left the East and went out West to school. Why there?"

"When Father died and the money gave out I was offered a scholarship there that took me through undergraduate school. After that came the job with the wildlife service there and in Alaska. Then I joined a museum research team in the Caribbean and through that worked with one of the editors of my publishing house. When they decided to do this natural-life series for the high school level, they asked me to come on the staff."

Diana smiled. "So if you can't be a vet and work with animals, you'll edit books about them—or maybe even do one of your own."

I'd forgotten that Diana could be both bright and shrewd. Barely in time did I prevent myself from saying that that indeed had become a dream of mine—to write books on animals and live in the country where I could take in as many strays as I wanted. There was no need, I thought, to give Diana more arguments for her case. Instead I got up. "I'm sorry, Diana, but I do have to go. I hope you find somebody and . . . and lay your ghost."

14

She looked up at me, "Whatever your salary is, Candida, I'll double it."

I stared down at her, angered by her open attempt to buy me. "I told you," I said. "I'm not for sale."

I expected her to be insulted. Instead, she just continued looking at me, as though she could read something in the back of my head. "Do you believe in ghosts?" she asked.

I shook my head. "No. Absolutely not."

She smiled then. "I didn't think you did. I remember your father's views on the subject. They were quite strong."

They were indeed. My father was, with great impartiality, against all churches. The Judeo-Christian religious teaching, he always said, had no place for animals in its scheme of things, and he blamed some seven thousand years of the wanton killing of animals on all the teachers going back through the calendar of saints, through the prophets, to Abraham. To the Eastern religions he was, theoretically, less hostile, but since there were no practitioners of Zen or the Hindu teachings in our neck of Westchester, his views on them remained academic. One result of all this throughout his life was his strong and often pungently expressed opposition to the concept of the supernatural in any form, an opposition I inherited.

"If you should change your mind," Diana said now, "I'll be at the Plaza Hotel for the next week."

As I scurried back to the office, it occurred to me that if she could offer to double my salary and stay at the Plaza, her idea of having no money was far removed from mine. My definition of that unhappy state meant, specifically, that I could not pay the next month's rent, and had to sit around waiting for Con Edison to turn off the electricity for lack of payment of bills.

But perhaps, as Diana said, it was meant.

When I got back to the office I found a note on my desk summoning me to an editorial meeting that had been called for two o'clock. The fact that it was now two forty meant that I had missed a large part of it.

15

Pushing my dress box behind the file, I took off my coat, combed my hair and fled to the meeting, and discovered that the axe had fallen in my absence. The natural-life series, which had not sold as well during the first year as the sales department had predicted, was to be—temporarily, I was assured—discontinued.

Profoundly aware that my not being there had not helped my cause, I pleaded and argued for the series to continue through another two books, both of which were in the planning stage, which would take another year. I pointed out that since books of this nature were mostly purchased by public and school libraries, who bought on the strength of reviews, any real sales would not show for at least another nine months; that the series had to put out a few more books before we could really see how well it would do. I was backed up in this by my boss and two of the local salesmen. But the figures were against us, and we might as well have saved our breath.

"By the way, Miss Brown," the office manager said as the meeting came to an end fifteen short minutes after I had come in, "what are your usual lunch hours? This memo was delivered shortly after twelve—as a matter of fact I delivered a few of the copies, including yours, myself—so I thought two a reasonable hour to expect everyone to be back."

Dead silence. Then there was a loyal outburst from my fellow workers, in which the words "agents," "authors," "editorial lunches," seem to drop in no particular order.

"I see," said the office manager, whose name should have been Legree or Himmler, but was actually Smith. "And which author or agent were you entertaining?" He stood up, a thin man with a thin mouth and thin slitty eyes and probably a thin mind, I thought to myself.

"None," I heard my voice say, rather to my horror. "I went shopping." And I walked out of the room.

"That was noble but rather dim-witted," my boss, Jerry Cohen, commented as we walked down the hall. "We were all trying to save your bacon."

"I know. Thanks. But I was furious. And not just over the lunch hour. He had a point there, damn him! Over the books.

Once they get accepted in the schools they'll make money for the firm hand over fist."

"I know. But he's got his files, his figures and his ideas. They're not going to work with books, but it'll take a few seasons for him, and Mother Corporation, to catch on. We'll get the books back, Candy, don't worry."

"But I was brought in to do them. I don't really have any qualifications to be any other kind of editor."

"You've done a beautiful job! You've written half the books that are already out, and they're very well written. If you don't believe me, look at the reviews."

"Thanks."

He gave me a buffet on the back as I wheeled off into my office. He was a kind man who grew up before the emotional revolution, and still didn't know how to express his affectionate impulses.

Things got worse.

When I arrived home I found a note from the super in my mailbox. He would like to come and see me that evening. Would I please call him to suggest an hour?

Since the super was someone who had an ability, amounting to genius, not to be there when one needed him, I read this note with a sinking stomach. In view of the more or less ongoing state of war between us—the tenants—and the landlord, I knew it did not bode good. To pick up any information I could about new developments in the apartment house that I might not be aware of, I knocked on the door of my next-door neighbor before going to my own. Terry O'Connor was a freelance writer who worked at home and who was therefore usually more knowledgeable about the nuances and stresses surrounding our current problem.

"It's probably something to do with the apartment house being on the point of being bought," she said when she came to the door. "The new buyer-to-be would like most of the tenants out, so they can renovate the place just enough to be able to slap a whopping new raise on to the rent. I've drawn up a petition. Will you sign it?"

She disappeared back into her apartment before I had a

17

chance to answer and reappeared with a piece of paper consisting of two standardized sheets Scotch-taped together. "Here you are. Here's a pen."

I stared at the pen being held out to me. "Look, Terry, I have an Achilles heel. My animals. When I first moved in they had that clause in the lease about no pets. I said I wouldn't sign it. But the super said it was just there in case some tenant had a monster dog that went mad and ran around biting people, and that it would never be invoked. I needed a place fast, I didn't have any pets then, so I talked myself into believing him and signed it."

"You were an idiot," Terry said unemotionally. "They've got you right where you operate."

I stared at her. "The super wants to talk to me. Let me find out what's on his mind before I sign that."

"Okay. But I'll bet you anything it's about your animals."

She was right.

I got home and greeted the animal kingdom and went around checking on the cages and habitats. Seth and Susan, the male and female Siamese cats; Pandora, the somewhat golden retriever; and Wisteria, the rabbit, pretty much ran free, although Wisteria would retreat to his open cage most of the time when I wasn't there—or so various visitors told me—and was good about using his cage for his bathroom needs. All four were lined up at the door when I opened it, the Siamese bellowing in their unmistakable voices, and Pandora leaping around and barking. Wisteria would simply hop on one of my feet and stay there as long as I was willing to stand in one place.

Picking Wisteria up, I greeted the tortoises, the fish and Mr. and Mrs. Gerbil, then passed on to the next important item, which was to take Pandora out for a walk.

The trouble was that Pandora's idea of a suitable walk grew longer as she got larger. A ball of tow-colored fluff when I adopted her from the Humane Society, she was now the height of my hip, and at nine months still had some growing left to do. A brisk trot around the block was nowhere near enough to sate her rambunctious energy. Fortunately, the apartment was near Riverside Park, where I ran with her for nearly an hour most mornings and took her for a short run before dinner.

Thirty minutes later I panted back to the apartment house, with Pandora charging beside me, not even breathing heavily. With the luck characteristic of the entire day, I ran into the super as I was closing the front door.

"What time should I come up tonight, Miss Brown?" he asked, plunging *in medias res* and without bothering to say good evening.

I have never been one who endured anxiety well. "What did you want to see me about, Mr. Ferro?"

He looked down at Pandora, who, with a lack of discrimination bordering on the insane, was leaping affectionately around him. "There's been complaints," he said ominously.

"Oh. What about?" Not that I didn't know.

"About them animals you keep. The neighbors say that the dog's barking disturbs them."

"Pandora only barks when my doorbell rings—which any good guard dog should—and when I'm just about to take her out."

"The neighbors—"

"And you can hardly say I shouldn't have a guard dog, not after the two robberies we had a few weeks ago."

"Your place wasn't broken into."

"Because of Pandora here."

His face settled into deeper lines of obstinate gloom. I had won that battle, but I could see he wasn't about to concede the war. "The neighbors say they can smell all those cages you have."

"That's nonsense, and you know it. They're cleaned out every day. What's behind this, Mr. Ferro?"

"Look," he said. "Why don't you find yourself another place—a bigger place, where you'll have room for all them creatures?"

"So that the people who are dickering for this house can slap another coat of paint on the walls, put in a couple of new stoves and decontrol the rents?"

19

"I'm just doing my job." He spoke the immortal words of those driven to the wall. "But my job is to tell you that you're going to have to get rid of those animals."

"Over my dead body, Mr. Ferro. You can just take me to court."

"We'll do that, Miss Brown." His voice rose. "You signed that lease, you know you did. I got your signature saying we could make you get rid of your pets."

"You told me that was just a matter of routine, and only if some animal went mad and bit people."

By this time he had retreated to his own door at the back of the hall. "I'm tellin' you, Miss Brown. For your own good. You better get rid of them." He shouted the words, probably, I thought, to make up for the fact that he knew just how crooked and phony the whole thing was and felt guilty about it.

But as I climbed the steps with Pandora leaping up in front of me, I discarded the idea of his feeling guilty. Nothing about him had ever indicated he had that much conscience.

"What did I tell you?" Terry said when I got to the top.

"I suppose you heard."

"The whole apartment house heard—witnesses to be called that he has given you so-called fair warning. You want to sign that petition?"

Well, I thought, the animals could not be in more trouble than they were already. "All right. Where's your pen?"

She produced it from her hand like a magician and I signed. "Do you think it will do any good?"

"Where can we go from this point but up?"

"I wonder how long I have."

"Just as long as it takes a smart lawyer employed by the prospective buyer to get some kind of court order, I should think."

"Well, I could get a lawyer, too."

"Do you know one?"

Mentally I went rapidly through my entire list of acquaintances and friends in New York. "No."

"Well, you'd better start looking either for a lawyer or a new apartment, and pretty fast."

20

The state of my morale degenerated as the evening wore on. Terry was a born fighter, picketer and protester, and, I suspected, enjoyed the battle for its own sake. I didn't. Temperamentally, I was unsuited to long warfare. And then there were the animals, my Achilles heel, as I so rightly called them. With me at the office all day and a determined and unscrupulous landlord with a passkey, how sure could I be of their safety? It was true, of course, that if I came home and found any mishap had befallen them—such as wholesale kidnapping —I could probably take the wretched owners to court. If I could find a lawyer. If I could pay the costs. . . .

Depressed, I went to bed, where I was shortly joined by both cats and the dog. Luckily, it was a queen-sized bed.

The next day my gloom persisted, and Jerry found me staring out the window when he dropped in for a chat.

"What's the matter?" he said.

"You mean aside from having my job neatly amputated from beneath me?"

He waved a hand. "I told you, sooner or later we'll be able to put the books on the list again. Is that why you keep eyeing the eleven-story drop to the pavement?"

"Not entirely. I'm having severe landlord problems." And I described the fracas. "I wonder if I really am paranoid or whether there is indeed a giant conspiracy to make me accept Diana's offer."

"Who's Diana?"

I told him about Diana and her offer.

"And you mean to say you turned it down? Twice the salary, plus rent and board and other perks? Candida, my dear, paranoia barely describes your condition. You must be raving. What on earth have you to lose?"

"My job, such as it is, or so I thought. Plus being in New York . . ."

"I know. I can hardly stand to think about what you'll be missing—the crime, the pollution, the potholes, the inflation, and now, from what you tell me, a hostile landlord who cannot be trusted not to gas your animals behind your back. Mind you," he went on rapidly when I started to say something, "I maintain, and have always maintained, that to live in a one-room apartment with—how many is it?—eleven other creatures who like to eat, none of whom contributes to the rent, is unquestionably a symptom of mental unbalance, but because I am a liberal person with liberal principles, I don't think that your landlord should be able to hassle you because of that."

Despite myself, I giggled. "Yes, but along with those perks you mentioned I'm supposed to help Diana with a bee in her bonnet that I find pretty off-putting."

"Such as?"

"You're not going to believe this."

"Try me. By profession, editors are trained to believe any-thing—almost."

"Okay. She wants me to help her in running down some ghost that she says is haunting her."

Jerry's brows shot up and he pursed his lips in a silent whistle. After a minute he said, "Do you believe in ghosts?"

"No."

"Then why should you care if she pays you to go groping around some ancient residence for something that isn't there?"

"Because I'd be taking her money under false pretenses."

"Did you tell her you believed in ghosts?"

"No. I said I didn't."

"Then I don't see what your false pretenses are."

"Then there are the books that are in the planning stage. I hate to leave them."

"Well, that's why I'm here."

I looked quickly at him. "What do you mean, Jerry? What are you up to?"

"Nothing. I swear. But I can read the writing on the wall as well as anyone. I have a feeling that things are going to go down here before they go up and Mother Multinational realizes what any proofreader could have told her—that you market books differently from the way you sell computers, shirts or cars. Please don't spread this around, but I have had an offer myself. From another house. Which I am going to take. And one of the first things I'll do after I'm settled there

22

is offer you a contract to write those books yourself. So it seems to me that while you're not helping your friend hunt headless spectres at midnight, you could be earning yourself some money and getting started on the kind of work I've long thought you ought to do."

I stared at him for a long minute. "It's not just the nonexistent ghost that's bothering me," I said. "It's Diana."

"Don't you like her?"

I was amazed to discover I couldn't answer that. "Yes... no... in a way. I sort of admire her... her style anyway. But there's something... something odd about her."

"Well, if she's going around looking for a ghost she's odd as all get out."

"No, that's not what I mean by odd." Then, as I paused trying to define the nebulous discomfort I could not explain, I felt for the first time a strange chill, and shivered.

"Still..." I began hesitantly, after a minute.

"Just keep your mind on all those fringe benefits," the eminently practical Jerry said.

"I'm tempted."

He got up. "Well, for heaven's sake don't fight it." Then he waved and left.

I spent the next five minutes staring out the window at the skyscraper opposite. I, too, had that hollow feeling about where this publishing house was headed in the immediate future.

Then I picked up the phone and dialed the Plaza Hotel. When the operator answered, I asked for Diana Egremont.

23

2

I thought Diana would go up to Tower Abbey first, leaving me a reasonable length of time to give notice at my job and to get my things in storage. But Diana was not exaggerating when she said she was afraid to be alone.

"I'll wait until you're ready and then we'll go together," she said.

The office manager seemed ungratifyingly willing to let me go with only ten days' notice.

"Don't be cast down," Jerry said, when I confided to him the wound to my ego. "It's nothing personal towards you. It's just that his heart leaps up and is made glad at the thought of saving your salary. One of these days, as I keep telling you, he's going to realize that no editors means no books and ultimately no sales, which he is going to have a hard time explaining to all the Big Brothers at the top."

"The trouble is, I'm not going to be around to enjoy the sight of that."

"No, but you'll hear about it. In the meantime, you'll be

banking all that lovely double salary, since you won't even have to pay rent. Look on the bright side."

It was good advice, and I tried to take it, rising also above the super's satisfaction over my announcement that I was going to move.

"It's a good decision, Miss Brown," he said. "I know you'll find something you'll like a lot better."

I tried to calm my resentment by reflecting on Terry's petition, which had now been signed by all the tenants.

"Maybe your boss's master plan is going to run into some trouble," I muttered to myself, going upstairs.

As the week wore on and I packed books, my few pieces of family silver and china and other objects in cartons destined for the storage loft, it occurred to me that when Diana had said "we'll go together" she probably had no idea that "we" included a dog, two cats, a pair of gerbils, a rabbit, two tortoises and some fish, all in or with their assorted living arrangements.

This thought struck me with full impact one evening when I crouched in the middle of the floor surrounded by boxes, sheets of newspaper, piles of books and bric-a-brac. Rising to my feet, I stepped over the various obstacles, went to the telephone and called Diana.

She answered promptly, as she always did. Never once had she been out when I called, which I found astonishing. Diana was not only a beautiful woman, she was an Egremont, which meant that her social circle around her native New York was wide and exalted. If she was penned in her room, it surely must be her own choice. If it were anybody but her—and, of course, if we were not about to be tied in a professional relationship—I probably would have made, with my customary lack of tact, some smart-aleck comment about this. But it was as though I fought off even the most casual involvement with her until the actual hour when I began work as her companion.

I explained to her then about my portable zoo.

She accepted the fact that she was going to be living with assorted animals without a blink and merely asked, "Why

25

don't you send them up separately by truck?"

It was an obvious solution that had occurred to me and which I had dismissed immediately. "I don't want them sitting in some warehouse, Diana, in unfamiliar surroundings, scared half out of their wits, and probably being handled by a bunch of toughs who think of them as cargo."

"I see." The voice on the other end of the telephone was dry. "Well, in that case I'll hire a limousine. You can go up in that with your animals and I'll drive my own car. I'm afraid it wouldn't be big enough to carry all your finned, furred and shelled friends."

I thanked her, and hung up. Then I sat cross-legged on the floor staring at the phone, wondering why the whole thing made me so uncomfortable. I had been sitting there for a while when it finally penetrated my consciousness that someone was knocking at the door.

"Who is it?" I yelled.

"Terry."

"Did I wake you up?" Terry asked when I let her in. She eyed the chaos in the room. "Although I don't know how you can nap in the middle of all this."

"I wasn't asleep. I was just—thinking."

"It seems to have a powerful effect on you." She looked at me out of her black square-framed glasses. "What's the matter? Aren't you happy to be moving out of this dump?"

The same, almost schizoid affliction that took hold of me when Jerry asked if I liked Diana seemed to get its grip on me again. "Yes . . . no . . . I don't know, Terry." I had given Terry a bare outline of what the job was going to be, without going into any of the whys or wherefores. Like Jerry, Terry had fastened onto the double salary and seemed to consider everything else irrelevant.

"I'd be delirious with joy," Terry said. "Why are you so down about it?"

"Oh, no, you wouldn't be delirious," I said crossly. "It would take the threat of a nuclear explosion to get you out of this city."

Terry regarded me thoughtfully. "There was one thing you

26

didn't explain. Why does this dame have to have a companion? Is she old? Or crippled?"

A vision of the exquisite Diana crossed my mind and despite my depression I grinned. "Not hardly. She's about thirty-eight and one of the most smashing-looking females you'd ever see. Her problems, whatever they are, are not physical."

"You mean they're mental?"

"Well, let's say emotional. She seems to be obsessed by an idea that she had a sister nobody told her about. She's looking for proof of some kind that she thinks is in that ancestral pile up the Hudson. And the reason she's paying me to be there is that she doesn't want to be alone." I paused. "You and Jerry keep telling me how marvelous the money is, and I suppose I agree with you. But if it weren't for the fact that they're axing my books at the office and I'm being threatened with eviction here, I'd never have taken it."

Terry sat down on one of the cartons. "But you've never been a city buff. You've always wanted to live in the country entirely surrounded by animals. Wouldn't saving all that money plus writing a book of your own on contract be a much faster way to getting that than staying here, hacking away at editing and rewriting other people's books?"

"Yes. It's just . . ."

Since I couldn't explain my discomfort to myself, it was useless to try to clarify it to anyone else.

"Is it to do with this Egremont woman?" Terry asked. "Or is it the idea of going up to that house?"

I took a while to answer. Then I said, "Both, I suppose." Curious, I thought. I hadn't, until that moment, actually thought about the house. And then, as though ten years had not passed since I had seen it, the huge gray pile, an anachronistic monster sitting on its hill, rose in front of my eyes, as clearly as though it had been yesterday that I had driven around the carriage sweep under those absurd towers and listened to the voices coming from the swimming pool and tennis court. It was there, in those days, that the brightest and richest of Westchester County, southern Connecticut and upper Manhattan would gather during the summer

27

months and discuss, between tennis and swimming (and with all the radical chic of the rich and protected), the people's revolution of the riotous sixties.

It was, quite suddenly, so vivid that I could feel the heat on my shoulder and smell the freshly cut grass of the long, sloping lawn to my left and the faint aroma of roses from the walled garden to my right. And there, stepping through the gate in that wall that led not only to the rose garden but to the court and pool, was one of the handsomest men I had ever known in my life, and I had known him most of my life. Moving towards me with his athlete's grace, he smiled—clear, sea-green eyes in a sunburned face under thick light hair bleached even lighter by the sun. I smiled back. The old, painful, disillusioning memory was still there, a child's memory of a fallen idol, but if Simon had ever realized how great that fall had been, he had forgotten. And already at sixteen and at my first grown-up party, I had spent five years trying to put the idol back on his pedestal.

"*Hello, Candida.*" Unlike most people then, he never called me by anything but my full name.

"*Hello, Simon.*"

"Hey!" yelled Terry. "Don't go off in a trance like that."

I came back to the present with a thump.

Terry looked down at me with concern bordering on severity. "If you can go off on some trip like that so easily, maybe you shouldn't go to that place. You spook too readily. But you never did before. It's not like you."

I laughed. "I wasn't in a trance. I was just remembering."

"Remembering what?"

"My first love," I said lightly.

She brightened. Terry believed in love, and the more the better. "At least it's a beginning. I've often thought you should transfer your affections from animals to people, especially those of the male persuasion. Is he still around?"

I shook my head. "He was in the Reserve and went to Germany with the Army Medical Corps. Of course I haven't been at home for several years, so all my information is about third hand. But I heard there was a ghastly accident that might or might not have been suicide. Anyway, he was killed."

"Too bad. Maybe there'll be somebody else. How are you getting up there?"

"Diana's going to hire a limousine to transport me and my zoo."

"Well, as the saying goes, the rich are different." She paused. "You mean once you get up there that's it? You don't have your own car?"

"You know I don't have a car. Where would I keep it?"

"On the street, like everybody else." Terry looked at me thoughtfully. "You know, that's the only thing you've said so far that I don't like, that you won't have a car of your own. I believe firmly that in doubtful situations one should not only have exits, but the means of using them. It sounds to me as though you're going to be stuck way the hell in the country with a female you're not sure you like and who doesn't sound as though she has all her marbles, in a house that you're not that fond of, and with no means of making a fast getaway. In other words, it stinks."

"Yes, all right. But I can't go out and buy a car with what's left over from my last paycheck."

"Not a new one. But how would you react to a beat-up old one? It's better than nothing."

"Do you have such?"

"No. But Mikes does." Mike was Terry's boyfriend. "He's got a station wagon that sounds as though it were holding together with Scotch tape and framing wire. Actually, it's quite reliable. He's on the verge of buying a new car—I mean a new secondhand one—and was wondering if he could get anything on this. Apparently the dealer he went to offered him a fast three hundred."

With my not very robust savings balance in mind, I said, "I'd give him that, or even a hundred more."

"Done!" Terry said, "It's yours."

"You haven't asked him."

"I don't have to. He'll be glad to sell it to you for four

29

hundred. It's big enough for you to carry your menagerie, and in the meantime I won't be wondering if you're up there with no way to skip the joint."

Terry's boyfriend was as pleased and willing as she said he would be. So one afternoon, a week later, Diana and I set out, she in her Jaguar and I in my ancient station wagon.

The arrangement had been for her to stop by my apartment before leading the way up to Westchester and Tower Abbey. When her sleek blue Jaguar turned into the street, causing heads on both sidewalks to turn, I was busy making sure that the aquarium, the terrarium and the gerbils' cage were wedged securely enough so that they would not slide or shift. The fish were in a special traveling affair with a top; their regular home, packed in layers of newspaper and rag, was on the floor in the front. Seth and Susan were in a large open basket also lashed firmly in the back so it wouldn't move. And Pandora was sitting bolt upright in the passenger seat in the front.

Terry and Mike were supervising the packing, both with fuzzy hair *à la* afro, both in jeans and white T-shirts, both wearing black-rimmed glasses. From the back they looked like twins, even from the front it was sometimes hard to tell which was which.

I introduced Diana, who was dressed in a pants suit that even my untrained eye could detect as something special and expensive from the world of the couturier. After the introductions were over Diana walked slowly around the station wagon.

"I just bought it," I found myself saying defensively.

"Had you considered a covered wagon?"

"That's a perfectly okay heap," Mike put in indignantly. "I know, because it used to belong to me."

"I didn't mean to insult it," Diana said. Her face still looked tired and strained. But her smile packed all its old voltage. The resulting visible melting of Mike made me think of wax left out in the sun.

"Come on, Mike. Let's get upstairs, we have work to do," Terry said, acting, for the first time since I'd known her, like an old-fashioned female with old-fashioned female responses.

"Have a nice trip," she said belligerently to Diana. And then to me, "*Ciao*." And she gave me a clenched-fist salute.

As the front door slammed, Diana said, "There's something about your friend that makes me feel like Marie Antoinette in one of her less fortunate moments."

"Well, to her you're one of the rich and mighty."

"And marked for extinction, I suppose."

"Something like that. But she's okay. I like her."

Diana looked at me out of her clear aqua eyes. "It seems to me a little unfair that I should be getting all the flak considered the just deserts of the rich when I'm not rich."

"Anyone who arrives in a Jaguar dressed in a model suit is rich around here."

"I see." She stared at me for a moment, as though she were thinking of adding something. But all she said then was, "Well, shall we get started? I'd better lead the way, I suppose."

"All right. But I don't want to go fast. It would upset the animals."

"I wouldn't think of doing that." She glanced at me. "Yes, Candida, I accept the fact that it's love you, love your animals. But then, you've always been that way, so it's no major shock."

What with stopping a few times, once for gas and twice to make sure the cages and aquarium weren't shaking loose, it was almost two hours before we turned off the freeway and bore northwest along secondary roads through wooded country to a village that at first glance looked as though it, in the fashion of Rip Van Winkle, had gone to sleep and awakened a century and a half later. But I had grown up not far from Tandem Village, and I was aware that behind a discreet Federal façade was housed a small but well-stocked supermarket; that just off the central green was a gas station; and that the row of shops, looking as though they were expecting the custom of Washington Irving, were expensive boutiques catering to those who did not have time to run into the city and visit Bergdorf's or Bendel's. In other words: that the village, quite genuinely old, was kept in a high state of preserve by a dedi-

31

cated and affluent population from surrounding estates.

But not everyone within a three-mile circumference of Tandem Village was rich and not every shopkeeper or professional man within the village itself catered only to the rich. As Diana drew to a stop in front of the decorously disguised supermarket, I could see, in a little alley just off the green, the white-fronted former stable where my father had had his surgery three afternoons a week. The people who brought their pets there were children and elderly inhabitants of the village who could not get to our home outside Tandem where my father kept office hours the rest of the time.

Diana got out of her car and came towards mine. "I think," she said, "we'd better get supplies now rather than later. There's nothing much at the Abbey to eat."

A thought, bizarre in its improbability, crossed my mind. "You surely don't mean you're doing the cooking yourself?" On the occasions, in the old days, when I had visited the Abbey, the servants had seemed to be even more numerous than the guests.

A smile flickered across her face. "You didn't believe me, did you, when I said I was broke? No, I don't have to cook all my own meals. A German woman named Elsa Klaveness does that most of the time. She and her husband, Hans, live in the old farmhouse halfway down the hill. But she comes up to the Abbey to cook the meals and keep the few rooms I use vaguely livable."

I frowned. "So you're not really alone."

"I am at night. And anyway, Elsa's reliable about coming, but . . . not exactly companionable."

"Do you want me to get anything?" I asked, nodding towards the supermarket.

"Well, I've made a list. I'll tear it in two. You could get half the stuff and I'll get the other half. We can meet at the checkout counter. Can you leave your menagerie?"

"Oh, sure. I'll just lock the door."

Twenty minutes later, when Diana and I emerged, each carrying huge bags, we found my car surrounded by children and one or two adults.

I put my bag in the back of Diana's car, along with her own. Then I went over to where mine was parked.

"Gangway," I said to the wall of small bodies surrounding the windows. I could see immediately what the fascination was. Seth and Susan, paws against the windows, were serenading their audience, their Siamese voices coming loud and clear through the glass. Pandora was contributing by barking, and Wisteria was staring out of his cage, his ears on the alert. Since the gerbils' cage was entirely surrounded by packing cases, they weren't visible.

"Are they all yours?" some child asked admiringly.

"Yes."

"Do you have a zoo?" This was another young questioner.

"Not officially," Diana put in. She'd come over to see what was going on.

The children and two adults looked up and saw her.

"Hello, Miss Egremont."

"Hi, Miss Egremont."

The voices, both children's and adults', were oddly formal. All at once, as though at a signal, they all stepped back from the windows and seemed to disperse.

"Come along, Susie. Time for dinner." This was one of the young women. She spoke sharply and pulled her offspring after her across the green.

"There are times," Diana said, "when I wonder if someone has me confused with Typhoid Mary."

I found myself trying to reassure her. "It's not that, Diana," I said, unlocking my car. "You know as well as I do that people around here—I mean the people in the village—have never felt too matey with the estate families."

"Yes. I know that. It's a pity."

I opened the car door. "But not entirely their fault."

Diana spoke rather sharply. "My family may all have been robber barons, but my own views have always been, on the whole, pretty liberal."

"You may have been the shining liberal light of your set, but when you hobnobbed with those of us from the other ranks, there was never any doubt as to who came from the house on the hill and who came from down in the village."

Diana's face flushed and then went white. I found myself remembering that that usually meant she was angry and was often the prelude to one of her stinging set-downs. I braced myself to meet it.

But all she said now was, "Yes. You see what I mean when I told you I valued you for your candor."

"I didn't mean to be rude. I'm sorry if it came over that way."

Diana made a face. "It's all right. As I said, it's part of your charm. But . . ." Her voice ran down.

"What?" Whatever it was she had on her chest about me, it was better that we have it out now, here in the village, while it was still easy for me to turn around and go back. *Back where?* a mocking voice asked. *Your apartment's gone. And if you did beg a bed from Terry, what would you do with your animals?*

It was at that moment that a sense of being trapped touched me. It passed immediately. If I put my mind to it, I reminded myself, there was always a way out. But the feeling left a residue. To get rid of it, I repeated my question. "But what?"

"But," Diana said, "strange as it may sound, I almost wish that your untactful comment about the distance between"— she made a gesture with her hand—"the big house and the village were the reason for the withdrawal you saw just now— that and others I've noticed."

"What else could it be?"

Diana shrugged. "It could be, as I told you, that I've put the house and land up for sale. They're afraid that some environmental wrecker will buy it and ruin the neighborhood."

"But would you sell it to somebody like that?"

"That rather depends on how desperate I am."

"But doesn't the township have zoning laws and boards?"

There was a pause, then, "Apparently there are loopholes— or so my lawyers tell me. Anyway, it's making the locals very nervous. We'd better get up there. It'll be dark before too long."

We drove around the two remaining sides of the green, passing the white-spired picture-postcard New England church, which was actually St. Stephen's Roman Catholic, and, farther up the climbing road, the large, gray-stoned gothic structure, as big as a small cathedral, that was All Saints Episcopal Church. As we passed the churches a memory assailed me that made me grin: It was of my father driving home past the two structures after a convivial evening, sticking his head out the window and shouting, "A plague o' both your houses."

It was a long pull up to the Abbey. The summer rain which had been falling on and off now came down again, soaking everything in sight—the trees that lined the road, the fields, glimpsed occasionally through the woods, and the road itself, where the water gathered in shallow puddles.

After a while the trees thinned out, with here and there a farmhouse showing, with barns attached. Vaguely I remembered stories that Diana's grandfather, who had built Tower Abbey and was known locally and unaffectionately as the French miser, had bought all the surrounding farms, including one that had held out to the bitter end when some kind of tragedy or disaster intervened and forced the stubborn farmer to sell to the tycoon. Then, when Egremont had put up his mansion and decided how much empty land he needed as a private park, he rented the remaining farmhouses outside the park either back to the original owners or to anyone who would take them, at extortionate prices. Not a nice character, Louis Egremont. At least according to local legend. More trees in sporadic patches went past the window, and then came the gate, standing open now, a not very distinguished affair of boards and wire.

I had never particularly admired the style of Tower Abbey —for me it breathed too much money and too little grace, as exemplified by the turrets that were affixed in every available corner of this basically Georgian house. According to tradition, the turrets were insisted on by Diana's grandmother, wife to old Louis, who had dreamed up the name for the mansion before anyone had thought to show her the plans. But fake turrets or no, it certainly had always had the kind of splendor that came with money lavishly, if not always tastefully, spent. It had been kept and manicured and trimmed as neatly as an

English seventeenth-century garden, complete with gazebo, with nothing growing in profusion, not even the roses in the rose garden, which had had the ordered spacing of a corps de ballet, and the creeper, which had been as disciplined as a soldier's haircut.

It was therefore a shock to see the changes that neglect had brought. The little round pond in the center of the carriage sweep around the house was empty, the metal pipes that had kept the water flowing rusted, the remains of plants and water lilies lying dead on the bottom. Rooms and houses are supposed to appear smaller to the adult who sees them for the first time since childhood, yet for some reason Tower Abbey appeared larger. Built in the basic H pattern, the crossbar was the main part of the house, and much longer than the two wings on either side, so that the H, as it would appear from above, was low and stubby. But the wings, which I had remembered as small, seemed much larger, as though they were arms grown disproportionately long and showing the first signs of beginning to meet in front. After a minute, as I drew the car to a halt behind Diana's, I realized the apparent difference came from vines and creeper that had so grown over the stone of the wings that they had seemed to thicken the walls.

Inevitably, my eyes strayed to the right, to the wall behind which were the pool, the tennis court, the toolshed and the little ornamental gazebo. Beyond that was the rose garden, through the door of which I had seen Simon Grant emerge that day long ago. My heart gave a small, remembering flutter. Then it seemed to stop altogether.

The wooden door in the wall had opened suddenly and a man came through it. He was still tall, but the athletic body in the parka was leaner and the thin face more lined. The blue-green eyes set under straight brows were the same, though somehow more remote.

But he's dead, something inside me screamed. *He committed suicide.* I was frightened then, frightened in a way I had never been in my life. Because any opponents or enemies I had ever known were the kind you could weigh and measure —not this ghost. At that moment I realized how quickly de-

risive I had been of Diana's cowardice before (I was sure)
some explainable mystery.

And then he spoke. "Hello, Candida," he said, just as he
had before.

And I heard my own voice. "Hello, Simon."

3

"But I thought he was dead," I said.

Diana and I were standing in the kitchen, our groceries in their bags on the table.

"To paraphrase Mark Twain—"

"Yes, I know. The rumors of his death were grossly exaggerated."

Perhaps there was something in my voice. Diana looked at me quickly. "I know a rumor did go around that he was killed in that awful accident in Germany. But he wasn't. He had a lot of broken bones and internal injuries and he was in the hospital a long time—maybe that's when the rumor got started. His parents were dead by then, of course, and he was an only child and didn't keep in touch with his friends, which was why, I suppose, nobody was really informed. Also, it was touch and go for so long as to whether or not he would pull through. And his state of mind was pretty grim about that time . . ." There was a second's hesitation in Diana's voice; then she went on. ". . . which probably gave rise to the suicide rumor. But I'm surprised, since you heard about the accident, that you didn't eventually hear that he was alive. You must have been out on the West Coast at that time, weren't you?"

"Yes." I could remember so clearly the letter from a school friend that had brought the news—even how the words looked on the page: *Have you heard? Simon Grant has been killed in some horrible accident over in Europe....Some people seem to think it was suicide. And speaking of that, have you been told about the uproar over . . . ?* I don't believe I ever read the rest of that letter, or if I did, I certainly didn't remember who or what the uproar was about.

"Yes," I said now. "I was at college. Somebody wrote."

"But nobody wrote and told you he'd recovered?"

"No."

"Which, I suppose, follows the same dreary logic that decrees that it's always the bad news that gets reported. That's rough. When did you hear?"

I could have told her the exact date, March 18, 1974. But all I said was, "Spring 1974, I believe."

"Umm. Well, that'd be about right. K—" She stopped herself, and then went on. "He'd been in the States on leave, then went back to Germany the previous fall and had the accident the following January. When did you graduate?"

"That year, 1974. In June."

"And you left the college for a job with the forestry service or something?"

"Wildlife. Yes."

"Well, that's probably why you didn't get the news of his recovery."

"Probably," I said. My voice seemed to be stuck in a monotone. I was still stunned. Automatically I took some of the frozen vegetables and fruit out of the big bag. "What was he —what was Simon doing coming out of the garden?"

"Strictly speaking, since he's my cousin, as well as an old friend, there's no reason why he shouldn't be here." Diana paused. I wondered if the slight chill in her voice was deliberate, or whether she was unconscious of it. I decided the latter was probably true. The devoutly liberal Diana was still entirely capable of responding to me, when she felt like it, as

39

though I were an impudent servant asking impertinent questions, and not know consciously she was doing it. Still, I thought, one of the better maxims that had come my way stated, "Begin as you mean to go on." Now that I was hired, sealed and, so to speak, delivered, Diana was finding it perilously easy to think of me as an upper servant, and was adjusting her manner accordingly. Unless I did something about it now, it would get worse, not better.

I was still shaken, but I put down the box of frozen vegetables in my hand and said as calmly as I could, "I'm not your servant, Diana. We're here together by mutual professional agreement, and because you wanted it that way. I'm your hired companion, but that doesn't mean the pecking order has shifted in your favor. If you don't want to tell me what Simon Grant is doing on the grounds of Tower Abbey, just say so and I'll shut up. But no put-downs." There had been more anger in my voice than I had bargained for. I decided to try to finish on a lighter note. "You don't want to spoil your liberal image, do you?"

Diana stared at me for a long moment, her face expressionless. Then she said with an equal lack of expression, "Sorry."

It was, I felt deep in my bones, going to be a bumpy ride.

"Do you remember the house at all?" Diana said a few moments later, "or would you like me to show you around?"

"I don't remember it too well, but I think I'd rather look it over myself, if you don't mind. Unless there's some part you don't want me to go into."

"Of course not, don't be silly," Diana replied. But I was aware of a fraction of hesitation before she spoke. "But before you go on tour, I'll show you your room. Or would you like a drink first?"

What I would have liked more than anything else was an explanation of why Simon Grant was coming out of the Abbey rose garden, of what he was doing in this area at all, and of where he lived. But pride and stubbornness would not allow me to ask it.

"I'd love a drink, Diana. But right now I think I'd rather

you show me my room so I can see where I can put the animals. They're not very comfortable out there, and they're probably frightened."

"I'd forgotten about your zoo. All right. Follow me."

We had come in through a side door opening at the end of the north wing, and had walked down a narrow corridor to the kitchen, so I hadn't as yet seen the big central hall and the main part of the house. I'm not quite sure what I expected. In my memory the hall, covered by red Spanish tile over which a magnificent Aubusson rug had been thrown, was as neat, planned and opulent as the exterior. Vaguer in my memory were the rooms, except that they had always seemed enormous and overpowering.

Now, with me trailing Diana, we went from the kitchen through an old-fashioned green baize door into a large square room, in the center of which was a round table of heavy mahogany.

"This is the dining room," Diana said shortly. A gray day outside had turned into a gloomy dusk. But even taking that into consideration, the room seemed extraordinarily dark.

"Isn't there a light?" I asked. "I've always hated dark rooms."

Diana put a hand out to the wall and flipped a switch.

I could see then why the room seemed so somber. Mahogany paneling that I remembered as reflecting a reddish golden shine was now dull, dry-looking and almost black. The wallpaper above it had long since lost whatever color it had once had and was something of the same murky shade. The candelabra, hanging low over the table, must have had years of filth on it.

"Yes," Diana said dryly. "It's not quite the same, is it?"

"What happened?" I blurted out.

"What happened was that when my father died there was far less money than anyone had thought. A lot on paper, but, when liquidated, only enough to provide me with a modest income—and I mean modest—if I lived in a one-bedroom apartment in New York. There were also debts of my own, incurred before I realized the extent of the financial disaster, which I have been paying off since. Hence the blank spaces on the walls."

She waved her hand towards the wall to my left, and, sure enough, barely visible in the overall gloom, were big rectangular spaces a shade or so lighter than the surrounding wall.

"You sold the Stuarts."

"And glad I was to have them to sell."

"Didn't you . . . I mean, Diana, I thought your husbands were rich."

"Unfortunately, only the second one was. And since I divorced him before my father died and the grisly financial facts became known, my liberal guilty conscience made it essential for me to refuse any settlement. My most recent husband was not rich—just distinguished and brainy in an obnoxious way. And since he got custody of James, and because I didn't feel like fighting, there was, again, no settlement."

"James?"

Diana reached up and switched off the light. "We might as well be moving on. At this rate, and with the number of rooms, it would take us until midnight, and your animals would be clawing their way out of the car. We go through here."

It was exasperating to keep my mouth shut, my tongue clamped between my teeth. But I was not about to let myself in for another cool set-down by asking what Diana would undoubtedly think of as intrusive questions.

Frustrated, I followed her into another smaller room, plainly a glassed-in porch, and then turned at right angles through a farther door.

"That was the so-called sun porch," Diana said. "I usually eat there, when I'm not snatching a bite in the kitchen. This is the living room." I saw her hand go out and another clouded candelabra sprang to a muted, dirt-encrusted light. This room was as wide as the dining room and much longer. Trying to keep that H pattern in my head, I saw that we had turned a corner and were now in the main part of the house. Lighter square and rectangular shapes along the walls spoke of other paintings sold. Here, the furniture was dust-sheeted, a long sheet over the carpet.

On the wall opposite the windows was a fireplace with a stone chimneypiece above it. Sunk into the stone was a coat of arms: a shield bearing a cross with a line slanted through it, and underneath that a scroll with some kind of a motto.

"The family crest?" I asked.

Diana made a face. "My grandfather's pet vanity."

"But I thought he gloried in being the compleat French peasant—wasn't that his nickname around here?"

"Oh, yes, but that didn't prevent him from digging up a noble—albeit illegitimate—ancestor. That's what the slant line is, the bar sinister. Anyway, he claims we were descended from a saintly cleric of noble blood."

"Not very saintly, if he went around having illegitimate children."

"Apparently he was like St. Augustine. He saw the light and abjured the flesh, but only after he had produced a son."

I leaned over and tried to read the French words in the scroll. "In my . . . my foolishness," I translated after a short struggle, "is my . . . my force? Strength?"

Diana was walking slowly across the room. "I once asked my grandmother about that. She seemed to have her own reservations about the motto, but she said foolishness there was meant in the religious sense. Like somebody or other—St. Paul, I think—saying 'we are fools for Christ's sake.' "

"What do you mean by reservations? Why should she have reservations? She sounds like me."

"Well, her manner was so odd I asked her if she thought the motto meant something else. And she just smiled and said that that was perhaps her own foolishness. And she wouldn't talk about it anymore. Why do you say she sounds like you?"

"Because I led a very protected life as far as religion was concerned. My father was against it in any form."

Diana looked amused. "I see."

I backed away from the fireplace and then veered to avoid a piano, a concert grand by the looks of its size, that lay mountainous under a dust sheet.

43

"Do you still play?" I asked.

She shook her head. "No. Simon does, sometimes." She glanced at me. "I never answered your questions about him, did I?" She had reached the door opposite to the one by which we had come into the room and waited there for me to join her. "He's now running a halfway house for young people who've been in trouble. It's one of those houses we saw on the way up."

I was almost as astonished as I had been that he was alive. "Simon? A halfway house?"

"Well, he had psychiatric training at the end of medical school, you may remember." She paused. "After he left Germany he...he went into training of another kind." She hesitated. "He'll probably tell you about it. Anyway, he now works with disturbed young people."

"He must have changed," I said with conviction.

Handsome, intelligent, full of charm and well aware of it, the Simon Grant I remembered was also possessed of an arrogance that sprang from having been showered with every possible gift of the gods. It was almost impossible to imagine that exceedingly attractive, but proud, young man in the role of warm, understanding therapist.

"He comes up here to stroll around or think or just get away from his charges from time to time," Diana said, emerging through the door out into the central hall. "This is the hall, that over there is the front door we should have come in by, except that it's easier to use the side when I'm headed for the kitchen. Opposite is what would be a back door, except that it faces over the valley, and in some ways is the real front door."

I looked around. The walls here were painted rather than papered, and the hall itself bare except for a scarred-looking table on one side and an equally battered chest on the other. Lighter areas of paint against the wall indicated that this time it was furniture that was sold. I looked down. There was no carpet now. Just scratched and faded tiles. I shivered.

"It's not exactly cosy, is it?" I said.

"No."

44

I looked up from the chilled stone of the floor to see her watching me. She had switched on the light overhead—inevitably another grimy candelabra—and was peering at me in an odd, intense way. "Do you find it cold, Candida?"

"Yes. Why? I mean, you sound as though you thought that to feel cold was a sign of some terrible disease. Aren't you cold? It may be summer, but it's hardly what you call warm."

"Yes. I'm cold."

"Then why—" I made a gesture with my hand, "why the meaningful question?"

Diana shrugged. "I didn't mean it to sound that way. Just ... just concern for your well-being."

I'll bet, I thought.

"About James," she said, successfully diverting my attention. "He's my son. By the last marriage. As I told you, Roger —my late, third and veddy English husband—had custody of him until he died a few weeks ago. He'll be coming over from England in a day or two to be with me."

Thoughts tumbled through my head: that this was a rather crucial detail she'd managed to leave out; why hadn't I known she had a son? That she had lost custody of him? That her third husband (whom I remembered) had died?

"How old is your son?" I asked, deciding that this question had priority.

"Nine." She glanced at me as she paused by the foot of a wide stone staircase. "I haven't ... we haven't lived together since he was five." She stopped and took a deep breath. "You might as well know. Roger—Roger Eliot, James's father— divorced me and got custody of James on the grounds that I was an unfit mother."

Her voice was as harsh as the words. They scraped in the silence. For a woman of her pride, it must have cost a great deal to say that. I knew that the worst thing I could do was to show sympathy. "I'm sorry," I said, with as little expression as I could manage.

"We'll go up here," she said.

"So your name is really Eliot."

She looked back at me and smiled a little. "Oh, no, it isn't.

45

I took back my maiden name—much nicer."

"Have you always taken it back—after each divorce?"

"No. Just after this one." The bitterness in her tone was unmistakable. She turned back and we started up the stairs.

How much better it would be, I thought, if the stairs had been wooden. Even if they were bare and unpolished they would be warmer than the grayish white stone of the wide, cold, shallow steps under my feet. The stairs were in two short flights, doubling back on each other, with a square landing in between.

"Now," Diana said when we got to the top, "I've chosen the old master bedroom"—she waved towards the left of the top of the stairs—"for my own." Pause. "There are rooms on the rest of the floor and more one flight up. You can have any one of them you want." There was another pause. Obviously she hadn't finished, because we still stood there. And then, before she spoke, I knew, with a pang of sympathy, what she wanted to say and for which she was trying to find the words that would save a little of her pride. I said them for her.

"But you'd rather I didn't choose one on the floor above."

"Yes. I hope you don't mind."

I didn't at all mind her asking. I did mind the lady-of-the-manor note that at that moment crept into her voice, and then I understood that it was a face-saving sop to her pride. Leaving her, I moved towards her room. Since the door was open I glanced inside and was struck by its quality of bleak chaos. Clothes were strewn over everything—the bed, the chairs, even on what looked like the dressing table. Yet it was not the untidiness that bothered me. I had had enough college roommates who never picked up a shoe or a skirt to be disturbed by that. It was a negative quality, as though everything warm or cheerful had been sucked out, withdrawn, leaving only desolation and abandonment.

"Maybe," I suggested, "new wallpaper would help."

An arm reached out past me and pulled the door shut. "I'm afraid I left in rather a hurry," Diana said coldly. "And as you know, I haven't been back since we met in New York."

"I'm surprised Mrs. Klaveness didn't tidy the room for you."

"She's here to cook and take care of the kitchen and the housekeeping. Not as personal maid. Feel free to look at any other room. I'm going to go downstairs for a while."

Diana turned on her heel and went back to the staircase. I looked at her smooth blond head disappearing.

Well, I thought. I'd rather look at the rooms and pick two for myself and the animals on my own. Shifting my shoulder bag into a more comfortable position, I opened the door to the room next to Diana's. It was much the same size and shape. Unlike Diana's it was bare to the point of austerity. I switched on the light, which was not much of an improvement. The blue of the papered walls was cold, whether or not because the color had faded I couldn't tell. Two brass beds stuck out from the wall. Closing the door, I went to the next room, which wasn't much better, except that the walls which may, once, have been yellow, were now mustard.

Sighing, I crossed the hall to the room opposite. The walls there were red. The beds were wooden, not brass. The atmosphere was just as depressing. Coming out of that, I went back to the central hall at the top of the stairs, and noticed that a small archway at the other end of the hall led, at right angles and down a few steps, into what was undoubtedly the south wing. Going over to investigate, I saw in the wall to my left a small door revealing a narrow, winding stair leading both down and up. Deciding I could explore that later, I went down the steps into the wing and along the short hall into the first of two bedrooms. Far less palatial—and less gloomy—than those I had seen in the main part of the house, this room was still, by ordinary standards, sizable, made more so by the fact that it contained one bed rather than two, and the white-painted furniture seemed less awe-inspiring. On the walls, I was relieved to see, were stripes of tiny blue, green and yellow flowers.

"That'll do nicely," I said to myself, and went on to the next and larger room. It, too, contained one bed, in this case a studio couch, and plenty of empty table and shelf space. It would, I decided, be perfect for the zoo. And the wallpaper, also cheerful, was a variation of that in the room before.

When I went back along the narrow hall of the wing towards the main part, I noticed again the small door giving on to the winding staircase. I paused, curious, because I was almost certain that, after looking in, I had closed that door. Well, I thought, I must have been mistaken, hardly remarkable, when I had spent the past twenty minutes opening and closing doors up and down the hall. Reaching in, I grasped the knob to close the door and was struck again by the chill that seemed to pervade the rest of the house. Probably because this was a stairwell, it seemed unusually marked here. Or perhaps there was a door open beneath. After all, there was an outside door in the opposite wing that Diana and I used when coming into the house. Therefore there must almost certainly be one in this wing.

Instead of marching back along the main hall and down that formidable front staircase, I thought I might as well use the stairs at hand to go out and collect the animals. Releasing the doorknob, I stepped through the doorway and turned to go down the narrow, winding stairs. Reaching out, I touched the stone wall and was almost shocked by its chill. This might be the coldest June on record, I thought, but it hardly accounted for the temperature of the stone. No wonder people in hot climates built stone houses. Such houses held on to the winter temperature and acted as their own air-conditioning unit.

Between the chill and the narrowness of the stairs I was extremely glad to reach the bottom. But the doorway leading from the staircase did not give on to the outside. Walking through, I found myself in what had obviously once been an indoor swimming pool, now empty.

Well, I thought, staring down into the stained marble cavity, a good eight feet deep at the end where I was standing, people of a bygone era who built great houses plainly did so with an unabashed consideration for every possible comfort and pleasure. Diana's liberal guilty conscience came two generations after her self-made grandfather. And self-made men were rarely, if ever, afflicted with a sense of guilt over their hard-won riches.

Looking up, across the width of the pool, I saw that there was indeed a door leading outside, set in huge glass panels that served as the outside wall of the pool. Walking around the deep end, where marble benches were set for the convenience of the swimmers, I slid the door open and stepped outside.

Almost a twin to the pool inside was the stone pond in the garden, shielded from the curious by hedge and wall, the same wall through which I had seen Simon step. A wide strip of bare earth next to the wall indicated what had once been a carefully tended English herbacious border. Dividing the lawn and the pond from the rose garden behind was the gazebo, a delapidated remnant from another age. Back of that, sturdy and serviceable, was the toolshed.

Behind the gazebo and the toolshed lay, I knew, the rose garden, with the trees as ordered and as handsome as a regiment of red, white, pink, and yellow soldiers. They were, I remembered, Diana's father's particular pride. I was there with my father the night of the sudden frost when Mr. Egremont left a black-tie dinner in his dining salon to rush out and cover his beloved roses with tarpaulin.

From where I was standing, I couldn't see the rose garden or what was left of it. Had Simon left? I wondered. Or had he waited until we had gone into the house and returned to the rose garden? More important, was he still there? Would I run into him? And why should the thought of that fill me with such dismay? I wondered, turning firmly away from that direction. In any case, I decided, I had no desire to see the waste of what had once undoubtedly been one of the loveliest sights I ever remembered. Also, my poor animals must by this time be frantic with claustrophobia and the need to relieve themselves.

Praying that they had managed to show restraint over the latter, I opened up the back of the station wagon and started to extract them.

Leaping over the cages, suitcases and boxes of books, Pandora greeted me with hysterical affection—did she, I wondered, believe that I had deserted her forever, after walling her up in the moving and cramped box humans call a car? "There, there," I crooned to her, stroking her yellow silky head, "I didn't mean to be that long."

Seth and Susan liked their confinement no better than Pandora did, but had, with regal scorn, settled themselves back in their carrier basket and stared at me with wounded crossed blue eyes.

"And you can get out and hunt," I said to them, hauling the basket out. "But not until you learn where your sleeping and litter boxes will be."

The sleeping box was simply a sop to what I felt was their due. In two years I had had them they had slept nowhere but my bed.

It took me another half hour to settle everybody in the bedroom beyond mine, to make sure that the cages, the aquarium and the terrarium were where their occupants would feel most secure. This time I used the front door and the grand staircase, partly because it was now dark, and the thought of that dark, combined with the chill of the narrow staircase, did not attract me. Also, I did not know how well I would navigate the winding stair with all I had to carry. After I had them all stashed comfortably, I made sure that everyone had fresh water. Food, I thought, could wait until they had settled in.

Then, preceded by Pandora and trailed by Seth and Susan, I went downstairs to try to find Diana.

Retracing our steps of an hour before, I went back through the long, dust-sheeted living room, the sun porch, the dining room and the kitchen, expecting to find her there. But the kitchen, though lighted, was empty. A little to my surprise, some of the groceries we had brought had not been put away. The household items in my bag I had left on the table, not knowing where to put them, and expecting to be told when I came downstairs. They were still there. But Diana's bag was also on the table, containing, still, a few packages of frozen food, now lying rather sodden at the bottom. She must have forgotten that we had not put everything away when she took me on the tour of the house, I thought. But how strange that she would not have finished storing the vegetables in the freezer before we started.

With a slight spurt of indignation, I wondered if she had deliberately left them for me to put away. My hands, which had been busy removing the wet packages from the damp bag, paused. Perhaps—in the spirit of starting as I meant to go on —I should find her and ask her if she intended to leave the frozen vegetables out to thaw. But my compulsive neatness— an antidote, perhaps, to the inevitable messiness of animals— was too strong. Mounds of thawed vegetables would involve waste, and I disliked wasted food in fact and principle.

Having stacked the packages of vegetables in the freezer, I then put the household items away, opening and closing cupboard and cabinet doors to find out as much as I could what went where. Either Diana was neater than I gave her credit for being, or Mrs. Klaveness's hand dominated this region of the house. Not only was everything stored according to order and logic, but the shelves and drawers themselves shone with cleanliness.

Although neat myself, I was wary of that quality in others— it so often extended to a hostility to the animal world. Thoughtfully I looked at Susan and Seth, who had sprung onto the kitchen table and were now inspecting the various interesting smells that had been left by the food. Among the groceries I had put away were some canned meals for the cats and Pandora. Their food dishes, however, were upstairs.

What I should do, I thought, opening and shutting cabinets to find the least elegant dishes, would be to go upstairs and get the three plastic dishes. But I was tired, and the animals looked hungrier than I thought they would be so soon after arriving in a strange place. I finally located two cracked saucers and a plastic container lying, dishonored, among the cleaning fluids and steel wool below one of the sinks. After I had washed them two or three times, I emptied Pandora's can into the plastic container, and Seth's and Susan's into the saucers. Pandora marched into her food showing no neurotic hesitation. Seth put his seal-brown nose into his saucer and sniffed delicately. Then he ate. Susan, a lilac point, her body almost as white as when she was a kitten, sniffed, walked around to the

51

other side of the saucer, sniffed again. Then she went and started to eat from Seth's dish. After a while he put out a brown paw and pushed her away. She put out a smaller, paler paw and pushed him back. I watched the contest with interest. It went on two nights out of three, but the results were by no means predictable. This time Seth, muttering to himself, went over to Susan's abandoned dish. Since each had half of the same can, the food was identical. I felt, as his loud voice complained and commented, that he knew this, and that he knew also that what had just happened was a contest of power.

"Never mind, Seth," I said, tickling his head. "You didn't lose. You just decided that it wasn't worth a domestic quarrel." Between bites, Seth sounded his views, bitter and chauvinistic. Susan, who always took a smallish bite, then dropped it on the floor outside her dish and divided it into even smaller bites, ate delicately, like the Prioress in the Canterbury Tales.

"If Mrs. Klaveness saw that, she'd turn into a pillar of salt with pure rage," Diana's voice said from the kitchen door.

I looked up. She was standing there, leaning against the door frame, a glass in her hand. She saw my eyes on it.

"I'm a drink ahead of you . . . or so," she said.

"I'll wash the saucers and container," I said. "And in future use only their own dishes. You don't have to tell her about this, do you?"

"I don't have to tell her anything. But one'll get you fifty she'll know."

A worm of doubt and worry established itself inside me, and instantly grew larger. "Does she dislike animals?"

"Who knows what she likes or dislikes? No, I'll take that back. She doesn't like disorder. She doesn't say so, but a blind idiot could tell."

"Diana," I said, "if there's the slightest chance she'd hurt any of these three, or any of the others upstairs, I'll leave now, tonight."

Diana took a swallow. "What would you do for an apartment, or a job?"

"I could stay with Terry for the time. And something would turn up. I'm not kidding."

Diana looked at me for a minute, then shrugged. "It's my house. There won't be any problem. I'll just tell her that if anything at all happens to any of your pets she'll be fired immediately. Okay?"

I was about to open my mouth to tell her that such high-handed methods didn't suit me either. But then I looked at Pandora, her pink tongue going round and round the container to extract the last crumb of food, and Seth and Susan, sitting side by side, as dignified as bishops, washing their paws. "Okay," I said.

Diana straightened. "Now that your progeny are taken care of, come have a drink."

"I'm starved, Diana. I'd rather eat."

She looked annoyed. "How dreary."

"Aren't you hungry?"

"Not at the moment. But help yourself." She started to go.

"Don't you want something?" The question came out despite myself because I was sure that the natural result would be for me to fix dinner for us both. And I was not hired as cook.

But she said, "I told you. I'm not hungry." She turned and wandered off towards the dining room. "See you later."

"Where are you sitting?" I called after her.

She glanced back, just as she was about to go through the baize door. "In the study, cater-cornered from the living room." And she disappeared through the door.

So there I was in the kitchen, a single powerful bulb hanging from its cord washing everything in a pale, glaring light, contemplating the unwelcome thought of having to get myself dinner. Truthfully, I acknowledged to myself, I would have preferred to get dinner for two with a little human companionship to help.

That thought was so surprising that I went about taking meat, vegetables and the fixings for a salad out of the refrigerator, trying to figure out why, for the first time in my life, I felt the need of another person's company when I could have my animals instead. Terry was not the only one to suggest that I transfer some of my regard from my four-footed friends to a two-footed lover. "Well, never mind kids," I said aloud. "I still prefer you."

Since I usually got a response—Pandora's bark or Seth's loud voice—I was astonished enough at the ensuing silence to turn around. They hadn't spoken, I discovered, because they weren't there.

Funny, I said to myself.

Well, I thought, I could go look for them, or I could get my dinner. Rather morosely, I took down from the overhead rack above the stove a small saucepan and a frying pan. Putting a little water in the first, I started a flame under it, and then, when the water was boiling, threw in the vegetables. After melting a little grease in the bottom of the frying pan, I slapped a handful of ground meat on top of it. While they were all cooking I made a salad, and all the time my mind was coming to grips with the question, Where did the animals go?

Of course, I thought, sitting down finally to my meal, they could have slipped through the baize door when Diana left. For some reason I didn't think they had. And how many other ways out of the kitchen quarters were there? And where did they lead to? In a house of this size the answers could be—in fact, almost certainly were—endless. In my mind, the house seemed to stretch, covering acres and acres. I put down my fork and stared at the half hamburger and wilted salad that had abruptly lost all interest for me. "Well," I said aloud, staring at the plate, "you've always wanted to go on a diet and lose weight. Now's your chance." The thought should have cheered me. But it didn't. The depression that had been descending steadily seemed to close around me in a fog. At that moment I wished with all my heart that I was back in New York, in my apartment, fighting my landlord, fighting the office manager, and coping with simple, straightforward problems like losing a job and getting evicted.

With an enormous effort, I shook off the paralysis that my blackening mood seemed to have brought and took the dishes to the sink. Scraping the remainder of my dinner off into the garbage, I washed and dried the dishes, a job I normally did not mind, but that suddenly seemed to be a chore over which

I had to clench my teeth. That done, I set out to find Pandora. Seth and Susan I trusted to find me and, I devoutly hoped, their litter box. But Pandora had to be walked.

If they had followed Diana, I reasoned, they would be in another part of the house, but I decided to make sure first that they were not in some corner of the rather extended kitchen quarters. Turning on lights as I went, I inspected a variety of storerooms opening off the kitchen itself, and then came to the beginning of the long narrow hall through which I had originally come. To my right was a door. Opening it, I found myself inside another enclosed porch which looked, by the way it was set up, as though it had served as a dining room for the domestic staff. On the far side of that was another door that obviously led outside. But I could see from where I was standing that it was locked.

Retreating from that, I went back into the hall and looked around. Another door was at my back. In the dim light of the hall I didn't see, until I was practically on top of it, that the door was slightly ajar. Pushing it farther open, I stared into blackness. There was probably, I thought, a light switch on the adjacent wall, and I extended my hand to see if I could locate it. Irritated that I had managed to miss it, I decided to step inside to see if I could find it more easily. The urge to do so grew. Pandora must be in there, I thought, playing games as she so often did, waiting for me to find her. Annoyed that she should choose to do this when I was unwontedly tired, I said out loud, rather sharply, "Pandora!"

Her bark came to me from the end of the hall. Stepping back, I went down there and saw Pandora through the screen door jumping around outside. The wooden and glass door behind it was wide open. The ease with which she had got out became obvious when I pushed the screen door open with one finger. But, of course, she would be unable to get in.

"You silly dog," I said, opening the screen door and letting her in. She bounded in and greeted me with her usual effusion. Well, I thought, she'd had plenty of time to take care of her various needs. She and I could go to bed. Closing and locking both screen and outer doors, I returned back down the hall, thinking a little grimly of Diana's apparent habit of leaving outside doors open. But . . . I stopped in mid passage, a clear picture of our previous entry vivid in my mind. Diana had led the way. I had followed, and I remembered very distinctly closing the door behind me. It was true, I had not locked it. But I had heard the click of the tongue as it went home. I was almost positive. Almost.

But, of course, memory is accommodating. I couldn't be sure. Perhaps I had only thought I heard the click, and the door had blown open by itself.

Feeling unsatisfied, I walked past the open door where I had been unable to find the light. Closing that automatically, I went back to the kitchen, followed by Pandora. But my eye caught the big box of kitchen matches. The cats might be in that unlighted room, I thought, the one whose door I had just shut. I'd better go and open it anyway. On an impulse, I picked up the matchbox and wound my way back to the hall. Standing in front of the door, I took one of the matches out and struck it. Then I opened the door.

A rickety-looking flight of wooden steps led directly from the door straight down to the basement floor. If, a few minutes before, I had taken the one step I had felt so impelled to do, I would have fallen to the concrete far below and almost certainly have been killed.

4

I felt much better the next morning when I awoke early to find the sun streaming in my window, my body in a snug cocoon consisting of Seth, Susan and Pandora lying, respectively, on either side and across my feet, and a breathtaking view across the valley to the hills beyond, visible as soon as I sat up.

I stroked Seth and Susan. "Where were you?" I scolded.

Pandora, assuming, as usual, that anything I said was addressed to her, went through a sort of morning dance, barking excitedly. The cats merely opened their eyes. A faint odor seemed to drift in my direction from them. I sniffed. Somewhere in the past I had smelled that smell. I closed my eyes and tried to fix the time and place, especially the place. Images stirred in the back of my mind, but wouldn't be brought out where I could see them. Never mind, I thought. Sooner or later they'd emerge.

Getting out of bed, I went over to the window, pushed it up, and took a deep breath of fresh air. The shock to my smog-accustomed New York lungs was so great I got giddy. After my head cleared, I stared over the soft, rolling hills, all shades of green, to the bluer hills beyond, and my old love of the country reasserted itself.

I glanced at my watch. Six thirty. Early, but I had eight and a half hours sleep nevertheless. As I stepped into the shower in the adjoining bathroom, I remembered passing back through the dining room, the sun porch and the living room, and going into the central hall on my way, theoretically, to finding Diana. But in the hall, caught in some kind of paralysis of fatigue and depression, I had decided the hell with it. The duties of a paid companion would, I was fairly sure, include going to make sure Diana was all right and didn't require company. But all she had wanted of me, she had originally said, was just for me to be there to keep her from being alone. My presence had accomplished that already. I would go to bed.

Once in my room, the depression had lifted, but the fatigue remained, and I was asleep within five minutes of slipping into my nightgown.

Now, bathed and dressed and ready for breakfast and accompanied by Pandora, Seth and Susan, I went downstairs, passing Diana's closed door on my way. It occurred to me that the formidable Mrs. Klaveness might already be presiding in the kitchen, a thought that somewhat dampened my spirits. I did not want to have to cope with a reproving and repressive personality before I had had my first cup of coffee.

But it was not Mrs. Klaveness who was standing in the kitchen staring out the window and holding a cup of something that steamed.

"Hello, Candida," Simon said, turning as I came in.

I had forgotten, I discovered, that curious jolt that looking into his blue-green eyes always gave me, and were giving me at that moment. His fair hair, I could see now, was mixed with gray.

"Hello, Simon," I said, trying to sound as casual as he.

"Are these yours?" He put his cup on the windowsill, squatted down and held out his hand. Seth and Susan approached, sniffed and then started rubbing against him, their purrs like generators that had just started up. At that moment Pandora, who had stayed behind in the hall to conduct an exploration of her own, hurled herself into the kitchen and then braked to a stop in front of the vistor.

"Yes," I answered his question. And then, "Down, Pandora," as the latter, having finished a cursory inspection, obviously decided to accept Simon as a close and valued friend.

"That's all right." Simon stood up and rubbed Pandora's yellow head. "Mostly retriever, I'd say."

"You'd be right."

"I remember now, you always had a private zoo, made up of the abandoned and maimed of the territory. It's nice to see that life in the big city hasn't changed you." He picked up his cup again.

The easy charm was there, I found myself thinking, but more aloof, as though an overbrilliant light had been dimmed.

"Speaking of the abandoned and maimed," I said, pouring boiling water from the kettle into a cup containing instant coffee. "Diana told me that you now run a halfway house down the road."

"That's right." He leaned back against the windowsill and gently swirled the coffee around in his mug. "What brings you here?"

I mixed milk and sugar into my coffee, then drank some. I was a little surprised at his question. For some reason I had assumed that Diana had told, or written, him about my coming.

"Diana hired me to stay here with her," I said bluntly. "Didn't she tell you?"

"No. She hasn't been around here for a few weeks. She was staying in New York, I think."

"Yes. That's where I bumped into her. Literally." And I told him about our encounter in front of Saks.

"I see. And she asked you to come up here to be with her?"

"Yes."

He stared into his cup. "That doesn't sound like Diana. Paying somebody to come and stay with her. If anything, she's always complained about having too many people around—relatives, friends, hangers-on."

"I'm not making it up, you know."

I was astonished at how swiftly I came back with that. I was not usually that defensive.

He looked up quickly. "I'm not suggesting for a minute you are, Candida. What's the matter? You've never before carried a chip on your shoulder."

There were so many easy answers I could have made: that a hired companion was a come-down from being an editor and my ego was therefore feeling sensitive; that anyone as blunt-tongued as I was unaccustomed to being doubted. I could even have just laughed and said, "Sorry." Instead the old memory came between me and Simon as it always did. As a result, my tongue clung to the roof of my mouth and I felt a slow, hot flush crawl up my neck to my face. At that moment I would willingly have killed Simon and then myself out of sheer embarrassment.

"So it's still that," Simon said. He put his cup down on the nearby table. "Look, Candida, that was fifteen years ago. I realize you were a child and it was a shock. But—"

"I don't want to talk about it," I said, furious at myself.

"We have to talk about it. If we don't, we'll never bridge that barrier between us, and I—"

"I told you, Simon, the subject is closed. Shut. *Geschlossen.*"

I turned my back on him, took out two cans, one of dog food and one of cat, opened them, and emptied the contents into the three big plastic dishes I had remembered to bring down. "There you go," I said to the three animals who closed in on the dishes. "Have a ball."

"What made you use the German word?" Simon asked.

"What German word?"

"*Geschlossen.*"

"I've always used it. I had a German refugee nurse after my mother died—you should remember that."

"I do now. I had forgotten."

"Why? Why were you concerned about the German word?

60

I must have used it in front of you before."

"I suppose so. But I didn't notice then. Perhaps Diana told you. I spent a while in Germany with the army."

"Yes," I said steadily. "She did. I also had heard before that that you had been killed—or committed suicide—in a bad accident. I thought you were dead."

"That explains your stunned look when you saw me coming out of the rose garden. I'm glad to know it was merely shock. I thought it was horror at finding me here—very debilitating to my ego."

"What did happen?"

"It's a long story. Sometime I'll tell you. Did Diana say why she wanted you to come and be with her?"

The change of subject was blatant. Ordinarily I would comment on it, and my soaring curiosity was almost more than I could swallow. But I had closed a subject on him. I couldn't very well probe into an area he wanted left alone.

I shrugged, unable to bring myself to betray Diana's outburst at our lunch about feeling herself haunted. To tell people who didn't know her, such as Terry or Jerry, was one thing. To tell Simon was another. Besides, I was remembering that she had had a certain amount to drink. Perhaps what she'd said to me she might not have put quite as baldly if she had been cold sober.

"Why don't you ask her yourself?" I said.

"Ask me what?" Diana said. "You're up early, both of you."

I looked up.

Wearing a long cotton robe, with her blond hair falling around her shoulders, Diana managed to look younger than her thirty-eight years, and therefore more vulnerable. Yet in some way that I couldn't pin down she looked not quite put together—almost blowsy.

"Ask me what?" she repeated.

It was her eyes, I decided, that made her look raffish. The lids were puffy, and the famous blue eyes seemed almost to have retreated.

"What is it that Simon is supposed to ask me?" Diana said. It was interesting that she asked me, not Simon, and that her

61

voice had the edge to it that I had heard the day before and resented.

"I was just curious as to why you asked Candida to come and stay here with you," Simon said.

Diana looked at him then, and the expression in her eyes when she did brought back within me the old, searing memory with a vengeance. "For company," she said.

"Would you like some coffee?" I asked her. "There's water boiling."

"No, thanks. Just some juice."

Moving past me she went to the refrigerator and opened it. In a second her hand emerged with a tall glass of tomato juice.

"You must have had that all poured and ready," I said.

"What do you mean by that?"

This time there was such a snap to her voice that I stopped with my own coffee cup halfway to my mouth. "Nothing—nothing more than I said. Why?"

"Is there any reason why I shouldn't have juice poured out and cooling?"

I put the cup down on the table. "Diana—" I started, more than willing, I discovered, to have a showdown of some kind. But Simon interrupted me.

"You know, Diana, that was a perfectly ordinary comment of Candida's. You betray yourself when you come out with some defensive comment like that."

Betray *what*, I thought.

Diana, both hands still cupping the glass of red juice, stared at him. "I suppose so," she said after a minute. Then she looked down. "Sorry, Candy, I'm afraid my temper is not of the best these days."

She was staring at the glass, which she was still holding in her two hands. Then, "I think I'll drink this in the study," she muttered, and swept past me out of the kitchen, bearing the glass in front of her as though it were a sacred vessel.

"I don't understand any of this," I said.

Simon, who was back studying his coffee, didn't say anything.

62

"Is there anything I should know?" I asked.

"Why do you ask that?" he said, still not looking up.

"Because I keep feeling that there is."

"Like what?"

"If I knew, I wouldn't have to ask." Tiny alarm bells seemed to be ringing in my head and were beginning to affect my normal cheerfulness, largely, I decided now, because I couldn't read whatever message they were sending. More to be doing something than because I felt hungry, I went to the refrigerator for bread, butter and eggs, passing, as I did so, the cats' dish. Then I stopped in astonishment. Seth's and Susan's usually incomparable appetite must have deserted them. Their dish was still almost full of their favorite food. I glanced at Pandora's. Hers was polished clean. All three were sitting in a corner of the kitchen, eyes half shut, in a collective post-prandial trance. Which meant, of course, that they were all full. Including the cats.

"I know what you've been doing and what that smell is," I said suddenly. "You've been catching mice."

"You sound," Simon's voice said behind me, "as though you've stumbled over a new law in nature—cats hunting mice."

"You mean there're mice around this antiseptic kitchen?"

"Hardly. Not with Mrs. Klaveness ruling the domain. Probably the cellar. Although—Oh, good morning, Mrs. Klaveness."

The tall, gray-haired, iron-faced woman standing in the kitchen door surveyed her realm with very much the same expression, I couldn't help thinking, that might have been on the face of an ancient Roman looking over his city after the sack of the Goths and other barbarians.

"Animals in the kitchen I do not approve of," she stated in a heavily Teutonic accent.

"Mrs. Klaveness—" I started, ready for battle.

"Just a minute, Candida." Simon put out his hand. "Let me explain."

I decided to ignore his high-handedness.

"I don't see why—" I started again.

"Yes, Mr. Simon," the formidable woman said, "tell me." What irritated me was that her voice had softened. Was every woman, I wondered disgustedly, regardless of age or national origin, and including myself, knocked flat by her hormonic reaction to Simon? He certainly was not as devastatingly good-looking as he once was. Resentfully I looked at the tall middle-aged man in the rough, navy blue sweater with his graying fair hair and tired lined face. But replacing the varnished handsomeness was something else, some other quality, that made Mrs. Klaveness's softened tone understandable. . . . Stop it! I admonished myself. Cease this maundering! And don't let him take the ball away from you. Filled with this worthy aim, I started to open my mouth again. But Simon was already talking.

". . . and because Miss Egremont and Miss Brown are old friends, and Miss Brown could not possibly neglect her—er—obligations towards the animals she adopted, they are now making their home here. I know that you will understand and be kind to them."

Why the old *fake*, I thought. Be kind to them indeed! As if their rights weren't fully as great as Frau Himmler's here. But my indignation receded, quite against my will, at the apparently magic effect Simon's hypocritical words had had.

"Yes. I understand. I do not like them in my kitchen. But I will be kind to them." She put out a large, tentative hand. "Kitty?"

Seth and Susan, regality in every move, opened their sapphire eyes and rose from their Egyptian cat positions. Then, with Seth leading, they stalked from the kitchen towards the back door.

But Pandora, the people's friend, ears flopping, went over to the granite lady, wagged her tail, rose up and put her front paws on the awesome bosom. Then, before Mrs. Klaveness could stop her, Pandora licked her face.

Germs, I thought, reading the housekeeper's mind.

"It's all right, Mrs. Klaveness," I said, hoping to repair matters. "Dogs' mouths are much cleaner than humans'."

"Just shut up, Candida," Simon advised, *sotto voce*. I saw,

64

too late, that my remark could be construed as having unfortunate, not to say lascivious, interpretations.

"Not that I mean—" I started, never learning.

But it didn't matter. The big square face had gone pink. "*Ach, du lieber hund,*" she said. And then, "You are hungry," she declared, rather in the manner of a theologian stating a dogma.

I was about to undo this gift of the gods with yet another ill-conceived, ill-timed statement to the effect that Pandora had already eaten. Fortunately, I noticed, just in time, that Simon was glaring at me.

"I have here," Mrs. Klaveness said, opening up a package wrapped in foil, "a little something that I have decided I do not wish for lunch."

And before my astonished eyes, she proceeded to feed what looked like a chicken sandwich down Pandora's ever-willing throat.

"Candida," Simon said, taking my arm. "I want to show you the rose garden. I know we can leave your zoo in Mrs. Klaveness's care."

And before I could object, I found myself, my arm clamped in a grip of steel, being led through the dining room to the sun porch.

"Well, you needn't act as though I'd just been promoted to the FBI's most wanted list," I said.

"If I don't get you out of there you're going to ruin all my good work. Don't you ever think before you talk?"

I yanked my arm away as we got to the door in the porch. "No," I said, regressing rapidly to childhood. "It's pompous to do that."

It was an old joke, dating from the days when I was a dazzled child, far gone in love with the handsome prince who embodied, as far as I was concerned, every masculine ideal. Pompous, a newly learned word, described everything I disliked. Therefore Simon, the cavalier-knight, *sans peur et sans reproche*, became the opposite of pompous, a fact I told him one day in a rush of love. He kissed me then, on the cheek, the only time he ever kissed me, and made me promise that if he ever showed signs of being pompous, I would tell him immediately.

Fortunately, I thought now, realizing how much my use of the word betrayed me, he wouldn't remember that.

But he did.

"Alack and weladay, Candida. How are the mighty fallen!" He stood looking at me, a crooked half smile lifting one corner of his mouth, his face lit in the sun that managed, somehow, to come through the dirty window.

And he kissed me again, on the mouth this time, his lips, warm and sweet, resting on mine for a few seconds. Electric volts quivered through me. Then I jerked my head away and hit him, because it was the better of two alternatives, the other being to cry.

The imprint of my hand had showed pink against the tan of his skin, revealing what I had not noticed before: scars, white against the pink.

"Mrs. Klaveness," he said as coolly as though both the kiss and the slap had never happened, "would look upon your animals as ambulatory disease carriers to be eliminated unless she could be made to see them first as orphans abandoned by a cruel world, in which case, so far from being eliminated, they should be fed and loved and given homes. See you," he said, and opening the door, went out into the garden, moving rapidly towards the gate.

"Damn, blast and hell," I said. "That *toad*. That unprincipled invertebrate, that conceited—"

"So you're still in love with him," Diana said. Her glass empty, she was standing in the living room door looking, I thought, miraculously better. I hadn't realized tomato juice had such restorative powers.

"I have not been in love with him since I was eleven years old," I said. "To be accurate, fourteen years, ten months and eighteen days ago."

"In other words since the day you walked in—without knocking—and found him making love to me. Is that why you're still so anti-sex?"

"I am not anti-sex," I said furiously.

66

"Then why, at the age of twenty-six, are you surrounded by wildlife instead of lovers?"

"That's none of your business."

I waited, hopefully, for her to fire me.

"You're absolutely right. It isn't." She surprised me by saying, "But I still think you shouldn't hold that against him."

"And I still think that that was an odd thing for him... for both of you... to be doing the day before your first marriage to somebody else."

"To quote you," Diana said firmly, "that is—and was— none of your business."

"Maybe then we'd better change the subject."

Diana stared at me for a moment. Then shrugged. "As you wish. I have two pieces of news. Eric Barrington is coming to lunch. Does that ring a bell? Do you remember him?"

A face, remembered from a famous (and disastrous) party, sprang to my mind. "Tall, dark and hardworking," I said. "Wasn't his father the man who started off working for some local company and ended up owning it?"

"And a few other things besides. Yes, he was our very own self-made tycoon."

"Since I approve of the Horatio Alger myth, why do I get unpleasant vibrations when I hear his name?"

"Who knows? Maybe you caught him kissing me behind the rose garden. He often did."

"In that case, I'd be against the entire male population of upper Westchester. And despite all your allegations about my being anti-male and anti-sex, it ain't true."

Diana laughed. "No. All right." Then her smile faded and she hesitated.

"What's your second piece of news?"

"James is arriving at Kennedy."

For a minute I didn't connect. "James?" Then I remembered. "Your son?"

"Yes..."

I looked at her stilled face. "Aren't you happy?"

"Oh, Candida, of course I am. But..." Her voice faded.

"But what?"

67

"Well, I haven't seen him that often. I wanted to," she burst out. "But Roger was so *stuffy* about it. And anyway, a lot of the times I went to London to see him, Roger had him out of the country."

"You mean he sent James out when he got wind of your coming to see him?"

"Yes . . . well, not exactly. Roger was connected with the Foreign Office. He was often posted abroad. . . ."

Since her voice seemed to run down again, I prompted, "And he took James with him? Wouldn't that be the normal thing for him to do?"

"I suppose so. Although it must have been hard on poor James to be chopping and changing from one environment to another. James, James, *James*," she said suddenly, and with an odd violence. "Anybody else would call a little boy Jimmy. But not Roger. 'His name is James,' he always said."

And as she spoke, a picture of the quiet, dark, enigmatic man who was Diana's third husband suddenly appeared in my mind. The second marriage had been a fiasco from the beginning. Diana had gone to Mexico within something like six months. Then, a year and a half later, when she was twenty-eight and I was sixteen, there was a wedding in the rose garden—after two divorces a church affair seemed a little out of place. I was there with my father, both of us invited to the wedding and to the big party which followed. I remembered standing off to one side, just after the ceremony, watching the happy couple. Diana in a powder-blue dress created for her by some great name in fashion, her blond hair up in the chignon that became practically her trademark, a glass of champagne in each hand. And Roger Eliot? His was an intelligent face, but a face that gave away very little. Somebody came up and spoke to them. Roger removed one of Diana's wine glasses, said something to her. She turned her face to him and replied and then he smiled. It was an attractive smile, but it still told me nothing about the man.

My father had spoken from behind me.

"She's going to have trouble with him," he said.

"Why?" I asked.

68

"Because she won't be able either to dominate him or buy him. And he will probably have no understanding at all of her problem."

"What problem?"

But at that point one of the waiters had come up and replaced my empty plate with a full one, and by the time that transaction was over my father had wandered off in the direction of the bar. I meant to repeat my question, but by the time that tragic and cataclysmic evening had come to an end I no longer remembered.

". . . so do you think you could drive in to Kennedy and pick him up?" Diana was saying now.

I could, of course, have asked her to repeat the first part of her request through which I had been daydreaming. But the general drift was obvious.

"What time?" I asked.

"The plane gets in at two, and then he'll have to go through the customs."

"I take it—" I stopped, wanting to make sure that I said this tactfully. "I take it he's coming to live here permanently."

"Of course." Despite all my tact the haughty note was back. "Exactly where he should have been all this time. I'm going to get some more tomato juice." And she went towards the kitchen.

Even allowing for the time it might take for James to go through customs, I felt that, to be on the safe side, I should leave no later than twelve. At eleven fifteen Mrs. Klaveness found me in the animals' room, where I was busy cleaning out cages and providing food and water.

"Before you go, you will eat a sandwich?"

I had never gone back to the kitchen to pursue the program instituted by my taking out the bread, eggs and butter, so I was hungry.

"Yes, thank you, Mrs. Klaveness, I'd love one."

She stood there, surveying the room. After a while she said, "You should be a vet."

"Yes. That's what I wanted to be."

"Your sandwich will be ready in the study at eleven thirty."

I changed out of my jeans and into a more respectable pants suit, and went downstairs to find the study.

It turned out to be on the opposite side of the main hall and on the far side of another, smaller living room. I was halfway across the latter when I saw that Diana, also in a pants suit (a much more expensive one than mine) and with her hair up, was in the study sitting opposite a man whose face was hidden by the wings of the chair but whose gray-flanneled legs were visible.

I paused as I entered. There was something about the two of them that suggested a tête-à-tête. But Diana looked up and smiled.

"Come in, Candida. You remember Eric, don't you?"

"Of course," I said pleasantly, as the legs went back and a head and torso arose above the chair.

"Hello, Candida. No time long see," Eric said.

Unlike Simon, he bore his years well. Tall and muscular, and without a touch of gray in his dark hair, Eric Barrington looked like a man who had become successful without being obnoxious about it. Even his "no time long see" sounded humorous, even witty, instead of banal.

"It's good to see you again," he said, holding out his hand, "and to know that you're going to be here with Diana."

It was a nice statement, and I ignored the pang I felt at this further evidence that wherever Diana went, and no matter how many husbands she had, there was always a covey of males hovering around to protect and comfort her. You're jealous, my girl, I said silently to myself. And felt myself acknowledge the accusation.

"It's nice to be here," I said.

At that moment Mrs. Klaveness came in behind me, a cloth-covered tray in her hands.

Putting it down on a coffee table, she drew up a chair near the unlit fireplace. "You will be comfortable here," she said, in the manner I was beginning to recognize of making statements.

"Aren't you going to eat with us proles?" Eric asked, smiling.

"Candida is going to meet James," Diana said.

"I'd forgotten. Of course. He's coming this afternoon, isn't he? What a pleasant thing for both of you."

There was an odd pause. I uncovered the tray. "That looks beautiful," I said to Mrs. Klaveness.

"But you want a drink first, don't you?" Diana asked.

"Not when I'm about to drive. Is there coffee?"

"I'll bring it immediately," Mrs. Klaveness offered in such a hearty tone that I wondered what I had done so right as to win this approval. Diana, I noticed, was still drinking tomato juice.

"You really like that stuff, don't you?" I nodded towards her glass. "Aren't you afraid you're going to get vitamin C shock?"

"What does that comment mean?"

I paused, a wedge of the sandwich halfway to my mouth. "Nothing. I was kidding."

Diana finished her tomato juice, then put down the glass. "Oh, well, you know what Linus Pauling says—the more vitamin C the better."

"An admirable statement. Let me get you some more." Eric stood up again and reached for her glass.

But Diana paused, not relinquishing it. "Maybe I'll wait."

At that moment Mrs. Klaveness returned with a coffeepot, cup and saucer, cream, sugar and a piece of chocolate cake.

I sighed. "We're going to have to have a talk about my diet."

"I do not like diets," Mrs. Klaveness stated. "They spoil cooking. Some people"—her little blue eyes seemed to fix on Diana—"do not eat properly all the time."

It took me a minute to work out that statement, but after I did I glanced over towards Diana. "I can't believe you're on a diet, Diana. You've always been slim." I was about to add that it must be all that tomato juice when I remembered that she hadn't taken my previous quip very well. She had become, I thought to myself, extremely touchy on a great variety of subjects. All of which I wished I had known before I accepted her job offer.

"I've never been much of an eater," Diana said airily. "But

71

you're right. I've never had to diet." Perhaps in my own super-sensitivity to the whole subject I read a degree of self-satisfaction in her comment.

"He jests at scars that never felt a wound," I muttered between bites of the cake.

"What did you say?" Diana asked.

"Just a quote." I swallowed the last bite of cake and rose. "I think I'd better be on my way. What time is it?" I glanced at my watch. "Ouch! A quarter past twelve. Good-bye, everybody. I take it I'll recognize James immediately?"

It came out in the form of a question. I stared at Diana. "Does he look like you or Roger, Diana? Dark? Fair? Large or small for his age?"

"I haven't seen . . . dark, and rather small for his age. Hadn't you better be going, Candy?"

"Yes. I'm on my way. Let me make sure I have my keys. Yes, there they are."

"Take my car," Diana said. "I'll get you the keys." She started looking around the room. "I know they're in my bag."

"Thanks but no thanks. My heap is a simple American car with an automatic shift. I've never driven those smart foreign jobs and I don't want to have to worry about four forward speeds and your son all on the same trip."

"Candida!"

I stopped, half out the door. Diana came after me. "I'll walk you to the outside," she said. Then when we'd left the study, "Please make him understand that I would have come for him myself, *of course*, if I hadn't had to have this business lunch with Eric, set up before I knew he was going to arrive on this plane."

"How *did* you know he was coming in today?" I asked, suddenly curious.

"They telephoned a cablegram to me this morning."

"Oh." It was odd, I thought. I didn't remember hearing a telephone ring. But then it was a big house.

"You *will* tell him."

"Of course. Don't worry."

Still, I thought, as I maneuvered my station wagon past her

72

Jaguar and drove through the gate, if I were her nine-year-old son I would find it strange that she considered a business lunch more important than meeting her son's plane. But perhaps, since he had never lived with his mother, or not since he was five anyway, he would have no particular expectations of her as his mother.

Several very obvious questions about the whole matter of James's arrival inevitably leapt to the mind of anyone involved in it: Who was sending James over? Obviously some adult or adults must have been looking after him since his father's death. But who were they? Lawyers? English relatives? In which case, why were they returning the nine-year-old boy to a mother his father had not only considered unfit but had persuaded a court to consider the same, thus giving him custody of his small son—not a usual procedure? And in what way was Diana unfit? I munched on this question as my car, rattling at every joint, swallowed the miles. A mother would have to be very unfit indeed for an American court to hand over the custody of a child to its father. But then American courts were notoriously sentimental about mothers. England, I had heard, was still a man's country. Perhaps it took less there to declare a mother unfit, and therefore was less of a disgrace. Maybe there were no English relatives and there was no choice as to where James must live.

But above all other questions rose, to me, the most puzzling: In view of everything Diana had said and everything she'd told me and the indignation she'd implied about having lost custody of her only son, how could she let the most important business matter in the world come before meeting his plane? And how could I convincingly explain this strange priority to her son? In fact, I decided, as I negotiated the bridge, she had been astonishingly casual altogether about James's advent.

My planned two-hour allotted time to get to Kennedy had been generous, so I had not been unduly upset at getting off twenty minutes later than I had intended, thinking that I would make up the time on the way. But about fifteen minutes past the bridge that nightmare that haunts all drivers bent on meeting or catching planes, especially those on the narrow

73

entry and exit ways binding Manhattan to the mainland, descended on me. I had been bowling along at somewhat over the speed limit when the cars ahead of me grew abruptly thicker. As, perforce, I slowed down, I saw, coiled ahead of me and visible as far as I could see, a long reptilian creature made up of bumper to bumper cars. I stared at it in dismay, then glanced in the rearview mirror. In those few seconds I had become part of the creature, with cars nose to tail back of me. In other words, I was trapped. Even if there were another back road to Kennedy, there was no way I could turn around and find it.

So there we inched, with periodic blasts of car horns sounded more to relieve the frustrations of the drivers than to serve any function. As the minutes passed with no breaking-up ahead, I tried to console myself with the thought that those trying to catch a plane were in worse shape than I. But it was small comfort. If James had been an adult, who knew that such things as delays and traffic jams occurred, instead of a small boy arriving in a strange country to meet a strange mother . . .

But thinking along these lines did no good. Nor did it help to remember an occasion when I was six or seven and had been taken to New York City by my father. His mind on something else, he had walked past the great library lions on Fifth Avenue, unaware that I, enraptured by the proud marble beasts, had stopped to admire them. After offering my child's homage, I turned to speak to him. But he wasn't there. There were only huge strangers, twice my height, walking past. As long as I live I will never forget the despair and sense of abandonment that swept over me. It was both terrible and timeless. I let out a great wail. Then my father was back, bending down, reassuring me.

Such a vivid memory, suddenly in my mind, did nothing for my peace and serenity. Angrily I blew the horn. Angrily the man in front turned around and glared at me.

What, I thought, slapping the wheel, could, on a weekday, at a non-rush hour, be causing this? The answer to that was obvious: Anything—most likely an accident of some kind,

74

not yet cleared off the road, that had narrowed the lanes to one.

Half an hour later, easing past a huddle of two cars in collision, now both empty, one with its front buried in the back of another, plus a tow truck and a police car, I saw that my guess was right. Much comfort, I thought, emerging from the single lane and then letting the car out as much as I dared in view of the traffic policemen just behind me.

There was no making up that lost forty-five minutes. I would just have to hope that airline personnel, seeing that the little boy had not been met, had had the good sense to telephone Diana and learn that I was on my way and would hold him until I got there.

It was ten minutes to three when, my car parked, I flung myself through the doors of the arrival building and paused, wondering where to begin looking. A few knots of people were standing around, some surrounded by baggage and looking very much as though they were waiting to be met. Others appeared to be waiting for someone to arrive. I could see no child of either sex, although it seemed evident the plane had long since arrived and the passengers had cleared customs and gone on their way.

The obvious thing to do, I thought, was to ask. Going over to the airline desk, I tried to attract the attention of one of the clerks. The trouble was, they were all busy. Finally I blurted out to the nearest one, "I'm looking for a little boy, James . . . James Eliot. He was supposed to come in on the two o'clock flight."

The man finished his conversation with the customer in a leisurely fashion, in the manner of clerks, tellers and salespeople the world over who, knowing their services to be essential, have found the perfect platform from which they may discharge any free-floating hostility that they have spent most of their lives harboring.

"I'll be with you in a minute, madam," he intoned in a voice nicely calculated to put me in my place and make sure that all within earshot had noticed him doing so.

I swallowed my ever ready anger. A lost child came first. "This little boy—" I started.

75

The clerk on the other side, an older woman, said, "He's in the upstairs waiting room. One of our attendants up there is keeping an eye on him. I'm afraid he's been there for some time."

"But how could he—?"

"The two o'clock flight, as you mistakenly described it," said the sadist to my right, "came in at one, as it was scheduled to do."

"One? But—"

"You must have been mistaken about the arrival time," the kind woman said, still working on the ticket for her customer. "Anyway, you'd better check on that kid. He—"

But I didn't hear the rest. I ignored the escalator and went up the stairs to the mezzanine two at a time. Except for a young woman in the blue uniform of a flight attendant, sitting at a desk on the other side of the room, the whole area up there was deserted. So I saw them immediately: a small boy in the longish gray-flannel shorts that English schoolboys wear, sitting on a bench, two bags, a roll and some kind of box at his feet, and sitting beside him, bolt upright, one of the largest black cats I had ever seen.

5

I walked over and stood in front of him. "You're James Eliot, aren't you?"

He nodded his dark head. "Yes. And this is my cat, Hannibal."

"How do you do, Hannibal?"

Hannibal's short black fur was glossy with good health, his lake green eyes were almost round, and he had a long Roman nose and wide jowl. Around his neck was a pale blue collar. He was a magnificent and impressive sight, and I said so.

"He's very imposing, James. Hannibal, I mean. Did you . . . did he come over in the cabin with you?"

A look of indignation came over the boy's pointed features. "No. They wouldn't allow it. I told them and told them that he would be perfectly good and would sit in my lap or on the seat beside me. We've traveled heaps together and he's always done that. But they said he had to go in this awful box and then in the bottom of the plane with all the baggage. I was very annoyed." One hand went out and rubbed Hannibal behind the ear. Slowly a loud purr filled the air like an expensive, velvet motor.

"Did you have a good flight?" I asked him.

"No, because I was worried about Hannibal. They tried to make me eat something, but I wouldn't."

"Not for the whole flight? That's seven hours."

"As a matter of fact . . ."

"Yes?" I prompted.

"I threw up the dinner I had before I left. All over the next seat," he added with satisfaction.

I tried to recreate the picture. "Did you travel first class?" I asked.

"Yes." He spoke indifferently, as one who had never traveled anything else.

I, too, had traveled by air, but never first class, and on my way back to the tourist cabin had often cast an envious glance at those wide seats, only two across, with lots of space in between, knowing that my own narrow berth awaited me in the back with the rest of the hoi polloi.

"That's why I had a whole seat to throw up on," James explained. "There was nobody beside me."

A powerful fellow feeling was stealing over me. "How much of that was on purpose, and how much was being airsick?"

"I wasn't airsick. I never get airsick or seasick. It was what they did to Hannibal. I was angry."

"I see." I held out one finger about three inches from Hannibal's regal nose. For a second or two he gazed at it, as though wondering whether to recognize its presence, then he leaned over majestically and sniffed for a while. After that, with the air of majesty deferring, he rubbed his head along my hand.

"He likes you," James said. I found the clear brown eyes regarding me with greater interest. "He almost never does that."

"I'm flattered," I said truthfully. "But I can't help wondering if he's smelling Seth and Susan, my two Siamese."

"Do you like animals?"

"Very much. As I see you do." Hannibal, still purring

loudly, was allowing me to rub his head.

"Well, I do like animals. I like them a lot. But that's not why I like Hannibal. Hannibal's a *person*."

There was an urgency in his voice that made me glance at him again. His hand came up again and rested on Hannibal's neck, covering the collar. Those dark eyes, so unlike Diana's, were trying to tell me something, and although, for the life of me, I could not have put that messge in words, on some level I understood it. And I felt, for a moment, as though a shadow had moved over me.

I dropped my hand. "Yes, I know he is, James. By the way, I haven't told you who I am. I'm Candida Brown, a friend of your mother's, and I'm going to be living with you, too, for a while."

"How do you do, Miss Brown?" He held out a thin boy's hand.

"I think I'd rather you call me Candida," I said. "If you don't mind. I'm more used to it."

"All right. If you'd rather."

"We're . . . we're probably a little less formal over here," I said. And reflected immediately that it was a stupid statement to make. There was something about James that was his own, and that went beyond the greater reserve of the average English child. Looking at the closely cut dark hair, blue blazer, collar and tie, I wondered what Diana would make of him. And again felt something like a stab of fear.

"My car is parked outside. I'll get a porter to collect the box and suitcases and carry them for us. About Hannibal—"

"Oh, that'll be all right, I'll put his lead on him."

"You mean he'll walk with us?"

"Yes. He likes walking on a lead. Then I can take one suitcase and you can take the other and the roll. We don't need a porter."

"What about that box or carrier or whatever it is?"

"I told you. Hannibal never needs that. They made me put him in it. I wasn't going to anyway, but Walker said that if Hannibal had to go in the luggage place, then the box would protect him. I could see that that was true, and that was the only reason why I let them put Hannibal in. He hated it. They put him in and I could hear him howling all the time he was being taken away on that horrible baggage belt. Come along, Hannibal, I'll put your lead on."

James stood up then, a thin, wiry child with a well-shaped head and narrow body. Deftly he snapped the blue leash onto Hannibal's collar.

"What's this?" I asked, bending down and putting the roll under my arm.

"Nothing," James said, "Just something . . . something that's mine." Then he picked up one of the suitcases. I picked up the other.

"You'd better let me carry both, James," I said. "It's a bit heavy for you, and anyway, you have Hannibal."

"I can manage." And he started ahead. Sure enough, Hannibal padded beside him with perfect aplomb. Somewhat dubiously I looked at the makeshift carrier. Well, the airline could have it with our compliments, a fitting return for the exquisite courtesy of the unpleasant man downstairs. Quickly I followed James.

When we got to the escalator I glanced down to the lower lobby. There were, as far as I could see, no mastiffs or Great Danes lurking to take exception to Hannibal. Lifting his friend onto his shoulder, James stepped onto the escalator, with me bringing up the rear. When we got to the bottom he put Hannibal down again and walked with him across the lobby to the front doors, both of them moving briskly. I could see the heads turning as we passed, and, feeling a little like Gunga Din in the train of the British Raj, followed them through the doors to the sidewalk.

"You wait here with Hannibal and the suitcases, and I'll bring the car around."

"Can't we go to the car?"

"No. It's in a parking place. I have to cross several roads with traffic, and I'd rather you'd wait here."

"All right."

"James, keep an eye on Hannibal. The porters come along here pretty quickly with trucks and carriers."

The little boy looked at me with his strange, adult dignity. "Yes. Of *course* I will."

I left him standing near the curb, the bags to one side, and Hannibal, looking like an ancient portrait of himself in the Metropolitan Museum of Art, sitting on the other side. With a prayer that no harm befall James and his stately friend, I made my way quickly to the parking lot and then brought the car back around to where James & Co. were waiting for me.

I stowed the bags in the back. When I got into the driver's seat I found James and Hannibal already installed, with the cat between him and me.

"How did you happen to name him Hannibal?" I asked a few minutes later, easing the car onto the expressway.

"Well, actually, my father thought of it. Walker and I had found him hiding in an areaway of a house that was closed up. He was terribly thin and his fur was all stuck together. Even so, I knew he was going to be handsome, like a lion, and was trying to think of a proper name, when Father said that Hannibal was a great African general."

He spoke of his father calmly, which made me wonder how he felt about his death. "I'm sorry about your father," I said.

James didn't say anything.

It seemed both unfair and unkind to prod the boy further. "Who is Walker?" I asked.

"He's my great friend, I mean my other one."

"You mean besides Hannibal?"

"Yes."

I tried to envision the child who was James's friend. The son of someone Roger Eliot called friend? Someone who lived near? Or who played in the same park, or went to the same school?

"Did he go to school with you?"

"Who?" The dark head turned.

"Walker, your friend."

"Oh. Oh, no. He was . . . well, he sort of buttled."

"Buttled?" I glanced sideways at the neat profile and then back to the road. "You don't mean he was a butler, do you?"

"Not exactly. He did everything, except cook, of course. He

81

looked after the house, and Father and me and Hannibal."
There was a pause. "You see, Father was away a lot. Sometimes I would be with him, but sometimes it wasn't . . . wasn't convenient. So I stayed at home in London with Walker."

"Where is Walker now?"

"He's got another job. He doesn't like it."

"But he saw you off?"

"Yes. He changed his day off so he could go to the airport with me. Mr. Stearns said it would be all right. Mr. Stearns is the family solicitor."

"Don't you have any relatives, James?"

"Not close ones. Father didn't have any brothers or sisters. The only ones Mr. Stearns was in touch with, he said, were abroad or very old and in Scotland."

"I saw your father once. When he was married to your mother. You look a little like him."

"Yes."

Conversation lagged for a while. Both James and Hannibal were sitting upright on the seat, staring straight ahead. There had been no emotion in James's voice when he spoke of his father, now dead, or his friend Walker, back in London. But I could feel the tension, as taut as a trapeze wire. What storms were going on behind that closed little face? I decided to change the subject.

"Sometimes here we call people named James, Jimmy."

"Like your President."

"Yes. Which would you prefer?"

"My name is James. I've always been called that."

"All right, James it is. And there, James, is the New York skyline." I felt a pride of possession in pointing it out.

"It's very phallic, isn't it?"

I nearly ran the car off the bridge. "Where did you hear that, James, from Walker?"

"Oh, no. He'd never say anything like that. Sir Arthur Bolton, a friend of my father's, said it once when he was having dinner with us."

"Do you know what it means?"

"Yes. I asked Walker first. But he just said what he always

82

does when he doesn't want to answer, so—"

"What's that? What does he say when he doesn't want to answer?"

James gave a little giggle and pitched his voice lower.

" 'That'll be quite enough, Master James. You'd better ask your father when he comes back.' " But the sound I was listening for in his voice, the hint of tears, was there in the last two or three words.

"So did you ask your father?"

"Yes. He always answered questions, though he did say Sir Arthur Bolton was an arrant ass."

I could almost hear Roger Eliot's emphatic, incisive voice.

Past the bridge and headed up into North Westchester, I became aware, the nearer we drew to Tower Abbey, of a descending depression. Diana Egremont, I silently assured myself, was James's mother, certainly she must love her son. But there was love and love, another part of me countered, and, unfortunately, it did not always go with wisdom. Would she know how to leave that tautness alone?

"James," I said, "we're awfully glad to have you here. And I'm so glad to meet Hannibal." I put out a hand and touched the cat's big head, and encountered James's hand. I saw the dark eyes look at me quickly and guardedly.

"I haven't told you," I said, "but I have a lot of animals of my own."

"What, besides the two Siamese you mentioned?"

I told him about Pandora and Wisteria, the gerbils, the fish and Anthony and Cleopatra.

"I wonder if the Siamese—what were their names?"

"Seth and Susan."

"If Seth and Susan will mind Hannibal?" He sounded anxious.

I glanced at the cat, who was still sitting up straight, and reflected that if size had anything to do with it, James had nothing to worry about concerning his pet. But, of course, size was not always the deciding factor in such matters.

"They may have a few discussions over turf," I said. "But, for one thing, Seth and Susan haven't been there that long

83

themselves. It wouldn't be as though Hannibal were coming into my former apartment. And, heaven knows, there's enough territory for them to argue about. It's a huge house."

Conversation lapsed again. Three or four times I thought of topics I could introduce that might open up some discussion, questions about his school, or friends, or hobbies that might get him started talking. But I was stopped by the feeling that he really didn't want to talk, that because of his upbringing he would probably be polite and answer, but that he would rather be quiet. On the whole, and given the huge change in his life that he was in the middle of undergoing, I didn't blame him. Under those circumstances, I would feel the same.

So we rode in silence for a while. Finally, as we came up the parkway on the last stretch, I said, "You can see the house from here if you look, right up there on the left. There are some gray-stone towers poking up among the trees."

He ducked his head down and forward and I slowed down. I had made him fasten the seat belt, but I didn't want to incur any possible danger that he would strike his head against the windshield.

"Is that why it's called Tower Abbey?" he asked.

"Yes. How did you know that?"

"My father mentioned it."

As James sat back, I accelerated the car.

"He also said it was an architectural abortion," James added idly.

Again I could hear Roger Eliot's voice. And it was no use wishing that he had kept some of his more acerbic comments out of his son's hearing, or even that James had something less than what appeared to be total recall for some of his father's acid sayings.

"He was undoubtedly right, James. But it would probably be more tactful not to say so to your mother. After all, it's the home she grew up in, and she might have sentimental feelings about it."

"All right."

And was I right to put my oar in like that anyway? Perhaps tact was not the right road for greater understanding between mother and son. Maybe . . . But it was no use second-guessing myself. Besides, in less than five minutes we'd be there.

As we came around the carriage sweep I saw the front door open and Diana come out. Unbelievably, she was holding a tall glass of tomato juice. As the words flashed into my mind and I realized how naïve I had been, I heard James's voice beside me.

"She's still drinking bloody marys, the way she was when I went to see her in her hotel in London, two years ago. That's why Father didn't want me to see her."

As I parked the car on one side of the carriage sweep, I saw for the first time the full wreckage of the situation and of the fact that I was now, whether I liked it or not, part of it.

"James—" I started, having no idea of what to say further.

But Diana had come out of the doorway and was walking to the car. Veering to her left, she headed towards James's side. For a moment he continued to sit there. Then, with a courage I admired, he opened the door and slid out so that he was standing, facing his mother, when she reached him.

"Darling!" Diana said. Somewhere she must have disposed of her glass, because she held out both arms, and I saw James disappear inside her embrace. Unfortunately, he was still holding Hannibal's leash, so that as James's arm was pulled forward the cat was yanked from his seat and half dragged from the car.

"Watch out!" I yelled.

"Mother!" James cried out. "Don't!" Somehow he pushed her away. Hannibal was part in and part out of the car. In some way his leash had gotten looped over the open door handle and he was nearly strangled and protesting loudly.

"You've hurt him," James said indignantly. "You jolly nearly strangled him. Here, Hannibal." Tenderly James got the leash unhung from the door handle and put Hannibal down onto the ground.

"Where did that cat come from?" Diana asked, hostility in her voice.

It is said that vodka is odorless, but I realized immediately that this was not true. I also knew that Diana, rudely pushed

85

away by her son, her faculties blurred, was in no condition to be able to handle the rejection. Because rejection it was, with elements far deeper in it than the mishap to Hannibal. In that, Diana's intuition was on target.

"That's Hannibal, my cat," James said.

"Diana—" I started.

But disaster had not finished with us. From out the doorway rushed Pandora, delighted to see me after several hours of separation, and then braked as Hannibal's back, the black hair a rigid perpendicular strip down the middle, arched. I lunged for Pandora's collar. Hannibal spat. A black paw snaked forward. Pandora, eluding me, sprang back and barked, drops of blood appearing on her nose.

"I didn't intend to set up a zoo," Diana said loudly and angrily.

Pandora barked again and sprang towards Hannibal. This time I got hold of her collar, but it was too late. Hannibal gave a yowl and streaked towards the gate to the rose garden.

Diana's loud voice, riding over mine, said, "James, I'm talking to you."

"You're drunk," James yelled. "Just the way you've always been. See what you let happen to Hannibal! Now he's frightened and gone. I've got to go and look for him."

Lightning thought has never been my specialty, but I knew I had to make a rapid decision: either to go help James, or stay and try to calm Diana. I decided to help James find Hannibal.

"I'll explain later," I called to Diana over my shoulder, and sped towards the gate.

James was walking slowly around the edges of the garden, where there was shrubbery and bushes against the wall behind which Hannibal was probably hiding. The trouble was, the gate led to other parts of the garden nearer to the house and, by extension, down the hill into the slope and fields.

"Dear God," I breathed, "don't let Hannibal be lost."

"It's all right, Hannibal," James said softly. "Everything's all right. There's nothing to be frightened of. Please say something so I know where you are."

But, apart from James's voice, there was silence. Any second now Diana, angry and wounded, would come through the gate, and she would certainly not respect the quiet that was essential if Hannibal was to allow himself to be found.

I stood where I was, still as a sentinel, trying to will the cat to come out of hiding or to let James approach him. Then I heard footsteps on the path leading to the rest of the garden, and I saw Simon, with Hannibal over his shoulder, approaching from the other side of the gazebo.

James swung around. Obvious fury at having the quiet disturbed gave way to joy.

"Hannibal!" he said and ran forward.

Simon handed over his armful of black fur, which seemed to cover the upper part of James's body.

"Where did you find him?" James asked.

"He came racing towards me, but then his leash caught on a branch of one of the shrubs. I took him out another gate, and your mother said he belonged to you."

"Thanks. Thanks awfully," James said. For a while he stroked the back that was draped over his shoulder. Then gently he lowered Hannibal to the ground. "I think perhaps I'd better take him straight up to my room so he can get himself familiar with that. Walker said to butter his paws as soon as I got here. The best animal books think it's just a superstition, but I wonder—"

"Would you like me to get you some butter, just to be on the safe side?" I asked.

The dark eyes looked up. "That would be super."

There was not only Diana. There was Mrs. Klaveness to get past. I tried to imagine myself saying, please Mrs. Klaveness, I would like some butter to put on the paws of an exceedingly important cat. . . .

"Could you?" James said, his eyes still on me.

"Of course."

There were two ways I could go: through the rose garden door out to the carriage sweep, or down the path that led right past the gate and towards the door into the swimming pool. Where would I be least likely to meet Diana?

As I hesitated Simon said, "Diana went up to her room."

James's small nostrils flared, making him look, suddenly, very like his father. "She jolly nearly killed Hannibal."

"She didn't know how important Hannibal was, James," Simon explained. "After all, not only had she not met him, nobody had told her about him."

"That's all very well, " James said, "but Miss Br— Candida here didn't know either, and she knew instantly how to act with him."

I was by no means impervious to praise. But for once I wished that my behavior had not shone so brightly at the expense of Diana's. "Well, you see, James. I'm an animal person."

"That's what I mean."

Simon touched James's head lightly. "You must give your mother a little time, James. After all, people aren't that different from animals. Hannibal's going to need adjustment, too."

I could see that the argument carried weight. My heart lifted a little, and I threw Simon a grateful glance. But ultimately, it seemed, not weight enough.

"She was drunk," James said flatly.

I thought about denying it and then, luckily, didn't. James was used to hearing the truth, however unpalatable, from his father. It would, in fact, be possibly the worst thing I could do.

"She probably had more to drink than she realized, James. And on an empty stomach. That happens sometimes."

"It happened *all* the time when she was in London."

"How do you know, James? Did you see her that often?"

Out of the corner of my eye I saw Hannibal, who had been standing, rather tensely, sit down and start washing a paw. His adjustment, I reflected, was getting under way.

"I'm not asking that to put you in the wrong," Simon said. "But I think that one should discriminate between what one knows to be true because one was there, or had direct evidence of it, and what one hears to be true. Do you understand?"

James's leaf-brown eyes gazed up into Simon's blue-green ones. Then the boy looked down. "I *saw* her drunk once. She tried to hug and kiss me the way she did this afternoon. I . . . I *heard* that she was drunk a lot."

"Did your father tell you that?" There was no judgment whatever in that voice. It was a simple question.

James was still looking down. Bending at the knees, he stooped and ran his hand down Hannibal's back. A purr broke from Hannibal, who was at work on the other paw. Then, without getting up, he looked straight up at Simon. "I heard it through the door. My father was talking to Mr. Stearns, our solicitor. I knew they were talking about Mother, so I listened."

Like most people with no children of their own or younger brothers and sisters, I'd always had a lot of theories about how to bring up children, what to tell them and what not to tell them. Now all my theories were proving as flaky as a piece of pastry that was coming apart in my hands. How could I say, you shouldn't have done that, when I probably would have done the same, and anyway, with an upbringing as eccentric as his, how could I be sure what scale of values to appeal to?

"The trouble with listening at doors," Simon said kindly, "is that one often hears something that, in the long run, one would be better off not to have heard."

"Isn't it true?" James said, straightening.

"Isn't what true? That your mother sometimes, but not always, drinks too much? Yes. It's true. That she loves you very much? That's true, too. That because she loves you and wants you to love her she becomes afraid when she's going to see you, and therefore drinks more than she ought? That's true, too. Truth isn't one single thing, a fact, like 1066. It's a lot of feelings and circumstances coming together, and if you're going to look at one, and make a judgment about it, then you have to look at all."

Pause. I could almost see James, like a master computer, accepting this astute piece of programming.

"For example," Simon went on, "someone who didn't like cats could say that Hannibal here proved as soon as he arrived that he was too wild to be kept in anyone's home."

"But—" James interpolated angrily.

"That no sooner had he got out of the car," Simon went on inexorably, "than he started yowling; that he attacked Candida's dog here, giving her a nasty scratch down the nose, and then ran away. And that further, when I tried to pick him up to bring him to you, he scratched me." And with that Simon pushed up the sleeve of his sweater and showed a long, pinkish line running up his forearm.

"But that wasn't his fault. He was dragged out of the car, and this huge, strange dog came running towards him, barking, and *of course* he stuck up for himself, wouldn't you?"

Behind his indignation there was, in James's voice, a desperate note that touched my nerve. I said quickly, "Simon isn't trying to blacken Hannibal—well, how could you get him any blacker?—but he isn't trying to make him look bad so that ... so that you couldn't have him or anything...." The whiteness of James's face made me reach out and grasp his shoulders. "I *promise*, James."

"Yes, James. So do I," Simon said evenly. "He's as welcome here as you are. I'm just trying to point out that there are lots of ways of telling the same story. Do you understand?"

James's face was once again its usual clear ivory, with just a touch of pink in the cheeks. "Yes, I suppose so. But"—the stoic armor cracked a little—"you *scared* me."

Simon smiled then. "Pax. By the way, I'm Simon Grant."

"How do you do?" James said politely. He considered Simon for a moment, then, "All right. Pax."

"James," I said, "I'm not sure which room has been prepared for you, but we could go in and find out. Maybe we'd better go and get your bags."

"I think Mrs. Klaveness has seen to them," Simon said.

He turned out to have been right. The housekeeper was in the main hall running the vacuum over the tiles. Obviously irritated at being interrupted, she turned off the motor long enough to say that James's bedroom was on the same floor as ours but farther down the hall, and that she had taken up his suitcases herself.

"It's the room across from Mrs. Egremont," she said, her hand on the switch, her gaze on Hannibal. "The blue room—blue wallpaper, blue carpet, blue bedspreads."

"I think I'll leave you here," Simon said. "I've neglected

my charges long enough."

James looked at him out of his wise young eyes. "Are you a schoolmaster?"

"Well, in a manner of speaking, almost. A sort of housemaster, more nearly. Only the boys are a lot older than you, and they've all been in trouble."

"Don't you live here?"

The consternation in James's voice was both flattering to Simon and comic. But why comic? my argumentative other self asked. James had plainly been brought up by men. Wouldn't it be natural for him to feel more comfortable with a man, and dismayed if he showed signs of leaving?

"No. I'm just a bit down the road. But Diana, your mother, is my cousin, and I'm up here a lot."

James's face lit up. "Then we must be cousins, too."

"That's right." Simon smiled down at him. "We absolutely are. Welcome, cousin." And he held out his hand. James's hand disappeared inside it. His cheeks went pinker. "I say, that's jolly good. Can I come over and see you at your house sometimes? Would the other boys mind?"

A vision of James, whose language, even by English standards, was ludicrously formal, hobnobbing with the (I supposed) hairy, angry and sullen denizens of Simon's halfway house was almost more than I could sustain.

"I'm afraid—"

"Not a bit," Simon said cheerfully. "But they're tough and very American and they don't talk the way you do, James, so you'll have to be prepared for that."

"I don't mind people being tough," James said. "But I don't like it when they pretend."

"On the whole I agree with you," Simon said. "See you." And with a wave of his hand he went back out the front door.

With a powerful, delicate movement Hannibal sprang from the floor up to the broad stone balustrade at the beginning of the staircase.

"All right, Hannibal," James said cheerfully. "You can walk up that way."

"That is your cat?" Mrs. Klaveness, who had started and

stopped the vacuum motor again, asked.

"Yes. This is Hannibal."

Mrs. Klaveness and Hannibal eyed each other. I held my breath. So much seemed to hang in the balance. Then Mrs. Klaveness nodded. "At home, when I was a child, they had, in the zoo, a panther like that. What does he eat?"

"Well, almost anything," James said. "He's quite fond of Yorkshire pudding."

"Perhaps Mrs. Klaveness doesn't . . . isn't fully acquainted with Yorkshire pudding." I was nervous lest this budding friendship get off on the wrong foot.

But it was my own foot that was in my mouth, it seemed.

"It just happens," Mrs. Klaveness said, "that I quite often make Yorkshire pudding."

"When you do, could you save some for Hannibal?"

The housekeeper bent down to turn on the motor. "If there's any left over."

James opened his mouth.

"I'm positive there'll be some left over, the next time we have it, James." I started up the stairs. "Come along and let me show you your room."

We made a stately procession up the stairs, Hannibal walking up the balustrade, James beside him, his hand clutching the blue leash that was attached to the cat's collar, and I on the other side of James.

"Do you think she likes Hannibal?" James said anxiously.

"As much as I can tell anything about Mrs. Klaveness, I would say yes."

"I wonder what she's frightened of," James said as we reached the top.

"Mrs. Klaveness? Frightened?" I stopped in my tracks. "I'm much more frightened of her than I can imagine her being of anything." I stared at the small boy who was now busy taking Hannibal down from his perch onto the floor. "What made you say that?"

"I don't know. She looked as though she wanted to give Hannibal the evil eye when we came in."

"Well, all that means is that she's an orderly housekeeper

92

who probably thinks there're three cats too many in this house, for all that she seemed to accept Seth and Sue this morning."

Turning left, I crossed the hall and opened the door opposite Diana's.

"It's blue all right," I said, "just as Mrs. Klaveness said."

Like all the rooms on this floor—guest and family rooms when Diana was growing up—it was large and high-ceilinged. Two beds stuck out of the wall on the left. To the right, on the other side of a wide expanse of blue patterned carpet, was a chest of drawers. Directly across, a desk occupied the wall between the two tall windows. Watercolors of various country scenes occupied the walls. To the far right, near one of the windows, another door led to what was obviously a bathroom. It was an expensive, comfortable, even luxurious room. Yet despite that, and even with the afternoon sun streaming in, it was almost bleak. And bleak or not, it was hardly a little boy's room.

"You know you can put up whatever pictures you like," I said for want of anything more encouraging to say. Then I looked down to where Hannibal was standing, his tail almost trailing the ground.

"Hannibal's collar and leash match the carpet," I said hopefully.

James didn't say anything. He stood, just inside the door, his black shoes touching the edge of the carpet, one hand gripping the loop of the leash.

If, at that moment, I had had a button that would have transported James and Hannibal back to London, back to Walker, back to wherever the two of them felt comfortable and safe, I would have pushed it.

"Your bag is over there on the luggage rack," I said finally. "Would you like me to help you to unpack?"

After a few seconds he said, "No, thank you."

If he had cried, I would have felt free to put my arms around him. If he had had a temper tantrum, I could have tried to argue rationally with him, or at least had an excuse to talk. But there was nothing I could do about that taut silence. As a wall, it was far more effective than his mother's wildest flights of arrogance.

"I think I'll unpack now," he said. "If you don't mind."

It was a dismissal.

"No. Of course not. And James."

"Yes," he said without turning his head.

"Look at me."

But it did no good. The eyes that met mine were remote and polite. Doggedly I said, "Across the hall to the right is a wing. You go down some steps, turn a corner, and there's my room. You can't miss it. If you're feeling . . . lonely . . . or anything, you can come there any time and knock on the door. Even if it's the middle of the night. If I'm there, I'll be happy to see you."

"Yes. All right. Thank you."

As I turned and went across the hall to the staircase I heard his door close behind me.

A depression, comparable to the one I had felt the previous evening, seemed to seep into me. For no reason that I could at first think of, I felt like crying. Then it occurred to me that one very likely cause was James himself. And it was more than just an overpowering empathy with his despair. It was because, as sure as though James and his Hannibal were a steel chain, they effectively bound me to this cheerless place. Until their advent I would have felt free to go, even without a job, even without a place to stay. Terry, or the vet I used to go to, would have taken the animals on a temporary basis until I'd found a room I could rent. I could have managed. And almost any external obstacle, difficulty, hardship, would have been better than this . . . this . . . whatever the right word was it eluded me. Standing there, looking at the afternoon sun through the windows over the staircase, I shivered.

But, hugging myself as though the temperature were below freezing, I knew that because of James, all options were closed. I could not leave him to face his mother and this house alone.

His mother. On an impulse I turned back, went towards her door and rapped sharply.

There was no answer.

I knew she was inside—or at least I was reasonably sure—and this time I beat a noisy tattoo with my knuckles.

"Come in," a blurry voice said.

I turned the knob and pushed open the door.

6

The blinds were slanted and the room was dim, but I could see Diana pushing herself up against the headboard of her bed and adjusting the pillow behind her. Over her was a quilt.

"Yes?" she said, sounding considerably less blurry. Then, "Could you please adjust the blind to let in the light?"

I had knocked on Diana's door with a burning desire to express myself to her on the subject of James, a desire stiffened by her lady-of-the-manor tone in requesting me to fix her blind. So I turned back from the window on the boil to say a great number of things, all of them to the effect that she had better shape up in her role of mother.

But the words remained unsaid. In the added light Diana looked ghastly. The clean, angular lines of her face now appeared soft and padded. The magnificent eyes were hidden between upper and lower puffs. And the hand that was trying to hold a match to her cigarette was shaking. I knew all of those signs well, having seen them, increasingly, the last years of my father's life. Nevertheless, the depredation within only twenty-four hours was incredible. Even allowing for Diana's

96

potations from the night before and the solid red stream of bloody marys that had poured into her today, it was hard to believe that that alone could produce in such a short time the pallid skin, the shadows under those swollen eyes.

"Well," Diana said, after finally getting her cigarette lit and inhaling deeply, "what is it?"

Perhaps there are angels, I found myself thinking. Or something. Because a force that seemed to come from somewhere else was quite effectively preventing me from pouring out my indignation on the subject of James. And as I registered that fact, I also realized that for reasons I did not understand the subject of James and her relationship to him was an area of danger both for and with Diana, and if, in speaking, I appeared to criticize her role, then I would make an enemy of her, and anything I would ever do or say about or for James would automatically be opposed or discarded.

"I wanted to ask how you were," I said lamely.

"You mean you woke me up for that?"

I could not let her get away with the implications of that tone. "For one thing, Diana, I didn't know you were asleep. I'm sorry I woke you. But if you wanted to go on sleeping you could have told me so, instead of asking me to fix the blinds. For another, when you asked me to come up here, you said it was because . . . because you felt haunted here." Saying it like that made it sound not only incredible but ridiculous, a figment of my own invention, instead of something I remember her saying, but I pushed on. "Haunted, you said, by a twin sister you never knew you had. And you could only find out about her here. But I wondered if your being back in the house had something to do with your drinking last night and then again today."

"Or whether it had to do with James's arrival." Diana was not stupid.

"Yes. Or that."

She stared down at her cigarette. Her hand, I noticed, was still shaking.

"I suppose you now wonder whether . . . whether my feeling haunted . . . comes from alcoholic hallucinations."

97

"Well, in the past twenty-four hours that had occurred to me."

"It occurred to me, too. So I stayed up here, by myself, for three months without drinking. Not a drop, not one drink. And she was here . . . in this room."

"Did you see her?"

"What's seeing? I thought I did, but when I put my hand out, there was nothing. But I could describe her, down to the last detail."

"And she looked like you?"

"Yes. Just exactly the way I did when I was nine. There are scores of pictures of me in family albums I could show you, so that you'd know exactly, too, what she looked like. The only thing . . . the only thing was . . ." Diana's voice quivered and stopped. For a moment I thought she would break down. But she swallowed and went on. "She wasn't dressed in any dress I remember having. In fact, she wasn't dressed in the style I was at all. I ran around mostly in shorts or slacks or riding pants. I can't ever remember having on a dress except when Donnie made me put on one for a party or something."

I was momentarily distracted. "Who was Donnie?"

The blue eyes opened wider now. "My God, Candy, you've got to remember who Donnie was. The whole world knew who Donnie was and what happened to her." Diana fumbled for a cigarette from the package on the night table and then, with a hand that shook more badly than ever, lit it from the old one. Exhaling the smoke, she stubbed out the old cigarette. "No, I suppose you wouldn't. I keep forgetting that you're such a baby. You weren't even born when that happened. Still, I would have thought that even when you came along people would still be talking, it was such a ghastly affair."

A memory stirred. "Was she the one who died in the elevator here?"

"Yes."

"I'd forgotten about that." I paused. "Didn't people go away and leave her? I can't remember the details."

98

"Lucky you. I wish I could forget them. No, we did not deliberately leave her, of course not. We, my father and grandmother and I, were going abroad. I was only a child. Apparently he had made arrangements for the electricity to be turned off for the summer. Donnie... Donnie didn't go with us, because she was leaving to get married. Anyway, after we, Grandmother, my father and I, left, and the other servants were gone for the summer, she was staying packing her things. Then she got into the elevator to go down, carrying her bags with her. It was while she was going down in the elevator that the current went off." Diana dragged on her cigarette. "She was found three months later when we all came back.... It was horrible. I got ill almost immediately. I don't remember that part very well. But I still have nightmares about what she must have gone through."

"What a horrible memory for you to have."

"Yes."

"Were you fond of her—Donnie?"

"Since she was, in effect, my mother, having taken me over when I was a baby when my mother died, yes. She was all the mother I ever knew."

That made things even worse, I thought. And then my mind veered back to Diana's obsession with her theoretical sister. "Wouldn't Donnie have told you if you had had a mysterious twin sister?"

"If she knew."

"Why wouldn't she know?"

"Candida, if I knew the answer to that, then I'd know the answer to why she's... to why I'm being haunted." Once again her voice betrayed how near she was to the brink of hysteria.

I still thought it was hallucinations, alcoholic or not. After all, people other than those who drank had them. People who were mentally ill.

Mentally ill. I had, I realized, stayed away from those two words in my mind. Suddenly Terry's and Jerry's flip comments about people who didn't have all their marbles didn't seem quite so amusing.

"You think I'm off my rocker, don't you?" Diana said, once again demonstrating her radar intuition. "Candidate for the funny farm. Well, you're not alone. That's what the psychiatrist in New York said. He didn't mention anything as crude as schizophrenia or having hallucinations. He just talked about a private sanatorium where I could—what was his phrase?— learn to stabilize my sense of reality. Then he learned that I could pay for about two weeks of that fancy place, and after that it would be Manhattan State. After that he lost interest. Anyway, I still don't buy his theory. I still think that child isn't all in my head."

I suppose I continued to look skeptical.

"Just wait awhile, Candy. I have a feeling you'll be aware of her, too."

"I didn't say—"

She swung her legs over the side of the bed. "You don't have to. By this time I'm an expert on seeing that look come over people's faces. The psychiatrist's, yours, even Eric's, for all his old loyalty to me when I was recovering from that awful illness when Father and I got back.... About the only person who treats me as though he thought there was a germ of truth in what I saw is Simon."

"Simon? A therapist? Believes your ghost story?"

Diana stood up, slipped off her loose robe, and pulled on a pair of slacks and a sweater hanging over the back of a chair.

"Being a therapist is only half of him."

"What's the other half?"

Her grin had a touch of malice. "Episcopal priest." She caught the look that must have been on my face. "Surprise, surprise."

All of my father's old prejudices surged up in me. "And a plague on all your houses," I murmured.

Diana paused in putting on her shoes. "What was that?"

"That was what my father used to yell when we drove past those big churches on the drive up here above the green. At least he used to when he'd had a bit to drink."

I said it without thinking, and glanced quickly at Diana.

"Yes, all right," she said sourly. "I know I'm supposed to

have a drinking problem. But I can stop whenever I want to."

"He used to say that, too."

She turned quickly. "I stopped for three months, remember?"

"I didn't say *you* had a drinking problem, Diana."

"Considering that you had to live with the problem, I find your remark this morning about overdoing vitamin C with all that tomato juice even more phoney-naïve than I did then."

"Yes. I can see now that you would think that. It *was* naïve, I suppose. But my father's drink was bourbon. If he was out of bourbon, he would, in a pinch, drink rye. But I never say him drink anything else. I've seen other people drink bloody marys, of course. I've drunk them myself...I just never thought...I'm sorry, Diana, I must have looked like I was running the needle in."

Diana was sitting at her dressing table brushing through her fair hair and, with unsteady hands, trying to put it up in pins. She saw me watching her in the mirror. "You don't know how lucky you are with that short curly mop."

I glanced in the mirror at the brown hair that I kept short because it did curl and was therefore easy to take care of. "I'd gladly trade it in for your smooth blond mane. But, since that's impossible, tell me, instead, about Simon."

"What's there to tell?" She sounded impatient again. "After he recovered from his accident and..." She paused as though she were going to add something and then changed her mind. "...after he recovered from his accident in Germany, he went through some kind of crisis or conversion, or something, got out of the army and went to England to study for the Anglican priesthood. He was ordained, and when he got back here, he—and, I suppose, the bishop—decided that he could contribute most by using both his ministry and his psychiatric training. Hence the halfway house."

"It's such an odd thing for him to do, becoming a priest, although I suppose that was what he meant this morning when he said that my telescoped version of what he was doing, that I'd just been describing, left out a step or two on the way."

101

"Why odd? His father was a doctor, but two of his uncles were priests and there have been bishops and priests all over his family for several generations."

"Oh," I said. "That."

Diana turned on the dressing table stool. "What do you mean by 'that,' quote unquote?"

I made a gesture with my hands. "I suppose I mean that it's like going into the family firm. Only instead of it being a corporation like Xerox or General Electric or some other company, it's the Church."

"That's a pretty cynical view, particularly coming from anyone as nature loving and animal loving and generally up and so on as you."

"What's that got to do with the Church? As a matter of fact, that's why my father loathed churches and used to shout his personal anathema to them when he got drunk. He felt they ignored the good of all nature and animals, and I inherited his prejudice, I suppose."

"Well, you'd better talk to Simon about it, hadn't you?"

"I haven't the faintest desire to talk to Simon about it. After all, it's a free country, he can do what he wants."

"Nice of you," Diana grinned. "I'll tell him you said that."

"Yes, do." And then, before I knew what I was saying, I asked, "Is he in love with you?"

She looked at me steadily. "Do you care?"

"Not really."

"Then why ask? What's it to you?"

"Since I'm here as a paid companion it might make it easier for me to know. If the two of you are having a thing going then his status here is one thing, and if I find him wandering around the house I don't stop and ask if I can do anything for him. If he's a casual visitor then maybe I do."

There was a flicker of something in her eyes that I thought I understood. "All right, if you must know. The answer is yes. We do have something going. And since he has keys to the house, you might find him wandering around at odd hours, so don't get into one of your virginal states over it."

"If you and Simon and whatever you have going—to say

102

nothing of his clerical calling—are none of my business, and I agree they're not, then I don't think my virginity, whether present or absent, is yours."

"Agreed," Diana said. "I apologize."

I started to leave the room, then stopped at the door. "What baffles me," I said, turning, "is how you think a family as rich and prominent as yours could cover up the fact that you had a twin sister—even if she did exist."

Diana came out of her bathroom wiping her hands on a towel. "What I should think would fairly leap to your mind—given your general anti-money slant—is that rich people can pay to have things done, such as a little hushing up."

"But *why*?"

Diana didn't answer for a minute, then she hung the towel on a rack near the bathroom door and said, "I don't know the answer to that. But, according to Eric Barrington, there was a rumor around the time I was born that there was a second child. It was denied again and again, but it persisted."

"Did you know about this rumor when you were growing up?"

"No. Of course not. I only just discovered it when I told Eric about . . . about my own trouble here."

"I thought you said he was among those who thought you'd gone round the bend."

"Being Eric, and being also in love with me—since you want to get everyone's status straight—he didn't put it that crudely. I think he thinks that I heard this story at some time, and what with stress and nerves and drinking and the state of the house and not having any money, I've built it into a 'haunt.' He thinks that when I finally get this place sold and leave it for good, the whole thing will go away."

Privately, I thought that the most sensible diagnosis of Diana's ghost problem I had heard yet. "And what does Simon say? You said he was sympathetic."

"He says he doesn't know, although he concedes there might be some basis in reality for my feeling about this house." Diana paused. "I've even asked him—in his role as priest—to conduct an exorcism."

103

"Good heavens, Diana!" Medieval tales and contemporary movies swam through my mind. "That's pretty far out!"

"Evidently he agrees with you, because so far he's refused. He seems to think that it would be a good idea for me just to leave, get out."

I was astonished at the surge of emotion that went through me at those glorious words. Leave the house? What a splendid idea! If I had had any doubts about how strongly I felt about it, those doubts were now gone. Twenty-four hours after arriving I was more than willing, I was eager to go.

Diana was watching me. "Nothing would make you happier, would it? You're sorry as hell you agreed to come up, aren't you? Is it me? Or the house? Or both? Simon said you wouldn't stay the course."

Who knows what I might have answered if she had just left off that last statement. The history of the next few weeks—and of my life—might have been different.

But she didn't leave it off. She said it: *"Simon said you wouldn't stay the course."*

So I bit. Right from the beginning, almost as far back as I could remember, Simon had the power to shape my thinking and life, and I didn't stop now to consider the import of my words.

"Well, Simon, as often, is wrong. I said I'd come. I've received half my first month's salary in advance. I'm not going to take your money and run."

"If it's the money, forget it. If you want to go, go."

Another possibility—not altogether welcome—occurred to me. "Do you want me to go?"

"Why would I want that, having gone to so much trouble to have you come up here, and having waited in town at an expensive hotel until you could get yourself together?"

"Maybe things have changed for you. Maybe Simon is willing to stay here instead of me. And you'd rather have that."

"And James?" she said.

My heart did its plummet to the bottom. I'd forgotten about James. Clever Diana. But if she wanted me to go (as I

104

had hoped) what was clever about reminding me of a reason to stay? And by the way, how come she knew I considered James a reason to stay?

"Well," I said, "what about James? If Simon were to stay here, James would have the two of you."

Diana lit another cigarette. "Even if Simon wanted to stay, and I wanted him to stay, it would not be exactly in his best interests as a member of the clergy, now would it, to stay here in this house with me?"

"I don't know. The clergy are getting pretty liberal these days."

"Maybe. But not a lot of the laity, who can withdraw their support and their money. And Halfway House is supported by the Church."

"Ah, their money. It comes back to that, doesn't it?"

Diana smiled maliciously. "Which supports your worst suspicions of just about everybody."

"You make me sound like Tandem's own homegrown revolutionary. I'm not against money. But now I'd like to ask a question. If Simon thinks you should get out, if you hate being here alone, if Eric, whom you respect, thinks you'd get rid of your problems if you'd just go somewhere else, why don't you?"

"I thought I made that clear. Because I'm quite convinced —and don't ask me why, because I don't know—that I can only find the origin of all this here. And I'm going to stay here until I find it." She went on more slowly. "I told you before I wanted you here because you wouldn't snow me, because in your own untactful way you tell the truth. I don't necessarily like you. And I know you don't like me. But I trust you."

In its own negative, backhanded way, it was a compliment. "All right, Diana," I said. I watched her smooth the quilt on her bed. "How are you going to try to run this thing—this feeling about your sister—to ground? I mean, do we all just wait here until something happens?"

"We may have to. But there's another thing I thought I would try first. I was going to ask you to help, but then you

105

said you'd signed a contract to do an animal book and I thought you wouldn't have time. After all, all I asked you to do was be here."

"What was it you were going to ask me to help about?"

"There's a diary or journal somewhere. I don't know whose it is, or where it is. But I know it exists and I know it's in this house. And I think I'll find it—the origin of this rumor about a sister—there. And if I find that, maybe I can find out what she wants with me now."

I suppose I hadn't really taken Diana's ghost seriously. Or perhaps it would be more accurate to say I hadn't really accepted that she took it—that any rational person *could* take it—seriously.

"You really think she—your ghost—is real and wants something from you?"

"If she isn't, then I'm not real."

I thought for a minute. "How do you know there's a diary?"

She hesitated, standing at the end of her bed, watching me. "You're not going to like this explanation any better than the rest of it, but . . . it's because I have dreamed about the diary, not once, but three times. Always in this house. I even know what it looks like."

It was no use going on saying to myself what nonsense it all was, however much I might think it. And despite myself, there was something about Diana's conviction that impressed me.

"And," Diana said suddenly, "if you have any doubts as to how . . . how much I believe this, let me tell you that by staying here, I'm passing up a once-in-a-lifetime opportunity to sell this mausoleum."

"Who'd want to buy it?"

"A school. Who on earth else could keep it up? It's a white elephant."

"And you're turning them down?"

"Yes. Because if I don't give them an answer in a week, they'll buy another place they've got their eye on. Apparently they like this best, but it's a question of concluding the sale and making the place usable before the fall."

106

"How much are they offering?"

Diana hesitated. "Not what it took to build it, which was back in the early part of the century and cost a million even then. They're offering five hundred thousand for the house and what's left of the land. The funny part is..." She stopped.

"What?"

"Well, their headmistress, or whatever she calls herself, is the granddaughter of the man who wouldn't sell his lot to my grandfather. That's why, at first, there was a small bite out of the land immediately around the house. The rose garden is on it. Then there was some family tragedy, and the owner finally agreed to sell. My father once told me that my grandfather took a certain pleasure over the fact that he got that particular piece for a lower price than he'd offered for it originally."

"It seems to me your grandfather's strength was not in his foolishness—religious or otherwise—à la motto, but in his ability to drive a killing bargain, in the great tradition of Yankee traders."

"True. He was very sweet to me when I was a child but he had a terrible reputation for being a robber baron."

"And you're turning down five hundred thousand and the opportunity of getting rid of what you call a white elephant so that you can run down this diary, whose existence you have learned of from dreams?"

Diana smiled, then, "Sounds lunatic, doesn't it?"

"Yes."

"Well, you certainly don't have to believe what you don't want to. It wasn't part of the agreement. Nor was it part of the contract that you had to help me look for that diary."

But I knew I was going to do everything I could to locate it. Because if Diana could be convinced that the wretched book did not exist, she might be persuaded at least to consider that her other illusions were—just that: illusions. "I'll help you with the search. Although—"

About to come out with one of my bits of tactlessness, I hesitated.

"You might as well say it."

I grinned. "Well, my father, who was at least an agnostic if not an atheist, once said that pursuing the supernatural was like looking in a coal cellar at midnight for a black hat that wasn't there."

To my surprise Diana's face broke into a smile. Then she laughed and came and put a hand on my shoulder. "I like that, even though I'm not an atheist, or even an agnostic. Tell Simon, he'd love it."

I could feel myself stiffen. "You tell him."

She looked at me. "But you'll help me search in this coal cellar for my black hat?"

"Yes," I said shortly. "I'll help." But I still had a bone to pick with her. "Why did you bring up James, as though he were some kind of added inducement for me to stay?"

"Isn't he?" she said, and took her hand away. "He seems to like you better than he does me."

I thought about the strange small boy across the hall. "I don't come to him surrounded by layers of family conflict, and . . ." She valued my candor, but I wondered how much she would take. "And," I said, deciding to go ahead anyway, "you weren't entirely sober when he arrived."

If I wondered how far I could go, I learned. "I like you when you're direct and truthful, as I told you," Diana said coolly. "I don't like you when you're being some kind of moralistic prude."

"If James doesn't care for you when you've been drinking, does that make him a moralistic prude, too?"

The reaching out, the friendship that had been there for a moment, was gone. Diana was back in her fortress. "That was an accident that will not happen again." And she went towards the stairs.

I let her go, and then called after her. "Just a minute. I said I'd help you with looking for the diary. Where do you think I should start?"

She paused at the top of the steps and stood staring the other way out the window. Fortunately, I managed not to say

108

what was in my mind at the moment, which was to suggest that she go back and have another dream, this time with more specific information.

"There's a library at the end of the southwest wing," she said. "I started to look there, but got . . . distracted."

"Well, if you're going to look for any kind of a book, that's a good place to start, I suppose. Although I would have thought . . ."

Diana turned. "What?"

She said it with such intensity, that I said, "Nothing earth-shaking, there's no need to look as though I had some kind of comic answer."

"Maybe not. But I'll tell you one thing I think. I think, whether you know it or not, that you're psychic."

"Come off it, Diana. I don't wish to offend, but I've told you I don't believe in that kind of stuff."

She didn't say anything for a minute. Then, "You started to say that you would have thought something."

For a moment I couldn't remember, then I said, "Oh, yes. Well, I would have thought that a diary would be more likely to be in an old trunk in the attic rather than a library."

A shade of disappointment passed over her face. "This house doesn't have an attic. There are a couple of rooms downstairs in the basement that are stuffed with old family things—mostly furniture, I think. But there could be some trunks or boxes. Would you prefer to start there?"

"No. If I'm going to be part of the search, I'd a lot rather be in a library than in a cellar. I'll begin where you suggested."

Both Simon and Eric were at dinner, to celebrate, as Diana said, James's arrival. She drank, I noticed, sparingly before dinner was announced, and not only looked her best in a sheathlike black dress but seemed attentive to James, whom she put on her right at dinner, with me on his other side. Opposite us were Eric and Simon.

It would be pleasant to report that the dinner was a success, that James warmed up a little towards his mother. But while he was (at first) perfectly polite, and answered all her questions and those of Simon and Eric, he presented a courteous, seamless front, astonishing in a child that age, and quite impenetrable. And then, suddenly, and prompted, unfortunately, by a question of mine, the evening became a disaster.

"How's Hannibal?" I asked, when conversation seemed to lag.

I expected the closed face to open a little. But it didn't. "All right," he said.

"Did you butter his paws?" Simon inquired. In his white shirt and striped tie he looked, I thought, like a bank executive. I found the fact that he was a priest more, rather than less, incredible.

I shook my head. "No, we meant to, but forgot."

Eric looked across the table. "Who is Hannibal?"

There was a time, I found myself thinking, when Simon's tense brilliance made Eric seem lumpish. Now Eric, also in collar and tie, looked the athlete, his tan face, rising above the white collar, making him seem much younger than Simon, who was the same age.

I answered him. "Hannibal is a magnificent black cat who came over with James."

"Oh," Eric said, with a noticeable lack of enthusiasm. He added, "I'm a dog man myself."

"Singular or plural?" Simon asked idly.

I saw Eric glance at him.

"Oh, come off it, Reverend," Diana said. "Anyone totally without vices is a bore—which should make you feel better, because you have your full share of them, round collar and all."

"How true," Simon said. He tapped his chest. "Mea culpa!"

"What dogs?" I asked, on the qui vive as always when animals were mentioned. "What are you talking about?"

Eric, who had looked at Simon with an expression I found hard to read, turned to me and smiled. "I've been known to place a bet," he said.

"Why not?" Diana asked. "And why the holy put-down, Simon? Half your kids were in the numbers rackets."

110

"As well as in others," Simon agreed. "I apologize for my fit of piety."

Diana's beautiful smile lit her face, rendering its usual transformation. Her feeling for Simon was suddenly transparently clear. "It's all right, darling. Just don't have those attacks too often."

Simon smiled back at her. "I'll try to repress them."

All this time I had been vaguely aware that James had been staring at Eric. "Are you an ailurophobe?" he asked sternly.

"I'm not sure," Eric replied. "What is it?"

"Somebody who doesn't like cats." James spoke with the air of one pointing out the obvious.

"That's a mouthful of a word," Simon put in. "Where did you learn it?"

Diana glanced at her son. "From his father, I would be willing to lay good money. Right, James?"

"That's right. He told me an ailurophobe hates cats and an ailurophile loves them. I'm an ailurophile," he added unnecessarily. "Probably," he continued, looking at Eric, "Hannibal would feel the same about you if he met you. He'd be a . . . a personphobe."

"Homophobe," I tried, having had, in college, a brief brush with philology. "But Hannibal isn't. Not with everyone."

"Just ailurophobes." James pronounced the word with relish, his eyes unwinkingly on Eric, who was beginning to look uncomfortable.

"I think that's enough on that subject," Diana said.

"How do you like the house?" Eric asked in a laudable attempt to turn the conversation to less controversial channels.

James shrugged. "It's all right. My father said—"

"Architecturally it's very interesting," I broke in loudly, plunging across his conversation, as I remembered Roger Eliot's description of Tower Abbey, treasured and almost certain to be repeated now by his son, as "an architectural abortion." "Especially the towers," I said, grabbing at anything.

Simon laughed. "Egremont's folly." Then he smiled across the table at James. "That's what the towers were called locally. The three of us, your mother, Eric and I, used to scour

111

through them regularly, looking for buried treasure."

"Why?" James asked. "Was there supposed to be some in the towers?"

Simon buttered a roll. "The family motto, which you can see in the living room, is 'In my folly is my treasure.' Everybody was convinced that your great-grandfather had buried treasure around here somewhere, and that that was the real meaning of the motto. So we used to spend our time trying to tear the towers apart to find it."

"Did you find anything?" James sounded, for once, excited, the way a small boy would at the thought of a treasure hunt.

"Alas, no. Finally somebody, I think it was Diana's father, your grandfather, explained to us that the meaning of the word folly in that context had some religious significance."

"Oh." James was plainly disappointed. He looked once more at Eric and then at me. "Can I go upstairs and meet your animals?" he asked. He had, I noticed, eaten little and long ago put his knife and fork down.

I was aware of Diana's tensing. As little as Eric, I thought, did she sympathize with James's idée fixe on the subject of Hannibal. Any neutrality she might have had vanished after their first meeting this afternoon.

"I'll see if I can round up Seth and Susan after dinner," I said. "Right now Pandora is out making love to Mrs. Klaveness. She may not be the brightest dog in the world, but she knew instantly who was in charge of food."

"Then there's the rabbit, Wisteria—" James went on, as though he and I were alone.

Diana interrupted him. "I think all of us, except perhaps Candida, are a little tired of the subject of animals, James. Your father, whatever his faults, was well informed. I'm sure you discussed other topics with him and I suggest we do the same now. Anyway, it's time for dessert and we have a surprise for you."

The last sentence, and the anxiety in her eyes, told me that Diana had probably not meant for her statement to sound the way it did. But I saw the flush of anger stain the boy's cheeks.

Before I could think of anything helpful to say, Mrs. Klave-

112

ness came in with a tray. An expectant look came over Diana's face.

"Ta-da!" Eric sang.

The housekeeper put the tray on a sideboard and came over to the table bearing a big dish of ice cream with three flavors mixed and blended, then she returned with a sauce boat of chocolate sauce, and a third time with a smallish devil's-food cake.

There was a pause. Mrs. Klaveness hovered back of Diana, her eyes on James. Diana was also watching James. A smile touched her lips.

I tried to will James to say something, and, unfortunately, he did. "May I be excused?" he said.

"Before you have your ice cream and cake?" Diana sounded incredulous.

"I don't like ice cream. Or cake."

"*Tcha,*" Mrs. Klaveness said. It sounded halfway between a spit and a sigh.

"Mrs. Klaveness made the cake especially for you," Diana said. "And Simon brought the ice cream and chocolate sauce."

"It's okay—" Simon started.

"Can I be excused?" James said, and sidled out of his chair. "I want to go up and see if Hannibal is all right." There was a barely perceptible emphasis on the word Hannibal.

Diana stared at him, a white look around her mouth. "First you must apologize to Mrs. Klaveness."

"Why should I say I'm sorry? I can't help it if I don't like ice cream or cake. Nobody asked me."

"I thought English children were supposed to have such marvelous manners. The least you could do is say thank you."

"Can I go to my room, please?"

"Yes. And you can stay there for the rest of the evening."

"Thank you," James said. And walked out.

Mrs. Klaveness had already left the dining room. For the first time I found myself feeling sorry for Diana, but I had the remaining sense not to say so.

"He's probably feeling homesick," Eric said. "It's got to be difficult for him. His father dead, his home gone. Don't take

113

it personally, Di."

Simon, who was folding his napkin, didn't say anything, which, since he was supposed to be some kind of counselor to young people, surprised me. It may have surprised Diana, too, because she looked straight at him and said, "What do you think I should do, Simon?"

He put the folded napkin on the table. "At the moment, nothing."

"Maybe if somebody took some ice cream up to him," Eric ventured, and my heart warmed a little towards him.

"No," Simon said.

"Could I have some?" I asked.

Diana pushed the big dish towards me. "Help yourself. I'm going into the study." And she got up and walked out of the dining room.

"I wonder why James did that?" Eric said. "If he'd tried for a week he couldn't have thought of anything that would have spat in his mother's face more effectively."

"That's why he did it," Simon said.

"I suppose," Eric said, "we can thank his father for that."

"Probably," Simon said. "If you don't mind, Candida, I think I'll go in and see how Diana is." He got up and pushed his chair in.

I waved my spoon at him. "Feel free."

Eric pulled the ice cream dish over towards him and helped himself. "To tell you the truth," he said, "I don't care much for sweets either. But—" He took a spoonful and swallowed it.

I glared at him. "I hate you. I hate all people who are thin and have good figures and who really don't like ice cream. I feel like an alcoholic who hates people who don't enjoy drinking."

Eric looked at me. "I seem to remember you were a pudgy little girl. But why the obsession? Your figure is as delicious as any man could want—or is that a sexist statement?"

"With comments like that, you can be as sexist as you like." I sighed. "But your compliment is not true. Only people like Diana have truly gorgeous figures. It's not fair. I do not grudge her her money. I grudge her her metabolism."

"Speaking of alcohol," Eric said.

"Don't. It's a sore subject. Diana says she hasn't a problem. And as long as she says that, there's nothing anybody can do."

"I've tried to get her to go to a doctor I know. He's a well-known expert. But she won't."

I eyed the chocolate cake. "As long as she says she has no problem, then she's not going to go to a doctor. I think we ought to make some kind of inroad on that cake, so that Mrs. Klaveness will think everybody else had some. I wish Simon had forced down a piece."

Eric pushed his empty ice cream dish away. "I tried to enlist Simon's help as regards Diana. But he seems quite determined that he can handle her and her problem by himself. I'll admit to you that it worries me."

I cut the cake, put a piece on one of the plates Mrs. Klaveness had placed beside it, and handed it to Eric. "Do your duty like a man," I said. Then I cut myself one. The trouble with being on a more or less permanent diet is that it ruins one's pleasure in eating forbidden fruit. But that didn't stop me from cutting myself a large hunk. "So as not to hurt Mrs. Klaveness's feelings," I said aloud, pulling the plate towards me. I stared at the dark, succulent, seductive icing. "Liar," I said, and picked up my fork.

Eric smiled at me, and I found myself thinking how nice his brown eyes were. They were warm and responsive and smiling back at me.

"Why don't I remember you as being around more?" I asked. "I have the clearest recollections of Diana—Diana with her show horses, Diana in the village, buying stuff for a party, Diana bringing one of her animals to my father's clinic. And Simon, too." Simon, the blue and gold knight, with his casual grace and bruising backhand at tennis. And Eric? Other than the scene at the infamous party, my clearest memory was of a rather hefty young man working behind the pumps in the gas station off the green in the village. "You used to work in the gas station, didn't you?"

"That's right." Eric was cutting off a second piece of cake with great precision but, perhaps feeling my gaze on him,

115

looked up and smiled again.

"But why? I mean—well, it's probably uncouth to mention it, but your father was our local tycoon, wasn't he? Horatio Alger who made it?"

Eric polished off the last of his cake. "He was. But unlike a lot of men who make money, he lost nothing of his faith in the work ethic. He always told me that he wasn't born a gentleman, and that I'd have to learn early to work just as he did."

"How very puritanical."

"Yes. But I think he was right. An awful lot of first-generation rich kids get into a lot of trouble when their old man decides they're going to have all the comforts and short-cuts he didn't have."

Puritanical or not, he was, I decided, okay. And then remembered that Diana had said he was in love with her. I sighed. "Haven't you ever married?" I asked.

He looked at me and laughed. "Of course. I'm divorced now, though. Why?"

"I thought . . . you seemed, well, sort of fond of Diana, and I'm afraid I just didn't think that you might have been married already and divorced. I somehow had this romantic, sentimental picture that you had been waiting around for her." All of which was a lot of fictionalized circumlocution to get me out of a tight spot and at the same time elicit some information.

The brown eyes regarded me thoughtfully. "You *are* a romantic," he said finally. "I didn't think anyone was anymore, in this day and time, what with the sexual revolution and women's lib. How did you get away with such anachronistic views in Fun City?"

"Oh, there're still a few closet romantics around."

He smiled. "And you're one of them. I wonder why."

You can't be twenty-six and living in New York and not visibly involved with somebody and not have to field comments like this all the time. Terry kept talking hopefully about my transferring my affections from the four-footed to the two-footed world. Diana—among many others—made cracks about

116

my virginity, and attributed it to my finding her and Simon *in flagrante* when I was of delicate and impressionable years. But there was another and much stronger reason that lay deep in a blurred and uncertain memory, pushed to the back of anything that I wanted to think about. By now, years later, I managed not to think about it most of the time, ninety-nine percent of the time, not counting dreams and occasional nightmares, which had been growing less and less frequent. But occasionally, something someone said set off vibrations that sent plunging me back into the past. And I remembered then, even before I knew I remembered, because I became aware of my pounding heart and the fact that the palms of my hands, which never sweated, were damp.

"What's the matter?" Eric asked.

"Nothing." I pushed the plate containing one last chunk of the devil's-food cake away, the one with the most icing. I got up. "Excuse me."

He caught my hand as I passed. "What's the matter, Candy? What did I say?"

"Nothing, Eric."

"You look like you've seen a ghost."

"That's an unfortunate remark to make around here."

He smiled. "Do you believe in them?"

"There are ghosts and ghosts," I said, realizing the truth of that comment a few seconds after I'd said it. "Some kinds. Maybe I'm here to learn about other kinds."

He stood up, still holding my hand. His other hand he nestled under my chin.

I said, as steadily as I could, "I've been kissed once today. For anyone like me, that's enough raw sex in any twenty-four-hour period."

"By Simon?"

I nodded.

"*Plus ça change,*" Eric murmured. It was a shock to hear him speak French so well.

"Yes," I said. "That's one reason why I slapped him. He may have metamorphosed himself into therapist and priest, but Simon the playboy still lives."

"Give a little credit to yourself," Eric said, and touched my cheek.

Gently I put away his hand. Perhaps I would, after all, have to do what I'd avoided doing for so long: fight my own ghost. But it had been a long day, and I was grateful to Eric for seeming (unlike Simon) to give me some choice. "Another day or hour," I said.

Eric smiled. "I'll wait until I'm asked."

A comment like that always evoked from me a comeback like, Don't hold your breath. Instead, this time I said,

"How clear does the invitation have to be?"

"One look out of those expressive dark eyes."

But I was still confused about something. I could not betray Diana and say that she had stated that Eric was in love with her. But neither did I like poaching around someone else's preserve. Especially not if I were living in her house. Besides, who was I to compete with Diana?

"You know," I said bluntly, "I'm not good at flirting. Aren't you in love with Diana?"

He didn't answer for a minute. Just stood there, looking down at me out of his own expressive dark eyes. "I'm sorry if I seemed . . . flirtatious. Yes. I do love her."

"Then why don't you marry her?"

"I'd like nothing better . . . if she'd have me."

It suddenly seemed to me such a glorious solution to Diana's problems (and therefore mine) for Eric to buy the house, marry her, adopt James and tear down or renovate Tower Abbey. The little matter of James's passion for Hannibal and Eric's ailurophobia I pushed to the back of my mind, where I also pushed Diana's insistence on tracking down her ghost. The clean wind of a new marriage and the renovation of her house should sweep that out of her head, I told myself. It would all work out. And Diana might even stop drinking. I realized that that was wishful thinking. Having encountered and studied the problem because of my father, I knew that a change of circumstance, however beneficial, never stopped the true alcoholic. But perhaps Diana wasn't yet at that point. And anyway, Eric would be there to catch the pieces and I would be free to return to New York City.

"Well," I said, rather eagerly, "why won't she?"

"Because, as I should have thought you'd have noticed, she's in love with Simon, who, to an extent I find worrying, has enormous influence over her."

"Why worrying?"

"I told you—he's against her being treated in a recognized rehabilitation place. I have strong reason to believe she's on pills as well as liquor, pills she could only get on prescription from a doctor—but I've said too much. I don't want to go around making hasty accusations. I am aware, or at least I strongly suspect, that Simon loves her, too, and is no doubt doing what seems to him best for her."

A little desolation settled down over my heart when he said that. "Yes," I agreed. "I guess so."

As I heard Mrs. Klaveness's heavy steps approaching from the kitchen, my eye caught the remains of my piece of cake. Leaning over, I picked up the icing-encrusted piece and put it into my mouth at the moment she emerged from behind the screen guarding the door to the kitchen.

"That was excellent cake, Mrs. Klaveness," Eric said, giving me a few seconds to swallow.

"Yes, it was," I agreed rather thickly. "Delicious."

The housekeeper didn't say anything at all. Just put the cake plate, the ice cream and the chocolate sauce onto the tray and went back into the kitchen.

"Her feelings are hurt," Eric said.

"I'm afraid so."

Eric was going towards the door into the big living room. "Coming?"

"No. I think I'm going to try and soothe Mrs. Klaveness's feelings."

"Blessed are the peacemakers," Eric said, and disappeared.

I found the big woman emptying the ice cream into a container.

"Please don't feel bad about James." I came straight to the point. "It . . . it wasn't directed at you."

"*Ach*, do you think I am stupid? It was to his mother. Such

119

a pity. So much trouble. Always with this house, so much trouble."

"What do you mean?" I asked, aware of a prickling sensation at the back of my neck.

She put the lid on the container and placed it into the freezer that stood to one side of a massive refrigerator. Then she took another container from the refrigerator itself, and, putting it on the table, started to empty the sauce boat into it.

"This is not a good house. You will see."

"How do you mean?"

"You will see," she said.

Silence. Mrs. Klaveness placed the chocolate sauce container in the refrigerator, then turned her attention to the cake.

"Mrs. Klaveness, I'd like to know what you're talking about." Suddenly it was very important.

The little blue eyes looked up at me over her busy hands, placing the cake in a box. "I will say nothing more. You will see. That's enough."

She meant what she said. I could get nothing further out of her.

7

I woke up suddenly, and then lay there, wondering what had waked me.

The moonlight streamed in through my window and across my bed, throwing a moving pattern of lace on the quilt and the floor, where the branches of the tall tree outside swayed in the light wind back and forth across the face of the golden disk. Without thinking, I put out a hand to where Pandora stretched beside me. Awareness of her paws quivering in some dream had been my last, amused thought before I went to sleep.

But my hand encountered only the rough, stitched cotton of the quilt. Hastily I slid my hand across to the edge of the bed. There was no silky coat on top of a firm, warm body. Pandora was not there. I sat up. Neither were Seth and Susan, who usually spent the night on my other side or lying against each other at the end of the bed.

"Pandora, Seth, Susan?" I said aloud.

I shivered, wondering if a cold breeze had sprung up, and glanced at the branches of the tree outside, expecting to see

121

them tossing about as they had been a few seconds before. But they were quite still.

Of course, still air could be cold, too. And this house was higher than sea level. Still, that chill was an odd phenomenon for June. But my mind barely touched on these points before reverting to the far more puzzling matter of the whereabouts of the animals. Idly I glanced towards the bedroom door, which I had closed . . . which I was almost certain I had closed . . . but which was now definitely open. Throwing back the bedclothes, I swung my feet over the side of the bed and groped around for my slippers.

Then I picked up my robe from where I had thrown it over a chair, wishing it were something warmer than thin cotton. Going over to the door, I switched on the light. The room was not large, and unless the animals were under the bed, it was immediately obvious that they were nowhere in the room. They weren't under the bed either, I discovered, lifting the flounce that fell from the bottom of the mattress to the floor. And the reason they weren't underneath was because they couldn't have been: The bed was a solid piece of furniture, the hard mattress (which I liked) resting over two large drawers whose pull-out handles faced me when I lifted the pleated flounce. Tentatively I pulled the handles. Then, "of all the fakes," I said aloud. Because that's what they were: fake panels fitted with brass handles to look like drawers.

Perhaps it was the sound of my voice, but almost immediately I heard what sounded like Pandora whining. Dropping the flounce, I went out into the hall and into the next room, where the rest of the zoo had their quarters. Turning on the light, I checked the fact that the blue and gold fish seemed to be pursuing their usual languorous swim around the aquarium. But Anthony and Cleopatra, all extremities pulled into their shells, had taken refuge under a lot of greenery in their terrarium, and the gerbils had dug themselves to the bottom of all the chips that covered their tank and were now only visible if one looked carefully. Wisteria was crouched in one corner of his cage, and when I put my hand on him, he tried to bite me, which he had never done before. The whine sounded again. The bed in this room, unlike the one in mine, was standing on legs and had no flounce. When I bent down to look underneath I found all three animals jammed at the far end.

"Come on out of there," I said.

Pandora gave her strange little whine, then came forward a little, mostly on her stomach. I reached underneath as far as I could and stroked her head. "What's the matter, Pandora? Did you see a ghost?"

The moment I said that my hand stopped what it was doing. I sat up on my knees. Then I said in a loud, clear voice, "I do not believe in them."

I don't know what I expected would happen. A thunderbolt to strike me? A clammy hand on my neck? The only thing that occurred was Seth's loud voice, followed antiphonally by Susan's, higher, less argumentative but more plaintive.

"You heard me," I said aloud. "Come on out of there."

But they wouldn't. Not even Pandora, who lay collapsed on the floor under the bed, a few feet from my outstretched hand, making her strange whimpering sounds.

"Well, I'm not going to go down there after you and get you out. You can stay there if you want. I'm going back to bed."

Now that I knew they were all right, I felt free to go back to sleep. If I could. "Of course you can," I muttered to myself, turning back into the little hall serving the two rooms and leading, by a few steps up, to the main upstairs hall of the house and—I stopped in my tracks—to the little staircase I had gone down the day I arrived. It was the same narrow stone staircase that led to the empty swimming pool below, whose door, I could see from the lights I had turned on, was now open.

Well, I thought, that explained the cold. No need to look for supernatural causes—not that I believed in them. Still, it was nice to have my skepticism affirmed so soon and so plainly.

Walking up the four steps, I approached the open door, somewhat narrower than the other, and reached in to pull it closed. But the door must have stuck wide open, though I couldn't imagine how. Stepping around to behind the door, I

123

pushed it hard and it abruptly slammed shut with me on the other side.

Horror and disbelief vied with one another as I stood, shivering, in the unrelieved dark. It could not have happened. But it had. The wind blew it shut, I said to myself, aloud. My voice sounded strange. I had the odd feeling that I was someone else, and had heard myself talking. Then my numbed shock wore off. Reaching out I grasped the doorknob in front of me, turned and pulled. But the door would not open. Turning it again, I pulled again. Still it would not budge. Desperately, I put my body next to the door and tried lifting it, thinking that the door itself and the jamb had gone out of alignment. Then I pushed it down. But if it had been locked and bolted from the other side, it could not have been more like immovable concrete. I kicked the door then, and pounded on it, and felt as helpless and as soundless as though I were in a tower with twelve-foot walls. And even if the sound got through, who would hear it? Diana, who could have easily drunk herself into a drugged sleep? James—a small boy—far down at the end of the hall?

I was afraid then. Really afraid. Standing there, I realized something that in all my cheerful skepticism I had forgotten: I didn't like the dark. And I especially didn't like it in a confined place.

Drawing in a breath, I put out my hands on either side of me and laid them flat on the cold, damp stone of the walls. No wonder the hall outside felt cold. With the door open, the chill could pour out.

Taking my hands away, I stood still, forcing myself to breathe slowly, in . . . and out, in . . . and out, in . . . and out. Finally I could feel my heart beginning to slow from its gallop. I continued to stand there, determined not to give into the panic that seemed to my overactive mind at that moment like an enemy, waiting for me to show the first sign of weakness so it could enter me and take over.

But the slow, regular breathing eventually had the effect I hoped it would have. The panic seemed to recede. Again I put my hands out, and this time shoved forward one foot, the flat mule sole scraping against the stone like the legs of a giant locust. In a moment, I felt the edge of the first step.

It was not easy going down. There was no banister, nothing to hang on to, only the sides and my own not very sound sense of balance to keep me from tumbling down uncarpeted stone stairs with square, sharp edges. The dark was total, black, thick, an entity in itself. A room that is dark, one with the blinds drawn and the curtains pulled, will look black, but when the eyes grow accustomed to that black, degrees of blackness can be seen, with fainter black around the edges of the curtains and blinds. But there were no degrees in this black. It was like a huge unshaped animal, or like those black holes in the universe that astronomers write about, black nothings that go on for eternity, refuting all theology and hope. . . .

"Stop it!" I said aloud.

I had the curious and frightening feeling that I was speaking to something outside and alien to me, something beyond my own panic-struck mind, something that was trying to tell me something . . . I stopped, both feet on a step, my hands out against the walls . . . trying to tell me something that would produce despair. And out of despair would come madness. Where had I read that? Somewhere. For a second I could almost see the words and the words themselves brought despair. Then, with a sickening certainty, I knew what had been beating against my consciousness . . . the door downstairs, the one that led to the empty swimming pool, that, also, could be locked. And if it were locked . . .

For a moment a fury against my father swept through me. In his angry iconoclasm he had deprived me of God and gods, of talisman and symbols, of belief even in luck or anything to pray to. Because now was the time when I could use something, anything.

Stout disbeliever and agnostic that I was, I said a prayer. "Help me," I said aloud.

What happened then was almost ludicrous. Because what filled my mind were not words traditionally thought of as providing peace, comfort, strength or support in time of trouble. What came to my tongue were the opening lines of a poem that my father, admirer of Kipling, loved to recite when drinking.

Ere the steamer bore him eastward Sleary was engaged to
marry
An attractive girl at Tunbridge, whom he called "my little
Carrie . . ."

Hardly the Twenty-third Psalm or the *Rubaiyat*, but Sleary's absurd adventures, ringing and jingling in my head, broke the spell, kept my feet moving and my tongue going, even between chattering teeth, till I got to what I could feel was the bottom.

And the door opened.

It was not pleasant standing looking into the shadows crowding the deep end of the empty swimming pool. But, with the rest of the marble room lit by the moon, it was a big improvement on the passageway, and considerably warmer.

There was a door leading outside to the garden. But if I got out, would I be able to get back in another door? The answer to that was most likely no. The next thing, obviously, was to see if there were a second door leading from the pool back into the house.

There was, down a short passage, a third door. Furthermore, it opened, inward. I paused there at the threshold, faced again by blackness. There was nothing on earth I could immediately think of that would induce me to step back into the confined blackness I had just left in the little stairway. On the other hand, the options were neither numerous nor attractive: I could spend the night in the swimming pool, or I could (if the door leading outside were open) go into the garden and wait till the morning there. After a few minutes what I had hoped for occurred: My eyes became accustomed to the dark and, after a while, with the aid of the pale moonlight from the pool area behind me, could distinguish what was immediately in front of me. More stairs down. But they were broader and only half a flight deep. I could also see something much more welcome—a light switch, which I promptly touched.

What was revealed was an entire changing area, with showers and rooms visible through doors open on either side

126

of the rectangular hall that lay at the base of the stairs.

By now thoroughly awake, I went slowly down the stairs, my mules clattering on the marble, making what seemed, in that silence, an unconscionable noise. The hall itself was fairly large, large enough for a Ping-Pong table, its markings now invisible under layers of dust and dirt, its net a mess of rotted string, cobwebs strung between the table and the legs. More than cobwebs, I realized, darting back. Two of the webs sported their creators, one small and brown, the other slightly larger with thicker legs.

Deep within me was my father's conviction that all nature, including man, was, at some level, one, a viewpoint that had a great deal to do with my feeling about animals. But it was hard to remember when faced with insects. A sense of kinship there competed with an even stronger revulsion. *All things bright and beautiful,* I muttered silently to myself, and gave the filthy table a wide berth.

The changing rooms, one on either side, contained old-fashioned marble showers with hooks on the wall, and in both rooms there hung dirty, ragged remnants of what had once been terry cloth towels and robes. Staring around, I had the curious sensation that I had wandered into a recently discovered Roman bath, so unrelated everything seemed to my own life, or even Diana's. Her name jarred something loose in my mind. My curious sense of timelessness vanished. What was I doing here, by myself, in the middle of the night? Hastily I glanced at my watch, only to discover that I had forgotten to wind it and that the hands had stopped at five minutes to ten.

"Damn!" I said aloud.

And then I stood absolutely still. My voice had echoed and reechoed between those marble walls, but that was not what had rooted me. Mixed with the sound of my voice was another sound, something that seemed like . . . But there my memory failed me. I could not remember what it was like. It happened too fast. Nevertheless, it increased my awareness of where I was, and how very alone I was.

Half turning, I glanced back. Behind me lay the swimming

pool, with its limited and unpalatable options. In front lay, possibly, some way of getting back upstairs that did not involve returning up the winding staircase, which I had decided, beyond any question, I would not do, even if it meant spending the night in the pool or the garden. *Ergo*, I might as well go forward to see if some other way could be found back to my bedroom.

I walked to the other end of the hall, went up more steps to another door and groped my hand around the wall for a light switch. When the light went on, I was astonished to discover that I was at one end of what was—I could hardly believe it—a bowling alley, running at right angles to the wall I had just left. A little cogitation made me realize that the bowling alley, which was undoubtedly below ground level, ran the full length of the house underneath the crossbar of the mansion's **H** shape. Many yards away, at the opposite end, a complicated wooden structure held and lowered the pins in place.

What the well-heeled tycoon can build for his own and his guests' amusement, I thought, starting to shut the door behind me. An upbringing drilled in thriftiness impelled me to glance at the wall for another light switch with which to turn off the light in the changing-room area. But even though the light switch was there, I did not turn it off. I still did not know how I was going to get out of this basement, and until I did, I wanted as much light behind, as well as in front of, me as possible. So, with mental apologies to whatever budget Diana might be trying to hold to, I left it on.

At the other end of the bowling alley was another door, another set of light switches and more steps down, and presently I found myself in what was plainly the working section of the basement. I walked slowly, turning on lights, leaving them on behind me, down one hall, then down another at right angles to it, this second with rooms opening off that I looked into as I passed. Here, obviously, were the storerooms that Diana had spoken of, furniture piled, boxes and more boxes, trunks, and piles of books. Twice, peering into the rooms, I started back before the scuttling forms of more wildlife—this time the huge relatives of the unlovely cockroach, called waterbugs.

"*Yuch!*" I said aloud, and then remembering what happened the previous time I had spoken, waited to hear, once again, the sound, whatever it was, that I couldn't remember.

But this time there was no sound, beyond some scrabbling that I took to be mice. Yet, as I stood there, my hand on the dusty doorknob, I had a sensation which I couldn't place, yet which made me uncomfortable. I'm going to get out of here, I thought to myself, and moved ahead.

It was just as I was entering a huge room, containing three massive boilers, that, for a moment, I identified that sensation that I hadn't liked: It was the certainty that I was not alone; that there was someone else in this area with me. The panic that I had felt on the staircase exploded inside me, paralyzing my ability to move, making my heart pound and my skin clammy.

"Who's there?" I said, my voice thready and hoarse with fear.

The lights went out. Something went past me. I could feel the air moving against my face. In panic I lunged in the opposite direction, felt my foot encounter something hard and crashed over it, hitting my head on the stone floor as I fell.

I came to sometime later, how much later I had no idea, with a pain in my head and a rising sense of nausea. But the nausea, unpleasant as it was, was not as unpleasant as the blackness around me. After a few moments the sickness passed and I realized where I was and what I was doing lying on the floor. What got me to my feet, regardless of my head and still unsteady stomach, was the clear memory of the waterbugs. Then I tried to remember what I had seen before the lights went out. Dead ahead of me there were boilers, as big, it seemed to me, as the ships' engines that I had once seen as a little girl; also boxes lying around over one of which I undoubtedly fell, and . . . I tried to reconstruct the picture before the blackness descended . . . yes, to one side a door.

It was as I moved, pushing one foot after another in front of me so as not to trip again, that I realized I was, despite my discomfort and dislike of the pitch dark around me, no longer

129

filled with that terrible panic. Somehow I was quite sure that whoever had been there had left.

It was a long journey across the room, my hands out in front of me, my mind trying to keep away from the thought of whatever might be running around my feet. Eventually I encountered a wall. After feeling along that for a while I came to the door, found a light switch and thankfully turned it on. Then I saw, opposite to where I was standing, back in the direction from which I had come, another door, standing open, revealing a room in which there was a soiled bed, with covers thrown back, and beside it, a broken chair with what looked like a shirt thrown over its back.

What I should do, I thought, was go over and inspect that room, but despite the fact that I no longer felt someone else's presence, I found myself powerfully reluctant to cross the boiler room once again, particularly since there were only two light switches, one by the door through which I had entered, the other under my hand beside another door leading out in the opposite direction. I would look at it tomorrow, I decided. Right now my most pressing problem was to get back upstairs.

It took me fifteen or twenty minutes, winding along passages, some of which had doors, others of which didn't. Finally I found myself confronting more stone steps leading up and ending in a door. Somehow I knew, or at least strongly suspected, that the only way up, other than the way I had come down from the swimming pool, was in front of me. If it were open, well and good. My journeys would be over. If not—then I would have to go back from where I came and decide all over again whether or not I would spend the night in the pool room or outside. Taking a deep breath, I climbed the stairs, turned the knob and pushed. The door opened. Waiting on the other side were Pandora, Seth and Susan.

"Guess what happened to me last night." I said.

Diana, James and I were having breakfast in the enclosed porch, sitting around a small round table that had been placed there.

"What?" Diana asked, with an unmistakable lack of interest.

130

Her face was not puffy this morning, but it was strained-looking.

I gave her a brief rundown of my adventure without mentioning my certainty—strengthened by the unmade bed and shirt—that someone else had been there. I wanted to see what she would say about the door to the staircase leading from my hall to the swimming pool.

"It often sticks that way," was what she said. Considering the anguish it had caused me, I found her unconcern maddening.

"Well, it's not just an inconvenience, you know," I commented rather sharply. "If I hadn't got back up by wandering through the entire basement, I could have had to make a choice between spending the night in the empty swimming pool or on the lawn."

"Well, why bother with the door? You could have left it open."

"With that cold, dank air filling the hall from the staircase?"

Diana was in the act of pouring herself some more coffee, but she was suddenly still, her hand gripping the silver pot poised a foot above her cup, her eyes raised to me. "Cold?"

"Yes. Cold. It must have something to do with the stone walls."

"Ghosts make the room cold," James said matter-of-factly. He had pushed his cereal around his plate and was now nibbling at a piece of toast.

Diana put the pot down on the brass stand with a snap. "Who told you that?"

"Walker."

"Who's Walker?"

"He's . . . he was sort of a butler."

"You mean that long-faced retainer, or whatever he was, that your father used as a general gofer?"

"What's a gofer?" James asked.

Diana picked up the pot again and finished pouring her coffee. "Dogsbody, lackey, messenger boy."

James's eyes flashed. "He was not a gofer."

131

There was a short silence while Diana drank some of her coffee. "If he was a friend of yours," she said finally, "then I didn't mean anything . . . anything offensive by it."

"He knew lots of things," James said. "History and stories and facts about animals and everything."

"And obviously served the kind of function your father should have served," Diana said, and then frowned. "I shouldn't have said that. I'm sorry."

James, whose mouth had already opened, closed it again.

"What . . . what did he mean by that statement about ghosts?" Diana asked.

"Just that in haunted houses you can always tell if a ghost is around because the room gets cold. He used to read me stories about that. Of course," James went on, rearranging on his plate the crusts that he had pulled off his toast, "it's only a bad ghost that makes the room cold. Walker used to tell me stories about that. Do you have one here? A ghost, I mean?"

"No," I said.

Diana didn't say anything.

"Because," James went on, "if you do, I shall say a prayer to keep it out of my room. Hannibal wouldn't like it."

"You might extend your prayer to cover my room," I said.

Diana glanced up at me. "I thought you were an agnostic or an atheist or something?"

"I am," I said, and then remembered my momentary desertion of my agnostic principles the night before, and the odd answer, if it was an answer, in the shape of the long Kipling poem that got me down the stairs. "Sort of," I finished off.

"Unbelievers will perish," James said with satisfaction.

"I wouldn't be too sure about that," Simon spoke from the door.

James, on the brink of arguing, turned around and saw who it was. His face relaxed. "Hello," he said in a more friendly voice. Plainly he approved of Simon.

"Hello." Simon, in blue shirt open at the neck, sleeves rolled up and jeans, came towards the table. "Is there any more coffee?"

Diana poured him another cup.

132

"Why are you so hard on unbelievers?" Simon asked James.

James grinned. "I heard it from a man talking at Hyde Park Corner one day.

"Well," Simon said, leaning over and helping himself to a piece of toast, "everyone is entitled to his opinion, but you don't have to buy it, lock, stock and barrel."

"We were discussing ghosts," Diana said lightly. There was a little pink in her cheeks, and her eyes, resting on Simon, seemed to be brighter. So much for true love, I thought sourly.

"What about them?"

"Candida was telling us that she got up to investigate some cold air last night, and James said—that Walker said—that cold air meant bad ghosts were in the vicinity. Is that true?"

For all her light air, I thought, watching Diana closely, she wasn't just kidding.

Simon didn't look up from the toast on which he was now carefully spreading some marmalade. "Tell me about it," he said.

So I went through the whole thing again.

"That stairway leading down to the pool *is* cold," he said when I'd finished. "But there's nothing mysterious or unusual about stone holding the cold. All people who live in the tropics know that. So there's no need to assume the presence of psychic phenomenon just from that."

"What are psychic phen— phen— ?" James asked.

Simon smiled. "Ghosts."

"You sound as though you think such things exist," I said, not at all pleased. "Diana said something to the effect that you might, but I couldn't take her seriously."

"Why not? Belief in psychic manifestations is not confined to kooks and fake mediums."

"Maybe not. But I think it's pretty odd that you, a clergyman, go along with that. I thought all the ecclesiastical powers-that-be frowned on that kind of thing."

"Frowning on people who meddle in the psychic world for their own amusement and profit is not the same as saying that world does not exist."

133

Quite suddenly I shivered. Simon was watching me. "Were you frightened when you were on that staircase?"

The memory of my panic came back as a present reality. I could feel again the thick texture of the dark, as though it were a living creature.

"Yes," I said. "I was. But I don't like the dark, and I don't like the feeling of being locked in, and I had both."

"Perhaps it was the ghost," James said.

"The thought doesn't appear to bother you," I commented.

"Walker said—"

"Who's Walker?" Simon asked.

James looked pointedly at his mother. "He's my friend."

"Roger Eliot's major domo," I put in.

"The world's greatest authority on practically everything," Diana said, "according to James."

Simon looked at James. "I see," he said. And then, "You must miss him."

James looked down at his plate. "Yes."

"Come along down to the halfway house," Simon invited. "I'll introduce you to some of my friends."

"I don't think—" Diana started.

"I'd like to," James got off his chair. "May I be excused?"

"Why don't you come too, Di?" Simon suggested. "I think it would give them all a boost."

Diana's face softened. "Another time. But take James, if you want to."

"By the way," I said, gingerly feeling my head. "One little detail about last night that I forgot to mention. When I got to the room where the boilers are, I'm sure there was someone there. The lights went out and somebody went past me. The trouble was, I tripped and fell on the stone floor in the dark and half knocked myself out. When I finally got up and turned on the light, whoever it was was gone. But in one of the rooms opening off the boiler room I saw what looked like a bed that had been slept in and somebody's shirt."

Simon was staring at me. "That was a pretty odd detail to have overlooked, wasn't it? I should have thought you'd mention that first."

134

"Oh, that was probably just Ben," Diana said. "He used to work for my father, and I sometimes let him have a room in exchange for doing odd jobs around the place."

"Ben Champreys?" Simon asked.

"Yes. He's been having a hard time of it. And he's pretty eccentric anyway."

"Not to say nuts," Simon added.

"Well, I'm glad I asked," I said. "Next time I feel presences zipping past me in the night I'll know it's Ben."

After a minute, Simon glanced down at James. "Ready to visit Halfway House?"

"Yes. Perhaps I should bring Hannibal."

"Why don't you bring him another time, after you've gotten to know some of the boys there? They might be a bit much for him all at once."

"All right. I'll just go upstairs and make sure he's had his breakfast and is all right."

We watched James's narrow form in its English garb disappear through the door.

"If Hannibal were a dog," Diana said, "I could understand all this better."

"You sound like Eric. Don't you like cats?" Simon asked.

"I put up with them," Diana said briefly. "Candida won't move an inch without her entire zoo, and now James seems to have some deep spiritual relationship with an oversized black cat that doesn't like me. As a matter of fact, I find it pretty odd that his only two friends—at least the ones he talks about —are a servant and a cat. If Roger were such an outstandingly fit parent—"

"There's nothing wrong in having animals for friends," I said.

"Well, I don't think—"

"This conversation can only get worse," Simon said. "Why don't we change the subject? I'm taking some of my crew up to White Deer Lodge next Tuesday. Why don't you come along?"

"Who are you inviting?" Diana asked. "Candida or me?"

"Both of you. Come along and lend the female touch."

Diana made a face. "Isn't that the place where they're always having those town meetings—the ones that end up sending me letters of petition?"

Simon grinned. "The Ad Hoc Committee to Save Our Village? They did have one up there, an impromptu one—usually those meetings take place down in the village hall."

"What meetings?" I asked. "Petitioning what?"

"Petitioning me to sell this place to the school I was telling you about."

"Why do they want you to sell to a school?"

"Because they know I'm going to sell eventually, and, as I told you, they're terrified that I'll let the land go to a builder who'll put up tacky houses on small lots and ruin their ancient and upper-class community. Which is why they're raising so much dust to counteract it. Anyway, as I also told you, the school people are trying to push me into selling immediately, and I have my own reason for not doing so. If and when I sell, it's going to be at my own convenience, not somebody else's."

"If?" Simon asked. "I thought you were hell-bent on selling."

"All right, when," Diana said. She looked up as James walked into the room. "I think I'll take you down to the village this afternoon and get you some jeans. Those flannel shorts must be hot."

James looked down at his trousers. "No, they're not. Anyway, shorts are cooler than long trousers."

"No kid around here is dressed like that," Diana said. "They'll probably laugh at you." There was a tight look around her mouth.

"Why should I care?" James said. "I'll wear what I like."

"Come on, James. Let's get going." Simon went over and put his hand on James's shoulder. Over it his eyes, looking green and cold in the morning light, regarded Diana. "See you later," he said, and pushing James in front of him, left through the sitting room door.

There were a lot of things I could have said to Diana, and many of them I would have considerably enjoyed saying, mostly to the effect that for a mother who had finally achieved her heart's desire—at long last having her son with her—she

136

was going about cementing the relationship in a very odd way. But some saving sense kept my tongue still. Nothing, I knew, that I could say along that line would help James. And in a minute or so I was glad. Glancing up again, I saw Diana, her head bent over the morning paper, surreptitiously wiping tears off her cheeks.

Then she looked up and saw me watching her. "I don't know why I do that," she said, and caught her breath. "I want so much for him . . . for us to have good relations. I mean to be a good mother, and then something like this pops out of my mouth and I don't know *why*."

"Maybe because he reminds you of Roger," I said.

"Maybe," she replied dully. She pushed the paper aside and got up. "I'm going down to the village to do some shopping. Do you want to come?"

I got up. "No, I don't think so. I don't suppose," I said, as she started to leave the porch, "that you've had any more dreams about that diary?"

She turned. "No. Why?"

"Well, I might as well begin looking for it. I'll start in the library. You said you even knew what it looked like. What does it look like? What am I looking for?"

Her sudden smile, which always made me forget some of her less likable qualities, flickered over her face. "You mean you're going to help me look for my black hat at midnight in a coal cellar?"

"Even though it isn't there," I finished. "Yes. Although I'll give you the benefit of my suspended disbelief for the moment and go on the theory that the diary is there. But I still have to know what it looks like."

"There's a cross on it," she said slowly.

"And?"

"Well, that's all I can be sure about . . . but I would recognize it," she added hastily when she saw the expression on my face.

"Diana, do you realize that that could describe half a dozen kinds of books, of any size or color, bound in any kind of material—bibles, prayer books, pious lives of pious people?"

"Well, you don't have to look. I haven't asked you to."

"Granted," I admitted. "All right then, is there anything else—anything at all—that you can tell me about the book that will help me?"

I saw her hesitate. Then, "Nothing," she said finally.

"You were going to say something. What was it?"

"Well, you probably won't like this any better than you like any other of my spooky ideas—"

"But?"

"I've dreamed about it three times," Diana said. "And every time, I have, in my dream, been frightened. In fact, terrified. And the dream is always exactly the same. I recognize the book, know that I have to open it and find something in it, and feel this terrible fear. But I open it anyway, and I read something, always the same thing. Then this awful terror comes and I wake up in a cold sweat with my heart pounding, and I know that what I have read has caused this fear but I can never remember what it is."

8

I spent most of the next several days in the library, a large room sitting over the swimming pool and lined with books on three sides from floor to ceiling. Diana had shown me there right after telling me about her dreams of reading something in the diary that had, each time, frightened her. All my skepticism had gathered itself at that to refute any connection between her strange dreams and the reality of what was in the book, or even the existence of the book itself. But after rationalizing away the dream and its weird contents on the grounds of the possible effects of drinking on the human imagination, or Diana's tendency (I told myself) to drama, or her taste for metaphysical sensationalism with a view to shocking the visiting innocent (me), I was left with a residue of something that certainly wasn't belief, but could most nearly be described as doubts about my doubts.

I was so absorbed in thinking about this, that, when we turned from the main hall into the shorter hall leading to the library, I almost missed Diana's casual statement. "There's the famous, or infamous, elevator."

I came to. "Where?"

She waved towards a door we were passing. "There."

"The one where your governess—what was her name, Donnie?—died."

"Yes."

I stopped. "Do you still use it?"

"No. Which is why I pointed it out. The door doesn't have a lock, of course. If you opened the door you might be tempted to use it. But I had the switch turned off in the basement, and you could stand there for half an hour pushing buttons and wondering why it didn't take off."

"Was it turned off permanently after the accident?"

"Oh, no. It was used all the time I was growing up. But when my father died I saw no reason to use it, so I had the main switch turned off. I was just warning you about it."

"I don't have any particular desire to use it anyway. Walking up and downstairs will be good for my figure."

When we got to the door facing us at the end of the hall Diana opened it and I walked in, looked at the tiers of books and whistled. "Going through all these can take some time, particularly as I have so little to go on."

"You'll know it when you come across it," Diana said.

"How will I know?"

"I don't know, but you'll know. I told you, I think you're psychic."

"I don't wish to be rude, Diana, but that strikes me as . . . well . . . garbage."

"Have it your own way. Good hunting!" she said, and went back down the hall.

That I would, by some mystic means, know the book I had no trouble in ignoring as so much idiocy, which did not make the prospect of what I had to go through easier. Particularly after I had done a rapid computation and discovered that there were more than five thousand volumes.

Oh, well, I said to myself, so I would begin at the beginning and look for a book with a cross on it. . . .

After all, I continued to cheer myself on, a diary was a diary, and would not be easily confused with novels or various types of nonfiction. And it wouldn't take me that long to mount the

140

ladder, moving on rollers attached to one of the upper shelves, and check on the titles.

But, for a variety of reasons, it did. The first discouraging discovery was that some of the shelves, though not all of them, carried double rows of books, but that there was no way of knowing which did and didn't without looking at the back of every single shelf. Another was that an astonishing number of books sported crosses, for the simple reason that a bookplate, almost as large as the page of an average book and bearing the Egremont coat of arms with its crossed shield, had been pasted onto the first blank page or, when that was absent, inside the cover itself, of every single book. So every book that wasn't demonstrably something else—such as, for example, *Civic Engineering in Westchester County in the First Two Decades of the Twentieth Century,* a tome resting with other engineering works in the second tier of books that I examined—had to be checked.

"I'm just looking for a handwritten book," I said to Diana the second day when she walked in and asked me why I was so hurriedly opening and shutting the books.

"Why are you so certain it's handwritten?" Diana asked.

I turned, almost falling off the ladder. "What do you mean?"

"There's nothing to say it isn't typewritten—or printed," she said slowly.

"But in this famous dream of yours, haven't you *seen* the page?"

"I suppose I must have, but I can't remember."

"That's a heap of help."

One way or another it took me a lot longer to get around that library than I could have imagined. Everything seemed to happen. The wheels at the top of the ladder that were supposed to roll effortlessly along the metal gutter stuck. Attempts to unstick it by me, Diana and Mrs. Klaveness were unavailing. It was Simon, who had dropped by for a drink, who finally discovered the trouble and, with a screwdriver, pair of pliers and an oil can, put it right. But a whole day had been lost.

141

"That ladder's unsafe anyway," he said, wiping his hands on a rag that Mrs. Klaveness had thoughtfully supplied. "The wood's rotten where the metal holding the wheels is attached and could just come apart some fine day."

"Well, short of having another ladder put up, which I can't afford," Diana said, "I don't know how else Candida's going to look for that book."

"Weren't the books catalogued?" he asked in astonishment.

"Of course. But I don't suppose a diary would be in the catalogue."

"Is that what you're looking for?" Simon looked at me.

"Yes," I said. I wasn't sure how much she wanted discussed in front of Simon, although, given the relationship between them, I assumed he was in her confidence.

"Whose diary?" Simon asked.

Diana hesitated. "I don't know. You might as well know, Simon, I don't really know what Candida's looking for, except that it's a diary—or journal of some kind—and it has a cross on it. I've dreamed about it three times, and I'm sure if I find it, I'll find out the business about . . . about what's bothering me. Candida said she'd help me look. While she's been looking in the library, I've been going through all the shelves and drawers in all the other rooms." There was a slightly defiant look on Diana's face. "I suppose, like Candida here, you think I'm tottering on the brink of going round the bend."

"Have I said so?"

"No," Diana admitted grudgingly, "you haven't. But you're about the only person who hasn't." She glanced at me and a gleam of mischief came into her eyes. "Candida says it's like looking in a coal cellar at midnight for a black hat that isn't there."

Simon's laugh rang out. "I like that," he said. "Where did you get it, Candida?"

"My father used to say it."

"Well," Simon said, stooping for the ladder, then raising it and placing its rollers gently on the gutter, "you'd better get on with your search, but remember what I said about the unreliability of the ladder."

Faintly the telephone sounded in other part of the house. Diana turned her head. On the third ring it was picked up. "I think that's for me," she said. "I've been expecting—yes, Mrs. Klaveness?"

"Telephone for you," the housekeeper said.

"Stay to dinner, Simon," Diana said, following Mrs. Klaveness out of the room.

"Tell me," I said to Simon. "Just how much faith do you put in Diana's dreams?"

"I take it you think it's all nonsense."

"Well, I don't think it's very solid evidence on which to place a long, dusty, boring search on a ladder that may come down at any minute."

"Then why offer your services? I take it you did, or did Diana co-opt them?"

I sighed. "I offered them. Mainly because I understood Diana to say something to the effect that the sooner the mystery that is bothering her is cleared up, the sooner we can all leave here. And that was what sounded so absolutely glorious to my ears."

"Leaving?"

"Yes. Leaving. But that was before I knew the library had five thousand books plus, often in two rows, practically all of them with a cross on or in them."

Simon smiled. "Poor Candida! I can see what you mean by feeling that you're looking for a black hat that isn't there."

"But you think it is." It was a statement rather than a question.

"You mean, do I have any faith in her dreams or in the reality of anything else that is happening to her, don't you?"

I nodded.

"Let's say I have an open mind." I must have looked skeptical, because he said, "All right, let's talk about the diary: It could, as you think, be all nonsense, or perhaps spring from some strictly Freudian interpretation of what a diary with a cross on it could represent in her life. Or, think about it this way: At some point in her childhood, she did see a diary, but for some reason either it, or what she saw in it, threatened her,

143

so she blocked it out of her conscious mind. But the diary, along with the threat or danger it represents, remains in her unconscious. And where does the unconscious most clearly exhibit itself? In dreams. That being so, there could, possibly, be a connection between what's in a diary and Diana's obsession about a real or imaginary sister."

"Oh," I said. "I hadn't thought about that."

"You can accept that?"

"Of course."

"Because psychology is by now a respectable study accepted by all so-called sensible people."

"That sounds like a put-down."

Simon went on inexorably. "You can accept the fact that somewhere hidden in Diana's unconscious memory is, possibly, a diary alluding to something or someone that would make sense out of a possible sister or her fixation that she has one. But where is that unconscious memory? If you opened up her head and poked in the gray tissue inside, you wouldn't find a picture of a child reading a book with a cross on it containing information that is so terrifying to that child that she immediately blots it out of one part of that thirteen-ounce organ, but leaves it—but only under certain conditions—in another. And no matter how you poked around in that other part you wouldn't find that memory, would you? The only way you'd know that would be for Diana herself, either consciously or under hypnosis, to tell you ... that is, to make, with her mouth and tongue, certain sounds that would be transmitted by airwaves to your ear"—Simon leaned over and tapped my ear—"and that would, in turn, produce a picture in your mind of the child reading the diary. But if anyone, at that moment that you were seeing it, anesthetized you and looked in *your* brain, they wouldn't find a picture of a child reading a diary and being frightened, any more than they did in Diana's own."

"So?"

"But you still accept the idea of a picture, invisible in Diana's brain, being transmitted to yours, where it is also invisible, because that is an accepted physical and mechanical explanation. But you balk like a mule at the idea that some-

144

thing else—a collection of energy, an impulse, in other words, a presence that is as invisible as the picture in your mind and that is not apprehensible to your senses—can transmit the same picture. That comes under the heading of a ghost or psychic phenomenon and therefore is not respectable or acceptable. In other words, is not true."

It was like opening a sealed door. Always in my life, inherited from my father's strongly held views, there had been two worlds, one objective, probable and therefore real. The other subjective, imagined and therefore, in any true sense, unreal. All the good guys, according to my father, were in the first world. All the spook fanciers (bad guys) were dabbling around in the other, which didn't exist anyway. Now Simon had struck a blow at that reassuring barrier, so that, for a frightening moment, it quivered and broke and the two worlds poured across the barrier and merged.

"I don't believe that," I cried.

Simon took hold of my hands. "There's nothing to be afraid of."

But I was shaking and couldn't stop. After a minute he put his arms around me. I stopped shaking. Something warm and pleasant started to happen to me, something sweet and tender. . . .

I don't know what occurred then, but a power quite beyond my own took hold. Almost as though I were outside I saw myself jerk away, digging my elbows into Simon's chest to get free. Then I walked quickly out of the room.

At dinner it was almost as though none of it had happened. Simon's manner towards me was the same as it always was, as though neither our conversation nor his arms around me had actually occurred. . . . I came up out of my fog to hear Diana's voice.

". . . and, of course, they will build small houses on small lots, but that can't be helped."

"Who?" I asked.

"The man on the telephone," Diana said. "He represents the contracting company that wants to buy the land."

145

"You mean that's the outfit that you keep getting petitions about?"

"Yes. But at least they're not pressuring me to sell within the week, the way the school was."

"Are you going to sell to them?" Simon asked.

"If their offer is still there when I'm ready to sell—and he says it will be—yes. Are you about to tell me that you're joining the village in opposing it?"

"I may. I don't know."

"That sounds pretty stuffy coming from a priest. I thought you were out to serve people, not middle-class values."

"Come off it, Diana," Simon said good-naturedly. "That's a bit of elite snobbery. I'm not against people in small houses, if that's who the contracting company is really going to build for. But we have no guarantee that it is. That company is awfully shadowy. Nobody seems to know who's behind it. Do you?"

"I don't see why I have to. They're offering me an excellent price at a time I badly need it, and they're not trying to stampede me with a deadline the way Catherine Timberlake is."

"Well, I know you're strapped for money and I'm sorry. But until the zoning board enacts new limitations on commercial enterprises I *am* against the sale. Because I think it could result in the countryside south and east of here being gouged for highways plus short-order eating places, garages and bars. If you've found a loophole in the old zoning law and are going to sell your considerable land to a contractor who's after a fast buck, there'll be nothing to stop this whole area from looking like the cheaper outskirts of any big city. And I don't know who'd benefit, besides the builder."

"I would," Diana said. "As I seem to have to remind you, I'm broke and in debt, and all this is a lot of windy speculation by a bunch of environment freaks who are running short of a cause. And by the way—" She shot a look at him that was both angry and curiously vulnerable, as though his words had hurt her—"all this eagerness for civic purity comes very oddly from you, considering you're the one who introduced the ur-

146

ban masses by putting your halfway house here. If Eric, who has no axe to grind, thinks this contractor is okay, and he does, because I've asked him, then I don't know why you're suddenly scrambling into the role of Mister Clean."

"So Eric approves of him," Simon said thoughtfully.

"Yes, he does. And considering what Eric and his family have done for the village, and that he's a businessman with unimpeachable contacts—"

"As opposed to my ruffians," Simon put in.

"As opposed to your ruffians," Diana agreed. "I think you have one hell of a nerve joining some protest march to keep me from selling. Quite frankly, and since you keep acting like you are for the people all the way, I wonder what *your* motive is? As for my elite snobbery, since when were you such a great friend of the aspiring middle class?"

Trying to read Simon's face at that moment was like trying to discover meaning in a steel plate. I found myself wondering, for no reason I could pin down, if Diana hadn't put into Simon's hands a weapon that he could—and perhaps would—use against her. There was something about his expression, unreadable as it was, that led me to believe she might have. And that she would be sorry. And back of that, somewhere else in my mind, was the nagging of another problem. It had never occurred to me that there could be any acceptable argument on the side of the opposition to Diana's right to sell her own land and the right of the new owner to put up small lots for small houses. Now I suddenly discovered I was by no means as sure as I had been as to where the greatest good lay, a very uncomfortable position for anyone as certain as I usually was on which side the angels could be found. Suddenly, and out of the blue, I thought of Terry back in New York and her fierce contempt for compromisers. With her there were the good guys and the bad guys, and neither side was ever complicated by elements of the other. How very comfortable that was, I was thinking when, unexpectedly, James's high, clear voice broke in.

"Walker says the middle class is the backbone of every nation."

"He would," Diana commented, "since he probably lives off it."

"He does *not*. Anyway, he says—"

"And I'm tired of hearing about him."

"You don't like Walker and you don't like Hannibal and you don't like my father. You don't like anybody I like, so I don't like you."

"What I can't make out, is why you never talk about children your own age. Don't you have any friends in your peer group?"

"What's a peer group? Like earls and dukes?"

"Of course not. Are you—?" Diana stopped suddenly. Glaring at each other, nostrils flared, mother and son looked, for a moment, rather alike.

"Peer group is a piece of American sociological jargon, Diana. There's no reason why James would have heard it." Simon almost visibly poured oil on turbulent waters. "What it means, James, is children of your own age."

"I don't know very many," James said rather sulkily.

"Well, I think it's time you did," Diana replied. "Tomorrow I'll ask over some of the local kids."

"I like the boys at Halfway House. Especially Enrico."

"Which one is Enrico?" Diana asked Simon.

"Er—he plays the guitar," Simon said.

"You mean that young thug that's spent most of his life in juvenile court when he's not stealing cars and mugging people on the street?"

"Halfway House is full of boys who've done that all their lives," Simon said. "After all, it's not Exeter or Andover." He stared at Diana. "You know you're the one who was for having a halfway house up here when the community objected. That's why it's on your land."

"Yes, I know," Diana said. She sounded, quite suddenly, tired. After a second she went on. "But I will invite Marje Pritchett and her kids tomorrow. You'll like them, James."

"I'd rather see Enrico."

"James," Simon and I spoke at the same time. I glanced at Simon, who went on, "There's no reason why you shouldn't

148

do both. And your mother is right about one thing, you should get to know children your own age here. It'll be much more fun for you."

Looking at James's face, I found myself wondering whether Simon was right. Peers could be cruel if a child was different, and James was indeed different. Abruptly there sprang to my mind a picture of Hannibal. It was such a powerful image that I said to James, "How's Hannibal?"

James didn't reply for a minute. Then he said, "He doesn't like it very much here."

Seeing Diana about to speak again, I said it quickly, "How do you know that?"

"Because he's under my bed so much. He never went under the bed in England, unless somebody came in the flat that he really hated."

"Maybe he should get out, too," Diana said. "After all, it must be a pretty boring life for him stuck in that room."

"It's not," James shouted. "He likes to be with me. We have lots of games."

"Well, there's no reason to yell, James. It's just that I think you should let him out sometimes. After all, Seth and Susan, Candida's cats, go out all the time. Don't they, Candida?"

Privately I had thought the same. Yet I found myself strangely reluctant to say so. "Well..."

"I won't," James said. "Please may I be excused."

"You haven't eaten your dinner. Of course not. Sit down."

But James was on his feet, his chair pushed back. "I'm not hungry."

"Then you can wait until the rest of us have finished."

"I have to go to the loo."

"All right," Diana said irritatedly. "Go to the bathroom, which you should have gone to before dinner when you washed your hands. But come back. You hear me? Come back."

But the words were wasted. James was out of the room.

"Diana," Simon said. "Why can't you leave James be for a while?"

"He's not like a boy at all. He's like a little old man."

149

"Maybe you'd be, too, if you'd had his life."

"And when I think that Roger had me declared an unfit mother, and I see what he produced in the way of an upbringing—"

"You can't take out your anger at Roger on James."

"That's an uncalled for comment."

"Leave him alone, Diana. Let him find his own way."

"His own way being to find his friends among the assorted cutthroats at your establishment, I suppose."

"He could do worse," Simon said coolly. "I was surprised at how well he got on."

"Yes, that is amazing, it makes one wonder about him even more," Diana said, angrily ringing the bell at her place.

"No. Not after you think about it for a bit. James, with his English accent and his strange, formal ways, offers them no threat; he's not some kind of American kid who's obviously had more advantages. He's so different that he's acceptable to them. And I suspect that that's the reason he likes them. Leave it that way for a while."

"I'll do what I consider best for my own son," Diana said. "Would you clear, Mrs. Klaveness? By the way, is there dessert?"

"Just fruit and cheese," the housekeeper said.

"Then we'll have coffee in the sitting room."

"He didn't eat," Mrs. Klaveness said, staring down at James's barely touched plate.

"I wish I didn't eat when I felt anxious," I said, my mind reverting as usual to my leading problem.

"Nobody forced you to have two helpings," Diana pointed out, getting up and pushing in her chair. She, too, had eaten little.

"You're just a charm boat all around," I said.

For a moment we stood, each behind our chairs, staring at one another like two men about to resort to fists.

"If you're going to have a fight, I'll be glad to hold your coats," Simon said, looking at us both, a faintly sardonic expression on his face.

With a final shove to her chair, Diana turned and went out of the room.

"What's the matter with her?" I asked. "I've never seen her this bad tempered."

"Withdrawal," he said simply. "It's tough."

For a minute I didn't understand. "You mean not drinking?"

"That's right."

"Wouldn't it be better then if she drank?"

"What do you think?"

I knew as soon as I asked that what the answer was. All I had to do was remember a few scenes from the first days here. I made a face. "Isn't there some kind of happy medium?"

"For people who have problems with alcohol, no. Did you know that half the boys in my house got in trouble from drinking? They have some kind of AA meeting every day, with local members of AA coming. Diana's been to a couple of them. That's why she's so hostile to them now."

"Oh," I said, absorbing that piece of information. Then, "Well, what do we do?"

"Nothing. Because there's nothing we can do, except to try and keep her relationship with James as uncomplicated as possible."

"It's probably a good thing then that she's going to invite this Marje whoever she is. The less time she and James have to collide the better."

"Have you met Marje?"

"No. Have you?"

"No. But I've met her children."

"What are they like?"

"I think I'll let you see for yourself. Are you coming for coffee?"

I decided not to have coffee in the sitting room, and without exactly planning it, found myself outside James's door. Knocking gently, I waited.

There was no answer. So I knocked again. "James?" I called softly, not particularly wanting anyone downstairs to hear me. There was still no answer. Perhaps he wasn't there, I thought, and put my ear against the door. But he was, because I could hear him singing. Rather than knock again, I opened the door and stuck my head in.

I was about to speak his name, when I stopped. Obviously James had not heard me come in. He was seated with his back towards me, cross-legged, at the edge of a small, tattered and dirty oriental rug. Opposite him, large and dignified and looking the very embodiment of an Egyptian statue, was Hannibal.

In a high, piping voice, James was singing a tune strongly reminiscent of "Here We Go Round the Mulberry Bush," but the words made no sense. What they sounded like was:

> *Beastie, bystie, boostie, bootsie*
> *Bulzartgay*
> *Bulzartgay, Bulzartgay*

At that point Hannibal raised his head and looked at me. James stopped singing and swung around.

"You have no right to come into my room without knocking."

"I'm sorry, James. I did knock, but I suppose you didn't hear me. That's a fascinating-looking rug, where did you get it?"

Slowly James got to his feet. "I suppose you'll tell Mother."

"Tell her what?"

"About the rug. Then she'll come and ask a lot of questions and take it away."

It was such an outlandish thing to say that I wanted to laugh. "James, why on earth would she take it away?" But the moment I said that I knew that he was probably right. What she would see was a torn, filthy scrap of rug lying on top of the expensive beige wall-to-wall carpet. As clearly as though I were a clairvoyant I could hear her demanding to know where it came from, why on earth James chose to put it down, and then, over his protests, insisting that she take it to be cleaned.

"Did you bring that rug with you?" I asked, rather unnecessarily.

"Yes."

152

My memory suddenly produced the roll that I carried out of the airport, along with one of James's suitcases. "Yes," I said. "I remember now."

"Are you going to tell about it?" he asked again.

"Not if you don't want me to," I replied, making a decision. "It must be something special for you."

Silence. Hannibal, who had been licking one paw, stood up on his four legs, arched his back, then jumped lightly onto a chair, where he sat with his front paws curved in, making a muff.

"Actually," James said, sounding English and deliberately casual, "it is. Special."

"I see." I stared down at the rug, wondering where to go from there, aware of tension in the thin figure in front of me. The pattern on the rug seemed common enough, I thought: a diamond-shaped blob in the center with red, blue and green ornaments in the middle. And around the edges of the carpet a thick, ornamental border in the same red, blue and green design, with small, boat-shaped objects between the border and the middle design. Boat-shaped objects, or simply, boats. Boats plying between the big island in the middle and the land around the edges of the rug . . .

"If you stare at the rug long enough," I said, "it looks like a map."

I heard him draw in his breath and looked up.

"You *promise* you won't tell?" he said.

"I *promise*," I said, meaning it.

"Well, it's a country called Bulzartgay. . . ." He paused, to see how I would accept that piece of information.

"I see," I said. And then inspiration hit me. "Was that its national anthem you were singing when I came in?"

He let out his breath, as though a great weight were off his mind. "Yes. It goes like this,

> *Beastie, bystie, boostie, bootsie*
> *Bulzartgay, Bulzartgay*
> *Bulzartgay*
> *Beastie, bystie, boostie, bootsie*

153

"That's a very nice national anthem," I said, feeling my way. "Do you sing it every day?"

"Yes. It has to be sung every morning and every evening, or the king will refuse to let the people have a national holiday with a fair and fireworks and parades and band music and a merry-go-round."

"And the king is you?"

"Oh, no. I'm only the national scribe. Hannibal is the king. And Walker is the prime minister."

I sat down and tucked my legs under me. "It sounds fascinating. Can you tell me more about it—especially as you're the national scribe and probably have to write up its history."

"Yes. As a matter of fact... I have. In a notebook." He shot me a look. "Would you like me to read you some?"

"I should love it."

As time passed and the thin piping voice read on, the world and people of Bulzartgay emerged in fascinating clarity:

There were two provinces: the Uplands, in the middle, where the mountain people lived, and the surrounding Plains, where the Flatlanders dwelt. Every morning there was a parade of the troops of both provinces before the king (Hannibal) and the prime minister (Walker). Should the prime minister have to be away, busying himself, it went without saying, for the good of the entire country, then the national scribe, James, would take his place in the reviewing stand. There were speeches by the leaders of the Uplands (Bootnag) and the Flatlands (Omneg), and a further discussion as to whether the daily ongoing war should be resumed or whether Hannibal should declare a joint national holiday to be celebrated by a fair with carnival, merry-go-round, races and band music.

In several aspects of its national life Bulzartgay was outstanding. Most outstanding of all were its four main laws:

No one ever hunted.
All animals, especially cats, were sacred.

154

No one went to school.
There were no parents.

By some happy, as yet unexplained, process all children were born orphans. There was a rumor in Bulzartgay that the UN had sent an investigatory team to find out how this was done so that the children of other nations could benefit, but the secret was closely guarded.

Frequently Bulzartgay was raided by a seafaring people who appeared out of the mists at the edge of the horizon (carpet).

Nobody quite knew where they came from, but they were fierce and predatory, sailing at night in their long, cunning ships with huge black sails and muffled oars, and slipping off again before dawn with captured Flatlanders and jewels and —if they were lucky—a maiden or two from the Uplands, because it was conceded everywhere that they were the most beautiful. Such a raid, of course, complicated the political situation in Bulzartgay further, because the need to defend themselves against the Seafarers interrupted the intricate ritual of war games between Uplanders and Flatlanders, devised over centuries to cause as much furor as possible, but no casualties. . . .

At this point James's voice, which had been reciting in a sing-song quality so seductive that I, too, had fallen spell to the reality of Bulzartgay, changed. He was no longer spinning off a chronicle. He was telling me something that was bothering him.

"There's a woman, or a girl, I think she's their queen. And she's evil, I know she is. We've never had anything before like that in Bulzartgay."

I came out of my spell and stared at James. Had he woven such a powerful charm that he was now unable to tell reality from the story? "What do you mean, James?" I asked.

There was silence, then he said, "I suppose you'll think I've made this up, like . . . like Bulzartgay. That's what people always say. Everybody except Walker."

I was beginning to see why Walker figured so largely in James's world.

"You've tried to tell other people about . . . about Bulzartgay?"

"Yes . . . once or twice. My father . . . a boy at school."

When he didn't go on I said, "What happened?"

"My father wasn't so bad, even though he did laugh a lot. He said I should try and write it down, which is how I discovered that I was the national scribe. But the boy . . . well, he appeared jolly interested, only then he told some of the other boys, and they thought it was the biggest joke of the year and . . . it was all rather rotten."

I could imagine that it was, and winced at the weapon for cruelty that had been put in their hands.

"But then my father took me out of that school because we went abroad for a while. So it was all right. And you know what happened? The school's roof fell in. My father told me at breakfast one day when he'd been reading the *Times* that was sent to him. He thought it was very funny. But I *knew*."

"What did you know?"

"It was just retribution. Hannibal said so."

I looked at the cat, whose big green eyes were fixed on me with an unwinking stare.

James saw my glance. "Just because he doesn't tell things when you're here, doesn't mean he doesn't communicate."

"I see." I looked at James again, concerned once more about his ability to differentiate fact from fantasy. But my mind, which had the uncomfortable habit, sometimes, of asking awkward questions, suddenly produced a new one: Was fact any more a reflection of truth than fantasy?

"Just as a matter of interest," I said, wanting not to make too much of a thing of it, "how does Hannibal communicate?"

James stared hard at me, then said almost belligerently, "If I tell, you'll say I'm not telling the truth."

Truth again, I thought. "No, I won't."

"Well, he thinks it, and then I know it."

"I see."

"And he's the one who told me about this evil queen of the Seafarers who's trying to put a bad spell on Bulzartgay, and even on Hannibal."

156

I remembered James's father, who laughed, and the boy who had told the others, so I said seriously, "What makes you think she's putting an evil spell on Bulzartgay and Hannibal?"

"Because sometimes Hannibal hides under the bed and won't come out when we're ready to start on the day's parade ... and even when I coax him out and unroll the carpet it's hard to imagine Bulzartgay. It just won't come ... it just looks like a carpet."

All of the things that were distressing James had obviously perfectly natural and rational explanations, yet I knew that any comment that sounded remotely like pooh-poohing the world of Bulzartgay would not only be useless, but it would alienate James and ensure his future silence. Furthermore, James was very near tears.

"I'm awful sorry," I said carefully. "I wonder what could be causing all this."

"Well," he started. But at that point Hannibal, who had been sitting on the chair, relaxed and immobile, suddenly galvanized into action, sprang to the floor and ran, his stomach dragging along the floor, under the bed.

"You see—?" James said, and then I heard the quick footsteps coming along the hall.

"Quick," James said. "The carpet."

I didn't stop to think. I found myself helping James to roll it up and push it under the bed. We had barely stood up, breathless, our hands slightly grubby, when the door was thrust open.

"I thought I told you to come back to the dining room when you had gone to the bathroom?" Diana said.

James and I stood speechless, like two culprits. My mind was blank, but one glance at James's face made me realize I had to say something and say it quickly. He was not only white. He was shaking.

"I'm sorry, Diana," I said. "It's all my fault. I came up here and James and I got talking about—" I was about to say Hannibal, when intuition told me to stay off that particular subject, "about cricket," I said. "James was explaining the rules to me."

I didn't know what magic lay in the words that had fallen, by purest accident, off my tongue. But some magic there must have been, because the tight, angry look disappeared from Diana's face. Despite what she had said, I had never believed myself to be psychic. But the least intuitive person in the world, at the moment she had flung open the door and walked in, would have felt the impact of the furious vibrations pouring out of her.

"Cricket?" she said. "I didn't know you played cricket, James. Your father always said he hated the game."

Which probably, I thought, explained why she seemed so willing, if not actually pleased, to hear of James's interest, or what I had said was James's interest.

"Well," he faltered. "I haven't *played* that much." His voice underlined the word. "But of course I know the rules. Everyone knows them."

For a few seconds there was silence, and, with a sinking feeling, I wondered if Diana was going to pursue the question of my interest in a game which I had neither watched nor shown any desire to watch. But, after a little hesitation, she said, "I also came up to tell you that I called Mrs. Pritchett and she and her two kids are coming over tomorrow afternoon."

"But tomorrow's the day we're supposed to go up to White Deer Lodge with the halfway house and Cousin Simon."

"I'd forgotten that. Well, you'll just have to go on an outing with them some other time. I've made this other arrangement and I think it's far better for you to meet children your own age. They can get you together with others, so that you can find friends here.

"But Enrico—"

"And I don't mean criminal teenagers from the city." Diana was beginning to be angry again.

"But—" James started.

I had managed, while Diana was talking to James, to move nearer to him so that I could nudge him with my arm.

"We can always go up to White Deer Lodge," I said. "I'm sure Simon will be taking his boys up there other times." I thought for a moment that James would go on arguing. But after a while, he lowered his eyes and mumbled, "All right."

Diana's face softened. "I'm only trying to do what's best for you, James. I want you to be happy here."

And the incredible part, I thought, watching her, was that she meant it. She did want him to be happy. As the angry look disappeared once more from her face, a sort of baffled wistfulness took its place.

She needed James so badly, I thought, as badly as he needed her. And yet any move on the part of one seemed to enrage— or frighten—the other. If only— And then it happened again.

In a gesture that was curiously arrogant, Diana stepped forward and reached her hands towards James's shoulder. Whether it was the demand inherent in her gesture or some inner revulsion of his own, I don't know. But he stepped back.

I saw the anger flood back to her face. Then she turned on her heel and went out.

9

I found it hard to go to sleep that night, which was possibly attributable to the fact that Pandora lay so jammed up against me on one side, and Seth and Susan on the other, that for me to turn over would cause a mass upheaval.

"Come on, kids," I said aloud. "Give me a little breathing space." All of which seemed to make them snuggle closer than ever. But since I had shared my bed with a variety of animals most of my life, and had often slept quite soundly curled like the figure S to accommodate them, I knew it wasn't that.

It was my growing conviction that things which had started out poorly at Tower Abbey were getting worse. Included in this grab bag of "things" was the relationship between Diana and me and the condition of Diana herself. It was true that, as far as I knew, she had stopped drinking. But the strain of staying dry was producing almost as many problems as the drinking itself. Whatever mystery she had come to clear up remained unsolved. Not only had I not found the diary, I did not, despite what Simon said, believe in its existence.

But more prominent in my mind and much more worrying

was the deteriorating relationship between Diana and James. Something deep within me responded to the solitary and difficult little boy and to his single-minded devotion to his cat, Hannibal. My emotional reflexes were all on his side. Yet I knew that Diana could not be entirely blamed for reacting to her son with something less than wisdom and tolerance. Their bad start was probably more her fault: She had obviously been drinking. But it became apparent soon after that James had arrived more than ready to find fault and well primed by his father's thoughtless and bitter-tongued criticisms. Given the formality of his upbringing, James had never been even normally polite to his mother, and in the matter of the ice cream he had been startlingly rude, a deliberate slap at his mother, as Simon pointed out, with Mrs. Klaveness an accidental victim.

Pushing the cats away, I turned over, and felt them, after suitable complaints, close around me again. And then, kicked off perhaps by the presence of my own animals, there started within me one of those internal arguments that always seemed, with me, to be a midnight specialty.

Wouldn't I, above all people, one side of the argument pointed out, be sympathetic with James's focusing of his frustrated affections on Hannibal? After all, he had hardly lived what could be called, emotionally speaking, a balanced life. Wasn't it natural that he should put all of his emotional investment in his pet? Hadn't I done the same?

Well, not quite. It was true, the other side of my inner tussle conceded, that my mother had died when I was young. But my father and I had had a good life together, not only as parent and child, but as friends. In my growing-up years, anyway, animals were an addition, not a substitute. But with James, Hannibal seemed something more than a pet—even a much loved pet. He was . . . what?

But when I tried to figure out the answer to that my tired mind balked. After all, I thought, zoology was my subject, not psychology. . . .

And then there was Simon. With no effort at all, like an arrow flying to its target, my mind, quite suddenly no longer tired, went to the moment that his arms were around me, to the feeling of sweetness and peace that their being there brought, and to the violence with which I rebuffed him a few seconds later. From its hiding place then slid an old fear and an old memory, and I was again my younger self, not the eleven-year-old child who walked in on a scene that shocked and wounded, but an adolescent at her first party, a party that took place here, at this house, on the occasion of Diana's third marriage, her marriage to Roger Eliot.

It should have been a glorious occasion: my first formal invitation, my first long dress, an all-ages affair that included my father, handsome and a little strange in his black tie and formal suit, giving off a faint smell of camphor and mothballs.

"Do I look all right, Candy?" he asked, sounding uncharacteristically uncertain, tweaking nervously at his black tie.

And my reply, "You look splendiferous!" My widower-bachelor father, who, unlike so many fathers of my various friends, still had all his dark wavy hair and flat stomach. I had been so proud of him, reconciled to not having a beau of my own to take me to the ceremony and the shindig following it at the big house, because I could walk in on my father's arm. . . .

The wedding itself had taken place in the garden out by the pond in the golden light of a late spring afternoon. Off to the side were trestle tables set up as bars, and, as soon as the nuptial itself was over and Diana and Roger pronounced man and wife, white-jacketed waiters appeared walking around with trays bearing, at first, champagne and, later, drinks. I had enjoyed my first glass of champagne and found it pleasantly exalting. But, being not quite sixteen, I had by-passed the drinks in favor of the fruit punch ordered specially for the young people and ladled out from a big silver bowl on one of the tables. Thirsty and nervous, I had found the fruity mixture delicious, and had drunk the whole tall glass almost immediately.

"What's in it?" I asked Diana, who had discarded her

bridal hat and bouquet to come around herself with a big silver pitcher, and who was waiting to replenish my near empty glass.

She looked up and smiled, her eyes the same aquamarine color as the silk dress that slithered down her body in a way that filled my adolescent heart with envy. Because it was quite evident that underneath that wedding dress Diana's slender and quite naked body was as lithe and firm as I devoutly wished mine to be. But all the exercise I had been able to take on the tennis court, on horseback and in the village swimming pool had not removed my hated puppyfat.

"What's in it?" Diana smiled as she filled my tumbler to the brim. "Snips and snails and puppy dog tails."

I took another large swallow. "Isn't that what little boys are made of?"

As clearly as though it had all happened yesterday evening, I could see her eyes crinkling up. "Precisely. That's why I think you should drink a lot of it. So that a nice boy will materialize for you."

I was all for that—theoretically. The trouble was that I had been in love with Simon for so long that—despite my early disillusionment with him—boys nearer my own age seemed, by comparison, callow and full of pimples and adam's apples. Or so I told myself. There were moments when I suspected that that was an elaborate defense to keep myself from minding the fact that the boys at school seemed singularly uninterested in me.

But as I drank my second glass of punch, and embarked on a third, my courage appeared from nowhere. Either that, or I saw my male classmates in a new light. A few hours later I found myself the center of a group being, it seemed to me, witty and scintillating as I had never been before. Exalted and euphoric, I decided it was the new me, an unveiled, hitherto unsuspected Candida, sparkling, unafraid and plainly far more attractive to the opposite sex (puppyfat and all) than I had dreamed.

The memories of the rest of that fatal evening came back

163

like separate camera frames: Simon, his blond head rising above his black dinner jacket, gliding across the polished floor of the sitting room (cleared that evening for dancing), his hair even lighter than Diana's, resting against his cheek... Eric, at the edge of the floor, watching them, something about him reminding me of a child with his face pressed to the window of a candy store... two of the callow youths, bent double with laughter as they described how they had emptied a quart of vodka into the fruit punch, already, they said, well spiked with white wine... Simon coming across the dance floor towards me, pulling me towards him and smiling that heart-stopping smile, so that I decided in that instant to forgive him all past sins... my hero-father, his black tie vanished, his white ruffled front smeared with lipstick, lurching against the bar table set up in the hall, and sending the whole to the marble floor in a splintering crash... Simon, his arm around me, leading me out of the house, my sense of bliss struggling against my growing queasiness...

After that the pictures became confused. I tried the next day, and on and off during the following years, to sort out some sequence as to what happened after Simon took me outside, to make some sense out of a jumble of memories and sensations only dimly recalled. But every time I thought an elusive memory seemed on the point of coming clear, a terror took hold of me, serving as a censor, and dropping a blank wall in front of any further recollection. And the pictures remained unconnected and therefore without meaning. . . .

I recalled being outside, my face on the ground with the smell of newly cut grass in my nostrils, of hearing someone screaming and realizing after another blank that it was my own voice making that terrible noise... of struggling not just with one person but several, only I couldn't summon their faces. All that would come back was a visual impression of white shirts and black suits, of fighting off a monster with many pairs of probing, tearing hands. . . .

And then, humiliatingly clear, the final degradation—being vilely sick, not once but again and again.

164

I looked up then and saw my father near me, weaving and faltering, his clothes as disheveled and soiled as mine. I don't remember how we got home. But the next day our car was in our driveway and the keys on the kitchen table.

Once, but only once, I asked my father what had happened. There was a deep, terrible disgust within me, both for him and for myself, and that disgust would not be reasoned away by the fact that I could not recall what had given rise to it. When I finally brought myself to ask my question, all he said was, "You got sick. It wasn't your fault. The Bigelow boys arrived fairly drunk and poured vodka into the punch bowl. The party was a shambles."

"But what happened afterwards?"

"Nothing. Nothing for you to worry about."

I knew it wasn't true. But I couldn't make myself press him further, because I didn't want to know.

The following Monday when I turned up at school, there were little silences that followed me down the hall to the classroom, silences punctuated by giggles. One of the Bigelow boys, a fair giant who captained the school football team, sang something about Dandy Candy being so randy, and the boys and girls he was with laughed. More than anything in the world I wanted to hide, but I stuck my head in the air and walked on.

Finally, when the agony of not knowing what happened overcame my pride, I asked a girl who had been at the party.

"What happened?" she repeated. "You don't remember?"

I shook my head.

She giggled. "Maybe better you leave it that way."

The only result that came out of that party—a party that became famous in the annals of that part of Westchester— was that my father, who had always liked Simon, would never again have anything to do with him. He didn't make a big thing of it. He just managed to be busy when Simon dropped by, or found that he couldn't come to the telephone when Simon asked to talk to him. But he would never tell me why. The only thing he did say was that it would be a good idea if I stayed away from Simon. And since Simon was so tied up with my fears about that night, every impulse I had was to do just that. . . .

More than ten years had passed since then. I had done as my father suggested and stayed away from Simon, barely speaking to him when we passed in the street. Once he caught me. I was sitting at a table in the village coffee shop, drinking a soda and reading a book, and he came in and sat down opposite me, putting his doctor's black bag on the floor beside him.

"All right, now, Candia. What have I done?"

How could I say, "I don't know. I can't remember what happened that night of the party." Even the possibility of saying it brought back the suffocating fear. So I fielded his questions about my father's odd behavior in avoiding him, and when he pushed for an answer about mine, I produced the memory of walking in on him and Diana, that I had always been uncomfortable with him after that.

"After all this time? You're grown up now, Candida. Surely the facts of life and men and women are no longer a deep shock to you now."

I shrugged, not being able to think of any reply.

"That's funny," he said, getting up. "I always thought we were friends. I guess I was wrong."

But still he stood, staring down at me. I didn't look back up at him, though I could feel his eyes almost through the top of my head. I kept my own at the level of his hand, broad in the palm, long of finger, a big strong hand. . . . Hands, probing, tearing hands.

"Does your . . . your hostility have anything to do with the night of the party?" he asked.

I could feel the sweat of fear break out on my body. "Nothing," I said. "Nothing."

"All right. I'm going into the army next week. So I won't be seeing you for a long while. I hope everything . . . everything works out for you."

And he left. I watched him run down the steps of the coffee shop, and then go to the curb where his car was parked.

And as I stared at the light, waving hair, a little shaggy around the edges, and the sharply etched nose, I started to cry. And I sat there, before my empty soda glass, the tears running down over my hands as I tried to wipe them away.

And now, I thought, we're back here together in this house, with Simon still in love with Diana, and with me still fighting my old ghosts. Ghosts. I sat up in bed. Why did that word keep coming back? And why had I been so stupid as to come back to this mansion, to this strangely cursed mansion, of which most of my memories were either unpleasant or—which was worse—missing altogether.

Sighing, I lay down again, and set myself to counting backwards, usually a successful way of putting myself to sleep. The system must have, once again, worked, because the next thing I knew I was abruptly awakened. But by what, I wasn't quite sure.

I sat up in bed. All the animals, I noticed, were gone. A full moon poured its light through my window. Something had waked me, something—and then I heard it again. It was Diana's voice. And she was calling me.

Flinging back the covers, I didn't wait either to put on slippers or a robe, but ran through my open doorway into the hall and stumbled up the steps leading past the narrow door to the little staircase and into the main hall. This was much darker, because the moon was on the other side of the house from the hall windows. But I could still see well enough to get to Diana's door and push it open.

My first thought was that the master bedroom, which she was occupying, must have been the only room of the house equipped with an air conditioner. Then I switched on the light by the door, and saw Diana thrashing around the bed in what was plainly a nightmare.

I went over to her and grasped her shoulder. She screamed again. I shook her.

"Diana! Diana, wake up!"

She stared at me, her eyes wide open. "She was in here."

"Who?"

167

"That child. My twin sister. The one I told you about and you didn't believe. She was here."

"You were dreaming, Diana."

She stared back up at me. "I'm not, Candy. I remember calling you. Then I heard you running into the hall. And you came in here. If I were dreaming, would I remember that so clearly?"

Truthfully, I didn't know. "Well, maybe you were just waking up," I said. "It's cold in here, do you have an air conditioner—here in the country?"

"Look for yourself. I don't. I told you. She was in here. That's why it's cold. What was it James said? 'Ghosts make the room cold.'"

I neither believed her nor wanted to believe her. Yet I did glance towards the windows and saw that there was, indeed, no air conditioner.

"Maybe it's on the windy side of the house," I said.

Diana sat up in bed and reached for a cigarette from the package on her night table. With a helpless feeling, I watched her try to bring the match, clutched in her shaking hand, up to the cigarette end. Was it fear or trying to stay off liquor that made it jump like that?

Diana finally got her cigarette lit and looked at me over the smoke. "Why don't you spend the rest of the night in the other bed in here?" In the bright, overhead light she looked so pale her skin had an almost bluish tinge. And I found myself forgetting about her frequent and unattractive attacks of arrogance, and feeling sorry for the fear that now seemed to pour out of her. I opened my mouth to say I would move into the twin bed, but no sound emerged. The words would not come. I discovered at that point that the thought of spending a moment longer than was necessary in Diana's room filled me with revulsion.

"What's the matter?" Diana asked.

"Nothing," I said, knowing that I could not let her know the strength of my feeling. "I was just thinking about Pandora and Seth and Susan." It was a weak grab for an excuse and a

168

disastrous one, as I would have known if I had given the matter even a few seconds' thought.

Diana lowered her cigarette. "Do you mean to say that when I ask you, as a favor, if you'll stay with me, you're going to refuse on the grounds that your animals might miss you?"

She had a point. "No, of course not," I lied. I took a deep breath. As though I were pushing the words against a solid wall, I said, "I'll stay. Let me just get my robe."

"No!" The word shot out. And if I had not been aware before I was now how much Diana did not want to be alone. "I'll lend you a robe, slippers, anything you want."

And how angry she was, angry that she had to plead with me! Nor did I blame her. To make up for it, I went over to the bed and picked up her hand lying on the cover. "Of course I'll stay, Diana. I didn't mean to sound ungracious. I just didn't think."

At which point, to my utter astonishment and consternation, she burst into tears. Dropping the cigarette on her counterpane, she put her hands up to her face.

I rescued the cigarette, stamping it out in the ashtray, and making sure there were no sparks smoldering on the bed or carpet. Then, feeling a little strange, I leaned over and put my arms around Diana and held her as she cried.

After a while she seemed cried out, exhausted.

"Do you think you can get some sleep now?" I asked.

She dug a piece of tissue from under her pillow and blew her nose. "Yes. I think so," she said dully. "I can try anyway." Then she straightened, so that my arms slid away from her. "Thank you for your . . . your sympathy." Ordinarily, the patronizing note in her voice would have sparked off a few inflammatory comments of my own. But it was so visibly an effort to step back into the security of her accustomed role that it was both pathetic and a little appealing.

I got up. "I'll go—" I started, meaning to say that I would go to my room to get my own robe, which I preferred to borrowing hers. But as I saw her lady-of-the-manor façade crack and terror jump into her eyes again, I changed course. "I'll go

169

and use your bathroom, if I may."

The terror receded. "Of course. There are extra towels in there."

It was a big, old-fashioned bathroom, with a tub on clawed feet, another door, undoubtedly leading to the hall, and hollow steam pipes on which to hang wet towels. Then, when I was washing my hands, I saw on the glass shelf above the wash bowl a plastic container of pills. I didn't have to pick up the container to see what the pills were. The name, typed at the bottom of the label, was facing me: Valium. Drying my hands, I went back to Diana's bedroom.

"What kept you so long?" she asked. Again, my tendency was to snap back, but the obvious strain in her eyes stopped me.

"I guess I'm just sleepy and slow moving," I said. I pulled back the covers on the other twin bed and got in.

"Lucky you. I wish I could sleep normally." Sitting up, she threw back the covers and disappeared into the bathroom, shutting the door behind her. She was gone several minutes. I heard the sound of the faucet being turned on, the clink of a glass, the water going off and then, a minute later, the flush of the toilet. When Diana came back she turned off the light that operated from a switch in back of her bed, as well as on the wall by the door leading into the hall.

"Good night," she said.

"Good night."

I had not lied when I had attributed my slow motion to sleepiness. I had indeed been sleepy, until I actually got in the bed and the light was turned off. At which point I became wide awake. Turning on my stomach, a position that I usually assumed before going to sleep, I tried my old recipe of counting backwards. Evidently I didn't start high enough, having begun at fifty and arrived back at one nowhere near sleep. Muttering to myself, I flopped over on my side and started at one hundred, counting backwards more slowly. Somewhere near forty-three, Diana started breathing heavily, and I knew she had gone to sleep.

Well, I thought ironically, lucky me, indeed. She was the

one giving every noisy indication of having finally drifted off. And then, as clearly as though they were hovering in front of me, I saw that phial of pills. She had gone into the bathroom after I had. She had drunk water and had spent a while in there.

Perhaps because of my father's experience with one drug—alcohol—plus my own disastrous adventure with the punch, or maybe because I came to adulthood at the end of the sixties and the beginning of the seventies when the young people had seen what havoc drugs could cause, I had developed a hearty dislike of any kind of pills up to and including aspirin. So I was not, at that moment, tempted to go in and steal one of Diana's Valiums to help me to sleep. What I was sorely tempted to do was to sneak out of bed and go back to my own room. But I remembered the fright in Diana's eyes and my word to her.

Sighing, I flopped over on my back, and decided to go back to an old college practice: run through various Latin verb conjugations—in the past a sure method of getting to sleep within five minutes, especially the night before a Latin exam.

Half an hour later, I had not only gone through what I could remember of the Latin verbs, I had embarked on the French, regular and irregular.

"Damn, damn." I sat up in bed.

I did not, I decided, like Diana's room at all. Whether it was because the shape was wrong or the wind blew cold or I resented Diana's loud, heavy breathing, I didn't know. I did know I never felt less like sleeping. I felt, in fact, as though I would never sleep again. I felt, my mind plodded relentlessly on, the way an old person must feel, tired almost beyond endurance, yet unable to sleep.

Bending my knees up, I put my head on them, aware of a depression that was like a terrible weight, making me immobile. Even if I had not given my word I couldn't have left now. I couldn't get to the door. I couldn't get to the door because someone was standing in front of it ... surely, surely, it must be an arrangement of light and shadow, that figure that stood in front of the door, a living presence, alone with me, because Diana was somewhere else. Diana, asleep, drugged, her breathing even louder, was, to all intents and purposes, out of the way. And whether I liked it or not, I had to stay and find out what the person standing there wanted, because...

I don't know what happened then. But I felt as though I had been yanked out of a trance by a loud, intrusive noise that was demanding my immediate attention.

Snapping my head up, I listened and then threw back the covers. Something had set the animals off. Seth's Siamese voice, frantic and loud, played some kind of obligato to another cat's, probably Susan's. And over all, like a wailing descant, was the steady, chilling howling of a dog.

What on earth had happened to them? I had to find out. But the thought of going to the bedroom door filled me with dread. I didn't think I could do it. "There is nothing there," I said aloud. "You don't believe in that stuff, remember?" I went on, even louder. And if my voice woke Diana up, so much the worse. I stood up and glanced over towards her in the dark. She was on her back, her breathing heavy and noisy. Considering her state of nerves forty-five minutes ago, she was proving amazingly hard to awake now. But that was not my concern. My concern, I reminded myself as the crying of the animals rose, was to go out there and see what was the matter. And still I stood. If I could just reach one of the two light switches, I thought. Clamping my teeth together, because they had begun to chatter, I went around Diana's bed to the switch near the bathroom door.... The bathroom. I seemed to remember that it had had another door, one leading into the hall. Going into the bathroom, I switched on the light and saw, with a sense of relief that seemed out of proportion, that, sure enough, past the bathtub was another door. I went through it in no time and found myself in the darkened hall. Somewhere around here, near the bedroom door, was a switch, I recalled. I put my hand out, feeling along the wall. Yes, there it was. I pushed the lever down. A cold high light flooded the hall.

The first creature I saw was Pandora, her tail between her

172

legs, her muzzle pointed to the ceiling, a howl breaking from her throat.

"What's the matter, Pandora?" I said, and went over to her. The golden fur was standing up in a ridge along her spine, and I smoothed it as I patted and stroked her head. The howl died in her throat and she whimpered as she rubbed against me. But this just made the carrying on of the cats sound louder. It was then I realized that one voice came from the direction of James's room. I had barely absorbed that fact when James's door opened, and his pajama-clad figure appeared.

"Hannibal is *howling*," he said in a frightened voice. "Is something going on out here?"

"Where is he?" I asked.

"Under the bed, screaming his head off."

James and I stared at each other.

"Is it the ghost?" he asked.

"There's no such thing," I said. "There has to be a perfectly rational explanation."

"All right. What?"

He had me there. I could think of nothing. My mind was a blank.

"My father had a dog," James said. "His name was Colonel. The week before my father died he howled every single night. I suppose," he added belligerently, "you don't believe that either."

But I did believe that. High as was my mental wall against psychic phenomena, I believed, because I felt I had experienced, a link between the world of people and of animals that enabled them to communicate, which was why I had not disputed James's statement that when Hannibal thought something, he, James, knew it.

"Yes," I said slowly now. "I believe it. But I don't see what that has to do with—" And then, suddenly, I did. It was as though I were a particularly slow pupil for whom everything had to be said or played twice, and because of that I heard once more the sound of the faucet turning on and off and the clink of the glass when Diana was in the bathroom.

173

"Oh, my God," I said. Running back, I thrust open the door into Diana's room and pushed my way in. And, as outlandish as that sounded and felt, it described perfectly my sense of a powerful resistance around the entrance to the bedroom that was making it difficult, physically and psychologically, to get into the main part of the room. Even more astonishing was the fact that I was not, at that moment, frightened, perhaps because a terrible urgency drove me forward. I barely glanced at Diana as I passed, though her breathing was even louder and heavier and her face a sickly color. But I ran into the bathroom and looked on the glass shelf. The container of pills was there. But it was empty. For a moment I stared at it stupidly, trying to remember how many pills it had held. My memory was that the phial was more than half full. But how many that would entail was only a guess.

My eyes strayed to the glass standing next to the phial. It had not been there before but, then, it seemed obvious, Diana had used it when taking the pills. How much water would be needed to wash down how many pills? Water? I still don't know what made me go over, pick up the glass and sniff it. Perhaps, unconsciously, I had been aware of a familiar odor in the bedroom but the fact had not registered with my conscious mind. Whatever the reason, when I put my nose over the glass, I knew that Diana had not washed down her pills with water. But where did she get the liquor? She certainly wasn't carrying any when she went into the bathroom. But I had not lived with my father during his last drinking years for nothing.

Opening the door of the medicine cabinet, I glanced along the shelves. There, in an unmarked plastic bottle, was a clear liquid. It could, of course, be rubbing alcohol. Unscrewing the cap, I sniffed once or twice. There was no doubt that the liquid contained alcohol in some form. Then I poured a little into the cap and tasted it. Vodka. I screwed the cap back on, put the bottle back onto the shelf and closed the cabinet door.

The mystery was solved, but my immediate problem was much more urgent. I was no expert, but from everything I had read and heard, the combination of liquor and Valium could be lethal.

At that point I did—for me—an astonishing thing. I found myself saying a prayer. Where it came from I didn't know. But the words were on my tongue, asking help for Diana and for me. Then I ran back into the bedroom to see if my memory was correct. Yes, there on the night table was a telephone. I didn't stop to think or consider whom I should call. Beside the telephone was a book for listing telephone numbers. Under G I found Simon's number. He was, after all, along with his various other callings, a doctor.

His voice answered on the second ring. "Halfway House."

"Simon? Candida. Diana's taken half a bottle of Valium on top of alcohol. I can't wake her. Can you come right away?"

He didn't stop to query the reliability of my information. "Can you get her up? No, probably not, she's a good eight inches taller than you. Make some coffee, black and strong. I'll be right over."

Curiously, it was easy to get out of the room. Whatever had been there before by the door—either in reality or in my head—was no longer there. Going into the hall, I saw James standing down the hall, as though he hadn't moved since I had first seen him come out of his room. There was something terribly forlorn about him. Perhaps it was the height of the ceiling, or the overpowering presence of the house itself—somehow more palpable at night than during the day. But he looked small and defenseless.

"James," I said quickly. "Come down with me. Simon is coming and he told me to make some hot coffee immediately. Come help me."

I moved rapidly towards the stairs expecting him to follow me. But he continued to stand there. "I don't like to leave Hannibal," he said. "There's something not right up here, and I'm afraid for him."

"Whatever you wish," I said. Sorry as I was for him, I didn't have any time to waste. I ran downstairs and through the downstairs hall, turning on lights as I went, and then through the living room, the dining room and into the kitchen. I had barely put some hot water on to boil when I heard a slight sound and there, crawling around my legs as close to me as

175

possible, were Seth, Susan and Pandora.

"Hello, kids." I was busy spooning coffee into the drip pot. "I don't have time for you now, but you're very welcome."

The words were barely out of my mouth when I heard the patter of slippers.

"Candida. Hannibal's gone. I've looked *everywhere*. He must have got out of the room when I was talking to you." James, his face distraught, stood in the doorway. "Please help me find him."

My heart smote me. Worried as I was about Diana, I could feel his anguish. As gently as I could I said, "James, your mother's very ill. I've called Simon, who is a doctor. He should be here any moment. But right now I'm busy making coffee for her when she ... er ... feels better."

James, his face pinched, said, as though I hadn't spoken, "Please, please, he could get out. I'll help you make the coffee after we've found Hannibal."

"James—I can't. I must do this first."

"She's just drunk," he shouted. "That's all. And Hannibal could be dead."

I put the top on the coffeepot. "You have no right to say that. And anyway, it's not true. I'm sorry about—" But at that moment I heard the front door close, and footsteps.

"Candida?" Simon's voice called.

"I'm here, in the kitchen."

"Cousin Simon!" James suddenly came to life and ran out of the kitchen. "Please help me find Hannibal. He's gone. I'm sure mother will be all right. . . . His voice, the words becoming unintelligible, grew fainter. Then I heard Simon's deep voice and steps coming back.

"But—" That was James.

"Listen, James. I don't think for one minute Hannibal has gone out. This is a big house, and as soon as we can we'll help you find him."

Simon looked in. "I'm going up now. Bring the coffee when it's ready. How long ago did she take the pills. Do you have any idea?"

"Not that long." I told him about being waked by Diana's

calling, and about going into her bathroom, and seeing the pills. "She took them—and I guess the liquor—right before she turned out the light. Although why on earth, after asking me to spend the night—but never mind about that. I tried for a while to go to sleep . . . then I must have dozed off because I had this weird impression. . . . Then I did go to sleep, and woke when the animals started to howl. Maybe she took them an hour or an hour and a half ago."

"You say she took half the container. How many would that be?"

"I don't know. Maybe ten, twelve."

"Well, I'll give her a shot. Bring the coffee up when you can." And he disappeared.

With one part of my mind I noticed that James was no longer around. But at that point the water boiled, and I busied myself with pouring it out and letting it drain into the pot.

I had never before been involved with someone who had taken an overdose of pills combined with alcohol, and such reading as I had done had not prepared me for how messy the next few hours turned out to be.

Whether from the shot Simon had given her, or the natural inhospitality of Diana's stomach to the deadly mixture she had absorbed, I don't know. But whatever the cause, Diana started, sometime during the proceedings, to bring it all back up, including, of course, the coffee she had been induced to swallow. After the first spasm was over Diana seemed a little more awake, so against her protests, with her head turning from side to side to avoid the cup, she was forced to swallow more of the hot black coffee.

"Let me sleep, damn you!" she muttered. And then again, "Let me sleep."

"No," Simon said. "Not yet."

But then she gave a terrible heave and that coffee went the way of the rest over the now sodden bed. But for the first time I had dreadful evidence of how people died from vomiting and then suffocating. If we had not been holding Diana's head so that at least she'd rid herself of all that was coming up and out, if she had been lying flat and still comatose, she

177

would have choked to death.

"She could have died," I said.

"Yes," Simon agreed grimly. "Which is why we can't leave her until she is sleeping naturally—not from drugs—and there is nothing left to come up."

After more long hours of struggling and mess and Diana's dead weight lugged back and forth between Simon and me—although for her height she was not heavy—I said, "Maybe we should have taken her to a hospital."

"We probably should," Simon said. "If it had been anyone else I would have. But from what you said and what I could see from the size of the pill phial, she hadn't taken that many, nor had it been that long, so it seemed worth the risk to try and help her here. Also, do you realize, Candida, how much of a news item it would have been if Diana Egremont had been brought into the local hospital out cold from booze and pills? Anybody else would have a reasonable chance of anonymity. But not Diana. The whole country would know it within twenty-four hours."

"I can't figure why she did it," I said. "If she was making a serious effort at suicide, why would she ask me to spend the night in her room?"

"Because I don't think for one minute it was a serious effort—at least," he amended more slowly, "not consciously. She took a couple of pills, which she's probably used to taking, without danger. The mystery is, why she took it with the liquor instead of water, particularly since she has been off the stuff now for a few days. But after a swig or two of that hundred-proof vodka, she probably couldn't remember whether she had taken the pills or not, so she took two more. And then some more liquor, and then, probably, because she was too drunk or too euphoric or both to know what she was doing, some more pills."

"Would a few swigs of liquor have that much effect on her so fast?"

"Sure, if her tolerance had diminished. People who once could drink everyone under the table, sometimes get to the point where one drink can render them drunk. It's a progressive disease. It gets worse, and that's one of the ways in which it gets worse." He glanced at my face. "I've had a lot to do with overdosing among kids, you know. With both liquor and pills."

"Yes. I suppose so. All right. I can see that having drunk the vodka she was beyond rational action. But why, with me in the next room willing to spend the night and keep off the ghosts . . ." My voice faltered for a minute as I remembered my conviction that something or someone was standing in front of the bedroom door.

"You were saying?" Simon said, putting various things back in his bag.

By this time Diana was in the bed I had taken, her own having been rendered unhabitable. And she was sleeping normally, her breathing quiet and regular.

"I don't believe in ghosts," I said loudly. "It must have been a dream I was having. I did doze off."

"Shhh! Come over by the window. For heaven's sake, don't wake her now. She'll be in the fiend's own humor, and not at all grateful."

I went over with him to the windows that looked south. Simon pulled back the heavy curtains and I could see the dawn sky with streaks of gray and rose.

"Why the passionate assertion that you don't believe in ghosts?" Simon said quietly. "What happened?"

I stared up at him. In the morning light his eyes looked as gray as the early sky. I wanted to tell him, and then I wanted him to tell me how childish and ridiculous I was being and that I had simply had a disturbing dream influenced by Diana's irrational statements about ghostly sisters. Part of me at that moment was sure of his calm good sense. Yet mixed up with this were images from the past, old angers, old mistrusts.

"I wish," I whispered unhappily, "I could trust you."

He didn't say anything to that for a moment. Then, "Well, that is something I can do nothing about. My telling you that you can trust me is not going to achieve anything. All con artists start out by doing that."

179

Perversely, that flat, realistic statement supplied some of the trust in Simon that I was lacking. "All right," I said, "when I was first in here, in the bed Diana's in now, I couldn't go to sleep. After running through my usual methods of putting myself to sleep, with absolutely no success, I sat up. I must have dozed off then, with my head on my knees." I hesitated, feeling, I suppose, that to tell Simon about my impression of a presence at the door would be to give it added reality.

"And?" Simon prompted me.

The hell with it, I thought. I might as well go on. I hadn't been able to exorcise it by pretending it hadn't happened. "I had a feeling—a terribly strong feeling, Simon—that there was something at the door. It sounds crazy, and I don't believe it. But for a moment I thought I saw it. But I couldn't tell you what it was like. Only I knew that I couldn't get through the door because it was there. It was then the cats and Pandora started howling, and I remembered that there was a door into the hall from the bathroom, so I used that."

Simon didn't say anything. He just stared out the window at a sky that was now more rose than gray, and a countryside that fell sharply from the hill where the house stood into a valley colored now in varying shades of green and gray-green.

"I'm waiting for you to tell me that I was dreaming," I said, a little desperately.

He glanced down at me. "Do you think you were?"

"Not to think that would be to give in . . . to give in to what Diana believes about being haunted by her sister's ghost."

"Not necessarily. There could be . . . something . . . without having to buy Diana's interpretation of it."

"What do you mean?" I asked, surprised at how angry I felt.

"I'm not sure—yet. But tell me something. What do you associate a dog's howling with?"

Without stopping to think, I said, "Death."

"Yes. So do I. And Diana was dying—would have died if we hadn't got to her."

A shiver shook me from head to foot. "Simon, I would like to get out of this house."

180

"Then go. You're free to leave."

"And what about Diana?"

"She has something in this house that she has to resolve—whether it's what she thinks it is, or not. In some way I don't fully understand, I do, too. I think Eric does. Perhaps because all three of us were children here together. But this does not mean that it involves you."

But he was wrong. All my own ghosts were tied up with this house. Theoretically, as he said, I could leave it. But if I did, what about Diana?

As though in answer to that unspoken question, her voice came from the other side of the room. "Candida?"

I went back to her bed. Diana's eyes were open. "I thought you'd gone," she said.

"No," I heard my own voice say. "Don't worry. I'm here."

She smiled a little. "Good." Then she closed her eyes. As I stood there her breathing deepened, and she was back to sleep. I went back to the window.

"Simon," I said. "I have the strangest feeling that there's something wrong with the house—not just us. But the house itself. Do you know what I mean?"

"Oh, yes. My father once said that the house was built over a tragedy. But he never told me what it was."

"Didn't you ask?"

"Yes. But he wouldn't tell me. I think it's something he knew because a patient inadvertently—when ill or in a fever or something—told him. So he felt it to be more or less under the seal of the doctor's confessional." Simon paused and then went on. "But what he did say once, before he stopped himself, was that this house was built at the cost of a life. And someday, somehow, that price would have to be paid."

10

It was shortly after Simon said that that I remembered James.

"Oh, my God," I said. "James. Hannibal. I'd entirely forgotten. That poor child must be frantic." I glanced quickly at Diana. "Do you think she's going to wake up again and have a fit if I'm not here?"

Simon went over to the bed, looked closely at Diana, picked up her wrist for a few seconds, then turned. "No," he whispered. "I think she's set for a while. Let's go find James."

We went first to his room. The door was open, the light on, the covers on the bed flung back, and the room empty. Getting down on my knees, I looked under the bed, not for James, but for Hannibal, remembering that before James had reported him missing, he had said Hannibal was under the bed. But he was not there now.

I got up and looked at Simon, who was standing in the door. For the first time I noticed that sticking out from under the bottom of his trousers were his pajama bottoms. "No wonder you got here so fast," I said dryly. "You just put on your pants and sweater on top of your pajamas."

182

He grinned a little. "That's right. Your voice was pretty imperative. It put the fear of God into me."

Or, I thought, your love and worry over Diana did.

He stared at me. "What were you thinking then?"

"Nothing," I said. Then, "Simon, where on earth do we start? This is a huge house."

"You were not thinking about nothing. One day I'm going to ask you that question again. And I want you to remember that I will. Because I believe you will have no trouble remembering what indeed you were, at that moment, thinking about." He paused, and then went on in a different voice. "Now, as to where we begin looking for James and Hannibal —I think we might as well start upstairs. We can easily check whether or not James is there, and of the two, at the moment, he's more important. Although he wouldn't agree with that."

But neither James nor Hannibal was in any of the many rooms and bathrooms on the third floor. Since the curtains were not drawn, it was now light enough up there to see under the beds and into the empty closets. The only oddity to emerge from the search was that the rooms in the wing opposite to mine seemed to me somewhat different in shape from my own.

"Are these the same as the rooms immediately below them, on our floor?" I asked Simon.

He smiled. "Don't you know? Haven't you been into the rooms in the second-floor wing opposite yours?"

"No. Diana threatened once or twice to show me over the entire place, but what with one thing and another we've been too busy."

"Well, the wings *are* different. For one thing, the wing opposite yours was a servants' wing. Those that didn't sleep in the basement, slept up here and on the second floor."

"Good heavens! How many servants did they have?"

"When Diana was growing up? I should say about twenty-five."

He grinned as my jaw fell open. "Yes. There was plenty of money then. Another reason for the difference is that the wing on your side was burned down a few years ago and then rebuilt. The new wing was supposed to be a match. But the original architect was, of course, long dead, and the one Diana's father hired quit in the middle over some quarrel. So yet a third man finally added the rooms you're in."

"That's probably the reason for the different quality of the rooms there. It's not very logical, I realize, because the dimensions are probably the same. But there's certainly a different feel. Why are you looking at me like that?"

"Nothing—I just had an odd idea."

"What about?"

"I think maybe I won't tell you now."

"I don't think that's at all nice."

"All right. I'll trade. I'll tell you about my odd idea if you'll tell me what you were thinking back there when I asked you."

Silence. It was a struggle, because I would have liked to know what Simon's odd idea was. I had a feeling it could be important. But I couldn't bring myself to bring up the subject of his being in love with Diana.

Instead I said rather coolly, "Shall we look downstairs in the basement?"

He waved a hand towards the staircase. "After you."

It was obvious immediately that James had been before us. Every light in that huge mansion was lit. By the time we had looked in every cranny of the basement and all the rooms, cupboards and closets of the ground floor, we were both considerably frightened. I knew I was. And I was fairly sure that Simon was, too. Because there was no sign of either James or Hannibal.

"Where now?" I asked, as we came up the cellar stairs and stood in the little hall behind the kitchen.

"Where would a boy, frantic over the loss of his adored cat, be?"

"Now that it's light, outside, searching and calling," I said.

"Yes. Let's go."

"What about Diana?"

"I think she'll be all right. If not, she'll at least be conscious, so there's no danger of her suffocating herself as there

184

was for several hours last night. We'll start in the front and work around the sides."

The garden was far larger than I had realized, with sections on different levels below the house, as well as the expanse of lawn practically surrounding the building and the rose garden beyond.

And it was in the rose garden we found James, sobbing and tugging at the sundial in the center. "I know there's a well underneath," he cried as we ran up. "Hannibal could have fallen in."

A strange look flickered over Simon's face, almost as though something James had said had caused him pain. "Let me try," he said, to my amazement, because I had no idea that the dial sat on top of a well, and said so.

"James is right about that," he explained. "There is a well underneath. If you look carefully you can see. But, James, if I can't lift this, how on earth could Hannibal get in?"

"There's a hole in the side, in the brick. You can see it if you look."

I glanced down to where he was pointing and, sure enough, there were at least three bricks missing and a gaping hole. "Hannibal could easily get through that."

"Have you tried calling him?"

"Everywhere. All around the garden and down the road. I'm *sure* he'd go into that hole, if he's drowning in the water he couldn't answer. Please lift off the lip."

It would have been unkind to point out that if he had drowned he would be beyond help anyway. "I'll get a crowbar out of the toolshed," Simon said, and disappeared to the corner of the rose garden and into the neat wooden shed.

James knelt down. "Hannibal? Hannibal?" he called.

I knelt beside him and put my hand on his shoulder. "James, if he didn't answer, maybe he can't."

The next thing I knew I was on my back among the remains of the rosebushes with a young fury standing over me. "Don't you *touch* me!" James yelled. "You could have saved Hannibal if you'd come to look for him right away!"

"I couldn't leave your mother," I said, trying to get up.

185

"I *hate* her. She's a wicked, wicked woman. You can feel it in that house. That's why Hannibal wouldn't stay. It's her fault. I wish she was *dead!*"

"That'll be enough," Simon said sternly. He had returned with a crowbar and a big flashlight, which he laid on the ground. "Don't say things like that."

"Why not, if it's true? I do hate her. And I do wish she was dead."

"Because hating her and wishing she were dead is not going to bring back Hannibal, it's not going to help you, hating never does, and it won't help your mother, who needs help."

James caught his breath on a sob. Simon stared down at him. Then put his arm around the child and pulled him close to him. James put his face in the middle of Simon's sweater and burst into tears.

For a moment or two Simon patted him. Then he said, "I've got now to look for Hannibal. If we don't find him here, and I think we won't, then we'll look somewhere else. Now apologize to Candida for knocking her over. She hasn't had an easy night either."

"James doesn't have to apologize to me," I said, astonished at how angry I was. "He's welcome to hate me if he wants."

"How pleasant for you both," Simon said.

Putting the point of the crowbar under the rim of the sundial, he bore down. For a moment nothing happened. Then there was a crunching noise and the dial flew off, revealing itself as part of a top on a well.

"Let's look with this," Simon said, and picked up the flashlight. Idly I noticed that his hand seemed to be shaking and wondered why.

It was a powerful light and lit up the entire well, including the water, which was far down. There was nothing there but water and scum.

"He's not there," Simon said, picking up the dial and hefting it back on.

"He could have drowned and sunk to the bottom, couldn't he?" James raised a white, tear-stained face to Simon.

"It's possible," Simon said, "but I don't think so. James,

please put this crowbar and light back. I have to leave you for a minute. Candida, please stay here, too."

"All right," I muttered, a little ashamed of my outburst. Poor James, I did know how he felt. And, like me, when he was hurt his immediate reaction was to push everyone away.

I watched him drag the heavy iron bar across to the tool-shed, and reluctantly conceded Simon's wisdom in enlisting the little boy's help, even though the bar was heavy. Somehow, having to do something difficult had calmed him. Once again, like a warning bell, came the thought that Hannibal was more to James than a pet—even the most adored pet.

In a few minutes he was back. He stared at me out of Roger's clear brown eyes. "I'm sorry," he said belligerently.

"It's all right," I said. "So am I." I held out my hand.

After a moment he took it.

We were standing there, more or less staring at the ground, having retrieved our hands, not knowing what to say, when I heard the sound of a step by the gate into the main part of the garden. The first thing I saw was Simon's fair head.

Then there was a shriek beside me. "Hannibal, Hannibal!" James yelled and flung himself down the path. I ran, too.

While James was hugging and kissing the cat, who seemed to be accepting his rhapsody with measured calm, I said to Simon, "You clever, *brilliant* man. Where did you find him?"

"Where I thought I would," Simon said. "In your room."

"My room?" I repeated stupidly. "But when—" Then, "Of course. He could have gone there anytime. I haven't been there all night." I turned and looked at James. "But I'm surprised he slipped past you."

"I went back to my bathroom after I first heard the howling and saw you in the hall. I thought I'd closed the door, but I suppose I hadn't. Bad, Hannibal, bad!" he said lovingly. A deep, contented purr emanated from the cat. "I'll just take him back to my room," he said, and headed for the gate, with Simon and me following.

As we walked past the gazebo I said, "Have you ever been in there?"

"Once, years ago. Diana found a key that fit and she and

Eric and I went in."

"What was it like?"

He made a face. "A tinselly horror, a sugarcake show, a nouveau riche gaffe that, so my father said, embarrassed everyone. I can understand why, after the old man's death, it was kept locked."

I stared at the rundown little anachronism. It was a desolate little relic with its stained paint peeling off, some of its louvers torn from their hinges and hanging loose, and the windows behind them broken.

"It does look pretty tawdry," I said as we followed James and Hannibal through the gate.

Back in the house, the procession, consisting of James with Hannibal in front and Simon and me bringing up the rear, started up the stairs. But when James reached the top and was turning towards his own room, Hannibal gave a convulsive leap, soared out of James's arms, landed on the floor and ran towards the little hall leading to my room. Blocked there by James, who sprang in his way, Hannibal turned and tore towards the stairs. This time it was I who stopped him, and got royally scratched in the effort.

"There's nothing wrong with Hannibal's claws," I said, hanging on rather grimly.

"James," Simon said, "move aside and let Hannibal go towards Candida's room if he wants. Candida, point him in the direction of your room. See if he'll go."

James had retreated back to the head of the stairs, a baffled, unhappy look on his face. Turning the wriggling Hannibal around, I pointed his head towards the hall and little staircase leading to my room and then gave him a slight shove. He went across the beige carpet like a black streak and disappeared.

"You'll probably find him under your bed," Simon said. Then glanced at James's unhappy face. "It's nothing to do with his affection for you, James. Let's go and see if I'm right."

Hannibal wasn't under the bed in my room, but he was in the animals' room beyond, and he and my three were delicately sniffing one another in the manner of animals getting acquainted.

"He's never liked other animals before," James said.

"And mine aren't that fond of strangers either," I added.

"They're all on strange turf, and therefore more tolerant here than they would be at home on their own territory," Simon explained watching. "And I think . . ." His voice faded.

"You think what?" I asked.

When he didn't answer I said, "I'm getting very tired of your starting to answer questions and then not finishing."

"Sorry." He sounded unrepentant. His eyes were on James, who had squatted down and was stroking the animals. All five. James and the animals, including Wisteria, who had just hopped up, seemed to be enjoying it thoroughly.

"James," Simon said suddenly, "do you like the bedroom you're in?"

"No," James said decidely. "And I don't think Hannibal does either."

"Would you like to be in this room instead? With all the animals? I'm sure Candida wouldn't mind." He turned towards me. "Would you?"

"No. Not a bit. In fact, it would be nice to know there was somebody in here with them, not with just Pandora and the cats, but Wisteria and the gerbils and the others. You won't mind the smell?" I asked James. "Because I'm forced to admit that on warm days, and even with changing the paper in the cages every day, it does smell like a zoo."

"I think it's a *nice* smell," James said. He looked happier than I'd seen him in some time. Then his face tightened into his pinched look again. "But I bet Mother won't like it."

I was willing to bet exactly the same, but I didn't say so.

"Let me talk to her," Simon said.

Whether it was because of Simon's influence with her, or because after her night's adventures Diana was too beaten down and drained to object, I didn't know. But later in the morning, after Simon, James and I had had breakfast, Simon

189

went up to see Diana and returned shortly afterwards to say that we could start moving James immediately.

We did this without further ado, with me carrying jackets and trousers on hangers, and piles of shirts and underclothes from the chest of drawers, and James transporting the far more important baggage: Hannibal and the rolled-up map of Bulzartgay.

Unfortunately, just as we were passing Diana's room, she appeared in the door, looking wan and hollow-eyed.

"Moving your things?" Diana asked unnecessarily.

"We thought it would be better now rather than later, when you might be asleep," I said, marveling a little at what a good liar or diplomat (or were they the same?) I had become.

"No, you didn't," Diana said, but without any of the anger or resentment I had so often heard in her voice. "You're doing it because James couldn't wait. Isn't that right, James?"

"Yes." He paused. His carpet was rolled up under one arm. The other hand was holding Hannibal's leash, and Hannibal himself was pulling with all his might in the direction of James's new quarters.

"Or is it Hannibal that can't wait?" Diana asked dryly, "What's that thing under your arm?" she said.

My heart felt as though it had plunged to the bottom of my stomach. I racked my brain for something to say that would not be a lie but that would safely deflect her.

James's face had gone as white as his shirt. Then he said, "Oh, it's just an old piece of rug that I keep for Hannibal to lie on."

It was a good effort, and James probably would have gotten away with it if his voice hadn't quavered. But the fates were, after all, with him, because just at that moment, as Diana's brows started to descend in a frown, the telephone in her room rang.

James almost ran across the wide landing and down the small steps into my hall. Moving slowly, so as to keep from dropping shirts and underwear, I followed.

"Phew," James said, when I reached the end room, "that

was a jolly near thing, wasn't it?"

Conscience, a sense of duty and all the rules of my upbringing pointed towards my telling James he should not lie to his mother. Instead I said, "Stick the rug in that cabinet with the sliding door, the one under the terrarium."

I left him stashing away the land and people of Bulzartgay and returned for the remainder of his underwear and socks. As I passed Diana's door she called me.

When I went in she was back in her own bed. Evidently the doughty Mrs. Klaveness had been able to switch mattresses, because in the other bedstead, the one where I slept, was a stripped mattress, the remains of what was obviously a coffee stain still visible and drying.

Diana caught my glance. "Well, you, at least, ought to be relieved. It means I can't ask you to spend the night in here, obviously not with a wet mattress. I suppose throwing up like that saved my life—in fact, I know it did—but it certainly wrought plenty of havoc."

I looked at her. "As I'm sure Simon has already told you, it was the lethal combination of booze and pills you took."

"Yes. He has already told me, so there's no need for you to belabor the point." She sat up and put her arms around her knees and rested her forehead on them. Then she raised her head. "You may not believe this, in fact you probably won't, but although I'd be the first to agree that I've always, as the old saying goes, looked upon the wine when it was red—in other words, drunk too much—I've never gone at it so compulsively as I have since we came up here."

My heart gave a leap. Perhaps she was suggesting that I leave. "You mean you think it's my presence?"

"No. Not your presence."

"James's?"

"No. Not even James. Although in my more beaten down and therefore honest moments I know we have a long and very rough voyage before he and I can arrive at any kind of modus vivendi."

So it was not my presence or James's. "You mean your—er—sister's."

191

"Yes. I take it you haven't come across that diary. Do you think, if I let James go up to White Deer Lodge with his beloved cutthroats, you could continue the search? I know you wanted to go with him. But—"

"I thought Marje Pritchett and her kids were coming over today."

"No. That was Marje on the phone. She's had to postpone it. Apparently some uncle who's turned up has promised them all a trip to the World Trade Center and lunch in the restaurant at the top. It didn't seem to occur to her that I have a little boy here, a stranger who knows nobody, and who might like to go along. Well, maybe it's for the best. Marje is an apostle of total permissiveness, and her kids can be pretty rowdy. I thought it might do James good. He's so . . . so *stuffy*."

"He isn't stuffy, Diana. It's just that he has been brought up . . . differently." I picked my way among possible words, feeling as though I were tiptoeing over a mined field. I saw her eyes on me, and I suddenly abandoned trying to be tactful. "Diana, when you're upset you have your fortress you retreat into—arrogance. Yes, I know you don't like me to say that, but it's true. And you wanted me to come here because I do tell you the truth. I've known people who retreat into a charming façade, and you can't break through that any more than you can through your hauteur. Well, James's retreat is a sort of formality—natural, given his upbringing. I think he becomes what you call stuffy when he's afraid."

"Afraid of what, for God's sake?"

I hesitated. As clearly as though I were in James's head I knew what James's fears were: that this strange, powerful woman who was his mother would sweep into his life and take away his imaginary hiding places, such as Bulzartgay, and the creature he loved best—Hannibal. And that he would be helpless to stop her. But equally clearly I knew—or feared—that if I told her that, I would be placing the weapons to hurt him in her hands. Following that thought quick as lightning was the realization that I didn't fully trust her. So, disastrously, I waffled.

"Oh, he's in a strange place, a strange country, and with people he doesn't know."

"Such as his mother."

"Diana—he's only nine years old. It's not his fault that he was brought up where and how he was. But all of this must be very baffling to him."

She had been looking at me, but she turned her head and stared out the window. I could feel her silence like an angry wave coming at me.

"Shall I tell him then that he can go up to White Deer Lodge?" I persisted.

"All right." Still she didn't turn her head.

"And I'll spend the afternoon looking for the diary."

She turned her head then. "I know you still don't believe it exists. But . . . I'd be grateful." The hardness in her face and voice had gone. Curiously and tragically, it was only where James was concerned that she wore her impenetrable armor.

James was overjoyed to be told he could go to White Deer Lodge. His one concern had been that Hannibal would be safe in his absence, and I was able to reassure him about that. Since I had spent a more than usually active night in Diana's room, I intended to take a nap that afternoon, and told James that I would keep Hannibal in my room while I was there sleeping.

"Do you have screens in your windows?" he asked anxiously.

It took me a minute to think. I had, of course, had screens in my windows in New York. But for some reason it had not occurred to me to check up here in Tower Abbey. "I don't know," I said.

"You don't *know*?" James disapproval was all too plain.

"No, I don't." I was somewhat defensive. "But you know, James, I don't think I could screen every window in this enormous house, so to some extent I just have to trust that if the cats want to get out, they can go by one of the doors on the lower floor."

It was a weak excuse and James spotted it immediately. "You should think about their safety before *anything*."

I stared down into the severe little face. "You know there's something very Calvinistic about you, James."

"What's Calvinistic?"

"Look up John Calvin and you'll find out."

"Well, what I said about the animals' safety is true."

"All right, so it's true. I'll go now and check on the window in my room." But I had only gone a few steps when something struck me. I turned back. "Speaking of thinking of the animals' safety first, did you check whether there were any screens in the windows of the animals' room at the end of my wing when you put Hannibal there?"

His blush gave him away. He opened his mouth but nothing came out.

"You didn't?" I said, with somewhat unkind triumph.

His reply was to shoot past me, leaping down the steps into the hall of my wing and flinging himself to the end door. I followed at a more subdued pace and found him staring at the open window, almost filled by the branches of a big oak outside.

"They've gone," James said.

I realized he meant the cats—all three of them. My own heart gave a jump of alarm, when two things sprang to my mind. One was the open door of the bathroom that lay between this room and my bedroom. The other I gave voice to immediately.

"Well, theoretically, your Hannibal and my Seth and Susan could jump outside via that tree. But with all the will in the world Pandora couldn't. And she's not hiding under the bed, because she wouldn't fit. She's too big. So the explanation lies elsewhere."

I walked past James to the bathroom, crossed it and on into my room.

"Talk about the Peaceable Kingdom," I said.

There, on my bed, lay all four, my three curled up in a knot together at one end, and Hannibal's splendid length at the other. As we came in the big black cat rose, stretched and arched his back. There was a soft, cushiony miaow from him,

194

followed by the beginning of a deep, rumbling purr. Then Hannibal leapt with the ease of a feline Nureyev onto James's shoulder and stood there, rubbing his head against James's.

A look of satisfaction crossed the boy's face, and I knew as well as though it were I and my cat, that at least part of his gratification lay in the fact that Hannibal's preference for my wing of the house implied no change in his loyalty to James.

"You know," he said suddenly, one arm curled up around Hannibal's head, "this room is nicer, too, like the one next door where Hannibal and I are going to sleep."

"Yes," I said. "I know."

Curiously, the knowledge did not make me feel better. Rather it underlined my growing fear that there was, indeed, objectively, something wrong with the rest of the house.

"Still," he said, with a single-mindedness that reminded me strongly of his father, "I wish there were screens—at least in these rooms."

I sighed. "I'll go and ask . . . Mrs. Klaveness . . . if she knows of any." I was, of course, about to say "Diana" but decided the greater part of wisdom lay with at least starting with Mrs. Klaveness. Appealing to Diana on behalf of James's concern for Hannibal did not strike me, at this particular moment, as prudent.

But since I was not optimistic about the existence of screens, I was therefore pleasantly surprised when Mrs. Klaveness, busily chopping vegetables, said, "Yah. In the basement. They used to be taken out each autumn and put back in the spring. But not for several years."

"Where in the basement?" I asked, remembering its size and the number of rooms.

She paused. "I do not remember. But surely—they are too big to hide."

So in the half hour before James was supposed to join the others at Halfway House, he and I went down to the lower regions to find the screens.

"Starting from here," I said at the bottom of the steps, "I'll go to the right and you go to the left. The first person

195

who locates a screen, give a shout."

A great novelist once said in one of her books that two things could not be hid: love and a cough. Well, to that I would add screens. Mrs. Klaveness was right: One could see at a glance that most of the basement rooms did not contain anything remotely like screens. Then, as I turned a corner and went into another passage I looked into the rooms I had seen before, the ones crammed with furniture, trunks, boxes and, I noticed again with a sinking of spirits, books—pile after pile of them, all of which I would, sooner or later, have to go through. It took much longer to discover that there were no screens in these storerooms, and I was just about to decide that I was right in my assumption that a house such as this located on top of a hill didn't need any, when I heard James's voice yelling, "Found them."

I ran him down finally in one of the rooms off the big boiler room, and there, sure enough, stacked in rows against the wall beside yet more books were the screens Mrs. Klaveness had mentioned.

I looked around. "There must be dozens here; naturally enough, I suppose, when you think of all the windows."

"Umm," was all the reply I got from James. He was seated cross-legged on the floor with one book open and several more beside him. "This is jolly good," he said.

"What?"

"These stories. They're sort of fairy stories, but I don't think I've read them before. I wonder—"

"James, at this moment guess who might be getting out the window?"

"I decided he probably wouldn't," James said in a calm way that made me want to shake him. "He looked quite happy in your room, and I think he would in the other room there, too. But you're right. We'd better put the screens in. I'll just take some of these books up with me. After all, we only need about four screens, so I can take two under one arm and you can carry two with you."

There were times, I decided, following James up the basement stairs, that his cool assumption of my role and duties reminded me strongly of his mother's.

After the screens were in place and James had departed for Halfway House and the White Deer Lodge, I went back upstairs, cleared a space in the middle of my bed, then lay down and went soundly to sleep. . . .

I was running through long corridors, through rooms opening out of rooms, and I knew that I was trying to find something that was running just ahead of me. Only I couldn't see it, and didn't know what it was. But a sense of urgency made me run faster and faster and I became increasingly aware that to capture this thing—whatever it was—was of overwhelming importance; in fact, my life depended on it. If only I could even catch sight of it. And then I did, almost. There was a cross, and something red, and I realized that it was Diana's diary. But someone was carrying it, someone who didn't want me to see it. And I knew that if I could find out who was running in front of me with the diary, I would also know what was in it that I must discover to save my life. And then the person turned—and I woke up.

I sat up shivering, yet damp with perspiration. Something had waked me. What was it? And then I heard the knocking on the door.

"Who is it?" I called out, and could hear how frightened my voice sounded.

"Mrs. Klaveness." The housekeeper's voice sounded exasperated as she announced her name. "Do you wish lunch? It is almost ready downstairs."

Scattering the cats, I got up and opened the door. "Oh, thanks. Yes. I'll be down in a minute. Just let me throw some water on my face. I was asleep."

"Mr. Barrington is here," she stated. "He will stay to lunch. Miss Egremont invited him, but she will have a tray in her room."

"Thank you. I'll be right down. Er— should you offer Mr. Barrington a drink?"

197

"I have done so. In fifteen minutes. Lunch." And her stout form plodded back down the little hallway.

I had taken five-minute showers before, and I did so this time, more to wake myself up and shake off that unpleasant dream than for any passionate dedication to cleanliness. My hair was still damp when I arrived in the study to find Eric sipping a sherry and gazing out the window.

He turned as I came in. "I hear that Diana is a little under the weather," he said after I greeted him and poured myself a Coke.

"Yes," I agreed, wishing I could confide in him, but wondering whether I should.

"Something she ate?" he said gently, "or something more serious?"

I have never been good at either lying or evasion. "Well," I began, and then made the mistake of looking at him. The brown eyes bored into me. "What is it?" he said quietly. "You'd better tell me."

So I did.

"And Simon was here." It was a statement not a question.

"He saved her life, Eric."

"It would save her life—and sanity—more if he would get her into a psychiatric institution. I've told him so. I think he's risking her safety by letting this kind of thing happen. This is the third time."

"He didn't tell me that."

"He wouldn't." Eric glanced at me and said quickly, "Probably loyalty to Diana, plus his feelings about her, would prevent him from saying anything. But I really think that it's time for him to stop playing God, whether as a doctor or a clergyman, and letting people who know what they're doing get to work."

I was bound to admit that that sounded like good sense. Before I could say anything further, Mrs. Klaveness appeared and all but marched us to lunch.

With a look almost of defiance, as though daring me to disapprove, Mrs. Klaveness put a quiche down in front of me and placed a large knife at the side. Then she placed a glass bowl of salad on the other side and left.

"Occasionally, she gives me the feeling that she likes me," I said after the housekeeper's heavy footsteps faded. "But other times, like now, I feel waves of disapproval coming from her."

"Be of good cheer." Eric passed his plate, on which I placed a generous wedge of quiche. "I think the bad vibrations are for me."

"Why? I mean, why should she disapprove of you?"

"I suppose because if Diana follows my advice and gets rid of this place, along with her obsessions about it, Mrs. K. will be out of a job. And since she supports an invalid husband, that could be a serious blow."

"Surely anyone as competent as she is, and who can make such delicious quiche, could write her own ticket. I should think the rich and well born of Westchester would be queueing up for her services.

"Not if her husband was suspected of being a former Nazi youth leader. Nobody really knows, of course, but there are lots of rumors."

"But couldn't that be proved, one way or another?"

"Given the conditions of Germany after the war, not that easily. Besides, whoever heard of a German who admitted to having been—even in his salad days—a member of the Party?" Eric cut off a large piece of his pie and speared it. "Ask Simon. His various activities in Germany when he was in the army covered a lot of strange ground." He put the pie in his mouth.

As soon as he could talk he swallowed. "Nobody seems to know what he was doing over there. If he were up to some spy stuff for us, why hasn't he said so? Unless he were an active agent now—and given the priestly-therapist bit it hardly seems likely, although you never know with the Church these days—why keep it secret?"

"You sound as though you don't like him," I said bluntly.

He hesitated. "Let's say we take very different views of where Diana's greatest good lies. And that—Diana's good—is a consideration that for me outweighs anything else."

199

"And if you had your way regarding her good, what would that be?"

Eric glanced at me and then smiled ruefully. "First of all, I'd marry her. Then I'd use all of my powers of persuasion to get her to stay a while at that rehabilitation place I told you about where they can really help her to get off both alcohol and pills. Then I'd take her around the world on a trip for several months which, of course, would mean that Mrs. Klaveness would be out of her job, which is too bad, but can't be helped. Diana's more important. And while we're on our trip I would—with Diana's permission—either tear this building down and have another one built by the time we got back, or I'd renovate it from scratch."

"But why? It's not as though it were a tottering old frame house on its last legs. It was built in this century by a very rich man who could hire the best architects. Its structure is perfectly sound even though it may be, in Roger Eliot's unkind words, an architectural abortion."

Eric grinned. "Is that the phrase you managed to prevent James from coming out with the other evening?"

"Yes. I think, for Diana, it would have been the last straw. Although, truthfully, things could hardly have been any worse."

"No, they couldn't. Where is James, by the way?"

"Out with Simon and his cutthroats—as Diana calls them. They're going up to White Deer Lodge."

"I see," Eric said.

I glanced at his face, which looked as though he were exerting considerable effort to hold it in neutral.

"You don't approve, Eric?"

"It's not for me to approve or disapprove."

"That means you don't."

"Well, I don't want to arouse your protective ire, and I've stated my views on this before. But I told you I wished Simon had less influence over Diana. Now he seems to be extending that influence to include James."

"Why do you find that so alarming?"

Eric put down his fork. "Candy, two groups of men who

have always had great power over others—especially, if you don't mind my saying so, over emotional and highly charged women—are clergy and doctors. And Simon is both. People will confide things to their priests and their physicians that they would not tell to another living soul. And the physician—physician to the body or physician to the soul, and Simon is both—will prescribe, counsel and supply guidance, all to the view of changing the patient's or the penitent's behavior."

"If you're implying that he's abusing his influence with her, then that's a serious accusation, about the most serious you could make."

"I told you before that I'm quite sure that Simon is in love with her and is doing the best he can for her according to his lights. The trouble is..." Eric paused and sat frowning.

"The trouble is what?"

"The trouble is that frequently the more power one gets, the darker those lights become. Most doctors and psychiatrists and priests who've ended up in the courts and on the front pages of newspapers for handing out drugs to dazzled celebrities started doing what they were doing because they wanted to help people. And then the game itself took over."

"What game?"

"The power game."

"You think Simon is in this for power?"

"Well, don't you think it's odd? Diana firmly believes she is being haunted by a ghost, here, in a fairly recently built house in the last quarter of the twentieth century. And Simon, the Reverend Dr. Simon, who could laugh her out of this, or analyze her out of this, or pray her out of this, seems to be treating it as though he believes in this spook as much as she does."

"Maybe he does."

"Then, my dear, he's behaving even more irresponsibly than I thought. To me it's a lot of nonsense, but if I believed there were a ghost here, specifically one troubling Diana, and along with being her doctor and her priest I were in love with her, I'd have her out of here before nightfall, and I'd urge her to sell to the first buyer and get rid of the place."

It made sense to me. "Then I wonder why he doesn't."

"Because I believe he's playing a power game."

"Power? Power for what? Over whom?"

Eric made a gesture. "I don't want to go into it any further. But if he is into the occult stuff, then he's playing the oldest and most dangerous game of all and is using Diana."

"I thought," I said, after a minute, "that you didn't believe in that."

"As a moderately good son of the Church I believe in its ancient rules to leave all that occult funny business alone."

Simon's own words drifted up from somewhere in the back of my head. "Let's say I have an open mind..." Was it more than just an open mind? Had he gone beyond that? And then, much more sharply, there came to me the memory of my own sense of confusion as, almost hypnotized by Simon's words, the two worlds of subjective and objective, which for me had always been so reliably separated, flowed together. And the truth was, he almost persuaded me that the two worlds were, perhaps one. . . .

I became aware of Eric's eyes on me. "He's started on you, hasn't he?" Eric said. "You're no longer sure what's real and what's in our heads? Be careful, Candida, be very careful. And if you have any influence at all with Diana, get her to leave."

"She doesn't want to leave until she finds the diary," I said.

"What diary?" he asked quickly.

"It's a diary or journal of some sort that she thinks exists ..." I glanced fleetingly at him, "and that she has dreamed about. She thinks that if she finds it, everything that is... that is bothering her will become clear. As a matter of fact ..." I took a breath and plunged ahead, "I've dreamed about it, too."

"So his influence is beginning to take effect."

I shook my head. "Fair's fair. I don't think I needed anybody to help me dream that dream. Diana's monomania on the subject would be enough."

"You mean you agree with me that the whole thing is in Diana's head and not outside in reality?"

Quite suddenly I remembered my own words to Simon: "I

have the strangest feeling that there is something wrong with the house."

Eric put his hand over mine, "Candida, Candida, I trust your strength and good sense. If it were not for your being here with Diana, I'd be in a state of despair over her. Don't let Simon talk you into some of his weird ideas." He paused, and then said, hesitantly, "Look, I've said a lot of things about Simon. That doesn't mean that I don't have a great affection for him. And, of course, there's the element of jealousy. He has what I want—Diana's regard. But I really do think that some of his more recent notions are—to use a current expression—off the wall. Do you understand what I'm trying to tell you?"

Gently I withdrew my hand. "Yes, I think so. By the way, did you tell Diana that there had been some kind of rumor at the time of her birth that she did, indeed, have a sister? A twin sister?"

"No, I don't know what I could have said to make her think that, although I know she believes I did report to her that Donnie, Diana's nanny, had said something to ... to somebody about it."

"Wasn't she the one who died in the elevator?"

"That's right."

"Whom did she tell it to?"

When he was silent for a minute I wondered whether he was trying to remember, or whether I had said something that he was turning over in his head. My feeling that it was the latter was quite strong.

"Do you know?" I persisted.

He put his fork down. "Yes. As a matter of fact. It was my father."

"Your father? The tycoon?"

"That was quite some time before he was a tycoon. And not too long after he had stopped being an ordinary electrician with an inventive mind." Eric looked at me for a moment in silence. "I gather you don't know, Diana didn't tell you, that Donnie, her nanny, was due to marry my father the summer she died."

203

"No, she certainly didn't." I thought about it for a moment. "But how horrible for him. He must not have known for weeks—months—what happened to her."

"He didn't. He thought that she had simply changed her mind and didn't have the courage to tell him so; but had left instead without telling anyone, including the Egremonts, what had happened."

"But didn't he try to get in touch with Diana's family, her father?"

"No. You see . . . It's difficult to explain."

Silently I heaped some salad on a plate and passed it over to him. "Try," I said.

"It sounds ludicrous nowadays. But this was just after World War Two, and things were different then—not as different as they were back in the thirties before the war broke out. But still different. I was a boy at the time, and knew about it only from a distance. And my father was not one to confide in a small son that being a widower was a lonely affair and that he wanted to find someone with whom he could build a new marriage. As a matter of fact, I heard about it not from him, but from some of my school mates who let fall a few choice tidbits of information."

"That must have been difficult for you."

"It was. But when I finally got up the courage to ask my father, he admitted it readily enough—there was no reason not to. And I felt better about it. I'd known Donnie, of course, for years through knowing Diana." He paused. "And I loved her for her own sake. She was a marvelous and warm woman. I just wish—it was such a tragedy that she died. My father never really got over it."

It was a frightful story. I sat there, not really knowing what to say, vaguely aware of some reaction of my own that was bothering me, though I couldn't figure out what it was. Finally I decided it must be because Eric's and Diana's accounts as to who told her about a possible twin sister didn't jibe. Then, mentally, I shrugged: One of them obviously remembered incorrectly, and of the two, I thought it was more likely to be Diana. Eric struck me as probably being reliable about such matters even at an early age.

"Anyway," he said after a moment, "to answer your question, yes, there was a rumor about Diana having a twin sister. But after Donnie died I never heard any more about it. It was probably one of those servants' pieces of gossip that get distorted. But one reason why I wish Diana would get out of here is that this mausoleum just keeps reminding her of it." He paused for a minute, and then, "Not to change the subject, I hope Simon keeps an eye on James. It's a steep climb up to White Deer Lodge. Much more difficult than people are prepared for here, so near the big city. Some experienced climbers have been surprised."

"I'm sure he will." I was surprised at how stiff I sounded.

"You think I'm being unfair, and it probably is not well done of me to say what I did. But—" He shrugged. "One can't help worrying. After all, it was on just such an outing—when they were alone that time—that his daughter was lost."

I stared at Eric stupidly, not able to take in the meaning of his words. "His daughter?" My voice sounded as though it had come from someone else.

"Yes. I'm astonished he didn't tell you. He and Diana had a daughter. Nine months to the day after her first marriage to Ken Dawlings."

Again, as though a picture had flashed in my mind, I saw the two of them, their bodies together, their faces turned towards me when I walked in on them the day before Diana's first wedding. My mind felt numb. Yet I was aware of questions hammering away behind the numbness. Two questions finally broke through: "Where ... where did she die? And how?"

"Where? Here. She and Simon were coming back from a picnic. He stopped to speak to somebody—Hans Klaveness, I believe. She ran ahead. Evidently she managed to get the top off the well in the rose garden. Anyway, she had drowned by the time Simon got to her. It's very deep. There was nothing to cling to—even if she hadn't hit her head and knocked herself unconscious as she fell. By the time he got there she was dead."

205

11

"Are you all right?" Eric asked me suddenly.

"Yes, I said. "A little numb with shock maybe."

"I take it you hadn't heard about Karin."

"No. Which is weird. I mean, Diana is one of the Beautiful People. All her life, if she sneezed, it made three columns. How could she and Simon have a daughter nobody knew about?"

"Money is very useful when it comes to hiding things, too."

What was it Diana had said to me? *"What I should think would fairly leap to your mind—given your general anti-money slant—is that rich people can pay to have things done, such as a little hushing up."* Only she had been talking about a possible twin sister.

"Eric, if she had had this daughter—what did you say her name was, Karen—?"

"Karin." He pronounced the first syllable as in "car," with a broad A. "It's the German for Karen."

"Well, if she had Karin, where was she—Karin—all these years? Why didn't anybody know about her? Why all the hush-hush? Why didn't she just call her Karin Dawlings? After all, the child was born during her first marriage."

Eric grinned. "Why, why, why? You're like a child, Candy, asking what makes the world round, how high is up?"

A spurt of anger went through me. "Don't patronize me, Eric. Those are perfectly reasonable questions. And since I'm here in the role of family friend and companion—and I wish to God I weren't—I think I have a right to be given some kind of answer. Not to be told in effect that curiosity killed the cat."

He held up his hand. "Sorry! I apologize. I didn't mean to be patronizing."

Didn't you? I wondered. Curious, I thought. Diana, Simon or I would show some irritation at this moment. I had not been exactly the soul of courtesy. Yet Eric looked—what did he look? I suddenly realized that I had seen only two expressions on his face, smiling and unsmiling.

"I suppose," Eric said, "I keep forgetting that you're so much younger, so that the rest of us knew things automatically that you didn't."

"Such as?"

"Well, such as the fact that Ken Dawlings married because he wanted two things: money and children, in that order. Diana certainly had money, and he counted on her giving him children."

"How did he know that Karin wasn't his?"

"He'd been married before, you know. With no children. Then his ex-wife remarried and had two, one right after the other. So he took himself off to some clinic and had his fertility checked, and found that while he wasn't sterile, his fertility rate or percentile or whatever wasn't very high. That it would take cooperation from everybody and everything—the woman, the time of the month, and probably many, many tries before he could father a child. So when Diana got pregnant, bingo, like that, instead of rejoicing, he got suspicious, and in an unfortunate moment when they'd been drinking, accused her of playing around. Well, as I said, they'd both been drinking, and Diana Egremont was not used to being

207

talked to that way, so she told him the truth. And he walked out. Both his moral righteousness and his machismo had been insulted." He paused.

"What about some of the other whys?"

"I'm not sure, but I think that Diana was persuaded to have the child abroad, and the persuader was her father. Because Ken was even willing to sacrifice himself, to the point of letting his low fertility be known, to get back at her. In other words, he threatened to make a big scandal. And Diana's father, like the old-fashioned guy he was, would do anything to avoid a scandal. There was going to be enough of that with Ken and Diana breaking up after such a short marriage—especially after such a big church wedding. He didn't want the illegitimate-child bit added to that. So Diana went abroad before too many people were aware that she was pregnant, and had her child in Switzerland, and put her up for adoption over there. Anybody who knew about the pregnancy was told she'd had a miscarriage—emotional upset and all that stemming from the breakup of the marriage."

"So what was the child doing back here?"

"According to Diana, Simon brought her back. It was with the Klavenesses, by the way, that Karin had been placed. When Simon found Karin and decided to bring her back to the States, he brought the Klavenesses along to take care of her. Anyway, he said he hadn't been aware that the child was his, or even that there was a child. He'd heard about the miscarriage. How he discovered that a child had been born and put up for adoption, and that the said child was his, I don't know. Maybe you'd better ask him. Anyway, he brought her back here—"

"As his child?" I interrupted.

"I'm not sure. You'll have to ask him that, too."

"And Diana was here?"

"Yes. And blamed herself for letting the child go on the outing with Simon. Or at least not going along, too. Just as she blamed herself for not having the child openly, which, she feels, started the whole process that ended up in Karin's falling down the well."

My head was still filled with questions. How could Diana have kept having a child secret? How could Simon have discovered her so coincidentally? And, if the child were brought over here, why had no one ever made the connection? Why had there been no gossip? Why—

But at that moment Mrs. Klaveness stumped in again, still radiating waves of disapproval, removed what was left of the quiche—which wasn't much—and the almost empty salad bowl.

"That was delicious, Mrs. Klaveness," I said, quite truthfully, but feeling as though I were performing some quite despicable act of sycophancy. "Quiche is one of my all-time favorite dishes." Worse and worse, I thought. About as convincing as who's for tennis?

Muttering some kind of Teutonic imprecation, Mrs. Klaveness placed a dish of ice cream and a boat of raspberry sauce on the table and went out.

I stared at it. "I had somehow thought that being up here would enable me to lose weight," I said gloomily, serving generous helpings of ice cream to both Eric and me.

"You look just fine," Eric said.

Since those were the exact words of an ongoing fantasy of mine, they should have made me happy. The trouble was, in my fantasy Simon said them. Irrationally, now that Eric had almost read the script from my mind, instead of my being happy, I was irritated, convinced that Eric was offering me the false coin of flattery. I was also reasonably sure that he was avoiding any further questions on my part. If so, he was being ably assisted by Mrs. Klaveness, who kept hovering around, clearing off the sideboard, making sure we had enough dessert, inquiring as to whether we wanted cake as well and fussing over the coffee. And after she finally left, Eric swallowed his coffee and stood up. "I have to get back," he said.

"Come on, Eric. As president of your own corporation, you're surely not afraid of being fired?"

"No. But, like my father, I try to abide by the same lunch hours that my workers have. I've never been a believer in the executive three-hour lunch."

This was a view I (theoretically) admired. On this occasion I had doubts and voiced them. "I think you're cleverly removing yourself from the possibility of answering any more questions."

"There's some truth in that," he agreed calmly. "But after all, all I have to offer are unsubstantiated rumors and hearsay. Why don't you consult the—er—horses' mouths?"

"You mean Simon and Diana."

"Precisely. Surely they're the greatest authorities on Karin and what happened to her."

At that point there was a crash from the kitchen, followed by an agonizing yelp.

"Pandora!" I said, and tore out to the kitchen area.

Mrs. Klaveness, her face very red, was standing over a stricken-looking Pandora, who had retreated to a corner. In the middle of the floor lay an inch or so of pie crust and a broken plate. When I came she made a noise, half whine and half yelp, and leapt in my direction. I glared at the towel in Mrs. Klaveness's hand. "Did you strike her with that?" I asked, wishing that I had a towel of my own in my hand with which to do a little chastising.

"The quiche she has eaten, all of it. There was for Miss Egremont and myself a piece left." In her agitation Mrs. Klaveness had become very Teutonic.

"If Pandora, or any other of my animals, destroys any of your food or . . . or equipment . . . I'll be glad to pay damages. But don't you ever, ever strike one again." I found, somewhat to my pleasure, that my voice had risen.

Mrs. Klaveness hurled down her towel and stamped out of the kitchen in the direction of the basement stairs. Pandora jumped up and tried to lick my face. "Bad dog," I said, not meaning a syllable of it.

Eric said from the door, "I can understand her aggravation at having half the lunch gone, but she had no right to beat poor Pandora."

"She certainly did not. Come on, Pandora," I said, leading the way out. "Stay out of the kitchen." Which was, I knew, about as useful a statement as telling Seth and Susan not to sharpen their claws on my quilt.

Eric took his leave and, now that I had made up for some of my lost sleep, I decided to devote the afternoon to finishing checking the books in the library.

As I climbed up and down the ladder and pulled books out of the front of the shelf so that I could haul out and look at those behind, I continued to worry at the questions Eric had raised: questions about Simon's hunger for power—specifically power over Diana—and about the hidden and unknown child, Karin. Eric had given reasonable explanations for the secrecy involving Karin's birth and adoption, and yet it all seemed so . . . so strange. But was it any stranger than anything else about this extraordinary house and its inhabitants, including, and especially, the ghostly sister?

One of the more obvious courses of action, I thought, shoving the books in and out and raising clouds of dust around my head, was to get off this shaky ladder and go up and ask Diana about her daughter. That being so, my mind ran on as I continued with my chore, why didn't I?

The answer, when it came, did nothing for my peace of mind. However skeptical I had been about the validity of Diana's beliefs—her dreams about the diary, her conviction that she was being haunted—I had always been sure that she told the truth as she saw it. Now I found I was no longer certain of that.

And then, as though they were "before" and "after" pictures, two images of Diana slid across my mind: one as I had seen her in New York, unhappy, emotional, but still magnetic and still, even with the amount she had had to drink at our lunch, a woman very much in charge of herself.

And the other picture?

It showed a woman who, in some eerie and unpleasant way, was no longer in charge of herself. It might, of course, be her excessive drinking, which had gone skyrocketing up since we had arrived. Or the pills she seemed equally addicted to. Against my will my mind added, *or Simon's influence.* As I shifted my feet on the ladder step and leaned for support on the top shelf of the last segment of books to be checked, something within me seemed to plead, *no, not Simon, not that. . . .*

If I hadn't put weight on that shelf, I might not be alive now, because it seemed to me that the ladder under my feet moved and swayed, as though the room itself was unsteady. Am I seasick? I thought in panic, and let out a yell.

And then the next thing I was aware of I was hanging from the top shelf, the ladder had crashed behind me and I knew if I didn't do something rapidly, I was going to drop to the floor.

At that moment two very ungentle hands closed around my waist. "Let go or I will drop you," Mrs. Klaveness's voice said.

For a second I clung on. If I let go, I would really be at her mercy, and while it was not a drop from a cliff, bones could break from a bad landing after a seven-foot fall. I turned and stared down into the tight-lipped face. Then I let go.

The housekeeper had used a footstool to stand on as she reached up to me. Big and strong as she was, she couldn't, of course, lower me to the floor, but she did succeed in slowing my descent. In fact, she was in more discomfort than I, because I nearly yanked her off her rather unsteady platform.

"Thanks," I said, not forgetting Pandora, but grateful for her help.

"It makes nothing," she said. She got heavily down and walked out.

Well, I thought, lifting up the ladder, once again in pieces, at least I didn't have to use that any more. The library was done. There was no diary of any kind among all those thousands of books. And while almost every volume contained a bookplate sporting a rather elaborate cross—the Egremont coat of arms—there was no book, red or otherwise, with a cross actually engraved or carved in the front. I was quite sure that the book was not there.

But what stopped me in my tracks as I was about to leave the room was the realization of a change within me: that whereas once I had had overwhelming doubts as to the book's existence, now, although sure that the book was not in the library, I was quite convinced that it did exist somewhere else.

"I wonder if I've been brainwashed," I said aloud.

"What?"

I was standing at the library door when I had spoken, and I saw James in the hall, about to go up the stairs.

"Hello," I said. "Did you have a good time?"

"Super. It was really terrific. Enrico and I went on a rock climb and then we explored a marvelous cave. He said I was very good, and that if I worked out..."

As I listened to James's voice, excited, expressive as I had rarely heard it before (except when talking about Bulzartgay or Hannibal), I stared at his animated face, now burned by the sun. He looked, I found myself thinking, like a normal boy. And then realized that in my own way I was as much a captive of that stereotype, the normal boy, whoever he was, as Diana.

I smiled. "I'm glad you enjoyed yourself."

"I'll just go up and see Hannibal," he commented.

"Did Simon come back with you?" I asked, and found myself waiting anxiously for the answer.

"No, he dropped me off here, then went back with the others." The last words were barely audible as they came from the top of the staircase.

I felt both relieved and let down. It was inconceivable that I should see Simon without questioning him about his and Diana's daughter, Karin. But if he were not here, I didn't have to do so immediately. And my relief at that was some indication of an odd reluctance to broach the subject buried deep in an overwhelming curiosity. And why did I feel reluctant? That, too, was something with which I didn't wish to occupy myself. He'll probably come to dinner, I counseled myself.

But I was wrong.

There were just the three of us around the dining table, Diana, James and myself. It was an odd meal. When I discovered that we were to be alone, that neither Eric nor Simon were to be there to siphon off some of the tension that always seemed to crackle between Diana and her son, my heart sank. And, as I had done of old when I went to my first parties, I made a mental list of reasonably neutral and harmless subjects that I could bring up to keep the conversation flowing.

213

But it wasn't necessary. As James rattled on about his day at White Deer Lodge, the cave, the climb, the swim in the lake up there, I kept a guarded eye on his mother. Enrico's name cropped up quite often and I waited for her to snap. But she didn't. When James finally seemed to run out of steam, I took up the refrain and went into considerable and boring length about some camping trips of my own.

Although uneventful, it was all a strain, and when dinner was finally over I felt exhausted. James went up to his room almost immediately after dinner to be, I assumed, with Hannibal, after a day's absence. Again I held my breath, waiting for Diana to make some sarcastic comment about James's patent lack of interest in his mother's company. But she didn't say anything.

"How do you feel?" I finally asked her, as she toyed with the tea she had chosen to have instead of coffee.

"All right." She spoke listlessly, and had, I noticed, only picked at the broth and chicken breast that Mrs. Klaveness had put down in front of her. She added, "Not exactly like conquering the world."

I wanted to ask her about Karin. I wanted also to ask her why on earth she had taken that vodka from her medicine cabinet when she'd made such a point for several days about not drinking. But I knew I wasn't going to be able to summon the nerve, or hardness of heart, or both, that it would take to ask any of those questions until she recovered some of her bounce.

In a moment or two she thrust back her empty cup. "I'm going up to bed. As I'm sure you remember I had something of a disturbed night." She went to the door and turned. "However, I haven't thanked you, have I, for your good work last night."

"I'm glad I was there," I said. And then, before I could stop myself, "Diana—"

"Yes?"

"Don't . . . try not . . . liquor and pills are a deadly mixture. And if you drink, you won't know how many pills you took."

"Yes," she said dryly. "I can hear Simon's voice saying that."

"It's true, isn't it?"

"Yes. Any other instructions?" The slightly haughty note was back. All of a sudden she sounded more like herself.

"Not an instruction. Maybe question."

"Well?" Her brows lifted.

"Why didn't you tell me about Karin?"

There was a long silence. Then, "I suppose Eric or Simon told you."

"Yes. Eric. Diana ... somehow it seems so strange. That you would tell me about feeling you're haunted by a sister that you're not sure existed, but you don't mention a daughter."

"Possibly because as far as the sister is concerned, whatever happened to her was not my fault. I've been responsible for a great number of wrongs towards a great number of people in my life. But I really don't have to take responsibility for whatever happened to an infant twin sister when I was an infant myself. But what happened to Karin is different," she said with sudden anger. "Do we have to go into it now? Was it essential for you to bring it up—part of the punishment for my alcoholic misbehavior?"

"No, of course not. I'm sorry. You're right. I shouldn't have mentioned it. Only you sounded better for a moment. Go to bed, Diana. Try to get some rest." I hesitated, and then, perhaps because I myself was feeling guilty, "Would you like me to spend the night in your room? Would it help you to sleep?"

"Such sacrifice is not required," Diana replied sarcastically.

I don't like sarcasm, but this time I managed to remember, before snapping back, that pain underlaid her guilt. "I wasn't trying to be noble."

"No. I know you weren't. Sorry. I'll tell you about Karin sometime. Not now. Good night."

I dreamed again about the diary. Only this time, instead of my chasing somebody who was running with it, I was looking through room after room of Tower Abbey. After a while I realized I had left Tower Abbey and was in another house. In some way I had opened what looked like an ordinary door, but instead of leading to the Tower Abbey rooms already familiar to me, it had led into a room I had never seen before and which I knew immediately was not part of the house. And that unfamiliar room had led into another and another, until I saw that I was in a different house altogether. But even though it was a mansion I had never seen before, I knew that the diary was hidden there somewhere. I was also aware that though I seemed to myself to be running distractedly here and there from room to room, I was, without my conscious volition, following some unknown plan that would lead me to the room where I would find the diary.

A dream, when recounted, sounds either nonsense, or, at best, a distorted, surrealistic version of reality. But what description cannot convey is the emotion that, to the dreamer, is such an integral part of the dream. And the two emotions that gave my dream its power were an urgency and a conviction, impelled by that urgency, that no matter how bizarre the dream seemed (and, like most dreamers, I knew that I was dreaming) it was underlaid by an impeccable logic, a karmic thrust of cause and effect pointing to the importance of finding the diary. Then, suddenly, I was no longer running hither and thither more or less in circles, but focusing in one direction through a chain of rooms that led one out of another. Finally I reached the last room. And there was stopped by something familiar which filled me with a kind of terror.

Then I woke up and smelled smoke.

I realized immediately that what had waked me, pulling me out of the dream, was the howl of the cats and Pandora's frantic barking. My door must have slammed shut, because I had remembered leaving it open an inch or two, in case James or Diana should want me. Now Seth, Susan and Pandora were all crouched before my door, under which, undoubtedly, came the odor of smoke. Plunging across the room, I pushed the animals back and yanked open the door. The smell of smoke was much stronger in the hall. Making sure that Seth, Susan and Pandora were back in my room, I closed the door and opened the door to the other room where James and the animals were sleeping. Being at the end of the wing it enjoyed cross ventilation, and there was no smell of smoke inside, although Hannibal was standing in the middle of the floor, his nose raised, sniffing delicately.

"It's all right, Hannibal," I said, pulling the door closed. James, sound asleep, hadn't even stirred.

I ran along my hall, up the steps and along the big hall to Diana's room. I knew, even before I got there, that the smoke was coming from under her door.

The rest seemed to happen in a blur. I pulled the door open and saw thick curls of smoke coming from Diana's mattress. There was, as yet, no flame. Without stopping or thinking, I ran over, yelling Diana's name, hoping to wake her. When she failed to respond, I realized that she was probably unconscious from inhaling the smoke.

Coughing and sputtering and with burning eyes, I managed to get into Diana's bathroom, where I soaked a towel in water, wrapped it around my mouth and nostrils and came out. Then I went around to the far side of Diana's bed, took her by the shoulders, pulled her off the bed and dragged her across the floor to the hall outside. Leaving her there, I closed the door to her room and ran into one of the other rooms, picked up the phone extension and called Simon. Dimly, with one part of my mind, I noticed that this time I did not have to look up the number. And I realized something else: Whatever doubts had been sown in my mind about Simon, it was still to him, in a crisis, that I turned first. As before, he answered immediately.

Briefly I told him what had happened and left it to him to call the necessary people. Then I came out. Diana was breathing, though still unconscious. As I knelt beside her, I knew that I didn't have the faintest idea what to do for her, so I simply concentrated on praying that competent help would arrive soon. In surprisingly few minutes my prayer was answered. I heard the sound of wheels on the drive outside and the slamming of a car door, then from a distance, a siren. The front door opened. Feet pounded up the stairs. Simon said, "Where—" then caught sight of Diana lying on the floor and came over.

217

I decided to greet the fire department and let them know where to go, and went down the stairs to the first-floor hall. As I reached there I saw through the open front door the blinking red light of the fire truck coming closer as the siren got louder. In another minute or two a burly young man in a huge helmet and carrying an axe came forward followed by several more.

"I don't think you're going to have to soak the whole house," I said. "It's just upstairs in the bedroom. Dr. Grant will show you when you get up there. What's that? Another truck?"

"The ambulance, ma'am. The doctor said there was somebody overcome by smoke."

When Simon summoned help, I decided, he summoned all of it.

Following the stretcher-bearers upstairs, I heard Simon say, "I think she'll be all right. But I want her in the hospital tonight."

Diana, who seemed to be coming around, stared groggily up at us as the young men were lifting her onto the stretcher.

"I didn't—" she started to say. "It wasn't—"

Simon bent down. "Didn't what?"

She tried to say something else, but wheezed and coughed.

"Don't talk now," Simon said. "I'm taking you to the hospital."

"No—"

"Yes."

The word came out of him like a hammer blow. Diana tried to shake her head and then obviously gave up the struggle.

Simon stood up. "Take her down. I'll follow immediately."

"Is there anything I can do?" I asked, knowing very well that there wasn't and feeling rather helpless about it. "I'd offer to go with her, but I don't think I ought to leave James."

"No. You shouldn't. Candida, I'm going to the hospital to settle Diana in. After that I'm coming back here and spending the night here in the house. I'd rather you wouldn't be alone here."

"Why not?" I said. I had never minded being alone in a

218

house, even as a child when, perforce, from time to time after my mother died, my father was yanked out of bed on an emergency call.

"Because I don't," Simon said shortly.

"Yes, your lordship," I muttered as I watched him run down the stairs after the stretcher.

Two of the firemen were still in Diana's bedroom, sloshing about, making sure that nothing could be smoldering away in some hidden corner. I went to the door and watched them, aware again of Seth's voice yowling away, highly audible now that it was no longer drowned out by the general clatter.

"Do you have any idea how it started?" I asked the men.

"We're not sure," one of the firemen said. "We're still trying to find out."

The soaked mattress now lay on the floor, I noticed, wincing slightly as I took in the total destruction of Diana's powder blue carpet. As I watched, one of the men came over to the blackened mattress, heaved it over on the other side, and started groping around inside the charred messy interior. Evidently he found something because I saw him looking at his fingers. "I guess that's it," he said after a minute.

"What?" I asked.

"A cigarette." He paused. "Funny thing, though. Would you know which side was up on this?"

"As a matter of fact, yes. She had . . . there was a mishap the other night." I decided that the kinder part of tact lay in being specific. "She got sick and threw up and I helped her to clean up, which involved trying to clean off the mattress. There was a big manufacturer's label on the upper right-hand corner."

"Yeah," the fireman said thoughtfully. "That's what I thought, too. When we hosed it and pulled it off, I was pretty sure we didn't turn it over. But we did just now, and it looks like the burn started underneath the mattress."

"But how could it?"

"Damned if I know."

"Did she maybe drop her cigarette on the floor?"

"Then the carpet underneath would be burned, and you

would have seen flames. All the fire was right inside this mattress. Joe, look under the bed again, see if there's any burn on that rug."

The younger of the two men unhitched a huge flashlight from his belt and went down on his knees. "Nope," he said after a minute. "It's sure wet, but it wasn't burned before. Looks just like the rest of the carpet."

"Then how could it have burned from the bottom?" I asked.

"That's what we were wondering. The only thing that would make any sense would be if she somehow dropped the cigarette on the edge of the mattress and it rolled off and down. But then I woulda thought it'd drop through the big coiled springs here to the floor."

I looked to where his arm was indicating. Diana's bed was a relatively old-fashioned one, and the springs were built into the bed itself rather than in a box spring to go with the mattress.

"I guess," he finally said, in a bewildered voice, "the cigarette must have dropped, like I said, and then in a freaky way, stopped on one of the springs instead of dropping to the floor and then burned upwards. It was a crazy fluke, a one-chance-in-a-million unlucky break, but as far as I can see it was the only way it could have happened."

The older man wiped off his fingers. "You know you oughta tell her about smoking in bed. It's the dumbest thing a person can do. Half the deaths in fires happen that way. More than half."

"I'll tell her," I said.

He looked at me severely. "And for Chris' sake don't do it yourself."

"I don't smoke."

"Well, that's something."

After the men had dragged out their hose and left, I closed the front door after them and climbed back up the stairs. I had always hated the bare marble steps, but I could be glad about them now. They were soiled and dirty from the hose, but soap and water would take care of that. The light beige carpet covering the big upstairs hall was, most likely, beyond the skill of any cleaner. I got to the top of the stairs and stood looking down at it. Well, I thought, tomorrow I would, with the aid of Mrs. Klaveness, investigate the subject of local dry cleaners, or rug shampooers or whatever was required.

And then, suddenly, standing in the now bedraggled-looking upstairs hall, I was overcome with a surge of homesickness for my own childhood home, gone since I was in college and my father died. As our house was filled at all times with animals that had been dumped on our door—including hundreds of kittens, plus the young that had been born in my father's clinic next door and brought back to the house for me to raise, to say nothing of all the pets I acquired—my father wisely had no carpets. There were rag rugs that could be washed in the washing machine. Other than that, the floors were wide wooden planks that were dutifully polished but that bore as many scars, stains and scratches as a school desk. And somehow, I thought, standing there, the house itself, bare floors, scratched furniture and all, was infinitely dearer, more attractive than this cold, rich mansion could ever be, even at its best.

Shaking off the depression that threatened to descend, I went into Diana's room to turn off the light. But before my hand reached the switch the telephone rang. Squelching across the carpet, I picked up the receiver.

"Is all well?" Mrs. Klaveness's voice asked.

"How did you know we were in trouble?"

"With the fire engine coming up the road, it could only be two or three houses, and I didn't think it was the others. But it came back down the road soon after and I saw no flames, which I would see if the house were really on fire, so I was sure it was all right."

"Well . . ." I paused, suddenly faced with having to give an explanation. To say that Diana had smoked in bed and set her mattress alight would be interpreted by everyone in the village as certain evidence that as well as smoking in bed, Diana was too drunk to make sure her cigarette was out.

"It was some kind of short in the walls," I said, and wondered at my protective attitude.

"More likely it was a cigarette in bed," the housekeeper said.

I debated insisting on my lie, and then knew it was no good. The firemen would probably chatter the truth to their wives. There was no way I could stop the village knowing.

I sighed. "All right, Mrs. Klaveness. It was a cigarette. I'm sorry I lied. It's just—"

"You think I do not understand? I am not foolish." She paused. "If I know those firemen, there will be a big mess to clean up."

"You can say that again," I replied with feeling. "All you can imagine and then some." Might as well paint it thick, I thought. So when she got to the house in the morning she might find it not as bad as she feared and be pleasantly disappointed.

I had barely hung up and started back again across the room when the phone rang again. This time it was Eric.

"What happened? Are you all right? Diana?" He sounded almost panicky.

"Fine. We're all fine," I said soothingly.

"I just woke up, looked across the valley, and saw the fire engine coming back down the hill road. So I called the firehouse and they told me that the fire was up at Tower Abbey."

I knew that Eric's handsome but much smaller house was on the hill across the valley and was surprised that he hadn't seen—and heard—the fire engine and ambulance, sirens wailing, on their way up. He must have realized what I was thinking, because he said, "I have the air conditioner on at night, which blocked out the noise on the way up, but I woke up thirsty later and got up to get some water, which was when I saw the truck coming back down."

"So I guess you missed the ambulance."

"What ambulance? Who for?"

"Diana. She's okay, Eric, just groggy from smoke inhalation. But Simon said he wanted her in the hospital tonight."

"I take it you called him."

"Yes."

There was a short silence. Then, "Next time, if there is a next time, which I hope there isn't, I wish you would call me." The emphasis on "me" was slight but unmistakable.

In response, I could feel my inner turmoil start up again—doubts about Simon warring with doubts about my doubts, the old love versus the old pain. It was simpler to give an uncomplicated answer.

"All right. If there's time. I called Simon and he called the fire department and the ambulance."

"Are you all right now? I guess you and James are alone, aren't you?"

"For the moment. Simon is coming back here after he gets Diana settled."

"Okay. Then I won't worry. But remember, I'm just on the other end of a phone."

"Thanks. I will." My heart warmed to him. "Good-bye, and thanks for calling." I was just going to hang up when he said, "By the way, how did the fire start? Was there much damage?"

"It's sort of strange. Diana must have been smoking in bed and dropped a cigarette so that it fell just under the mattress and rested on the springs or something so that it burned upwards. Anyway, the fire started inside the mattress. Luckily, the animals smelled smoke and started howling. And I hope," I interpolated, "that this will once and for all shut up all the good people who like to make comic comments about me and my animals. If it weren't for them, Diana might be dead—not to mention the rest of us. They woke me up and I then smelled smoke. And, as they say, the rest is history."

He laughed. "All right. And all due thanks to your animals. Not that I ever thought there was anything wrong with them. I also think that you're not acknowledging how much you're responsible for saving Diana."

It was, I reflected, very good to hear. Nobody, which meant Simon, had bothered to thank me for my share in saving her. Until Eric spoke, I had no idea how much I had noted—and resented—that omission. "Thanks," I said. And then honesty pushed me further. "To be truthful, it wasn't that heroic."

"Maybe it didn't require you to rush through a wall of flame, Candy. But if the net result is saving Diana's life, why belittle it?"

As I hung up the receiver, a feeling of satisfaction stole over me. It was nice to be appreciated.

But as I stood, surveying the wreck of the room, the warm feeling of satisfaction drained out of me. The overhead light of the room was white and powerful, which was probably why Diana nearly always preferred, instead, the soft lamps on the two bedtables and on the wall above her dressing table. Now, underneath the overhead light, the blue walls looked stark and bleak. Outside, I knew, the night was hot, unusually so this far out in the country and up on this hill. And there was no air conditioning. Yet the coldness from the walls and the light seemed to fill the room. Quite suddenly the fireman's words were in my mind: ". . . a crazy fluke, a one-chance-in-a-million unlucky break . . ." Was that what it was—just ill luck, combined with Diana's bad habit of smoking in bed? Or was Diana right—that there was something profoundly wrong with the room itself?

Following fast on that thought was the memory of how I had felt before—was it only the previous night?—just prior to Diana's taking her lethal mixture of pills and vodka. Only, I told myself, I had been half asleep, dozing. That was why I had felt so strongly the presence at the door, a presence that had driven me into the bathroom and out of that door into the hall. . . .

"Candida?"

I whirled around. There, standing just outside the door, looking disheveled with sleep and scared, was James. "What's happened?" he asked.

"Your mother . . . there was a small fire in the room. Your mother inhaled some smoke. So she's gone off in an ambulance to the hospital. Simon is seeing that she's all right. Then he'll be back. I suppose all the racket and the sirens and firemen stamping around woke you."

He rubbed his eyes. "I don't know. I don't remember hearing anything. I just woke up. Then I had to go to the loo and saw the light. Gosh, it's a terrible mess, isn't it? What's that smell?"

"Smoke and burning mattress."

"Why is everything so wet?"

"Because the firemen came and hosed everything in the room to put the fire out. We're all going to have to do a massive job of cleaning up in the morning."

James started to walk forward. Behind him I saw Hannibal and Pandora.

"It feels funny," James said.

"What feels funny?"

"I don't know." He shivered. "Aren't you coming out?"

"Yes." I paused, aware, suddenly, of a powerful disinclination to go back through that door. My eyes detected nothing there. And yet— "I think I'll just step into the bathroom for a minute," I said, grabbing at an easy excuse. "I can use the door to the hall in there when I've finished." It sounded lame even to me.

"Then you won't need this light, will you?" James asked, surprisingly and put up his hand to turn off the overhead light from the wall switch.

For a second I felt rather sleepy, as though my eyelids were heavy. It was Hannibal's voice, incredibly loud, like Seth's, that jerked my eyes open. I saw first the two animals, crouched against the hall floor: Pandora, tail down, whining; Hannibal growling in an odd, uncatlike way, the ridge of fur on his back blacker against the other black. Then I saw James's hand, almost in slow motion, going up to the naked light switch, his bare feet resting on the sodden carpet. . . .

The naked light switch . . . Something had happened to the plastic plaque that ordinarily covered the light switch. In the general melee it must have come off. The switch itself was left, the stripped wires like metal capillaries leading from it.

"Stop!" I screamed. "Get back. Don't touch it!"

My last thought as I plunged forward was a question: What was it Eric had said about going through a wall of flame?

12

This time it was I who came to lying in the hall. Simon was bending over me, looking, I thought, rather grim.

It took me a second or two to realize where I was. "What—" Then I sat up, or tried to. "James . . . the light," I said. But I felt so queer that I lay down again.

"Hasn't anyone ever told you," Simon asked in a far from friendly voice, "that it is unwise to touch electric wires when their insulation has been stripped off and you're standing in what amounts to a pool of water? It's lucky you had on slippers."

"Yes. Of course." I tried, more slowly this time, to sit up, and was successful. "That's what James was about to do. That's why I had to stop him."

Simon sat back on one knee and didn't say anything.

"Well, it is," I insisted. "He came to the door and asked me what happened. I told him I was going to go out into the hall by the bathroom door as I had before. He said then that I wouldn't be needing the light and raised his hand to flip the switch. *I saw him*, Simon. And I saw the wires and his feet on the soaked carpet. . . . Why are you staring at me like that?"

"Because I heard your voice scream something just as I came in the front door and I got up here as fast as I could. James was standing there in the hall just in front of the room. He said nothing about trying to turn off the light switch before you did. I sent him back to his room."

"But I saw his hand go up. It was like slow motion."

"Well, he's in his room now. Can you get up?"

He put his arm around me, and with that aid, I wobbled to my feet. "My hand feels burned," I said.

"It is. You're lucky to be alive. Even with a relatively low voltage like that you could have been killed. Your heart and breath could have stopped. And might have. If I hadn't just happened to come in at that moment."

I took this in. "You mean you saved my life."

"Yes, if you want to be dramatic about it. Anyone trained in resuscitation techniques or a paramedic could have done it. The important thing was being there. Not great medical skill. How do you feel?"

I tried to establish some kind of sense of balance. But my head was fuzzy and my stomach felt odd. "Not too sharp."

"Well, getting an electric shock is no joke, even when it wasn't a bad one. I'm going to see you to your room and then I'm going to give you something to make sure you'll sleep."

"No," I said, surprising myself by my firmness.

Simon, who was walking with an arm around and holding me up, looked down. "You sound so definite. Why not? To put it at its mildest, you've had two very disturbed nights. You'd benefit by a good night's sleep."

"Night's sleep? It'll be dawn any second now."

"What I meant was, a good eight hours' sleep."

"No," I said. "I'm not going to take a pill and render myself unconscious and therefore useless. Something ... something uncanny is going on."

Simon leaned forward and opened the door to my bedroom. "Anyone would think that, after all those passionate disclaimers, you do believe in ghosts."

"Let's check on James first. I want to find out if he remembers reaching up to turn off the switch."

227

But when I opened the door I saw James in the same abandoned position of sleep that he had been in when I first woke up. On his bed were the three cats and Wisteria, the rabbit. On the floor, her nose between her paws, was Pandora.

I stared at them. "It looks like the entire cast of *The Sleeping Beauty*," I whispered.

"Yes, it does. Now come to bed."

But I was far from happy or satisfied. I was bothered by the memory of James's voice saying, "It feels funny," by the picture of his arm going slowly up, and by my strange, abnormal sleepiness as I watched his hand creep towards the naked switch. If it hadn't been for Hannibal's voice... Tired, confused and more frightened than I wanted to admit, I let Simon take my robe and I got into my bed under the window.

Simon put the robe over a chair. "I'll go down and make you a hot drink, and we can talk about your taking a pill then."

"I don't want a pill." I stared at the black night outside. "What time is it?"

Simon looked at his watch. "Three thirty. Why don't I go down—"

"No," I said, surprised at my own fierceness of feeling.

Simon stared at me, then leaned forward on the bed and took one hand in both of his. "What's the matter, Candida?" He held my hand for a minute, and then said, "You're shaking. Why?"

"I don't know."

He didn't say anything for a minute. I went on stubbornly, "I don't want to be alone. Not till it's light."

Gently, his eyes staring out the black window, he started to rub my hand between his. Handsome Simon, Simon the playboy, with his chivalric, romantic arrogance, I had been able to resist.... But this tender, comforting gesture knocked my defenses flat. The next thing I knew tears were streaming down my cheeks and I was groping around for a tissue.

"Candida, Candida," Simon said. "You are not making things easier." His hands stopped rubbing mine and gripped it hard.

228

At that the dam broke. "I don't understand," I wept with overwhelming illogic, "why are you being so *nice*? It's just not fair."

"A cad's trick, in fact."

"Yes." With my other hand I rummaged behind me under my pillow. "I know I had one," I said, and cried harder than ever.

Somewhere along the line he must have released my hand, because it was, with my other one, locked behind his neck. And his arms were around me. This time some final resistance broke. I didn't move away, or shove him away. He was kissing me, gently at first, and then harder, and I was kissing him back. I was shaking, shaking almost to pieces. And he had moved so that he was over me. He said, with an odd breathlessness in his voice, "This has been a long time in the making."

I woke up with the sun streaming in on my face. Outside the birds were making a fine racket. I was filled with an immense sense of well-being. In fact, I floated in it, and for a second wondered what had caused it. Then I remembered, and turned my head. But I was alone in the bed and in the room.

I thought then about Simon and Diana and Karin and waited for my well-being to subside. But it didn't. There was a knock at the door. My heart beat faster. "Come in," I called hopefully.

But it was Mrs. Klaveness, bearing a small tray on which were a pot of coffee, and a jug with a napkin over it, a cup and saucer and a sugar bowl. "Dr. Grant said to bring this up to you at ten."

Wondering what else Dr. Grant had seen fit to say, I murmured my thanks and tried hard to suppress the blush that I could feel coming up over my face. Then I sat up and made a discovery. I was naked. Blushing even harder, I pulled the sheet and light blanket up to my chin. "Just put it on the table there," I said.

But Mrs. Klaveness was made of sterner stuff. Putting the tray down on the dressing table, she took my robe from behind the door and brought it over to me. I had never had a nanny in my life, but as I wiggled into the robe, I felt I wouldn't be surprised if the housekeeper said something like, Now just slip on your robe and don't give me any argument, Miss Candida. And then you can have your bread and milk. This was so real that I giggled a little.

"Now," Mrs. Klaveness said. And bringing over the tray, put it on my lap. A copy of the local newspaper, a weekly, was folded neatly behind the pot.

"Any news of any kind?" I asked, slipping effortlessly into the role of mistress and personal maid.

"Dr. Grant said Miss Egremont was doing very well in the hospital. James is in the garden with Hannibal. Pandora..." she went on stiffly, and I remembered our contretemps over Pandora the previous day, "Pandora is in the kitchen. With me." Pause. "I bought her a new dish and gave her some leftover chicken," the housekeeper finished belligerently.

I realized that she was upset over her misunderstanding with Pandora, and that she was (a) apologizing, and (b) informing me that she was not a dedicated brute towards animals.

"That's lovely," I said, still washed by my euphoria. "Pandora adores chicken. I'm afraid she'll never want to leave."

Mrs. Klaveness's stern, wooden face relaxed. I picked up the little paper. "How nice of you to bring this up."

"Mrs. Egremont always wanted it when I brought up her breakfast," Mrs. Klaveness said, and marched out, starting to close the door behind her. Then, "So—come in!" And Seth, looking more cross-eyed than usual, came in, his long body moving with lanky grace across the room, his voice loud and talkative as he came over and jumped onto the bed. With the accuracy of his own inner radar he made for the jug of milk.

"No," I said.

His yowls rose. His tail lashed. Sitting back, he extended one brown paw and knocked off the napkin.

"I said no," I repeated, as his muzzle tried to push into the small mouth of the jug. He gave another howl of pure frustration. Rearing back, he squinted at the jug in rage and then started to put his paw in.

"No," I said, taking his paw out. I glanced up. Mrs. Klaveness was watching the proceedings with what could almost be called a smile.

"Now wait," I said, pushing his paw back again. I poured a little of the warm milk into the saucer under the cup, and placed it in front of Seth's nose. He sniffed, lapped once or twice, sniffed again, turned around twice, settled his back against my side, and started meticulously to groom his tail.

"So it is not good enough for you," Mrs. Klaveness said.

"He's inclined to judge milk by the high butter-fat content. In other words, the thicker the cream, the better."

After the housekeeper had left I poured my coffee, added milk and, feeling somewhat guilty, sugar. But, I told myself, I did not wish to disburb Seth in order to get up and find my saccharin.

"Anyway," I said aloud, "people say it's bad for you."

Seth turned around, fixed his crossed eyes on me, and gave a bellow. I wondered uneasily if it were a comment on the comparative evils of sugar.

"Quiet!" I said, drank some coffee and opened the paper.

I saw the announcement immediately, on page one: MS. CATHERINE TIMBERLAKE TRIES TO BUY TOWER ABBEY FOR SCHOOL. IS TURNED DOWN. SWEARS SHE WILL TRY AGAIN. And then, in small type underneath the headline: Teacher's grandfather balked Tycoon Egremont. Gave in after tragedy.

The body of the article, which turned out to be all about Tower Abbey, its past and its present, reported that Ms. Catherine Timberlake, principal of St. Margaret's School, a well-known and distinguished academy that had outgrown its old quarters, had approached Ms. Diana Egremont, present owner of Tower Abbey, who was rumored to be desirous of selling the mansion, which had become a white elephant, and had offered a large but unnamed sum. The story went on that Ms. Egremont had turned it down, giving no reason. Ms. Timberlake, on being interviewed, had refused to speculate on the possible reason. But, the reporter stated, it was well known that Ms. Timberlake's grandfather, Henry Timberlake, a

231

farmer in the Tandem area, had refused to sell a portion of his property that ran up the hill on which Tower Abbey now stood, thus foiling for a while the plans of Louis Egremont, who had selected that same site for the home he was about to build.

At this point the story went back to recount the beginning of the Egremont-Timberlake controversy. Apparently Louis Egremont, after inspecting many sites, had carefully selected the place he had finally chosen and had managed to persuade the various owners of the hill and its environs to sell to him which, considering the money he was offering, was not difficult to understand. All except old Timberlake, who wouldn't budge. Since the Timberlake farmhouse was at the bottom of the hill, a good distance away from the area Egremont wanted to buy, no one could understand the farmer's stubbornness. Rumors of minable riches under the not very fertile soil began to flourish. Egremont, who grew up on a French-Canadian farm and who loved to point out that he was descended from a long line of French peasants—a role he carefully fostered by donning a black beret when he went walking around the local countryside—was credited with craftily trying to obtain land containing treasure of some kind. It was then he acquired the sobriquet that so delighted him and that he cherished the rest of his life. "They call me the French Miser around here," he was, according to the article, given to saying to any and all guests. "They seem to think I follow the ways of my ancestors and keep everything in an old sock." And he would chortle with pleasure at the exquisite humor of it. The richer he got, the piece went on, the more he liked to tell the story and play the part, affecting, as time passed, along with his beret, a cane and a stooped walk. This was reputed to afford the tycoon the added satisfaction of embarrassing and irritating his son, Diana's father, who preferred to dress in accordance with what he was, president of several of his father's companies, and who fancied the executive uniform of pinstriped suits and striped ties. All that, of course, was much later, many years after Timberlake had sold his precious strip of land and Tower Abbey had been built.

But at the time when Egremont was dickering, apparently futilely, over Timberlake's property, the reason for the farmer's opposition finally became known. It seemed old Timberlake doted on his orphaned grandchild, whom he called Totsie, aged about nine. And Totsie liked to climb the hill with her puppy and play around the site of an old well, usually in the company of her aunt or her grandfather or some other adult. The well itself, long since disused, was considered safe because of the heavy iron top to it, a top which could barely be moved by a strong man and was therefore assumed to be safe for a child.

At this point in reading the story I made an exclamation, disturbing Seth, who had gone to sleep. A series of pictures chased each other through my mind: James, his face distraught, standing at the side of the well, pushing away the weeds so Simon and I could see the hole in the side, the strange look of pain that flickered over Simon's face as he watched James, Simon wrenching the top open with a crowbar.

"That's funny," I said aloud, and was responded to by Seth, who woke up and gave me an answering bellow.

"Okay, okay," I murmured, and rubbed him between his ears. He got up, smashed his way across the sheets of the newspaper, and, declaiming at the top of his powerful voice, rubbed his head against mine.

"All *right*," I said, exasperated. "I love you, too. Now go back and lie down."

After I reassembled the loose pages of the newspaper I read on.

Louis Egremont had not had to take no for an answer for years, if not decades, and he could hardly believe the repeated refusals as sincere, assuming instead that they were simply bids for more money. Money, of course, was not a problem with the tycoon. So he raised his offer. Henry Timberlake refused again. With rising irritation at what he considered exploitation of his wealth, Egremont upped the ante once more. Timberlake still refused. Convinced that he was being considered fair game for scrounging, Egremont stopped playing the haggling French peasant and started playing chairman of the board, setting his squad of lawyers on to a minute examination of Timberlake's rights to the land. The lawyers were high-powered, well-paid and anxious to keep their jobs. But they still couldn't find anything wrong with Timberlake's ownership.

By this time it was fairly obvious where the newspaper's sympathies lay. The tone of the article could easily be summed up in the imaginary headline: BIG TYCOON TRIES TO PUSH SMALL FARMER. Timberlake figured in the story as David to Egremont's Goliath. And little Totsie continued to run up the hill to play with her puppy, also, for some strange reason, called Totsie.

With the lawyers stymied and the money powerless, it looked for a while as though Louis Egremont had met his match and would have to sell the land he'd already bought and find himself another site for his mansion, the foundations of which had already been dug at the top of the hill.

Then tragedy struck. The child and puppy one day ran up the hill without an accompanying adult. After they were missed, Henry Timberlake himself went up and found the iron top to the well lying on the ground, and the two small bodies floating in the water far beneath.

It was possible, the reporter speculated, that if old Henry Timberlake had retained his health, he would have held out against Louis Egremont to the end. But the tragedy brought on a stroke from which Timberlake never fully recovered, although, according to one rumor, the story said, he regained his powers of speech enough to curse old Egremont, his family and, remembering Totsie, every child who would ever live in that benighted mansion. But it was impossible for him to live in his house alone, and a son, younger than Totsie's mother and (the story implied without actually stating) dazzled by all that money, accepted Egremont's offer. The Timberlakes moved out. The farmhouse was demolished. Tower Abbey rose on top of the hill. The land around the well was made into a rose garden. A new iron top, this one bearing a sundial, was fitted.

I lowered the paper and stared at the window. Wasn't Karin, Diana and Simon's daughter, nine years old when she died by falling into the well? Queer. Very queer.

I turned my attention back to the story, which had already occupied one full page of close print and was carried on to another.

Now, it went on, not sounding at all unhappy over the turn of events, after much spending and mismanagement on the part of the next generation of Egremonts, and more recent financial reverses, the current owner, Diana Egremont, had been rumored to be eager to sell. If this were true, however, why had she turned down the offer of Ms. Catherine Timberlake, daughter of the son who sold his land to the tycoon, granddaughter to old Henry Timberlake, first cousin to the late little Totsie? Particularly since the sum offered was rumored to be generous.

I put the paper down. Diana had told me the sum. She may, of course, have told others—notably Simon and Eric. Yet I couldn't imagine either of them gossiping about it. So those rumors more likely came from the other side, from Ms. Timberlake, who, according to the headline, swore she would have another try at buying Tower Abbey. . . .

What was it Diana had said? That she had passed up that generous offer because she would not leave the house without finding the diary that held the supposed secret of her twin sister.

As though my euphoria, my sense of well-being, were contained in a vessel that had suddenly tipped, I felt a little of it drain out of me. What had happened between Simon and me after we reached this room the previous night had effectively drowned out the memory of everything else. But it came back now: the fire, the door I couldn't go through, the sense of a presence at the door, a presence that (insane as it sounded) controlled, or tried to control, what James and I did. James's hand approaching the switch, Pandora and Hannibal out in the hall crouched in terror, and then the memory of a memory, Eric's words: *a wall of flame,* and my recollection of them as I plunged forward. . . . And I remembered also, with gather-

235

ing unhappiness, the other recollections that had always served as a barrier between Simon and me, the childhood scene, the punch-induced blackout at that calamitous party when I was sixteen, and now Karin . . . Karin, another child of nine who had fallen down the well in the rose garden and drowned.

I knew suddenly what people meant when they said they felt the hair on their neck stir. And it was not a pleasant feeling. I pushed the tray to the end of the bed. By this time my sense of well-being had vanished. How, last night, could I not have remembered Simon's other intrusions into my life? Every time they had marked me, and for the worse, not the better. So many of my inhibiting fears and confusions I could lay at his door. Why on earth had I allowed last night to happen?

Listlessly I picked up the paper again. The story, which ran for another column of fine print, said that it was no secret that Ms. Timberlake and her school was not the only prospective buyer of Tandem's richest and largest property. There was another: one which would, according to charges made by Tandem's Environmental and Civic Association (TECA), do its best to overturn or get around some loophole in Tandem's rather archaic zoning regulations. And if it succeeded it would put up cheap houses on small lots or low-to-middle-income high rises to accommodate an expected influx of workers in the new electric plant across the county line. And, the editorial concluded gloomily, there would be nothing to prevent the weedlike growth of small, cheap commercial enterprises that always sprang up to service such areas.

It was clear from the context of the story that the reporter was biased in favor of Ms. Timberlake and her school and was violently opposed to the prospective purchaser of middle-to-low-income houses who wanted to get zoning for smaller lots and, perhaps, multiple dwellings.

At the bottom of the story was a note in italics: *Please turn to Page 4 for editorial and letters on this subject.* Which I obediently did.

In the pontifical and oracular style used by editorial writers from coast to coast, the paper, like its reporter, came out for the Timberlake school offer and expressed itself as unalterably opposed to the would-be builder of small houses. Curiously, its most inflammatory rhetoric was reserved for members of so-called old Tandem families who—the editor implied severely—seemed more interested in accumulating wealth than in helping and serving the community.

Unfair, I thought. Diana's dire financial straits were widely known. In addition to which it seemed grossly unjust that she should be publicly scolded for, in effect, being her grandfather's granddaughter. I was perfectly willing to admit that old Louis Egremont was every kind of robber baron, a fraud posing as peasant, despoiler of the countryside, ruthless trader for land he wanted, and a persecutor of widows and orphans. But I'd never felt it was right to blame people for what their ancestors did.

After finishing the editorial, my eye went to the letters that followed, most of them angry and all of them filled with the kind of civic righteousness that a battle of this sort inevitably engendered. The combatants appeared to be divided into two camps: on one side was an alliance of self-styled liberals, conservatives and ecologists who did not wish to see Tandem begin to look (in the words of one letter) like some of the seedier boroughs of New York City. In violent opposition were yet more liberals who felt that to oppose middle- and low-income houses on small lots connoted racial prejudice and was a greater disgrace to the community than the worst that the commercial builder could do.

After reading through the editorial and all the letters twice more, I found to my unspeakable disgust that there was something to be said for both sides.

"Damnation!" I said aloud, and threw back the covers.

Seth, treated thus with less than the respect due him, let out a loud squawk, but I ignored him.

I showered and dressed rapidly and went downstairs, carrying my tray, and walked through to the kitchen.

"Did anyone say what time Miss Egremont was coming home?"

"Dr. Grant called and said he was keeping her in the hospital for another night."

I almost blurted out the question, Did he ask for me? But managed to bite it back in time. Besides, the answer to that was obvious. If he had asked for me, Mrs. Klaveness, a stickler about messages, would have told me.

"Did you say James was out?"

"Yah. First he took Hannibal for a walk. Then he went down to Dr. Grant's Halfway House."

"Did he take Hannibal with him? Or did he bring him back first?"

"That I do not know."

"Did Hannibal get anything to eat today? Not that I know why I'm asking. James would remember to feed him before he remembered to feed himself."

"I am preparing a little something for him for dinner. It a surprise will be."

Suddenly there seemed to me something very pathetic about the big housekeeper. Who could know that under that iron Teutonic front she courted even the animals for love and approval. Or perhaps she was just an animal lover, even as thee, my mind added for me.

After I'd finished a sort of brunch, I found myself at something of loose ends. With Diana in the hospital and James at Halfway House, there didn't seem much for me to do. Well, I thought, I could start working up a good outline for that animal book I was under contract for, drawing up lists of those whom I would have to consult and others who might be willing actually to contribute.

Or, my inner nag reminded me, I could continue to look for that wretched diary. An unpleasant mood, half depression, half lassitude, seemed to descend on me at the idea of pursuing the diary....

Pursuing the diary, I thought, and remembered my dream of someone I couldn't see running ahead of me with the diary. Someone... for a flash I almost saw him. But then he was gone.

"You know," I said suddenly to Mrs. Klaveness, "you once said that this was not a good house. I agree with you."

"Yah?" The housekeeper's little blue eyes regarded me

238

Never
hugging a
up here?"
"Well,
pockets,
you were
support t
this place
"It's al
off her T-
"Who'
"She is
You mea
Terry g
one of th
here over
went on,
that inste
income p
should be
will have
Having
working l
a little. S
neither sh
People, p
cated mo
them, goo
"Well,
She loc
comprom
"I'm so
have this
the peopl
some of t
what Sim
loophole—
"Zonin

above the knife with which she was chopping some cabbage. "You feel this?"

I was back to the depression and anger of the morning. But before that ... before that there had been euphoria, brought on by Simon.

I got up. "I'm going to look for that diary."

"What diary?"

I realized at that moment that very likely Mrs. Klaveness didn't know about the diary that seemed to turn up so prominently in people's dreams. "It's just a diary or maybe a journal, an old one, that Diana, that Miss Egremont—er—wanted me to find."

"And this will make everything clear?" I revised my assumption. Evidently she knew something.

"Did Miss Egremont speak to you about this diary?"

"She talks, when she is alone, when she does not know I can hear."

I stared at the housekeeper. "Well, Mrs. Klaveness, if you were going to look for it, where would you look? I've gone through every book in the library. It's not there."

"There are books in the cellar. Hundreds of them."

"Yes. I know. I suppose I was avoiding going there." I started to move out and then glanced at her. "Do you have any idea what Miss Egremont hopes she will find in the diary?"

"Perhaps," Mrs. Klaveness said, not taking her eyes off the cabbage falling into slices under her knife, "why so much evil happens here."

Only that? I muttered to myself, winding back through the living room. Mrs. Klaveness was too stout and corporeal to look like my idea of a witch, but it occurred to me that in another age she might have found herself tied to a stake.

There was nothing to do but what I knew I had to do, look through the books in the cellar, much as I disliked the cellar. Going upstairs I changed my skirt for some jeans, T-shirt and sneakers. The job promised to be dirty.

Coming back down again and through the kitchen I went down into the basement, turning on lights as I went, and

239

word for discrimination, for excluding—"

As Mike's indignant voice went on and on, laying down the gospel as he saw it, I realized that instead of being astonished that he and Terry, my friends from another world in New York, were here, I should have realized instantly that it was simply a matter of time till they turned up. They might devote the bulk of their energies to underground and above-ground newspapers from Soho and the East Village, but the promise of a zoning fight in Juneau, Alaska (let alone neighboring Westchester), would bring them as surely as a patch of clover would summon distant squads of bees. Which, in principle, I approved of. The trouble was, the snow-capped peak of principle that I had always admired had, for me, given away to the gritty surface of reality. Living in Tower Abbey, I could understand far better than before Diana's need for money. I could also—although this was more difficult, given her reasons and obsessions—sympathize with her need to sell on her own time schedule. On the other hand, despite, or along with, my doubts about Simon and his motives, I certainly found myself in accord with the horror he and people like him felt over seeing short-order diners, bars and heaven knew what other sleazy commercial enterprises take the place of the hills, fields and trees surrounding Tandem.

"...and it's not like you to sell out so fast," Mike finished sorrowfully.

"I'm sorry, Mike. I don't think I've really sold out. And—please don't eat me—it *is* more complicated. Truly."

"Okay," Terry said reasonably. "Explain to us."

"Come in and have a drink while I do."

It was really overwhelming, I decided, as I led the way to the study, how delighted I was to see them, as though they were troops who had lifted a siege, which was, in itself, a strange analogy. Granted, Tower Abbey itself was not my native turf, Tandem was. I had grown up in this town. So why should I feel besieged? I was here of my own volition because I was being paid. Diana was my employer, not my jailer. I could (theoretically) leave when I wanted to, and as for any opposition she might try to bring to bear—well, she

242

was in considerably worse shape than I. And Eric, with whose views on Diana's drinking, pill-taking and need for expert hospitalization I so agreed, was a reassuring note of sanity on whom I knew I could call for help. (But why should I need it?)

As for Simon . . . But Simon was the one who made me see that the whole question of who bought the Tower Abbey land for what purpose was not as simple as I, along with Terry and Mike, once would have thought. All of which put Simon, guide and mentor of the ghetto kids, on the side of the lily-white suburbs. Or so my two rescuers from New York would certainly think.

"You see," I said, "it's not just a question of rich estates against the people. As Simon—he's a cousin of Diana's who's very involved with local affairs—as Simon pointed out, which I hadn't seen before, if there *is* a loophole in the zoning regulation that Diana could use, and the building company who wants to buy could also use, then they, the company, could put up not just middle- and low-income houses, but cheap, tacky bars and garages and short-order diners and gyp joints and whatever else they wanted. And I don't think that's what you and your protest group have in mind either."

"Simon who?" Mike asked.

"Simon Grant, a cousin of Diana's who also runs a halfway house here."

"So it was him," Mike said gloomily and ungrammatically. "That figures, that he'd be for the rich estates' interest. Did you say running a halfway house?"

"Yes. Why? Do you know him?"

"Not like *know*. When you're a private in the army, or even a corporal, you don't exactly *know* a captain. But I thought I recognized him." Mike sloshed his beer around in his glass. "He was attached to the medical corps in our division when we were in Germany."

"You sound as though you didn't like him."

"I told you. I was a corporal and he was a captain. What kind of halfway house?"

"I gather for urban and ghetto kids who've been in trouble

with the law and drugs. That kind of thing."

"Drugs again," Mike said.

For no reason that I could think of, a little chill chased itself up and down my spine. "What do you mean?"

"Well—now I don't know, mind you, that wasn't my scene—but a guy I hung around with was a medic working in the army hospital there, and there was some big stink—hushed up, of course—over drugs being stolen and sold on the black market, even of being shipped into the Eastern zone. And according to him, my friend, Grant—Captain Doctor Grant—was in it up to his eyeballs, only nobody had real evidence, and, besides that, he was an officer with a lot of powerful contacts in Washington and the Pentagon. So no charges were brought. Anyway, he had some kind of accident soon afterwards and was in the hospital himself a long time, so the whole thing faded away. But I can't help wondering what kind of so-called guidance he's giving those kids."

So did I. My mouth was dry and my heart was hammering in a strange way. Mike and Terry were looking at me. "You haven't heard it all yet," I heard myself say. "He's not only a doctor, he's an Episcopal priest. Not just Doctor Grant, the Reverend Doctor Simon Grant."

Mike stared. "Far out!"

And at that point the Reverend Doctor himself walked in.

13

The light coming through the window was on Simon's face as he entered the room. For a second, until he saw Terry and Mike, who were standing a little behind the door, his face was open as I had never before seen it. The reserve, the aloofness, that he had always worn like a garment was gone. If he had come half an hour earlier, before Mike had spoken, adding his quota to the growing evidence that everything Eric had implied about Simon was true, my heart would have jumped out of my chest with sheer joy.

Oh, Simon, Simon, I thought. Women and his power over them, drugs, and the power they gave him, those, perhaps, were the vices that Diana—who should know—had alluded to that night at dinner. And yet, as I relinquished some final hold on my faith in him, a faith reborn the night before, I knew that I loved him, had always loved him, and always would. Faithful Penelope was considered either outmoded or sick by most members of my own generation. Yet I knew now why she had unpicked a tapestry night after night for twenty years to hold off her suitors and wait for her tiresome (and unfaithful) husband to come home. Undoubtedly I needed some consciousness raising, but I couldn't help it. Despite everything Simon had done, despite all his power games, I loved him.

"Hello," he said, the inner as well as the outer light still illuminating his face. And then he saw, in the same moment, my own face, which had been in the shadow, and Terry and Mike standing behind and to one side of me. "Oh." He stopped short, and the change in his face was like the closing of a door.

"These are friends of mine from New York," I said. "Terry O'Connor and Mike Cominsky. Terry, Mike, this is . . . this is Captain Doctor the Reverend Simon Grant."

I don't know what made me come out with that string of titles except that it seemed, quite suddenly, irresistible and ironic.

Simon's worst enemy could not have accused him of not being quick. His hand had half gone out towards Mike, but at my words he glanced quickly at me, dropped it and looked back searchingly at Mike.

"We've met?" he asked. "In the army?"

"I remember you," Mike said. "We didn't meet. I was a corporal in Germany when you were a captain connected to the army hospital there." Since Mike was incapable of any kind of polite concealment, his words came out like an accusation rather than statement.

"I see," Simon said. And he did see, I thought. Probably much more than Mike realized. "Just visiting up here?"

"No. We—Terry and I—came up to cover the protest over what's going to happen to this land—whether it's going to be integrated housing or another high-class expensive school. I hear you're on the side of the rich estates who want the school so they can keep this place pure and white. Naturally." If anyone, I thought, spoke with his fists metaphorically up, it was Mike.

Simon strolled over and stood with his back to the empty fireplace. "We're not against either integrated or smaller houses. We're against some of the sleazier restaurants and

246

gin mills that will go up like mushrooms—before the houses themselves are all up—if we don't get a new zoning ordinance passed before the sale."

"Yeah? That sounds to me like the usual upper-class sell-out—we're not against minorities, we're just against quotas, that sort of thing. By the time you've got your ordinance passed, the exclusive school will have bought the place and this whole area will stay rich and white."

"You don't let facts interfere with your prejudices, do you?" Simon said genially.

"What facts?"

"I just told you. We want the new area zoned for residences." He paused. "Come here, let me show you something."

Like ducks in single file, we followed Simon's tall, narrow figure out of the study, into the hall and then to the porch that looked out over the valley.

"Look down there," Simon said.

The land fell away in shades of green, different greens for different kinds of trees and yet others for the grass of the fields. Some children, their T-shirts bright against the soft, yellowish green around them, were playing with a russet dog, for whom they were throwing a ball. Here and there in other fields were young people lying, sitting on blankets, jogging and walking. Far in the distance, a white ruled line, ran the main road.

"All that land now belongs to the house here, but ever since Diana Egremont came into possession, she's let other people use it. If the school bought it, it would buy only the land immediately around the house, enough on which to build playing fields, tennis courts and so on. Some of the rest should, I believe—a lot of us believe—go for smaller houses, but enough of the open land should be left for the people who live around it to have an open common. That's what we mean by zoning it. If this commercial outfit bought it now, what you're looking at could become a string of short-order joints punctuated by pool halls and bars, with here and there a house squeezed in on twenty square feet of land. Do you

247

think that would bring happiness to the people?"

Mike looked at it for a long time and then said, "That's what you say. That's a pretty picture you paint, but who's to say that the school won't buy the whole lot? Or that if some of it's sold it won't be divided into five-acre lots for more big houses? Everything you say could be like some oil company getting a franchise from the government for digging for oil with the promise of cheap fuel for the people, and then when they've got the oil up raising all the prices." Mike paused and took a breath. "The profit motive—"

"Oh, spare me the economics lecture," Simon said. His face now looked tired and drawn. "I've heard it before. I hand you a fact and you hand me a lot of hot air. Very easy."

"What the hell do you mean by that? Why should I believe what you say?"

"For that matter why should I believe you? You come up here with your power-to-the-people rhetoric. But the fact is —fact again, not theory—that you're on the side of this contractor who wants to buy the land to squeeze as much money out of it as possible. How do I—how do any of us—know you're not a clever bit of propaganda they're sending up here? Just because you look and dress like the East Village doesn't mean you can't be taking his money."

"Why you—!"

Terry and I both sprang and each of us grabbed one of Mike's arms. "Come on, Mike," Terry said. "Let's get out of this place. Don't hassle with this jerk. Didn't you tell me he was some kind of drug pusher anyway?"

"Let go of me," Mike said furiously, yanking his arms. "I won't hit him." Which had a delicious irony that I didn't think anybody but me—at that particular moment—was appreciating: Simon, though lean, towered over Mike by about six inches, and though he was probably fifteen years older, could, I was quite sure, in a hand-to-hand contest, more than take care of himself.

"I'm sorry," Simon said now. "I shouldn't have said that. But there's a lot of hot air on both sides with people shouting

248

from their prejudices rather than examining what's best for this land at this time in a very specific context. By the way, what was that drug-dealing comment all about?"

Terry, who had spoken in the heat of the moment, looked surly.

Mike looked mulish, but he wasn't one not to meet a problem head on. "There was a lot of talk when you were in Germany that you had a good thing going shipping drugs from the hospital to the black market in the Eastern zone and also to the West."

"Yes," Simon said calmly. "I know that was the talk. It wasn't true. But I suppose a simple statement like that isn't going to cut much ice with you is it? You're going to believe what you want to believe."

Mike stared silently, a pugnacious look on his square face. All this time I had said nothing because my own feelings were in such turmoil. I knew I loved Simon. I also knew that loving him did not necessarily mean knowing him, and as time passed, I seemed to know him less, not more. All of which tied up my tongue. I saw Simon glance at me and I found myself wondering if his words, "You're going to believe what you want to believe," were directed at me as well as Mike. Could that be some kind of silent appeal? I studied the austere features. Impossible.

"If it's not true, if you weren't using your job with the hospital there to get drugs," Mike said, "than what's that Nazi who opened the door for us doing here? Yeah, I know that's reaching. But when she let us in a while ago, and right after seeing you down in the village, the whole thing came back. The kids here in Tandem—the ones involved in the protest —said something about a German woman, whose husband had been a Nazi, working up at the house here. And I remembered then that the talk going around Germany was that you had some local connection, rumored to be a middle-aged woman and her husband, that you'd see regularly."

"Well, if I can't clear myself, at least I can clear Frieda Klaveness." Simon hesitated for a moment and glanced at me, and I realized he was about to tell them—and me—about Karin, and didn't know that I had already been told about her.

"It's all right," I said. "I know about Karin."

"Who told you? Diana?"

"No, Eric."

"I see. Well, that makes this a little easier." He turned back to Mike, who was watching him warily. "I had a daughter, Karin. She was... she was illegitimate. I didn't even know she existed until she was seven or eight, at which point I discovered she had been placed as a foster child with the Klavenesses. It's perfectly true that I pulled a few wires to get them into this country. Hans Klaveness, Frieda's husband, had belonged to some Hitler youth organization. I think even at that age he would have joined anything that marched to a band and supplied beer. But he was only eighteen when Germany surrendered, so I didn't see him as a dire threat to the nation's security. And Frieda Klaveness, who had had no Nazi connections and who had been very good to Karin, was the only mother my daughter had known. Maybe it was to make up for my own guilt about Karin, but I thought that if, at the age of nine, she were going to change countries, cultures and schools, she should at least have the continuity of the same foster parents."

"Did she know she was your daughter?" I asked.

A shadow crossed his face. The lines in it seemed suddenly deeper. "No, I was going to talk to her about it. But to go that far without telling her also about her mother... I wish now I had. She wasn't a pretty child—she looked too much like me for that—but she was intelligent and very curious and had a... a poignant quality, as though she knew she didn't belong anywhere." Simon stopped abruptly.

There was a silence. Terry asked, "What happened to her?"

Simon didn't answer for a minute. Then he said, "She fell down the old, disused well in the rose garden and was drowned. Frieda Klaveness had gone out on an emergency call for a neighbor, leaving Hans to watch Karin. As usual, his attention was mostly on his beer. As I said, Karin was a

250

curious child. . . . Anyway, she was dead by the time anyone thought to go looking for her." He took a deep, uneven breath, and looked past Terry and Mike at me. And it was as though the other two weren't there. I saw then that he had said what he had said, had gone into the explanation, for me; that it was almost as though it were a conversation between the two of us.

"Did any of that have anything to do with the accident you had? The one everyone seemed to think was suicide?" I asked.

"I suppose so. Somehow it seemed to me that Karin was paying, or had paid, for my misspent life. I didn't—consciously—set out to commit suicide. But I certainly was showing no wish to keep myself alive."

Mike cleared his throat. I looked at him, and I could see, in his scowl, a resolution not to be conned or persuaded out of his righteous suspicions. "Yeah, all right. I'm sorry about your daughter and all that. But to get back to the question of the housing—"

But I knew that was a discussion that could go on forever, so I interrupted. "Before you get into that, I have a couple of questions. Simon, how is Diana?"

"She was shaken, but seems to be doing well." He smiled. "Thanks to you. If you hadn't waked and pulled her out, I think that would have been the end. In fact I'm sure of it. And I know that she knows that. When she wasn't insisting that I conduct some kind of exorcism rite here, she was talking about her gratitude towards you."

"Exorcism!" Mike, Terry and I said all at once.

"Well, it's not a completely new idea for her," Simon said. "She's asked me about it before."

"Yes," I agreed. "She mentioned it when I first got here. But I didn't take it seriously."

"You mean you have a ghost here?" Terry asked, an odd look, between scorn and eagerness, on her face.

"Diana thinks so," I said. "And I think Simon half or three quarters agrees with her. Am I right, Simon?"

"I'm not about to say it's all nonsense," Simon said. "Although I'm not an expert in psychic phenomena."

"What kind of a ghost?" Terry asked.

Simon didn't say anything. I didn't like to betray Diana's confidence so I said merely, "Of a child."

"I had a friend who took part in an exorcism out in Brooklyn," Terry commented. "She said the house was fine after that."

That Terry would do anything but look with the utmost scorn on this astonished me. "I still don't believe in it," I said, and then caught my breath, remembering my words to Simon the night before, that there *was* something there, that because of it I did not want to be alone. . . . I looked over at him and found him looking at me. He smiled slightly, and I smiled back and could feel the warmth stealing up into my face.

"Well, why don't you do this exorcism for her?" Terry asked Simon. "Aren't you a priest?"

"Yes. But . . . you don't just march off and do an exorcism like that, even if I were persuaded that was the thing to do. I've talked to the bishop—"

"So you have thought of it," Terry said. Idly, I wondered where she seemed to have gotten all her information on the subject.

"Yes. He told me to go ahead if I became convinced it was the right thing to do. But I would have to be convinced that there is, objectively, something . . . someone here . . . who shouldn't be here. And I'm not, quite. Diana, my cousin, has . . . does . . . well, she could be hallucinating. I have to be sure she isn't, that the odd things that have happened in her room —and some of them, I'll agree, are pretty odd—don't spring from some perfectly rational and practical explanation. I feel I must—" He turned his head suddenly. "What on earth are you doing here, Diana?"

We all turned. Diana was standing in the doorway of the study, clutching around her the short robe I had put, along with slippers and one or two toilet articles, in a canvas tote bag for Simon to carry when he took her to the hospital.

"I thought I told you to stay where you were," Simon said.

"You can sign me in, but there's nothing to prevent me from walking out," Diana replied. She stared rather pointedly at Terry and Mike. "We've met, haven't we?" It was amazing, I thought. Diana might be clad only in a robe having just come from a hospital where she had been taken after an accident caused almost certainly by her own careless drinking and smoking, yet it was she who looked at ease, and the rest of us, especially Mike and Terry, who seemed out of countenance.

"Yes," Terry said, her nervousness showing in her belligerence. "In front of my apartment house, the day you and Candida came up here."

Diana's stiff, almost haughty look relaxed in a smile. "Oh, yes. I remember now. Terry, isn't it? And Mike." Diana turned and smiled at Mike. "Did you come up to see Candida? How nice!"

"They came up to cover the protest over who you're going to sell this house and land to, Diana," I said. And then the irony of Diana, Terry and Mike finding themselves on the same side of a housing argument seemed too delicious not to be pointed out. "They're on your side. They think you should sell to the contractor who'll be building those little houses."

"Allies!" Diana said, as Simon made a wry face. "I could use them. Are you up here for the day or are you going to stay a while?"

Still funnier, I thought, were the expressions on the faces of Terry and Mike. Even in her robe, with her fair hair in a pony tail and her face drawn, Diana retained the manner of her birthright and presented a powerful class symbol. And Terry and Mike, who were staring fixedly at her, looked as though they were in the process of discovering for themselves for the first time the truth of the cliché concerning politics and bedfellows.

"Well—er," Mike said, "we have some gear in the car. We thought we might camp out. There's certainly plenty of land around here."

"Stay here. God knows there's enough room." Diana moved

towards the bar.

"I wouldn't," Simon said, his eye on the glass she had pulled out for herself.

"Wouldn't invite Terry and Mike, or wouldn't fix myself a drink?" Diana said coolly. She glanced at Simon's face. "The latter, I guess. Well, Doctor, I'm afraid your advice is not going to be followed. One way and another it's been a trying twenty-four hours." She poured herself a fairly stiff vodka and tonic and threw in some ice cubes from a bucket to one side. "We could use more ice," she said, and, moving towards the mantelpiece, rang the bell there. Then she glanced a little mischievously at Simon. "Why not fix yourself one?"

"Because I don't want to," he said.

"Do stay," Diana said, turning towards Terry and Mike just as the housekeeper came in. "Mrs. Klaveness? Could you get us some more ice? And I think we're going to have two extra guests for the next day or so." She smiled at them. "I need your moral support. All my friends are against me on this. So is most of the village, and Simon here, as you probably know, is on the other side, with Candida sliding in his direction."

"Well . . ." Mike glanced at Terry. "Our camping equipment isn't that great," he said to her. Of the two, he was obviously much more in favor of accepting Diana's invitation. And I remembered his rather rapid melting under the power of her charm the day Diana and I drove up here. I sympathized with the reluctance revealed by Terry's more balky expression. But I found the idea of their staying very comforting. "Come on, Terry," I added my voice. "Do say yes. Please."

Perhaps there was more urgency in my tone than I had meant to show. Terry, who, I was quite sure, had just about made up her mind to say no, paused and looked at me for a minute. Then she said, "All right."

I hadn't realized how much I wanted her to stay until she'd spoken. I smiled at her in relief. "Thanks."

"I will prepare the rooms," Mrs. Klaveness said. She looked

at Diana and hesitated. "You are better? Perhaps you should rest."

It was a common enough statement, an unexceptional expression of concern. Yet I saw Diana flush. She put her drink down on the bar with a snap. It was plain she construed the housekeeper's remark as a comment on her drinking. "Much better, thank you, Mrs. Klaveness. Now if you'll just bring us some ice and prepare bedrooms for Miss . . . Miss . . ."

"O'Connor," I put in. "And Mr. Cominsky." And I smiled at the housekeeper. "They're friends of mine and I'd be grateful for your help."

As Mrs. Klaveness left the room Diana picked up her drink and said to me, "It is, after all, her job."

"Perhaps, but speaking as a wage earner, I still like to get thanked when I do it."

There was a little pool of silence. I could see Terry and Mike going through their good-guy, bad-guy, upperdog, underdog confusion again. And since I didn't want Terry to get an attack of conscience about staying with somebody she didn't approve of, I said quickly, "By the way, Diana, how did you get here from the hospital?"

"Taxi," Diana replied. She glanced at me and the others. "If you're rich enough," she said a little acidly, "as I'm sure you'd be the first to agree, people will accept anything. All the cab driver said when I hailed him as he drove past the hospital door was, 'Home, Miss Egremont?' The big joke, of course, is that not only am I not rich—I'm poor and in debt. Most people know that—theoretically. But it has no reality for them. Which is one reason why I'm in the trouble I'm in over selling the house. I think it honestly doesn't occur to most of those opposing the sale to the contractor that I'm not trying to make an indecent profit. I'm just trying to pay off some creditors who are hounding me. Right, Simon?" The words were joking, but there was more than a hint of appeal in her voice.

But Simon did not reply in kind. He put his hands in his pockets and said almost coldly, "You know very well I don't

255

think you're profiteering. I do think—"

"Yes, we have been over this before." Diana, who had picked up her glass, put it down again. "I'm going to bed." She moved swiftly to the door, then turned and once again smiled at Terry and Mike. "Please feel free. I'm going to take a nap and will probably not be up for dinner. But I'm delighted you're here. *Ciao!*"

Mike shifted his feet awkwardly. "Do you think we ought—?" he started.

"Yes," Simon and I said in chorus. Simon went on, "Both Diana and Candida will be the better for your being here."

"Okay," Mike muttered. He and Terry once more looked like children who'd been told the wrong ending to a familiar story. Mike glanced at Terry. "We'd better go and find out what's happening."

Terry put down her half-empty glass. "Okay."

"Do come back to dinner," I said. And as they continued to look dubious, "Diana'll be in bed, I need your company and Mrs. K is a super cook."

"Okay. No promises, but we'll try." Mike lifted his hand and the two of them went through the next room into the hall.

And I was alone with Simon. "I guess I'll go back to looking for that diary," I mumbled and started to move towards the door.

"Just a minute." Simon said. He came over and stood in front of me. "Something happened to change your . . . your attitude since last night. What was it?"

Since I didn't know what I really thought, I didn't know how to answer him. So I stood there like a dumb thing, trying to find the right collection of words to tell him that I had discovered it was possible to love someone without trusting him.

"Who's been saying what? Eric? Diana? Those two aging hippies?"

Out of many unanswered questions in my head I picked one. "Why don't you want Diana to go away to a decent

256

rehabilitation place where she can get unhooked from pills and alcohol?"

"How do you know I don't?"

"Well, Eric said he had been doing his best to persuade Diana, and you, that she should go and get off the stuff once and for all."

"And that I'm preventing her because I don't want her to escape my Svengali-like influence."

"Okay. So Eric's prejudiced. But he's in love with her so he's entitled to his bias. What's in it for you?"

"You just told me. Power."

How could I have ever believed he could be gentle? What I had seen in his face before must have been a trick of light, because he looked about as yielding as Mount Rushmore. "Like most doctors I don't care to have my treatment interfered with and I don't appreciate advice from the sidelines by a layman, or laywoman."

Some small voice far back in my mind was saying in a whisper that I was going about all this the wrong way. But it was drowned out. "You mean Simon knows best."

"As far as Diana is concerned at this moment, yes." There was another prickling silence. "You're very changeable, aren't you, Candida? God help the idiot who ever decides really to trust you!"

"That's unfair!" I cried.

"Is it?"

He turned and was about to walk out when I said, "Simon?"

He half turned back. "Well?"

I had a terrible feeling what I was going to say would turn out wrong, and it did. "I'm sorry about Karin."

"Spare me your pity. I don't need that."

"Oh, what's the matter with you! I'm telling the truth. I *am* sorry. It was an awful thing to happen. And I have a feeling you blame yourself."

"Inevitably. If I had left her alone in Germany she'd probably be alive and well now. But I had to act like my notion of a good father, which involved bringing her over here. I

257

can't even claim that I cared for her—then. I came to. She was . . . she was—" He made a gesture with his hand. "I've described her."

"Simon, I was reading this morning . . . Mrs. Klaveness brought up the newspaper. I read about the Timberlake child, Totsie, who died, and about how her grandfather sort of put a curse on any child who might ever be here." I paused. Simon was looking at me unwaveringly.

"Well?" he finally said.

"Then there's this child—her twin sister—that Diana thinks she sees." It was hard for me to turn tail on years of thinking, but I knew I had to put into words a growing fear. "Do you think there was something in his . . . his curse? I think I must be going mad to ask you this. And my poor father must be whirling in his grave—" this last brought a faint smile to Simon's mouth, "but—"

"But do I think there's some danger to children in this place?" he finished for me.

"Yes." Now that he'd said it, it seemed so simple. "Do you?"

The question hung there as we stood a few feet apart, staring at one another.

Then Simon said slowly, "If I thought that, if I really thought that, then I'd have to do what Diana asked me to do."

It was like something cold and wet slithering down my back. "An exorcism?"

"Yes. An exorcism."

After Simon had left without saying anything further, I was visited with a sudden, overwhelming need to visit my zoo, to have a moment of being surrounded by those whom I loved and trusted, and who loved and trusted me. Well, I thought wryly, as I went along my little hall and pushed farther open the door of James's room, who else had an eleven-piece security blanket?

All my animals were there and greeted me, in their various ways, with enthusiasm. I even shut the door and let the gerbils out of their cages and the tortoises out of their terrarium so that we could all have a love-in on the floor and I sat there happily playing with them and feeling like Niobe surrounded by her children before Apollo and Diana (the mythological one, the goddess) killed them out of jealousy and revenge.

After a while, though, I became aware that there was a negative, or lack, that was bothering me and I finally focused on what it was: Hannibal was missing. Of course, I thought, as Anthony and Cleopatra made their stately way across the carpet, necks extended, James could have taken Hannibal with him when he went to Halfway House so he could show his pet off to his new friends. Automatically, my eyes went to the hook behind the door where James had carefully hung Hannibal's blue leash. Sure enough, it was not there. Still, I wished he had told me. Hannibal was not just a cat. If my eleven furred, finned and shelled friends were my security blanket, Hannibal was that and much more for James. If anything should happen to him—

"Damn," I said aloud, and got up. Gently and with much explaining myself, I took Mr. and Mrs. Gerbil back to their home and restored Anthony and Cleopatra to their glassed-in rocks and shrubs. I could, in fact, should, be doing a lot of other things, such as looking for the diary....

Perhaps it was that word in my mind that brought sudden significance to something that my eyes had been fixed on for some minutes past, something red, a narrow red slice barely visible underneath the pillow of James's bed. Trained, undoubtedly, by his beloved Walker, James was a neat little boy, and he made his bed without being asked, even if there was a rather shoved-together quality about the pulled-up blanket and pillow on top. Obviously he had put what looked like— from the spine that was showing—a red book under that pillow. Probably, I thought, not moving, so that people wouldn't know he had it, or was reading it. Otherwise, surely, he would put it on the night table.

At that moment I was filled with the absolute certainty— as though it had entered me from the outside—that this was the diary that Diana and I had both dreamed about, and were both looking for, and were both so completely sure was in this house. Going over to the bed, I pulled out the book. Just as I knew it would, it had a cross on the front, and, underneath, in golden letters, Agnes Medora Egremont. I opened the cover. In the middle of the page was the date 1912. Over it was the legend, *A Diary For The Christian Year*. Under the date were two lines in fine print:

Be not deceived, God is not mocked, for whatsoever a man soweth, that shall he also reap.

Galatians, Chapter 6, Verse 7

And underneath that in old-fashioned, sloping writing, *If this is true, then who will pay for the death of that child? I am so afraid she was murdered.*

I stood there and stared. *My father once said that the house was built over a tragedy. But he never told me what it was.* Simon's words, which I had not, curiously, remembered when I read the story of Totsie and Totsie, child and puppy, in the paper, now came back to me.

I glanced again at the spidery writing. Whoever Agnes Medora Egremont was—and I was fairly sure that she was Diana's grandmother, wife to the tycoon—she suspected that Totsie's death was not accidental. And the particular horror of it for Agnes was not hard to guess, if she feared that her husband, who had learned to remove obstacles from his path, had reached out his hand and disposed of the final barrier to his total ownership of his chosen site.

"Ugh!" I said aloud. The book dropped from my hand to the bed. I stood looking down at it, at the gold cross and lettering, set into the red taffeta cover, now rotted and discolored in various places.

But wasn't it odd, my mind went on, that Diana should be dreaming of this diary, a diary for the year 1912, to tell her about a possible twin sister born—I did a quick mental calculation—some twenty-eight years later. In fact, it didn't make sense.

Another thing that would be interesting to know was whether James had any notion how frantically his mother and

I were looking for this book tucked so casually under his pillow. Searching my memory, I couldn't recall whether we had ever mentioned our eagerness to find the diary when he was present, or discussed my laborious search through the library shelves.

I turned the book around. How long had he had it? Where had he found it? And then there came back to my mind my conversation with Simon a few minutes before, when he put in words the question I was trying to ask: *"But do I think there's some danger to children in this place?"* he had said for me. The child Totsie, whom Agnes Medora Egremont seemed to fear was murdered, the child Karin, the infant sister Diana claimed to have had, the child James ... *The child James.*

What if I were right? That there was some danger to any child who lived in or had anything to do with this house?

That same icy fright seemed to flicker up and down my back again. My hands must have loosened, because the diary dropped to the bed in a puff of dust. As I bent to pick it up something fell out of the pages. As I picked it up I saw it was an old newspaper picture, so old that the corner by which I was holding it broke off and the picture dropped again. This time I scooped it up more carefully and, holding it on the flat of my hand, carried it to the window.

The picture was not only on rotting newspaper, it must have been grainy to begin with. Even so, the child's face was clear, the hair, which looked fair, tied back in a bow, the skirt long with little boots underneath. Under the photograph ran the caption: *Teresa (Totsie) Timberlake, drowned last week in the abandoned well at the top of her grandfather's property.*

I raised my head, startled, as another memory surfaced. This time the memory of my conversation with Diana in her bedroom started to unroll, our voices alternating, as though the whole scene had been jolted clear by that photograph in my hand:

"So I stayed up here, myself, for three months without drinking. Not a drop, not one drink. And she was here ... in this room."

261

And my question: *"Did you see her?"*

"What's seeing? I thought I did, but when I put my hand out, there was nothing. But I could describe her, down to the last detail."

"And she looked like you?"

"Yes. Just exactly the way I did when I was nine. There are scores of pictures of me in family albums I could show you, so that you'd know exactly, too, what she looked like. The only thing was . . . she wasn't dressed in any dress I remember having. In fact, she wasn't dressed in the style I was at all. . . ."

I looked down, startled. I wasn't even born when Diana had been a child of nine, so obviously had no memory of her. What was it she had said about family albums? There had been albums in one of the cabinets in the library, stacks of them.

Slipping the photograph back into the diary, I put it under my arm and went downstairs, propelled by a great urgency to find those albums immediately.

It didn't take long to locate what I was looking for. Diana had been right. There were pictures of her, pages of them, in several of the albums, and quite a few were of Diana, aged nine. She was, indeed, dressed in slacks, shorts, riding breeches, even once or twice in a blouse and skirt. But the clothes were not important. What was important was the almost uncanny resemblance between Diana Egremont and Totsie Timber-lake—at least according to these pictures. That shiver that I disliked so much quivered through me again. Taking out a magnifying glass that I remembered lay in one of the nearby drawers, I examined the photographs again.

Having been struck by the uncanny likeness between the two children, I now saw the differences: There was a more coltish quality about Diana, although that could have been the modern dress. Diana's features were bigger and more strongly marked. Totsie had a doll-like prettiness, but there was a set quality or expression to that small mouth and in those round eyes that made me decide she might not have been such a lovable child. . . . Or was I seeing something in

262

that face that was not there . . . that I myself recalled from . . . from what?

"That's enough," I said aloud, slapping the album closed and putting it back in the cabinet. It was immensely important, I thought, that I hang for dear life on to every grain of rational skepticism that had been, all my life, such an integral part of my makeup.

Leaving the library, I paused in the hall, prompted by an impulse to go looking for James and Hannibal. On the other hand, there was the diary, and equally strong was the impulse to look through that now, while there was time, while no one knew that I had it. . . .

The diary won and I took it up to my bedroom.

Two hours later I put it down, not sure of what I had learned, yet with the odd feeling that I had learned much more than I had realized. Agnes Medora Egremont, the schoolteacher-daughter of a haberdasher in a small town in Maine, was no writer. But perhaps, I found myself thinking, the journal's power lay in the very baldness of the flat prose that recorded her domestic activities and her observations in the same prosaic voice. And from the pages of slanted writing arose a rather sad picture of an immensely wealthy woman who would have been much happier if she had been able to manage her own household and kitchen with the aid, perhaps, of a single servant, rather than to try to find things to interest herself in with all the time left by the twenty-odd retainers that were there (at her husband's insistence) to keep her from having to pick up a dropped handkerchief.

And what was equally clear was the portrait of old Louis himself, a portrait all the more deadly for its innocent intent. Because Agnes Medora, with very few lapses, and despite that one entry on the first page of the diary recording her worry over the manner of Totsie's death, had nothing but wifely devotion and admiration for her powerful and successful spouse. So that if the portrait that emerged from his wife's journal was of a crafty, conniving, ambitious, and vengeful

263

business genius, it was not because Agnes Medora saw him that way—at least not consciously. There were indeed moments when a slightly dry note would creep into the entries, when the former Yankee schoolmistress would triumph over the adoring wife: *Le Grand Louis* [went one entry, using one of her pet ways of referring to him] *today bought Mr. Baker's bank. It was Mr. Baker who once referred to him as a Canuck, which was very rude and he shouldn't have done it.* A few days later: *The Bakers put their house up for sale. I saw Mrs. Baker down in the village. She didn't bow.*

Well, I thought, propping my feet up on my bed, good for Mrs. Baker. But I could see, as I read on, that Le Grand Louis had a massive chip on his French-Canadian shoulder. No Anglo-Saxon was too small for him to outdeal, buy up or rout financially if he could manage it. And I suddenly had a picture of the French-Canadian boy, his patois thick in his mouth, trying to make it in a New England public school. The anger behind the pose of the French peasant striding around his acres wearing his black beret suddenly came clear. Not only had the hated Anglo-Saxons defeated his fellow Quebecois on the Plains of Abraham in the eighteenth century, the descendants of their cousins across the border had now sneered at Louis himself. And he never forgave them.

Louis insisted on building the gazebo when he got back from France, the diary recorded. *"You shall have a Trianon, a folie, just like Marie Antoinette," Louis said to me today. I told him I thought the whole thing was most unsuitable, but he insisted. So the gazebo is now being built. I can see it going up from this window. I sometimes wish Louis would not get these ideas in his head. They seem so pretentious. . . . But when I tried to tell this to Louis, he said, "It will be for you and the grandchildren. No matter what happens." I didn't have the heart to tell him I didn't really want it. He's the gardener, not I. I would never use those tiny, toy-sized gardening tools that he said he bought especially for me and put in the gazebo. But I feel so ungrateful.*

I put down the book. What had Simon once said about the gazebo? A tinselly horror inside, a kind of sugarcake show, a nouveau riche gaffe that embarrassed everyone. And so, after the old man's death, it remained locked. I shrugged and returned to the book.

I felt sorry for Agnes Medora, who would have loved to bake a cake but who was too frightened of her servants to go into her own kitchen and do what she wanted there. But the more I read about Le Grand Louis the less attractive he seemed, and since he appeared in one out of two entries the portrait grew apace: No aspect of his wife's life was too small for Louis's personal and unflagging attention. There was Louis insisting that his wife, who knew English literature quite well, should know French letters even better, and to that end he had submitted a list of suitable books—all of Victor Hugo, all of Balzac, the plays of Corneille and Racine. . . .

Poor Agnes Medora. Le Grand Louis had little if any use for Anglo-American writing, with the possible exception of Poe, whose story "The Purloined Letter" he admired extravagantly. *"That man, Poe,"* he was recorded by his faithful wife as saying, *"he must have been French. The idea was too good, too subtle for the stupid brain of an Anglo-Saxon. . . ."*

After two hours I was no nearer to finding out why Diana thought—or rather dreamed—she could resolve the mystery of her (supposed) twin sister and I had had all of Le Grand Louis I could take. So I decided I would stroll down to Halfway House to check on James and Hannibal. For all its prosaic qualities—or perhaps because of them—Agnes Medora's diary had left me with a nagging feeling of depression, attributable also, possibly, to the shadow of Totsie lingering over the pages. Some fresh air would do me good.

With these worthy thoughts in mind I went downstairs and out the front door, and was about to walk around the carriage sweep and through the gate when I caught sight of the absurd cupola of the gazebo rising above the brick wall enclosing the garden. On an impulse I decided to go and look at it. Perhaps it was no longer locked. Turning left, I went through the wooden door in the wall leading to the garden and walked over to Le Grand Louis's fit of madness, his effort to put sober Agnes Medora in the company of the luckless

French queen Marie Antointette.

As I approached, one of the louvers, hanging on one hinge, creaked back and forth in the faint breeze. And then, as I came closer, I heard the thin, piping voice:

> *"Beastie, bystie, boostie, bootsie*
> *Bulzartgay*
> *Bulzartgay, Bulzartgay ..."*

Smiling, I walked up the little narrow steps and thrust the door open.

14

It was like walking into another world. A little sunlight filtered in from the half-open louver. The rest from a candle sitting in its holder on the floor and throwing a yellow, flickering light over the octagonal walls and high ceiling from which a myriad sequins and small mirror fragments reflected back the tiny writhing flame.

"Ye gods!" I said aloud, then looked down to the floor. James's white face stared up at me from where he was sitting cross-legged. Opposite him, Hannibal maintained his Egyptian cat stance and between them stretched the small rug that represented the world of Bulzartgay.

"Hello, James," I said. "How on earth did you come to discover this place? And how did you get in? Simon said it had been locked since old . . . since your great-grandfather died."

"Hannibal and I were out one day and he jumped through a hole in the window and blind. So I got in after him and opened the door from inside. It wasn't hard." James sulky tone made it abundantly clear that he considered my presence an unwelcome interruption.

267

I sniffed the rather close atmosphere. "No wonder Hannibal came in here. I think he must have smelled mice."

"Yes," James said proudly. "He caught two and ate them. I watched him."

I winced a little. "Well, it's his nature, but I'm just as glad I wasn't around when he did." I glanced at James and said, half teasing, "I thought there was no hunting in Bulzartgay."

"There isn't, except for Hannibal. But he's the King. So he can do anything."

Something made me repeat, "And, of course, he's a cat, and cats hunt mice."

"I *told* you. It's because he's King."

All of a sudden I was swept with an unease I had felt before. I glanced over at the big cat, whose slanted green eyes seemed to glitter along with the sequins and glass fragments. There was, I thought, especially in this half-light, something both imperial and mysterious about Hannibal that reminded me strongly of the images of various Pharaohs I had seen in museums. It was not hard to understand how James could cross back and forth between his imaginary world, where Hannibal was King, and the real one that was so much less satisfying. But did James know when he had crossed that line? I found it important to repeat firmly, "It's Hannibal's nature, of course. He's a *cat*." I could hear myself, without having intended to, emphasizing the word. "And cats hunt mice."

"He's King," James said. "King of Bulzartgay. He *makes* the laws."

There was silence. "Aren't you going to go away?" James asked.

"You certainly don't do anything for my ego, James. I thought we were friends."

"I thought we were, too. But you don't understand about Hannibal."

"I love animals, too. But they *are* animals, James. We can ... can communicate with them. And I do believe we're all part of nature. But I don't think it's ... it's wise, either for you

268

or for Hannibal, to forget that he's a cat and you're a human. Because—"

But at that James scrambled to his feet. "This is Bulzartgay and Hannibal wants you to *leave*."

I don't know what I might have done at that moment, but as James and I were standing there, staring at each other, Hannibal himself took a hand. Getting up, he stretched his front and then his hind legs, yawned, showing an immense pink mouth, and made his stately way towards me across the map of Bulzartgay.

"See," I said, as Hannibal brushed against my leg purring loudly, and then turned and brushed it again. "He doesn't misunderstand me, do you, Hannibal?" Bending down, I scratched the big, wide head.

James didn't say anything, but the stubborn, angry look lifted a little from his mouth.

"Where did you find the candle?" I asked.

"It was in here."

"And you decided this was a good place to ... to celebrate Bulzartgay? By the way, where did you find the diary?"

"In the basement, when I was looking for the screens. It was in the drawer of a little table down there. Only the drawer was open, so I saw the diary. I didn't think anyone would mind. Anyway, when I read in it about the folly I suddenly remembered the motto—you know, the one you talked about at dinner: 'In my folly is my strength.' And this is a folly."

"A folly?" I remembered suddenly the words in the diary: "A *folie* ... a Trianon." "Oh, you mean where the diary reported Louis Egremont as saying his wife must have a *folie* or Trianon like Marie Antoinette."

"Not just that. It *is* a folly. That's what we call this kind of house in England. Lots of the great houses have them. You call it a gaz—gaz—"

"Gazebo," I finished. "And in England you call it a folly?"

"Yes. And I thought the treasure might be in here. And if we found it ... but it wasn't."

There should be a little light on this conversation I decided, and went over and unhooked the other closed louvers one by one, pushing them, squeaking and protesting, open. Since most of the windows were broken fresh air poured in along with the sun.

But with the late afternoon light, much of the magic went. Le Grand Louis's folly really was a tatty, tinselly little horror, just as Simon had described it. Dotted around were once white, now grimed, little straw tables, chairs and sofas, their upholstery rotting under years of dust. Four small chests and four cabinets were under the windows. On the floor, beneath James's carpet, were rag rugs.

"Whew!" I said, pulling my hands from the dirt-encrusted mirrored and sequined curtains that hung in the angles of the octagonal structure. Dust floated in the air.

As my eyes became more adjusted to the dim light I saw that hanging at eye level on all eight walls were miniature painted garden tools: spades, hoes, rakes, trowels, scythes, plus others I had no name for—all fashioned as though for children.

Fascinated, I reached up and touched a little hoe, disturbing a lacework of cobwebs. Under a generation's accumulation of dust, dirt and cobwebs, the hoe must have been a pretty toy, its metal handle painted blue, its business end made of steel.

The little implements somehow made vivid old Louis's purpose in creating this whole illusion. The folly was indeed, or was meant to be, a real little Trianon, everything miniature, everything stylized. Perhaps, when new, it wasn't so tacky. Perhaps the cheap-looking pink material and the now stained and cracked blue walls were delicate and once pretty, the toy tools, their paint new, their steel ends shining, appropriate and appealing. Now everything looked worse than silly. It looked decadent and corrupt.

"What's in those chests?" I asked, looking around.

James shrugged. "More tools and pots and gardening stuff."

"But no treasure?"

"No. I looked to see if there was a trapdoor under the rugs. But there wasn't any. The floor's solid. And there's no proper

270

ceiling. Just the roof."

I glanced up. James was right. There was nothing up there but the wood itself. I looked down again at the little boy. "What would you have done with the treasure if you'd found it? What would you have bought yourself?"

"I wouldn't have *bought* anything," James replied with great scorn. "At least, I'd have bought *first*-class tickets for Hannibal and me back to England. I learned that sometimes in first class, if there aren't too many people, they let you take your pet in the cabin. He'd have had a whole seat to himself."

"And you'd have gone back to England?"

"Yes. And with the rest of the money I'd have bought a cottage, and Hannibal and Walker and I would have lived there for ever and ever."

I couldn't prevent myself from saying, "Don't you want to be with your mother at all?"

"No. She doesn't like Hannibal and she doesn't like me, and I wish she was dead!"

"James!"

"Well, I do. She made me leave Walker and come over here and live in this horrible haunted house which Hannibal doesn't like and I don't either. It's *evil*. And if she was a proper mother she wouldn't want us to live here." And at that his formidable and unnatural dignity left him and he burst into tears.

"Oh, James," I said. Leaning over, I put my arms around him and pulled him to me. He was, after all, a bewildered, frightened little boy taken away from everything he knew that spelled security. "Your mother loves you and wants the best for you," I said, and realized as I said it that I was parroting a conventional piety. Mothers didn't always love their children. And Diana? Who knew what Diana thought or felt? Did I believe that she loved him and wanted what was best for him? Sometimes she did. I was sure of that. And other times? The trouble was, I could not make myself believe that she put James's greatest good above—well, alcohol, for one thing. Simon for another!

Still huddled against me and punctuated by hiccoughs,

271

James started to sing Bulzartgay's national anthem, very much, I felt, in the spirit of whistling in the dark, and the thin, light melody of "Here We Go round the Mulberry Bush" floated out of Louis's folly.

"Who's that?" a voice snapped from the doorway.

James jumped away from me. I peered into the stronger light outside where it poured over the shoulders of a large object. "Eric?" I said.

"Candida?" He came in. "What's going on?"

"Nothing much." I did not wish to give away James's Bulzartgay. "James and I were exploring."

"And Hannibal," James said, belligerence back in his tone. Belatedly, I remembered Eric's ailurophobia.

His eyes on Hannibal, who, paws curled in front, had assumed a sphynxlike pose on the floor, Eric said, "I see."

"We were looking for treasure," I said. Since both Hannibal and Bulzartgay were out of bounds as a topic of conversation, I felt I had to produce something.

"Why here?" Eric eased his tall figure into the house.

Feeling that James might consider it a betrayal, I tried to divert the conversation. "Simon was right when he called this ... this folly a tinselly horror, a sugarcake show. I'm sorry to say Louis showed up his nouveau riche bad taste."

"Every riche is nouveau at some time," Eric said evenly. "Even the noblest family began with brigandry—with the sword or the black flag in one era, with stocks and bonds and wheeling-dealing in another."

"Eric," I felt I had committed a gaffe. "Don't make me feel terrible! You're not nouveau riche!"

"Oh, yes, I am," Eric said, looking around. He gave me a tight smile. "As compared with the Egremonts or even the Grants."

"What nonsense!" There was an odd rigidity about Eric that made me uncomfortable. "Whoever gave you that idea?"

"Donnie, for one." He put a hand out and touched one of the filthy curtains. "Phew!" Dust flew out.

"Donnie? You mean Diana's nanny? The one that died? Who almost married your father?"

"That's right. She had a strong class sense. In front of strangers always she said, 'Miss Diana.' Simon was Master Simon. But I was plain Eric."

I looked at him and remembered suddenly my picture of the young man standing on the edge of the floor, looking like a child with his nose pressed to the window. "Did you mind?"

Eric glanced at me. "No." He laughed. "I just thought it was funny. Like something out of an old movie. What did you call this place?"

"Well, actually, it was James. He called it a folly. Apparently that's an English name for a gazebo."

"I see." He looked at James. "And were you looking for treasure because of the old motto, 'In my folly is my treasure'?"

"Yes," James said sulkily.

"I don't want to dishearten you, but I think the religious meaning is probably the right one—dull as that may sound."

"I know that now," James said.

"I'm sorry to disappoint you." Eric glanced down. "That's an interesting-looking rug. Was that here?"

"It's mine," James said, rolling it up. "Mine and Hannibal's." Defiantly, I thought, he started singing Bulzartgay's national anthem.

That tight look I had noticed on Eric's face returned. After a moment, as James's voice went on, he said a little sharply, "That's not my favorite tune."

James, slipping a piece of string around the rolled carpet, continued singing, his dark eyes on Eric.

I was curious. "Why don't you like it?" I asked. "What's wrong with 'Here We Go Round the Mulberry Bush'?"

Eric opened one of the chests. "It's probably foolish, but it has unpleasant childhood associations."

"Hannibal likes it," James said. "Don't you, Hannibal?" And he started up again.

"James, stop!" I said.

A little to my surprise, he did.

Eric moved towards the door. "It can't be healthy to be in here breathing all this dust and pollution. I'll walk you back to the house. By the way," he continued, as I went towards

273

the door hoping James would follow, "how's Diana?"

"She's much better. She's back, you know. Discharged herself from the hospital—to Simon's obvious disapproval—and walked in cool as you please when we were all there having drinks."

"Yes, Simon doesn't like things to slip out of his control. Who's we, by the way?"

"I forgot to tell you. Friends of mine from New York, Terry O'Connor and Mike Cominsky, came up to cover the protest on behalf of low- and middle-income integrated houses. They write for one of the East Village papers, and Diana, who sees them as allies, invited them to stay. It was really funny," I added, walking down the steps of the gazebo, "when they saw it was Diana's side they were on. She's not exactly their idea of a power-to-the-people symbol. Are you coming, James?"

"I don't think—" James started, when the matter was abruptly taken out of his hands by Hannibal. With his species' perverse fondness for those who don't like cats, Hannibal slipped between James's legs and, tail aloft, came padding rapidly down the steps of the gazebo and made for Eric, who was standing on the grass a few feet away. Instinctively, he stepped back. Undaunted, Hannibal followed, rubbed against Eric's trousered legs, then stood on his hind feet and put his front paws just above Eric's knees, sharpening his claws in the cloth for good measure.

"Hannibal," I said, and reached to remove him. But I wasn't fast enough. Automatically, in reflex action, Eric slapped him away.

Eyes blazing, James tore down the steps. "You beast! You hit Hannibal! How dare you! You should be killed! Walker says that people who are cruel to animals should be hung by the neck until they are *dead*. You—"

"That's enough!" I yelled over the noise. I grasped James by the shoulders. "Now that's enough," I repeated more quietly. "Hannibal's not hurt. And it's not Mr. Barrington's fault—"

"Yes, it is!" James twisted from me. "He's a horrible person!" And with a final tug of his shoulders the little boy lit out across the lawn in the direction Hannibal had taken.

"I'm sorry, Eric," I glanced at him. The tight, set look was now marked. "He . . . he's got some kind of imaginary kingdom in which Hannibal is King. He doesn't always . . . he is not always sure of the difference."

"So I gather." As Eric turned, the late afternoon sun hit his face and I saw how white he was.

"Eric!" I put my hand on his arm.

"It's okay." He covered my hand with his and looked down at me. "If you invited me in for a drink I wouldn't say no."

"Consider yourself invited." He started across the lawn. "By the way, did I tell you we'd found the diary?"

His hand closed over mine. "You did? Where?"

"James did. We were looking in the basement for screens to put in the upstairs windows for the safety of Hannibal and the other cats. Apparently James came across it while he was looking. I noticed him in one of the basement rooms surrounded by books, reading, but didn't think about the diary until I found it under his pillow."

"I see. And did it have anything about this sister Diana thinks she had?"

"No. Which is what makes the whole thing so strange."

"How so?"

"Well, Diana dreamed about it. . . ." I looked up and saw his skeptical expression. "Yes, I know you think it's a lot of nonsense. So did I until I found there was a diary. Because—I didn't tell you this—I dreamed about it, too."

"Not surprising or at all mysterious since you've been looking for it."

"No," I said doubtfully and a little deflated. "I suppose not."

"You were going to tell me what was so strange about the diary when it finally turned up."

"Just that Diana seemed to think that it would make everything clear, about her twin sister and so on, but there wasn't anything about that in the parts I read."

"Did you read through the whole thing?"

"No. I skimmed bits and missed others altogether. Heavy

helpings of Le Grand Louis were more than I could take."

"Yes. I gather he was quite overpowering."

"You didn't know him, did you? I mean, was he alive when you remember?"

"Barely. He was a very old man. My father was the one who knew him. I trust you put that wretched diary under lock and key, considering all the trouble you've taken. Particularly since you didn't finish reading it. I can't think of anything better to exorcize Diana's fixation on this sister than a diary proving that none existed."

I was about to explain that the diary was for the year 1912, many, many years before Diana was born, with or without twin sister, when the word *exorcise* jumped out at me. "Did you know that Diana's been trying to make Simon conduct an exorcism ceremony to get rid of this ghost?"

"Good heavens. How did you find that out?"

I opened the gate in the garden wall and stepped out onto the carriage sweep. "Simon said so. And, as a matter of fact, Diana herself told me when I first got here."

Eric stepped through the gate and closed it after him.

"That's dangerous stuff, Candida. And I'm not just talking about popular movie versions. I've known houses to catch fire when people fooled around with that."

"That's funny. I thought you didn't believe in it?"

"Basically, I don't. But I'm willing to admit that there are more things in heaven and earth than are dreamed of in my philosophy. And I wouldn't want anyone I cared about mixed up in it."

I smiled at him. "Such as Diana."

"Or you."

"Come on now, Eric. Let's not play games."

"As I told you once before, you don't give yourself enough credit for attractiveness." His hand touched me as we walked through the front door of the house. It was nice to be liked, I thought, and balm for the ego, but I found myself moving away from his hand.

"Now for the drink," I started, and looked up to see James, Hannibal over his shoulder, going up the stairs. The green

276

eyes, peering over James's narrow shoulder, regarded us unwinkingly. Then after a moment, slowly, as though taking thought, Hannibal spat.

"Hannibal!" I said. "I thought you were a gentleman."

James turned and saw us. He seemed on the verge of speaking, but to my relief turned back and continued on his way up.

"There's nothing like popularity to make a man feel loved and wanted," Eric said dryly, as we turned into the study.

"Never mind, Eric." I put some glasses out on the bar and opened the ice bucket. "Diana's handling of James isn't . . . well, she isn't used to kids. But she's absolutely right about one thing. James is alone far too much and always has been, which is why these . . . these fancies about imaginary countries are so real to him. He needs to be with children his own age. I think I'll go get some ice. I realize if I rang the bell Mrs. Klaveness would come in. . . ." My voice trailed off as I picked the bucket up from the bar.

"You have to be born to bells to be able to use them with ease and conviction," Eric said, the bitter note back in his voice.

"I suppose so. But their day is on the way out."

As though trying to make up for his tone, Eric smiled. "You are a revolutionary, aren't you?"

"Not really. In fact, not at all. I'm a real member of what my friend Terry would call, *not* admiringly, the upwardly aspiring bourgeoisie. My objection to ringing for Mrs. Klaveness is not on principle. If there were twenty servants here I don't think I'd hesitate. It's for practical reasons. I think taking care of this house as well as cooking is more than enough for any one woman, however Nordic and muscular. I'll be right back."

It was while I was busy extracting ice cubes from the rather ancient refrigerator that I heard the telephone ring. Since I thought Diana should not be disturbed I moved towards the wall extension in the kitchen. But the phone was picked up somewhere before I could reach it. Perhaps, I thought, Mrs. Klaveness, with the same motive, had answered it. But then I knew she hadn't, because at that moment the housekeeper appeared in the doorway leading to the back hall, a newspaper containing some earthy-looking vegetables in her hand.

"You didn't answer the phone just now, did you, Mrs. Klaveness?"

"No. I have some vegetables picked from the garden."

"Do you grow your own here? How marvelous!"

"*Ach*. It is nothing. A few small vegetables. In Germany, I grew all my own, and put them up, preserved them myself for the winter." She laid her improvised basket down on the kitchen table, and said, "You wish something?"

"Just getting some ice."

I was about to leave when she asked, "There will be how many to dinner?"

I stopped. "Well, my two friends, James and myself. Maybe Dr. Grant. And I was thinking of inviting Mr. Barrington, if it wouldn't be too many to cook for?"

"I make a casserole. A few more does not make much." She looked at me, her little eyes level, and, I thought, sad. "And Miss Egremont?"

"I don't know. Probably not. She should certainly stay in bed."

Mrs. Klaveness started breaking the ends off some string beans. "I fear for her," she said.

"Why? What do you mean?"

When the housekeeper didn't answer I repeated, "What do you mean, Mrs. Klaveness?"

"I do not know. I am not sure. But I feel it here—" and she put her hand on her considerable bosom.

"You feel what?"

"I do not know. If I knew I would tell you. But I feel that, soon, she . . . that she . . . that she will die."

I could get nothing further from the housekeeper, and went back to the study. "And that's all she would say," I finished up telling Eric. And I've arrived at the point where, whether I believe it or not, *I'm scared*."

"You have reason to be," Eric said, gently rolling his liquor around in his glass.

"Et tu Brute? Where's that skeptical common sense that I was depending on to laugh me out of this?"

"I may be skeptical about the spook aspect of this, but I do believe in human intuition, and I think it's more than likely that Diana is in some danger."

"But if it's not her spooky sister, then from whom?"

"If I told you—oh, hello, Diana. I'm glad to see you up. How are you feeling?"

"All right," Diana said briefly, moving towards the bar. She had on a long graceful robe that should have set off her willowy good looks. Perhaps, I thought, it was the color, a deep blue, that made her look so white. More likely, it was because she was far from well. Her face was not only white, it was haggard.

"Diana," I said, "are you sure you should be up? You look awfully . . . tired," I finished.

"Yes. I know I look terrible." To my consternation, she took out a large, wide glass and, without even bothering with ice cubes, poured two or three inches of vodka into it.

"You should be back in the hospital," Eric said. "I don't think this house is healthy for you or anyone else."

Diana took a large swallow of her drink. "That's something of a turn around for you, isn't it? I thought you scoffed at all that."

"Since Candida found the diary, I've become less of a scoffer." As Diana stared at him, he added. "She told me about your interest in it."

Diana lowered her glass and turned to me. "When did you find the diary? Why didn't you tell me about it?"

"First of all, Diana, I didn't find it. James did. And I only discovered it a couple of hours ago. I was going to tell you as soon as I woke up."

"Did you read it?" Diana's anxiety could be felt from across the room.

"Yes. Or at least most of it. There wasn't anything at all about a twin sister of yours in there. It was mostly about your grandfather. The only thing about a child," I said, wondering how Diana would receive this news, "was about the grand-

279

daughter of the Timberlake who originally owned this land. Your grandmother seemed to think that she might have been ... that her death might have been engineered."

"By my grandfather? What utter nonsense. That's an old story that's been going about for years, put out by the Timberlakes, no doubt. Donnie used to call it the family curse. You know, Candida, considering how I felt about that diary, I think you should have brought it to me. Where is it now?"

I tried to remember that with Diana arrogance meant she was feeling defensive. "I put it back where I found it, under James's pillow."

Diana looked at me, put down her drink and walked to the door.

"James," she called.

There was no answer.

"James!"

Whether or not James heard, I was reasonably sure he wouldn't answer. "I'll go up and get him," I said.

"That won't be necessary." Going to the chimneypiece, Diana rang the bell.

We waited in silence for a few minutes until Mrs. Klaveness appeared, bearing more ice.

"Please go upstairs, Mrs. Klaveness, and ask James to come down, bringing the diary with him."

There was a tiny pause. Given the hour, Mrs. Klaveness was fairly certain to be in the middle of preparing dinner. A spurt of anger went through me.

"Diana—" I started, about to say again I'd go up.

But I was stopped by a tiny shake of Mrs. Klaveness's head.

"Yes, Mrs. Egremont," the housekeeper said, and disappeared out the door.

Diana turned towards me. "You spoke?"

I could see why Mrs. Klaveness had stopped me. Diana's eyes were bright, her cheeks flushed. She looked better than she had when she came downstairs a few minutes before. But by now I knew the signs. And out of the corner of my eye I could see her glass was empty.

"Nothing," I said, and added lamely, "sorry about the

diary. But I didn't want to wake you."

Diana made a gesture with her glass. "Well, the phone did that."

"Oh—you answered it."

"Of course. It's right by my bed." She hesitated. "It seems that Ms. Timberlake is about to make another and larger offer. Whatever other house she had in mind for the school has fallen through. Back to square one. This should get the proschool protesters all het up again. Which makes the whole thing even jollier for me."

"Why?" I asked.

"Because with her out of the picture, I had a much stronger case for selling to the building outfit. Everybody knows, at least theoretically, that I'm broke. But with Ms. Timberlake back with a large offer—although not as large as the building company's—I'll look even more of a pig if I take the construction company offer."

"I wonder how much Simon had to do with that?" Eric said.

"What do you mean?" Diana and I asked together.

"Just that I saw him talking to Ms. Timberlake not an hour ago down in the village."

"Come on, Eric," Diana said. Walking over to the bar, she filled her glass again and took a swallow. Then she smiled up at him. "Isn't that just plain old jealousy?"

Eric flushed. "Granted. But you also have to admit that he doesn't approve of your selling to the building outfit, does he? His father was physician to that school at one time and he probably has pull with Catherine Timberlake."

There was, I couldn't help feeling, a certain plausibility to it. Simon made no secret of the fact that he opposed the sale of Tower Abbey to the building company. If he could exert a little influence, a little power . . ."

"Do you know if Simon is coming back, Candida?" Diana asked.

"No, I don't. Why?"

"Because I want him to get on with what I've been asking him to do."

"An exorcism?"

She raised her eyes from the glasses she'd almost emptied. "Yes." She looked at Eric. "You don't approve, do you?"

"As I've said again and again, I don't believe in playing with the supernatural."

"Well, I don't feel I've a lot of choice," Diana said. And this time the desperate note in her voice was clear. "I feel that there is some . . . some evil here, and I can't leave or sell the place until it's gone, until I know what I've done."

"What do you mean, what you've done?" I asked. "Why on earth should you feel it's something you've done?"

"I don't know, Candida, I don't know." Her hand shook as she put her drink down on the bar. The flush was gone. Curiously, she seemed sober. "I had a nap and I dreamed about Donnie. She was standing there in the hall with her bags, in her hat and coat, in front of the elevator, looking at me in this terribly sad and accusing way, and I woke up crying. I felt that I had killed her."

"What utter nonsense, Diana. You know how she died. You were abroad, you told me. And anyway, what has this to do with the twin sister you thought you had?"

"I don't know, I don't know. But it has. And I am afraid, afraid for James." She was looking over my shoulder as she spoke and I saw her face change. "James," she said again.

I turned. James was standing in the door. "I couldn't bring the diary," he said. "It's not there."

"James, darling," Diana said. "What do you mean it's not there?" Her tired, drawn face was wet with tears. For the first time I heard in her voice the affection and reaching out that should have been there from the time James arrived. I held my breath. Perhaps the bridge between mother and son could be built after all.

"Still in an imaginary world, James?" Eric said gently.

He meant, perhaps, to be helpful, but his words broke the fragile, tenuous bond. "No, I'm not," James said. "I left it under the pillow but it's not there now. You can go up and look if you like. But if you do I'll take Hannibal into another room where he'll be safe."

282

"What's all this about?" Diana asked. She glanced at Eric. "What did you do to his cat?"

"The shoe's on the other foot, or rather paw," he said. "He tried to sharpen his claws on my leg, and without thinking, I pushed him away."

"You hit him," James said. "Jolly hard."

"I don't think I hurt him, James. And I'm sorry, but it was reflex action."

"Where did all this happen?" Diana asked.

"In the folly," Eric said. "James told us about the English meaning of the word, as in gazebo. He was out there to see if old Louis had buried his treasure out there, because of the family motto."

"Oh." Diana paused. "Wouldn't it be funny if he had. In my folly is my treasure. Funny—it would be marvelous, if true!" She looked smilingly over at James. "Did you find anything?"

"No. There's nothing really much there. Just a lot of dust."

"But it's always been locked. How did you get in?"

"Hannibal got in, actually. Through one of the open shutters. So I got in after him and it was easy to open the door."

"I must go out and look at it."

"Haven't you ever been in it before?" Eric asked.

Diana sat down rather suddenly in the chair. Her face was again white. "No. At least not since I was a child."

"I'm surprised your father didn't make some kind of little pavilion out of it for entertaining," Eric said. He glanced at me, and I realized he was waiting for me to sit down so he could also. I sat down on the window seat and he lowered himself into the other armchair.

"I think there was something about it in my grandfather's will." Diana said. "He wanted it kept as it was in memory of his wife. Something like that. Anyway, it was locked and in those days the shutters were firmly closed. So, without the key—and I still don't know where that is—that was that."

After a minute or so I became aware that James, who was loitering around the other end of the room, was humming the national anthem of Bulzartgay. Without thinking about it, I glanced at Eric. His face had tightened, as though a drawstring had been pulled. Diana put her head back against the back of her wing chair. "That was Donnie's favorite song, wasn't it, Eric? Remember? She used to make us play it all the time, mostly, I realized later, to keep us moving and get us so tired we wouln't get into so much mischief. Do you remember the time—"

"I don't think Eric is crazy about it," I said, trying to help Eric out. "Unlike you, Diana, he has unpleasant childhood associations with it."

Diana raised her head. "Oh? What would they be? I thought Donnie, with her Irish Catholic foundling home upbringing, was the only one old-fashioned enough to produce all the old nursery rhymes, as she was always doing. I wonder why she's on my mind so much. That was a depressing dream." Suddenly Diana got up. "That was all thirty years ago, or nearly. I thought I was over it." Going over to the bar, Diana poured herself some more vodka. "You know, when I was a child, after I was getting over that awful illness I had when we came back from Europe, I used to think I could hear her singing at night. That same tune." She looked at James. "Here We Go Round the Mulberry Bush." She turned to James. "Why were you humming that?"

James, looking both scared and sulky, didn't say anything.

"Well?" Diana said.

"All children sing it, Diana," I said. "There's nothing unusual about it."

"Yes, there is. I know there is. James is just doing it to defy me, aren't you?"

It was like watching someone you know and care for—because despite everything, I did care for Diana—go mad while you're watching. One second Diana was reaching out towards her son with love and warmth, and the next she was turning into another creature. "How dare you? You know how I feel about that tune. It's all tied up with Donnie and my sister and the diary. The diary you have and are lying to me about. Aren't you?" And, still holding her drink, she started walking towards James. Terrified, he started to back.

284

"Don't you walk backwards when I'm trying to talk to you," she said.

Unfortunately for James, he had left the vicinity of the door and was now cornered. Backing, he reached the wall.

"Now," Diana said.

Without forethought, I ran across the room and stood in front of her with James behind me. "Diana," I said, "James isn't defying you. Truly." I knew I would be betraying his confidence, but it seemed, at that moment, the lesser of two evils. "James has ... has an imaginary kingdom with a national anthem and everything, and it sounds just like 'Here We Go Round the Mulberry Bush.' He's told me all about it. It's all right. There's no reason to be angry." All the while I was talking I was thinking that her eyes were strange, wild, like those of some other creature. And my skin seemed to crawl over my flesh.

"So you're in it, too," Diana said.

"There's nothing to be in, Diana. I think you're tired and worn out from the hospital and ought to be in bed."

"Not until I've dealt with James."

"James hasn't done anything wrong," I said. "There's nothing to be so upset about—" My head went back as the liquor from her glass splashed over my face. I don't know what would have happened then if Simon hadn't walked in.

"Simon," I said, "help me tell Diana that James hasn't done anything wrong, because he really hasn't. I don't know what's gone wrong with her."

It was funny and it was a nightmare, the little boy and me crowded into a corner with this fury standing in front.

"Diana!" Simon said. And quite suddenly I knew what Eric must have meant when he talked about power. "Diana!"

Slowly, she turned and looked at him. Then she looked down at the glass in her hand, and back up again to my face, which I was trying to wipe off. Then she burst into tears.

Simon went over and put his arm around her shoulders. "I'm taking you back to the hospital."

But there his power over her failed. She refused flatly to go. "I won't go," she said, crying. "I won't. I have to stay. I have to find out. I have to protect James."

It was pointless and even unkind to point out that she herself seemed to provide the greatest threat to her son. Finally, Simon and I got her upstairs and helped her to bed.

"Are you going to give her a shot?" I asked quietly.

Simon shook his head. "I don't have my bag with me." He looked down at Diana. "Do you think you can sleep?"

She stared up at us. "Yes, I think so." She closed her eyes. Then she opened them. "I'm so tired," she said. "So terribly tired."

Simon bent over her again, taking her hand in his. "Diana, once more, let me take you to the hospital."

Wearily she shook her head. "I can't."

When we got outside Simon said to me, "She had a fair amount to drink, didn't she?"

"Yes. Although she didn't appear that drunk. At least not all the time."

"It should help her sleep anyway."

We were about to start down the stairs when I suddenly remembered the diary. "I'm going to James's room to take another look for that diary. James may have missed it."

"You mean you found it."

"And lost it again." I explained about James finding it and about my discovering him in the folly.

"Folly?"

"It's what the English call a gazebo, and he remembered the motto, 'In my folly,' etcetera."

"Well, I'll be damned!"

"And then Eric came along and there was an . . . an incident with Hannibal." I told him about that. "Then back here, when Diana learned that we'd found the diary, she sent Mrs. Klaveness up to tell James to bring it down. But when he got down he said it was gone. Then he started singing that wretched song again, the one that Eric dislikes and that seems to be associated with Donnie."

"What song?"

"Oh, it's a song James made up to the tune of 'Here We Go

Round the Mulberry Bush.' Anyway, that's what started her off again, which is why I want to look for the diary myself. It could have slipped behind or under the bed, and I'm not sure that James would be that eager to locate it for his mother."

"Probably not," Simon said. "I'll come with you."

As we opened the door to James's room, a large heap in the middle of the bed separated into its component parts and became Pandora, Susan and Seth. Hannibal, by himself at the foot of the bed, raised his head and watched us, but stayed where he was. Over in their cages the gerbils scampered round among their cedar chips.

Simon sniffed. "No offense, Candida. But it does smell a little like a zoo in here."

"So what's wrong with a zoo? I can think of a lot worse smells."

"Come to think of it, so can I." He lifted the pillows and looked in, around, under and behind the bed. We then searched the rest of the room, but there was no sign of the diary.

"When was the last time you saw it?" Simon said finally, emerging after a search along the baseboard of the wall behind the bed.

"This afternoon, before I went out and found James and Hannibal in the folly."

"So theoretically it could have been stolen any time since then."

"Yes, but unless James told someone he'd put it there—but who would he tell?"

"Possibly Mrs. Klaveness, though I doubt it. Did she know about the diary?"

"Yes, I remember talking to her about it."

"Did you tell anyone?"

"Just Eric."

"Would he have had a chance to take it?"

"I don't see how. Well, I left him to get some ice, so I suppose he could have nipped upstairs and gotten it, except—no, I remember now, he couldn't have, because James was already up there. Anyway, why would he want it?"

"He might have his reasons."

"Between the two of you, you make me feel like the rope in a tug of war."

Simon walked over and touched the light switch. "There," he said. "I can see your face better." Until the light blazed I hadn't realized how overcast the long summer evening had become, although I was increasingly aware of the heaviness of the atmosphere, usually the prelude to a storm.

"I remember now," Simon went on, looking at my face, "you were telling me this morning that Eric thinks I'm on some power trip."

"He thinks you're trying to play God with Diana. And that she'd be much better off going to a proper sanatorium, after which he would marry her, take her around the world on a honeymoon, and in the meantime renovate this place."

"Neat," Simon said. "And what's in it all for me—other than power?"

"He thinks you're in love with her."

Simon didn't say anything.

"So do I," I said, "although for a brief while last night I forgot it." Angrily I turned to go down the hall. As I walked ahead of him, something in me hoped, against common sense and what I knew, that he would contradict what I had said. But he didn't.

When we got downstairs we found Terry and Mike had arrived and were in the study with Eric and James.

"I take it you've all introduced yourselves," I said.

"We have," Eric replied. "How is Diana?"

Simon went over to the bar and poured himself a drink.

"She's resting." He took a swallow and strolled from behind the bar. "How's the protest going?" he asked Terry.

"Protest?" Eric asked.

Simon looked at him. "That's right. Terry and Mike are your allies—yours and Diana's. I gather from Diana that you've put your seal of approval on the contracting company that wants to buy the house."

"They seem a reputable outfit and Diana needs the money."

288

"Why don't you marry her and take her away from it all? If she's married to you she won't need the money."

"I should think you, above all people, would know the answer to that."

"You mean that, contrary to popular belief, you don't have any money left?"

"No, I don't mean that."

"You mean then you've proposed and she's turned you down?"

Eric hesitated, which surprised me. Then he said, "Not once, but many times." He put his own glass down and looked at Mike and Terry. "I did hear something about sides forming up in the village. I'm delighted to hear you're with Diana and me."

"We're for putting low- and middle-income integrated houses into this white preserve," Mike said, repeating his formula.

"Well, I think the matter is academic now," Simon said. "Diana's going to accept Catherine Timberlake's offer. They're going to sign the papers tomorrow."

"How do you know?" I asked. "You weren't even here when Diana got that phone call from Miss Timberlake."

"I told you," Eric said. "I saw him talking to Catherine Timberlake this afternoon. He's been pulling the strings behind it from the beginning."

"Yes, but that was before the call here. How could Simon possibly know that the sale had been settled? Diana didn't say so. In fact, she strongly implied that she was still just considering it."

"That could also be part of the agreement," Eric said. Vaguely, I noticed that his rigid expression was back. "No announcements until the thing is signed, sealed and settled. But the thing was agreed on, and Catherine told Simon before he got here. Isn't that right, Simon, old boy?"

"You seem to have the rudiments of the plot," Simon said agreeably.

"Well, of all the double-dealing," Terry sounded furious.

But there was something that bothered me. "If you've been

289

stage-managing the sale to the school, why did you ask Eric if he'd proposed to Diana? I don't see what that has—"

But I never completed that sentence. From upstairs there was a terrified scream.

15

For a half a second we all froze. Then Diana's voice screamed again and we were pounding up the stairs. Simon reached her door first and thrust it open, plunging in. Eric and I were barely behind.

I couldn't at first see Diana. Then I saw Simon, who was on the other side of her bed, bend down. "My God!" He said.

By the time I got to the far side of the room, Simon was kneeling over Diana, who was on the floor. As I watched, he felt her wrist, called her name and shook her. When she didn't respond, he put his head down to see if she was breathing. Evidently she was not, because he knelt across her and with his fist gave a sharp blow to her chest. Then he put his mouth over hers. Seeing her bluish face, I was afraid it was too late. But after what seemed a long time, I saw her chest rise and heard her take in a breath.

"Candida," Simon said in a voice I hardly recognized, "call the hospital immediately and have them send an ambulance."

"Do you think—?" Eric started.

"At once!" Simon's eyes and voice were icy.

Going to the other side of the bed, I picked up the phone, got the hospital and told them to send an ambulance. "They said it would be here in ten minutes," I reported, hanging up.

Simon had lifted her onto the bed and wrapped her in a blanket. Just as the receiver went back on the phone, I saw her blond head move.

"Simon," she said.

"I'm here." He bent over her. "Don't try to talk."

But her eyes had opened. "Simon, I saw her. She was standing there, at the door. I know you don't believe me. But she was there. She was there. I swear it. And she was coming after me. I know..."

I saw Diana's hands come out from under the blanket. "Simon—"

He leaned over her. "Now listen. The ambulance is coming. You're going back to the hospital. And there'll be no signing yourself out this time."

"No. I won't go. Simon, I won't go. If I go she'll get James."

"No, she won't get James—"

"I won't go!" Her voice, weak and a bit thready, gained strength. She tried to sit up. "You can't make me, Simon."

They stared at each other. "You know you can't," she repeated. There was a silence.

"Is there anything that will make you consent to go?" Simon said.

"Yes." She sat up, the blanket drawn around her nightgown, her face without color and drawn. She looked older by a decade or more than I had ever seen her. Suddenly the thought came to me: Mrs. Klaveness was right. Diana's going to die. And she knows it. I pushed the thought away immediately as absurd. But a residue remained, a sick, frightened feeling, as though I who had always lived in and taken for granted one plane of consciousness had been touched by another.

"Yes," she said. "There is." I could see her body shaking, but her voice was steady. "You're a priest as well as a doctor. I want you to put on your vestments and go through this house room by room, banishing... banishing the evil that's here. I know you think I'm crazy. But it doesn't matter. It's here. I

292

know it's here. I want you to tell . . . whatever it is . . . to be gone, to go and leave us alone."

Simon said, "Diana . . . I'd rather . . . you don't understand."

"You're wrong. I do understand." She was shaking more than before. But her voice was strong, and her eyes were firmly on Simon, who looked lost, unsure and embarrassed. Diana went on, "You think you've lost your faith. Well, it doesn't matter whether you have or haven't. I won't leave unless you promise you'll do this for me. Tonight."

Once again I heard at a distance the sound of a siren, and could picture the ambulance belting up the narrow winding road, past the fork, past the farmhouse that once belonged to the Timberlakes, past Halfway House. . . .

"Promise me," she said. Her eyes were fixed on Simon. "You may have lost all your belief, but if you give your word, you'll keep it. I know that. Promise me. I won't go unless you promise me you'll do that tonight."

The siren was now wailing up the last stretch and with a sudden crescendo of sound came through the gate and around the drive.

"Well?" Diana said, her voice again breathy. "Promise. Otherwise I'll send them away."

"All right," Simon said. He sounded tired and defeated. "I promise. I'll take you to the hospital. Then I'll come back and do as you ask."

Leaving Eric to see Diana and Simon off in the ambulance, I returned to the study.

"Look," Mike said, as I walked in, "maybe Terry and I ought to go and find some other place."

But I didn't want them to leave. "No, stay. I need you. I don't want to be here alone. There are plenty of rooms upstairs where you can find beds." Then, as Mike, plainly ill at ease, walked around and around the carpet, I said, "What's bothering you?"

"I'm not sure. I think it's this house. I mean, this place is *spooked*."

293

I stood there, rooted to the floor with astonishment. Of all the people in the world, the least likely to have said what he just said was Mike Cominsky—hip, with-it Mike.

"You mean," I said slowly, "you think this place is haunted."

"For cryin' out loud," Terry said. "Don't you? My goosebumps haven't stopped going up since we arrived this evening."

I stared at them. "You didn't feel it earlier this afternoon?"

"Maybe we didn't stay long enough. Maybe we were so busy trying to get a bed for the night we didn't stop to get the feel of the place. But the moment I walked in tonight I started to —and Mike feels the same. You mean to say you don't feel it? What about Mrs. Egremont and whatever it was she saw?"

"I thought . . . I guess I thought it was just in her mind, from too many pills and too much liquor. She has a drinking problem."

"Well, I don't," Mike said. "And I haven't smoked any grass for a month. But this place has really bad vibes."

Eric said, "He's right, Candy. It does. It's a good place not to be in."

It was like seeing my last support sink below the surface. "Eric, I was counting on you for solid, practical, down-to-earch sense. I thought you agreed with me a while back that what was in Diana's head was a combination of too much booze and pills, some early unpleasant memories that have sunk beneath the surface, and assorted fears."

"Maybe my faith in the materialistic, psychological approach was shaken when you said you found the diary. I put that down as all in her head, only it turned out not to be."

"By the way, where's James?" I asked, suddenly aware that he was missing.

"I meant to tell you," Terry replied. "He said to say that he'd been invited to bring Hannibal, his cat, to Halfway House for dinner. It was when you and Mr. Grant and Mr. Barrington were upstairs with Mrs. Egremont. Should I have told him to wait until you got back? I didn't blame the kid for wanting to leave."

"No. It's all right. I don't blame him either. I suppose he went up and got Hannibal when we were in the bedroom. But I think I'll call down there and make sure he's arrived."

"You don't have to," Eric said. "After the ambulance left I noticed them walking down the road and watched until they turned into Halfway House. Like Terry, I thought it was a good idea for him to be out of here for a while, but I wanted to be sure that he wasn't decamping permanently." He smiled at me. "Rest easy."

"Thanks, Eric." I smiled back. After having to contend so much with so many unknowns about Simon it was a relief to deal with someone less shadowed and hidden.

Mrs. Klaveness's heavy tread sounded and she appeared in the doorway. "Dinner is served," she said dourly.

Understandably, it was not the most cheerful of meals. Having, apparently, publicly admitted that he was no longer quite as certain that the psychological and materialist approach could explain everything that had happened, Eric bent his efforts towards persuading us all to leave. "I have no explanations for what's going on," he said. "But whatever it is, this is not a good house to be in."

"Having flip-flopped over," I replied, a little crossly, "you're now taking a far more extreme tack than Simon, who's always conceded the possibility of psychic phenomena, but doesn't seem to be bent on driving everyone out."

"Simon may have other fish to fry," Eric said shortly.

Mike, Terry and I all looked up at once.

"Meaning?" I said.

"Still in love with him, Candy?" Eric said softly.

"Of course not," I snapped.

"Were you?" Terry asked. "Is that why you never seemed interested in anybody else?"

"No."

"He's a dangerous man to have a *tendre* for, Candy," Eric said.

Don't I know it, I thought. Nevertheless I said, "What makes you say that?"

"After that humiliating experience he subjected you to, all those years ago at Diana's wedding party, I wonder you can ask."

Those tearing hands, I thought, *the hands that were so gentle last night—or rather this morning.*

"Perhaps with the shock," Eric went on, "not to mention that lethal punch, you don't remember. Do you?"

As always, my tendency was to flee the subject as fast as I could. In fact, I sometimes wondered if my inability to remember exactly what happened sprang as much from the fact that I didn't want to remember as from the fact that I had been, that fatal evening and thanks to the royally spiked punch, in and out of an alcoholic blackout. Yet now some feeling other than fear and horror stirred within me. I looked at Eric.

"What do you mean, exactly, about what happened to me?"

"I mean that Simon, seeing you were drunk, took you off the dance floor and out to the garden. Maybe at that moment his motives were of the best. You were certainly sick. That was more than evident when I got worried and followed you out. It's also entirely possible that once your head and stomach quietened, and given your giant crush on him—which by the way he could be very funny about—you came on strong. Sexually strong, I mean. And Simon was not a man to turn that down. Whatever it was . . . I only know that when I got worried and went out to look for you, you were fighting like a tiger to get him off you, but it was like a kitten trying to fend off a tomcat. Unfortunately, it was obvious that I arrived—er—after the fact. But you were still struggling, so I tried to pull him off you and he turned on me, and the next thing I knew the two of us were on top of you, fighting tooth and claw. It was all highly uncivilized. But I felt desperately sorry at what had happened to you, and even granted Simon was drunk himself, there was no excuse for what he did. Just as well you don't remember. Though if you did, you could exorcise that particular devil." His dark eyes were on me, compelling, as though forcing me to rid myself of this burden I'd carried around for so long.

"You mean he raped her?" Mike had small patience with euphemisms.

"So that's it," Terry said. "That's why you've always been so anti-sex."

I could feel myself blushing. Eric smiled at me. "Are you, Candy? If so, it's a pity, but understandable." He glanced at Mike. "Rape is a strong word. As I said before, between the liquor and the childish passion she's always had for him, Candy probably led him on—quite innocently, I mean. But he didn't get his reputation as the local playboy for nothing, and he, too, was drunk. So I suppose, technically—and legally—it may not have been rape."

"What do you mean, legally?" Terry said. She looked at me. "How old were you?"

"Sixteen," I said. But her question only hit the outer part of my mind. Inside, something was bothering me. I should, I told myself, have felt additional tongues of anger at Simon, but I should also have felt relieved, because the mystery was cleared up. Instead, something was battering at some door in my mind, something that was disturbing me very much. But I couldn't think what it was . . .

"Sixteen!" Terry almost shouted, successfully routing whatever it was that had been hammering at my attention, "then no matter how much you led him on—if you did—that's statutory rape!"

"Yeah, it was," Mike said. He glanced over to Eric. "You don't like Grant either, do you?"

Eric shrugged. "As I've told Candy, I've known Simon Grant all my life. We were boys together. I'm old enough for that to mean something. But there are . . . things . . . which I don't like about him. Look," he said suddenly, "we can discuss this at length some other time. But this house is trouble. It's always been trouble. Simon will be back here to carry out whatever esoteric ceremony Diana made him promise to perform. I can't help feeling that the three of you would be better off somewhere else. You can stay with me. You can go to the local inn or motel—"

"Why?" Mike asked. "What do you think's going to happen?"

"I don't know. But Simon's more deeply connected with the sale of this land than anyone knows. I don't know what kind of deal he has going with Catherine Timberlake, but I find the fact that her offer to Diana came after he'd talked to her this afternoon, plus the fact that he knew Diana had accepted, pretty fishy."

So did I, I thought, as my feeling for Simon collided with and argued against that, added to what Eric had just told me about Simon's role in the nightmare episode of a decade past. How could I possibly love him? With one hand I rubbed my head, wondering if this was the way people felt just before they went mad.

"Well, what do you suggest—?" I started, when there was a sound at the door and Simon walked in. He was, I noticed, carrying a suitcase. His face seemed to be a mask of lines and shadows. His first words struck us all dumb.

"I think, Candida, your friends may want to spend the night in the village. They can go to the inn or the motel."

"Why?" Mike asked.

"Because I don't know what will happen to the house tonight."

"Meaning what?" Eric said. He had risen from his chair at the table and was standing, his hands hanging loosely.

"I mean I'm about to carry out my promise to Diana."

"That nonsense about exorcizing the ghosts?"

"Yes. Only it isn't nonsense. Far from it."

"You're the expert in the field. You should know."

"I don't claim to *know*. But whether you call them evil spirits or psychic phenomena or disturbances, I believe they exist and can make a place uninhabitable and dangerous. And I have finally come to believe that that's what happened to this house. Fortunately, as I told you, I've already talked to the bishop about this. I spoke to him again on the phone from the hospital and he has given me permission to carry out the rite of exorcism. I wish very much . . . but a promise is a promise."

298

"You wish what?" I asked.

"I wish I had more time. The exorcist—in this case I— should be better prepared."

"How?"

"By prayer and fasting."

"Somehow," I said, "prayer and fasting doesn't sound like my image of you."

"Which image?" he said dryly. "Your view of me seems to change from hour to hour."

"Any image. Fasting and prayer makes me think of a . . . a holy man of some kind."

"I thought it was against your principles to believe in that kind of thing."

There was, suddenly, in my head, a sense of chaos. I had always known what I believed. Now I didn't know. It was curious and unpleasant, almost as though I were dizzy. I glanced up and saw his eyes on me. "Well, whatever I believe or don't believe, I find it hard to associate any kind of a . . . a holy man with you."

A half smile touched one side of his mouth. "It doesn't sound at all like me, does it?"

"No. It doesn't. Do you believe in . . . in this exorcism?"

"Yes. But if, among those with the priest performing the exorcism, there is anyone who is not absolutely serious about it, then the whole thing—at the very least—will disintegrate."

"That leaves me out," Eric said. "I wouldn't want to spoil your little show."

"And you?" Simon asked, turning to Mike and Terry. "I still think you ought to go to the inn."

"Well . . ." Mike said.

"I don't think this is our scene," Terry said.

"I'm going to stay," Mike said suddenly.

Terry stared at him. "Yeah, but if you don't believe—?"

"Who said I don't? And besides, he didn't say you had to believe. He said you had to be serious. And I am."

"Even if not about that," Simon said dryly.

"I'm staying," Mike said stubbornly. "You can't stop me."

"No." Simon sounded weary. "I can't stop you."

299

"Then I'll bid you farewell," Eric said, "while you have your fun and games." He paused at the door. "What about Mrs. Klaveness? Is she going to be included in this ceremony?"

"Yes," Simon said. He had taken off his sweater and was buttoning on the cassock. The long black garment made him look even taller than he was. "Mrs. Klaveness is invited to join," he said. And then, his hand on a button, he paused.

A long look seemed to pass between the two men, and my mind, which was playing strange tricks on me, suddenly produced a drawing I had seen once in an encyclopedia of two fencers, foils raised, saluting one another before a duel. Then Eric was gone and Simon went on buttoning his cassock.

"I wonder if he'll find it," he said.

"Find what?" I asked.

"The treasure."

"What treasure?"

"The one in what you—or James—call the folly."

"You mean you think there *is* one hidden there?"

"I'm almost certain. That's just what that sly old fox, Louis Egremont, would delight to do."

"But there *isn't*," I said. "We looked everywhere."

"It's there."

"Well, if you're so sure, why aren't we there trying to find it?"

"Because I believe in first things first. And what I'm going to do in a few minutes has priority. By the way, where's James?"

"Down at Halfway House having dinner. According to Mike, Terry and Eric, he split as Diana was being taken to the ambulance. He said he'd been invited."

"I see."

"He's all right there, isn't he?"

"Where? At Halfway House? Yes, he's fine as long as he's there."

But there was something that bothered me about Simon's manner, or perhaps about what he didn't say. I suddenly remembered Diana's frantic concern about James's safety. "Do you think James is in danger of some kind?"

300

"Yes."

"Then why in the name of everything don't we go down and get him?"

"Because I have to do now what I am about to do, and because Diana was right. James would be in worse danger here if I didn't. Don't worry. I think there's still time."

I stared at him. "I don't know what you're talking about. And I don't know why you're implying that Eric is down at the folly trying to find the treasure all for himself."

Simon fastened the last button of his cassock and looked at me. "Do you love him?"

"I should think you of all people would know the answer to that."

He reached out and touched my cheek. "I told you. I think we have time."

"Everything's going to be all right, isn't it?" I felt like a child, begging for reassurance.

Simon didn't answer.

"Isn't it, Simon?"

"Candida, I don't know. I think James will be safe. But I know that something . . . something—but I don't know what —is going to happen."

"Something bad?"

"Yes. I'm afraid so."

Simon slipped a white cotton, loose, knee-length garment over his cassock and put a long narrow scarf around his neck. I had never before seen him dressed as a priest and it was, in its way, shocking.

"Candida, would you call Halfway House and tell them to hold James until I can pick him up, and then ask Mrs. Klaveness if she will join us?"

I will never forget that night. There are visual flashes that come back to me sometimes: the whiteness of Simon's surplice, the flickering candle, the dull metal gleam of the aspergill and diamond points of holy water flung from it, the strangely peaceful look on the face of Mrs. Klaveness, as, prayer book in hand, she gave back to Simon, the priest, the

301

liturgical responses, my astonishment at her serene participation in the liturgy of the Church and her obvious familiarity with it.

But the powerful memories are the aural ones, the sounds: Simon's deep voice, sometimes calm and strong, occasionally faltering, once or twice tight and strained as though he were forcing himself to continue doing what he was doing, forcing himself not to run away. And finally, towards the end, his own fear that was like a cry in his voice and that matched my growing terror. At some point I glanced towards Mike and Terry. They were huddled together like two frightened children. But that was all hours later.

When Simon was robed and I had brought Mrs. Klaveness from the kitchen, he said, "Now we're going to go into the living room."

"What are we going to do there?" I asked, as suspicious as Mike.

"We're going to pray."

"Pray! You know I'm an agnostic, you know how my father felt. I don't know any—"

"Do you want your animals to be safe?" Simon said.

"Yes. Of course, but—"

"Then add your prayers, whatever they are. Come along."

Strangely, after that short outburst, we all followed meekly enough.

"All right," Simon said, when we had entered the living room and turned on the light. "I've brought two or three copies of the Book of Common Prayer and one or two of the Roman Missal and a few Bibles. We're each going to read. Here"—he handed some small black volumes to Mrs. Klaveness, who was standing next to him—"pass these around. We shall begin with the ninety-first psalm. I'll read a verse, then we're going to each read one going around."

It was true that my father, angry at the Judeo-Christian world as a whole, had managed to keep me—as he thought—protected from its wrong-headedness. So the richness and might of the Elizabethan English of the King James Bible and the Book of Common Prayer burst on me that night in all its glory, and, standing there in a circle in the well-lit living room, I forgot what we were assembled for and reveled in the sonorous beauty of the words, thinking less what they were actually saying, than their manner of saying it. Then slowly, little by little, individual words and phrases assaulted me on some deeper level of understanding, and I remembered our supposed purpose:

"*Thou shalt not be afraid for the terror by night. . . . There shall no evil befall thee, neither shall any plague come nigh unto thy dwelling.*" That was Simon's voice.

Then the Elizabethan words emerged with a German accent as Mrs. Klaveness read, "*I will lift up mine eyes unto the hills, from whence cometh my help.*"

Then Terry. "*The Lord is my shepherd; I shall not want. . . .*" Even I knew those words as I heard my own voice take up the next line. "*He maketh me to lie down in green pastures; he leadth me beside the still waters.*"

After a while Simon said, "Each of you, in your own words, in any language that is comfortable to you, say a prayer, but say it aloud."

If he had said that an hour before he would have been laughed at by Mike, Terry and me, if not by Mrs. Klaveness. But something had happened in that hour as the psalms and other portions of Scripture unrolled. Somewhere along the way we had stopped being five separate and slightly warring people. Whether or not it was the reading of those ancient, potent words, one after the other, going round and round the circle, I didn't know. I did know that after a while I had to make an effort to register who was reading, even if it was myself. And when Mike, following Simon's direction, started speaking in what I finally realized was Hebrew, it seemed natural, as though we all knew Hebrew. And out of the silence at the end of Mike's Hebrew came Mrs. Klaveness's German. Terry's voice came next.

"*Ave Maria, gratia plena . . . Pater noster, qui es in coelis . . . Angus dei, qui tolis peccata mundi . . .*

Strange, I thought, that must really come out of Terry's early memory, because, unbeliever that I was, I knew that she must

303

have been a child when Latin had given way to English. . . .

The reading, the speaking, the praying went on. For me it seemed to go in three stages: the first when the curiosity and strangeness of it absorbed me, the second when I felt time dragged, my feet hurt, my back ached. . . . Then that, too, passed, and it was like one body and one voice that went on, tirelessly, not diminishing, but growing in strength.

". . . *they shall mount up with wings as eagles; they shall run, and not be weary; and they shall walk, and not faint.*"

The lights flickered. Through the window I could see lightning, like fiery needles, flash and disappear. After a short, heavy silent space, there was a crash and thunder rolled through the sky. The storm that had been threatening finally broke. Then the lights flickered again and went out.

The reading stopped. "What happened to the lights?" I said.

"Maybe a fuse?" Terry's voice sounded beside me.

Strangely, I thought, that sense of being knitted together hadn't gone. Nevertheless the blackness was total, and because the curtains in the room were drawn, there was not even the outside grayness to show up against the inside black.

Simon's voice said. "Nobody move. We must stay together. Mrs. Klaveness, do we have any candles anywhere?"

"Yes. In the kitchen. I always keep candles. I will get them."

"No. Just a minute. Let me think."

There was a pause. Simon's voice sounded. "I seem to remember that Diana had a flashlight in here in one of the table drawers. All of you stay where you are, and keep on talking or saying prayers. I can tell where you are then if I get disoriented."

So we went around the circle again, while I heard Simon's feet drag across the carpet. After a few seconds there was the sound of a drawer being pulled out. Then, suddenly, a pale shaft of light went on, so pale that I think if we hadn't been in darkness, we wouldn't even have seen it.

"These batteries are barely alive, but I think they'll get me out to the kitchen. Mrs. Klaveness, where are the candles and matches?"

"I will come—"

"No. You will stay here, with the others. Now link your hands together. I want you to be touching one another. Tell me where the candles and matches are."

I felt my hands go into those of Terry on one side and Mrs. Klaveness on the other.

"In the kitchen, on the left, as you go in, there is a cupboard. Inside the cupboard, on a shelf that is about five feet high, there are candles, and one is in a holder, with matches in the tray of the holder."

"All right. That's definite enough. Stay where you are. Keep your hands together in one another's. I'll be back in a minute."

And, in about two minutes, he was, this time carrying an old-fashioned candlestick with a handle, in which was propped a lit candle. He came back into the circle. "Here are some more candles, without holders, of course, but you don't need them. Mrs. Klaveness, take this."

I saw her hand go out and take a slender white candle and light it from the one in his holder.

"Now you, Candida."

When all our candles were lit we stood in the circle, our faces barely showing above the flickering, pear-shaped flame.

I glanced at my wrist and saw that I had left my watch upstairs. "What time is it?"

"Ten past ten," Simon said. "Let's go on with the reading."

"Shouldn't we find out what happened to the lights?" Mike asked.

"No," Simon said. "We have to do this first. Then we can worry about the lights." He sounded very sure.

"Is this the exorcism rite?" Terry said in a puzzled voice.

"No. Not yet. I said we should pray first. And we should pray collectively, as a group."

It was more than strange, I thought. Terry, Mike and I, if asked, would have sworn to our distrust of Simon. Yet there

305

we were. I looked at his tall head, glinting yellow in the light. If I so distrusted him, why was I here?

I didn't know. I did know I had to stay.

For what felt like a long time we went on reading, one after the other, until, once again, it seemed like one voice.

Then Simon said quietly, "All right." Reaching over to a table, he picked up a long metallic object and examined it.

"What's that?" Mike asked.

"It's the thing priests use when they spray holy water over a congregation," Terry said.

"An aspergillum," Simon explained. "Now—" I saw him make the sign of the cross. "In the name of the Father and of the Son and of the Holy Spirit, Amen." Then, holding the candle over his prayer book, he read, "St. Michael, the Archangel, illustrious leader of the heavenly army, defend us in the battle against principalities and powers, against rulers of the world of darkness. . . ."

St. Michael, I thought. I had seen pictures of this warlike angel in armor, with a sword. I tried to imagine him now, but the armor and the sword seemed child's toys. What I saw was . . . was what? The light from my candle seemed to grow and become white. There was a brilliant flash outside and another roll of thunder. What were angels, anyway, or archangels? Spirits? Good spirits? Thoughts of God? But I didn't believe in God. . . .

Suddenly Simon's voice came back, ". . . that the mercy of the Lord may quickly come and lay hold of the beast, that serpent of old, Satan and his demons, casting him in chains . . ."

Demons. If I didn't believe in God, did I believe in demons? What was it that Diana had seen, or thought she had seen?

Simon's voice, in ordinary speaking tone, dragged me back.

"Now, all of you, come close beside me. I'm going to say a line now, and when I'm through, I want you to repeat it. All right?"

We murmured an assent. A little chill crept up my arm.

Suddenly Simon said loudly, "Holy God, holy Mighty, holy Immortal One, have mercy upon us."

306

Tentatively, a little discordantly, we repeated what he said.

Then Simon said it again. After that, he said, "Lord, have mercy, Christ have mercy, Lord have mercy. Our Father..."

It was Terry and Mrs. Klaveness who followed him in that. Mike and I had obviously never learned it.

Then Simon went over to the door. "Come here and stand with me," he said. Stumbling a little in the dark we crowded around him. Then he turned towards the room, all the blacker for being on the other side of our candles. "Take this," he said, handing me his candle. "And hold your candles up high."

Raising the candle in its holder above my head, I saw him take from his pocket a large crucifix, which he also held high. Then he cried out in a loud voice. "Thou wicked and tortured spirit, in the Name of Jesus Christ and by the Sign of his all-conquering Cross, I bid thee come out and be gone!"

The chill I had felt before seemed to flicker over my whole skin. Then I saw Simon raise the aspergillum high and shake it towards various parts of the room, each flying drop reflecting the golden light.

"Now," Simon said, in an astonishingly matter-of-fact voice, "we're going to do this in every room."

And we did, room by room, hour by hour in the blackened house lit now only by gashes of lightning outside and the yellow flickering of our candles. After a while the surrounding blackness itself became a living substance, thick, alien, part of the armed camp opposing us, the ground of the enemy against whom our only weapons were the old, sacred words we were speaking....

But I pushed that fancy from my mind, telling myself that we were ordinary people in an ordinary house whose lights had been struck by the storm. And I sought reassurance by looking at the mundane articles revealed by our candlelight, tangible objects blessed by their very ordinariness: a table, a chair, a bronze horse, a row of books, the white oblong of a letter lying on a desk blotter... "The Purloined Letter."

The words sprang into my mind and seemed to hang there. Where had I read them recently? In the diary, of course, Agnes Medora's diary, of which the central character and leading actor was Le Grand Louis himself, a tyrant of the old school who wanted his way to the point of ordering a child pushed down a well. Don't think about that, I told myself, as the chill quivered over me. Think about something else—the books Louis wanted his wife, the long-suffering Agnes Medora, to read: Balzac, Hugo, Poe,—Poe, whose "Purloined Letter" Louis considered worthy of a Gallic intelligence. There was something about that that was trying to tell me something—but what?

"Candida," Simon said. And I realized as I looked at his face over our candles that this was the second time he had said it. "You have to be with us in mind and spirit as well as body, you know."

"Yes, all right. Sorry," I muttered, and tried to concentrate as Simon went on reading:

"... *Thou who didst, for his disobedience, cast down to earth the ancient enemy of our race, and together with him, all his messengers and spirits of evil that they might exist in the darkness of their own choosing....*"

Terrible words, I found myself thinking, frightening words, *the darkness of their own choosing,* so we choose our hell ... and suddenly I thought of my father. Did he choose his hell? It was hard to believe. Yet I knew, however sad it was to admit, that he had refused the help that from time to time had been offered to him.... Images, as fast as though from a movie camera, slid through my truant, wandering mind: my father, lurching against the table at that terrible party, faces close to me as hands tore at my clothes and body, a letter lying on a table where everyone could see it ...

Guiltily I yanked my attention back to the business at hand. We were upstairs now, huddled at the far end of the hall opposite to the wing containing my animals. As Simon started to speak the familiar words that he had said in every room, it struck me that his voice had subtly altered, that it was tighter, more constrained, as though he were forcing the sounds through. I looked at him then and saw the shine of sweat on his upper lip and forehead as he spoke,

"... *Grant that this our exorcism, which we accomplish in*

308

Thy Terrible Name, may be found unendurable by him, and that he, the master of evil, and all them fallen with him may thereby be put to flight. Command him to be gone from this place forever. . . ."

We were standing together, exactly as we had done a dozen times on the floor below, hearing those same words. But suddenly, as I noticed the sweat on Simon's face, I noticed also that I was cold and growing colder. And then, for the first time, I felt something. Often afterwards I tried to define what it was that I felt, but the only words that came near to describing it were: an opposing force, an adversary, an opponent . . . It was a person, yet it was not a person, it was there, but my knowledge that it was there did not come from any of my senses, because I knew, although I did not know how I knew, that while it was related to the cold, it was not the cold. . . .

"Simon," I whispered.

"Hold on," he said.

In the candlelight I saw him raise the crucifix and the aspergill, *"Thou wicked and tortured spirit . . ."*

As he finished the words, whatever it was lessened its pressure, as though it had retreated.

"There is something here." Terry's voice quavered a little.

"Hush," Mrs. Klaveness said.

Foot by foot, room by room, we went down the hall, as though a huge cleansing force of which we were the instrument scoured out one tainted, corrupted space after another. No wonder, I thought, as we stood at the edge of James's room, that the little boy was so unhappy, that Hannibal was so unhappy. . . .

"Candida," Simon said, "we must all concentrate on this. We will look for James and Hannibal later, I promise you."

Did what he was doing grant him the ability to look into my head and see the anxiety-charged pictures my brain was producing, the way he had once described it?

"St. Michael the archangel, illustrious leader of the heavenly army . . ."

And on we went. Everything got worse, the cold, the sweating, and now I was sweating as well as Simon, and I saw, as I glanced at them above the small flickering flames, that the others were, too.

"We've done enough," Mike said in an odd, whiny voice.

"No," Simon countered. "We must go on." But his breathing rasped, as though he were asthmatic.

I wanted very much to stop, and then, as we approached my wing, I became terrified. "My animals," I said.

"We're not going into the wing," Simon said. "Those rooms are all right. Just to the small staircase."

I wondered why my wing was all right and then remembered that Eric had said that wing had burned down and the rooms there now were new. "Simon—" I started.

But at that moment, he opened Diana's door.

There was a rush of icy air. Some of the candles went out. I saw her then, beside Diana's bed, a fair-haired child with a ruffled skirt a little above her ankles, a ribbon around her hair and a small dog at her feet. But the look on her face was not that of a child, or of a woman, or even anything human. It must have been at that moment that I dropped my candle. The carpet ignited as though it were straw and flames streaked across the room.

Calmly, almost in slow motion, Simon stepped into the room. In his raised hand was the cross, and I saw that the skin of his hand and arm and the sleeve of his cassock had been burned. There were flames all around him as the bedclothes caught. But he went on. "*I abjure thee . . .*"

The words I had heard again and again flowed out. Whatever it was there by the bed seemed to shrink and diminish against the flames. Then for a second it seemed to grow clearer, larger. There was a hissing noise. I saw the drops from the aspergillum fly out, but they seemed too few for a noise that rushed into my ears and grew into a torrent that could be a flood of water or fire.

In that second I knew Simon was in terrible danger.

"Simon," I cried, and tried to rush to him. But there seemed to be a wall of fire in front of me. Who was it who had said I didn't have to run through a wall of fire? Oh, but I did. I started to go forward pushing against the hands that were

310

trying to prevent me. "Let me go!" I yelled. Dimly behind me I heard voices I recognized, but I knew I didn't have time to listen to what they were saying. I made a huge effort and pushed forward towards Simon, who was falling. The blazing red rose in front of me. All of a sudden I understood something else, something my mind had been trying to get through to me.

Then I passed out.

16

I came to lying on somebody's raincoat on the wet lawn beside the house in a scene of pandemonium. The now familiar fire engine was parked in the drive, there were lights trained on the house, and some of the surrounding countryside seemed to be driving up in various stage of nightwear. Far away a mutter of thunder indicated that the storm had passed over and beyond us.

"Simon," I said, and turned my head away from the hand that was waving some powerful smelling salts under my nose.

"Yes." He was on one knee on the other side of me. As I spoke he lowered the smelling salts. "All right?" he asked.

"What happened?" I struggled to sit up.

"Is your head all right?" he asked.

I put my hand up. "Yes. I think so." And again I asked, "What happened?"

He hesitated. Then, "The room caught fire. But the firemen were able to put it out fairly quickly and it didn't spread. They're getting their stuff out now."

"I must have been out a long time," I said.

"Yes. You were. You had me—us—worried." He started to get to his feet.

"Simon!"

On the point of getting up, he paused and glanced down.

I took hold of his sleeve. "Simon, I saw her. I saw that child. Did you?"

"Yes." He spoke reluctantly.

"It was Totsie. You know, the Timberlake child who was drowned in the well. The story was in the paper this morning. I didn't get a chance to tell you, but in the diary, Agnes Medora, old Louis's wife, Diana's grandmother, was afraid that Louis had arranged to have her . . . have her murdered. There was an old newspaper picture of her in the diary, and it was the same child I saw, quite clearly, before I ran into the room and passed out."

Simon didn't say anything, just stared at me somberly.

"You saw her?" I said again.

"Yes. That is, I saw a child. But I couldn't be sure what . . . or who . . . was using her."

That stopped me, because I suddenly remembered that what went through me like an electric bolt was the sight of her face, which was not the face of a child or anything human.

"Did anyone else see her?" I asked finally.

"Not really."

"But something . . . whatever she was . . . was there."

"Yes."

I looked up at him. "But *not* there now."

"No."

I paused and looked at him. "But you don't seem relieved, or happy or anything. You still seem worried."

"I'm not sure that that is the end."

"What do you mean?"

"I'm not sure what I mean, but there's a price that has . . . has to be paid, I think. And I'm not sure it has been."

"What are you talking about?"

"Perhaps . . . nothing. Candida, I'm going over to the folly. You stay here." He got up.

"Simon, you were burned, weren't you? I saw—I thought

313

I saw—your arm on fire."

"My sleeve caught fire but I beat it out almost immediately. My skin is a little singed, but not too badly. It's all right."

"My animals!" I said, and struggled to my feet.

"They're safe. The fire didn't touch that wing, although they were all pretty scared with the noise and sounds of confusion. I checked on them. They're all right now."

"James is still at Halfway House, isn't he?"

"No. Enrico telephoned. He said that James and Hannibal had left more than an hour before when he had gone out of the room. But he said he hadn't realized they'd left. He'd assumed they were in another part of Halfway House with some of the kids, and only when they'd heard the fire engine did they discover James and Hannibal weren't there. Then one of the boys said he'd seen them leave about an hour before that. That's one reason I want to go over to the folly. There's something going on there. I can see some kind of light through the window. Why don't you go back into the house with Mrs. Klaveness or stay here with Terry and Mike. They're over there talking to the fire chief and—"

"I'm going with you," I said.

"Candida—"

"It's no use, Simon, I'm going with you."

"All right. But—I'm sorry if I sound like something out of an old movie—please stay behind me."

We started to move off towards the folly.

"Hey!" Mike and Terry called in unison. "Where are you going?"

"To the gazebo."

"For Pete's sake, why?"

"Because Simon thinks there's something going on there."

"Well, of all the queer times," Terry started.

"No, he's right. There is something going on there," Mike said unexpectedly. "When we came out I thought I saw a light moving inside, but what with everything else I forgot it. Can we come, too?"

"I think it may mean trouble," Simon said.

"So what else have we been having?" Terry asked.

"Let me go speak to the fire chief for a minute," Simon said.

In a few seconds he was back. "They're leaving now. He told me the inside of Diana's room is destroyed, but the rooms on either side are hardly touched and the rest of the house is fine. Of course the place is a mess. . . ."

"Yes . . ." Something was beating at the surface of my mind. Something that was there before I passed out. "Simon," I said, as he and I walked swiftly towards the gate to the rose garden, "there's something that's bothering me. Something about . . . about . . . about the letter I saw on the desk in the middle of the exorcism."

He stopped. "What about a letter?"

"I don't know. 'The Purloined Letter'—that's it. Does it say anything to you?"

"Nothing, except that it was the title of a story by somebody or other."

"Poe. Le Grand Louis, according to Agnes Medora, considered Poe the only American or Anglo-Saxon writer who could be mentioned in the same breath with the French."

"Yes, that sounds like him. But I don't know what that has to do with anything," Simon said, and moved forward again through the gate. Back of us, with a great deal of shoving and yelling, the firetruck drove off. Oddly, for all the mess and noise and upheaval they caused, I found I was sorry they were going. They offered a measure of normality, and I was surprised to discover that seemed more and more valuable the nearer we came to the folly.

"You see, I was right," Mike said. "There's a light. I guess the electricity there didn't get hit by the storm."

"Or the light doesn't come from electric current," Simon said. He stopped. "Let's all keep very quiet," he said softly. "I'm not sure what we're going to find, but there's no need to advertise our arrival."

"What do you think is going to be there?" I asked.

"I'm not sure. Let's wait and see."

"You're right about the light, I think," Mike whispered. And I could see why he said it. Through the closed louvers, some of them broken and hanging crazily from their hinges, the light flickered and changed.

We walked quickly over to the gazebo, and, as though arrested by some common impulse, stopped. Then, in one leap, Simon went up the stairs and pushed open the door. We all crowded after him.

We saw immediately the reason for the shifting eerie light. Candles stuck in their own wax were here and there on the floor and their flames writhed and danced against the angled walls and narrow roof beams. But I had barely registered that fact before I was hit with the full impact of the destruction of the dusty, anachronistic little pavilion. Nothing had remained untouched. The chests were open, their small, silly play tools scattered everywhere. The wicker furniture was overturned, the cushions ripped open, their wadding lying all over the floor. The curtains were torn and hung in streamers, and all over the floor, at more or less regular intervals, boards had been pried loose and either stuck up in the air or, totally detached, lay discarded.

I dont know how long we all stood there, probably only a few seconds. But I became slowly aware of a quiet noise, a kind of crooning that came from over near the wall on the other side of the door. By this time my eyes were more used to the shadows and I saw it was James. His face was in shadow, but one hand was gripped around Hannibal's blue collar, and it was plain that the big cat was struggling to get away. With his other hand James was rhythmically, if somewhat frantically, petting Hannibal and talking to him in a low voice.

"It's all right, Hannibal . . . everything's going to be all right . . . there's nothing to be afraid of." There was something very gallant in the gesture even though it was hopeless. Fear was thick in the room, and Hannibal, like all animals, would, I knew, be intensely aware of it.

"All right," Eric's voice said out of the shadows. "I suppose it was inevitable that you'd get here, so just come in, all of you, stand over there and be very, very quiet. If one of you moves or makes a sound, James gets the first bullet."

I saw him then, standing in another angle of the eight-sided folly, a gun in his hand, the muzzle only a few feet from James's head. "Come in and close the door behind you," he said. He sounded as calm and as much in command as the president of a bank showing a would-be investor over the premises. "Over there now, opposite the door. You'll have to pick your way through the floorboards."

"You could get a broken ankle," Terry said.

"That's your problem. You shouldn't have come here."

"How could we know you'd be in here tearing everything up," Mike said. "What the hell are you doing? What are you looking for?"

"Hunting for buried treasure," Simon said dryly. "What else?" As he spoke, his foot hit one of the toy gardening tools. He glanced down, then stooped and picked it up. A startled look came across his face.

"The treasure that is in old Louis's folly, right, James?" Eric said. "He's the only one bright enough to have figured that out, or maybe it's one of the side benefits of an English education."

"I still don't get it," Terry said.

By now we were backed, like a police lineup, against the angled arc of the wall opposite Eric.

"In my folly is my treasure," Simon said. He was standing next to me at the end of the row. "So this is where Eric came to find the treasure after all these years. We've always known that old Louis put it somewhere, haven't we?"

"I don't get any of this," Mike said.

"The family motto is 'In my folly is my treasure.' Ever since he died people have been saying that Louis Egremont left a treasure somewhere," Simon explained in an even voice. "But until James came along and called the gazebo here the folly, everybody—all of us when we were kids—looked for it elsewhere. But that's what you're after, Eric, isn't it? To get you out of all those embarrassing debts."

"What debts?" I asked. "Eric's rich."

"Oh, no, he isn't. He's gambled away not only what he inherited, but most of his family firm, haven't you, Eric?"

"So that's what you meant that night at dinner when you

317

made that crack about Eric's gambling and Diana said you were being holier than thou."

"Yes. I had a hope—not a very strong one—that I could stampede or embarrass Eric into giving himself away."

"But you didn't, did you, Simon?" Eric said, picking up the crowbar. "One up on me. Because you've been watching me like a hawk for weeks, waiting for me to make a mistake. And I've been watching you watching me."

Far away I heard the fire engine pause, then accelerate as it turned the angle by the fork down towards the town. If only they were here, I thought.

"Now," Eric said quite genially, "I have a few more boards to pry up. Just remember, if you're planning to jump me, that you're across the room, that there are holes in the floor and boards sticking up in between, and while you might succeed, James's brains might also in the meantime be splashed on the floor. It's a risk for both of us, but James is the one who'd pay." He glanced at the toy in Simon's hand. "And put that thing down." He watched as Simon did so.

Whenever I've read about hijackers and terrorists I've sometimes fantasied how, if I were there, I'd make a heroic rush when they were not looking. And just before sleep, when anything seemed possible, there has moved in front of my mental vision a delicious headline: CANDIDA BROWN RUSHES/ JUMPS/TRIPS HIJACKER. SAVES PLANE AND THREE HUNDRED PASSENGERS. How clever I'd be! How obvious it was!

But reality was different. What Eric said was true: One of us might successfully rush him. But James might be dead.

"Not too many more now," Eric said, rather as though he were a kindly dentist filling teeth. And he went on kicking aside the little gardening tools, prying up boards, dropping the crowbar, picking up a flashlight lying beside him, shining it down into the hole he'd just made and then going on to the next board.

I glanced over to James. "How do you happen to be here?" I asked him. "You were supposed to stay at Halfway House."

James stopped whispering to Hannibal. "Hannibal wanted to come home so we just left. And I was walking back with

318

Hannibal when he suddenly took off and jumped through the window. So I followed him and *he*—" James looked angrily at Eric—"was here with a gun."

"You've got to be crazy," Terry said after a while, and started forward. But she stopped as Eric dropped the heavy crowbar and swung the gun to face her. "Just stop right there," he said. "I'll be through in a moment and will get the hell out of here. But if you try to stop me, or make any sound or any move, James will get a bullet in the head." And he moved the pistol back so that it was a foot from James's temple.

"Understand?" he said.

"Yes," Terry said. She sounded scared.

"Even if you find the treasure, or whatever it is," Simon said in a detached sort of voice, "what will you do with it? There are a lot of us here. Are you going to kill us all? Don't you think you'll be stopped somewhere on the road, or on the way to the airport, if that's where you're going?"

Eric barely glanced at him. "Wherever I'm going I've decided James goes with me. If I'm safe, he's safe. If I'm stopped or interfered with, then he'll pay."

"And holding a pistol on James," I said, "you think you're going to get through all the checkpoints in an air terminal and onto a plane? You're dreaming!"

"You've forgotten the company's private plane," Simon said to me. "But I'm sure Eric hasn't."

Eric ignored Simon and glanced at me, and to my great shock, smiled. "Don't you wish I were dreaming! No, I'm not going to oblige you by telling you all my plans. Just the fact that if I am not harmed, when I arrive . . . where I am going . . . then James will be freed unharmed. Now, if you'll excuse me," and he bent to his task.

I think it was the sheer ordinariness of Eric's manner that kept me from being more frightened. He seemed like any businessman trying to get on with a tiresome but necessary task. There was about the whole scene something of the Mad Hatter's tea party. Perhaps because, despite everything, I couldn't quite believe it, I moved a small, and, I thought, invisible step forward.

"Don't! Simon breathed beside me, his voice barely audible.

Even so, Eric heard. With his long legs he took one stride towards James and jammed the gun up against his temple. I could hear the slight crack of it across the room.

"Stop, Eric!" I cried.

"Then step back to where you were," Eric said, and watched me retreat. "Don't do that again," he said quietly. He turned his head towards James. "And you shut up. Stop making that noise." It was the first indication to me that his own nerves were on edge.

"I'm just trying to keep Hannibal happy," James said. "He's upset."

"It would give me the greatest pleasure to ease his upset—for good," Eric said. He lowered his gun a fraction so that it was pointed at Hannibal. "So watch yourself."

I heard James's intake of breath. "I've *always* said you were a *beast*!"

As calmly as I could I said, "James, be quiet. Be very, very quiet. It will calm Hannibal and then everything will be all right."

In the short silence that followed the tension almost crackled. It was hard to see people's faces in the dim, changing light of the candles, but it seemed to me that Eric's eyes had an odd shine to them. Then the stiff arm, pointing the gun at Hannibal, relaxed. Almost in slow motion Eric lowered his arm. Then with the other hand he lifted the heavy crowbar and jammed it down into the brittle, already splintered wood and pulled up the end of the board. It was obvious that the rotten condition of the wood offered little resistance.

Involunarily, without thinking, I must have moved or shifted weight, because the boards under my feet creaked. The gun in Eric's hand snapped up again. "I told you," he said. "Now watch it!"

After that, since I didn't dare move anything but my eyes, I glanced at James, worried at how well he was holding up. He was seated on the floor, his back in an angle of the wall, one arm holding Hannibal against his chest, the other stroking the fur on the cat's head and back. James's face was next to his pet, and I could hear the faint whispering as he tried to soothe him. But, as I knew all too well, cats, highly nervous animals, were more sensitive than most to tension and fear. And Hannibal's response to the tension was becoming more and more evident as his tail, which had been twitching, was now beginning to lash back and forth. Watching it whip from side to side I became aware that somewhere off in the distance a telephone had started to ring. It must be in the house, I thought, my eyes and attention almost mesmerized by Hannibal's tail. Lash, lash. Back, forth, back, forth. I glanced up to the cat's head and saw that his ears were flattened—not a good sign. A strong sense that there was a disaster in the immediate offing took hold of me. Hannibal was reacting to everything in the room, including, and perhaps most of all, the crashing, splintering sound made by the crowbar as it was driven into the floor. Almost any moment now, Eric, who was busy shining the flashlight into the hole he had made would put down the flashlight and pick up the crowbar. Hannibal, who had become more frightened each time he had done this, was now plainly terrified, and a small space that contained an animal on the verge of panic and a man with a gun had all the ingredients of a catastrophe.

My mind scurried around, trying to figure out how I could avert a calamity, or, conversely, how I could use it. It was only when the telephone started ringing again that I realized it had stopped. But it was ringing once more . . . four, five, six, eight, nine, ten rings.

"Somebody must want to reach the house pretty badly," I said idly, with some idea of lessening tension.

Eric paid no attention.

"I think it must be the hospital," Simon said quietly. "I don't suppose, Eric, you'd let me either answer the phone or put a call through myself?"

Eric looked up, clicked off the flashlight and stood up, holding the crowbar. "Just how much of a fool do you think I am?" he said.

321

"Why do you think it's the hospital?" I asked Simon.

"Who else would be calling at what must be after one in the morning?"

"Do you think Diana is worse?"

"Yes. I think she is seriously ill."

"If you thought that, why didn't you stay with her in the hospital?" Eric asked.

"It was that or keep my promise to her. And she was so insistent that I perform the exorcism, and so increasingly upset as I delayed doing so, that I decided that it would agitate her less if I did as she asked."

"Too bad you didn't go back to the hospital after Candida came around," Eric said. "Instead of snooping here."

The phone finally stopped. Then, unbelievably, started again.

"I have to get to Diana," Simon said. "Eric, you're wasting your time looking under the floor. The treasure isn't there."

Eric raised his head and stared at Simon. After a moment he said in a voice that sent an added chill through me, "I see, you've known all along where it was." Moving abruptly, he walked over to James. Again I heard the slight thunk as he pushed the gun against James's temple.

"Don't do that!" Simon said, his voice sharp. "There's no need. I'm perfectly willing to tell you. The damned treasure is right in front of you, all over the floor and hanging on the walls."

"What the hell do you mean?"

"I mean those stupid child's gardening tools. If you don't believe me, pick one up and scrape off the paint. I don't know which particular precious metal you'll find—gold, platinum, whatever. But that's where the old miser hid his treasure, out where everyone could see it and ignore it."

" 'The Purloined Letter,' " I said. "My God! That was what he was talking about."

"That's right. It finally hit me when I kicked the hoe and then picked it up. It was far too heavy to be a real child's toy."

So that, I thought, was why he looked so startled.

Eric stared. "You're lying," he said. Then he turned and rummaged in a canvas bag on the floor, emerging with the scarlet-covered diary.

"I'm not your literary type, and I don't know what the hell you're talking about. Show me in here."

"So it was you who took it," I said.

"Obviously."

"When I was in the kitchen, I suppose. But I thought James was upstairs in his room. How could you take it if he was there?"

"I was in the loo," James said disgustedly. "I caught him coming out of my room and he said he was just checking to see if I was in the house because you wanted to know. I should have known he was telling a whopper."

"I haven't got all night," Eric said. "And I don't believe Simon's fairy story for one minute. He's done that kind of thing all our lives, he and Diana, anything to make me feel like the illiterate jumped-up electrician they used to call my father. Donnie taught them that, with her Master Simon and Miss Diana and just plain Eric. . . ."

And once again I remembered my impression going back to that night, ten years before, of Eric, standing on the edge of the dance floor, looking, for all his black tie, like a boy from the village with his nose pressed to the windows of the rich. . . .

"I think Simon knows where the money is, all right, and he wants to distract me so he can get it. No," he said as Simon reached for the book. "Not you." He looked at me. "You find it."

It didn't take me long to find the page. "Here it is, Eric." And I read him Anges Medora's prim statement, finishing, ". . . that man Poe, he must have been French. The idea was too good, too subtle for the stupid brain of an Anglo-Saxon. . . ."

"You see, Eric," I said, "the whole idea of 'The Purloined Letter'—of Poe's story—was to hide the letter by leaving it out where everybody could see it and therefore ignore it."

Eric stared at me, his eyes narrowed. "I don't believe it," he said.

And I realized then he didn't want to believe it. After all his effort and digging and staring through holes into the floor it made him look—he was afraid—a fool. Then he bent and picked up one of the little tools, a rake, with its powder blue handle. With his fingernail he tried to scrape off some of the paint, then, putting the gun on the floor, he took a little penknife from his pocket, opened the blade, and succeeded, finally, in removing a few chips of paint. He stared at this for a while. "It's soft," he said, in an astonished voice.

"Yes," Simon said dryly. "Gold is soft."

Ignoring him, Eric put down that tool and picked up a hoe, some of whose paint had begun to peel off by itself. Rubbing along the edges of that, he removed a fairly wide strip. Even across the room in the dim light I could see the gold.

"My God, my God, my God . . ."

I could hear Eric's whisper across the room.

"All the time . . . all these years . . ." He looked down and around and up at the walls where the tools were hanging in rows. "Dozens of them, all gold . . ."

He could have been a sixteenth-century pirate or conquistador, another Count of Monte Cristo, stumbling on a hoard of gold coins of some ancient kingdom.

Caught by the old magic of gold, we all stared as Eric picked up one tool after another, some from their nails on the wall, some from where they lay scattered over the torn-up floor. The functional end of the implements were ordinary metal. But the handles, underneath their paint, were gold. How many were there? My eyes shifted over the walls and floor—twenty? thirty? thirty-five? And how much was gold worth? My memory groped for figures read casually from financial headlines, heard over radio business news: one hundred and sixty dollars per ounce? And how many ounces per handle? I was still trying to arrive at a figure when my mind focused on something far more important and I forgot the gold and its worth: Eric, lost (like the rest of us) in his dreams of Eldorado, had forgotten the gun.

324

I was not as near to it as James, but I was much nearer to it than Simon. The boards would I knew, creak, but if I moved fast enough . . .

Perhaps if I had carried out the idea immediately, everything would have been different. But something stopped me, something much more powerful than anything that was going on in the room. It was the sudden knowledge that Diana was dead, exactly as though, at that moment, someone had told me. I had heard no words. Nevertheless they had been transmitted to my awareness. Then, as I paused, astonished and afraid, I became aware that Diana was beside me. It is almost impossible to describe the reality of that fact. Because it was a fact. That I could not see her was irrelevant. Her presence was as real as Eric's or Simon's. And in a way that did not involve sound I knew she was telling me something.

"James, watch James," she said. "Please. He's in danger."

"James," I whispered.

Far gone in some exultation of his own, Eric was staring at the tools a little to the right of his head. He took a step and reached out.

I jumped as Hannibal gave a yowl of pain and saw that Eric's foot had come down on his tail. Then Hannibal's teeth were buried in Eric's leg.

"You goddamned cat!" Eric yelled. With his bitten leg he kicked out. Then, like the football player he had once been, he drew the other leg back and kicked again.

Hannibal gave a terible cry as he soared across the room.

"Hannibal!" James screamed.

I moved as fast as I could, and jammed into Simon, who also moved fast. But it was James who got the gun.

"Hannibal!" James cried, holding the gun, and running to where Hannibal half lay, half crouched, cries coming out of him with every breath. "Hannibal, Hannibal," James cried, and got down on his knees.

I suddenly knew why Diana had spoken to me from whereever she had gone. James was in great danger, not of being killed, but of killing, and this new seed of Totsie's death would create another cycle of blood and death.

"James," I said, trying to make myself heard above Hannibal's cries. "James, give me the gun. Please give me the gun."

"No," James said, bending over his pet. "No. I'm going to kill him."

"It's more important to get Hannibal to a vet."

James didn't say anything. He was kneeling down, the gun looking enormous in his hand, whispering to Hannibal. "Hannibal, it's all right. It's all right. We're going to take you to the doctor right away." He looked up to Simon. "Go and call the vet *immediately*. Tell him to come here. Now. Now!"

"Not until you let Candida have that gun," Simon said. He was talking to James, but his eyes were on Eric who was staring, mesmerized.

"James," I said, trying to sound calm. "Let me have the gun. Then I'll run to the house and call the vet immediately and tell him to send an animal ambulance. I know he has one because he bought it from my father."

James started to cry, making no sound, but with tears falling down his cheeks. "He's going to die," he whispered. "I know he is. And it's all his fault." He pointed the gun at Eric.

Simon walked over to him. James swung the gun towards him as he did, in a weird imitation of Eric. "Don't you come near."

Simon's eyes were on the gun. "Give it to me," he said quietly. "James, give it to me. I know how you feel. But shooting Eric is not going to bring Hannibal back, and you're delaying our calling the vet. Now give me the gun and I promise you that I will get a vet here as fast as I can."

Another cry came from Hannibal's throat. The green eyes were half closed. It was obvious that the cat was in pain. More than a little I sympathized with James's desire to kill Eric. At that moment I could have killed him myself—almost. But in that "almost" lay the difference between fantasy and reality, and between perpetuating or bringing to an end the consequences of old Louis's greed and determined self-will.

"James," I said, "please give Simon the gun so that we can do something about Hannibal."

326

James stood there, the gun steady in his hand, pointing towards Eric. His face bore an old, unchildish look and I was afraid again that he would disappear into his own mind, into his fantasy world and would find it logical—indeed necessary —to execute Eric for killing Hannibal, King Hannibal, ruler of Bulzartgay.

Diana, I thought, wherever you are, help James.

And then relief washed over me, because as the words formed themselves in my mind I saw James become again a child, a bewildered, miserable, unhappy little boy—but a child aware of who and where he really was.

With a gesture that tore at me more than anything that had happened, James put up a dirty hand and rubbed away his tears. "All right," he whispered. Shakily he rose to his feet, the gun dangling like a cannon from his hand. Simon reached out. None of us, unfortunately, was watching Eric, who lunged forward towards the gun. James, startled, stepped back. His foot started to slide into one of the holes and he fell backwards, the elbow of his gun hand striking the wall behind him. The gun went off echoing and reechoing in that tiny space.

Eric stood quite still, as the blood stained the neat glen plaid vest. "He shot me," he said, astonishment in his voice, then slowly he crumpled forward.

It was Mike who ran to the house to phone for the ambulance for Eric and to Dr. Stevens, the vet. I had told Mike, "Tell Dr. Stevens that Candida Brown asked you to call, and to bring his station wagon ambulance for Hannibal. I'm sure he remembers my father and he'll know I'm not getting him out in the middle of the night for nothing."

When Mike had gone I turned back to the shambles in the folly. Simon and Terry were bent over Eric. James was lying on the floor, his arms around Hannibal, and was singing to him.

Beastie Bystie, Boostie, Bootsie
Bulzartgay, Bulzartgay
Bulzartgay

327

I couldn't see Hannibal's face, but I could see that his breathing had become rapid and shallow.

Suddenly Eric's voice rang out, amazingly strong. "Stop singing that. Stop it!"

"Why?" Simon asked.

James, off in the world of Bulzartgay, went on singing.

There was a pause. I leaned over Simon to look at Eric and saw him lick his lips. "I'm thirsty," he said.

"The ambulance will be here in a few seconds," Simon said. "Why don't you like that song?"

I wondered at Simon's nagging him about that at this moment. As though feeling my gaze, Simon glanced up at me and then, as though anticipating my saying something about it, shook his head. Then he repeated, "Why don't you like 'Here We Go Round the Mulberry Bush'? It's just an old nursery rhyme we used to sing as children, you and Diana and I, and, of course, Donnie."

Eric had closed his eyes. Now he opened them. "Donnie," he said. "That's what she sang, for hours and hours and hours. I could hear her. That was after she stopped screaming and calling."

"In the elevator," Simon said, making it a statement rather than a question. "After you turned off the switch and trapped her there. It was you, wasn't it?"

"Yes. I thought she would die much sooner. But it was days. It seemed to go on and on. Each day I'd sneak back into the house, hopping she'd be dead, that I wouldn't hear anything. . . . The last two days she just sang that song . . . sometimes other nursery rhymes . . . but mostly that . . . and I could hear her talking to Diana as if she was there. . . ." He moved his head restlessly. "She was out of her head," he added.

I shivered, feeling, for a minute, the terror of the trapped woman.

"Why did you kill her?" Simon asked.

"I couldn't let her marry my father . . . she was just a servant . . . and it was easy. My father once showed me where he installed the switch controlling the elevator. That was when

328

he worked for the elevator company. All I did was turn it off...."

His voice faded. Simon straightened, took off his jacket, folded it and put it under Eric's head. Then he knelt down beside him. "The ambulance will be here in a minute," he said again.

Eric opened his eyes. "She went to the top floor to get her bags," he said, as though Simon hadn't spoken. "My father was away. She was supposed to meet him somewhere. They were going to be married."

His voice, which had come out quite strong, weakened again.

"Better not talk anymore," Simon said.

But it was as though Eric were carrying on a conversation with somebody else altogether. "Diana said that after they were married I'd have to call her Miss Diana and you Master Simon.... She was just a housekeeper." He stared up at Simon. "This bullet... I can't feel much... I'm not going to make it... am I?"

"No. I'm afraid not."

"It's funny," Eric said, his eyes dark and wide open. "I don't really care. After all that, I don't... care."

There was a silence. My ears strained for the sound of the ambulance. It was strange, I thought, I felt sick and horrified at Eric, at what he was saying, yet I felt sorry for the boy he had been, for the boy who was afraid that he would have to call Diana and Simon, his playmates, miss and master....

"I didn't plan it," Eric said, his breath was sounding more labored. "When she went upstairs, I just found myself in the basement... with the switch in front of me. She was screaming and hammering on the elevator door when I left the house. After a while... some days... she was like an animal ... whimpering."

"My God," I said, no longer sorry for the monster who had been able to hear that. "How could you stand it?"

"I wanted to be like Simon and Diana." It was a statement terrible in its simplicity.

"And no one discovered her?"

"No," Eric whispered. "My father . . . thought she'd walked out on him. . . ."

Something was coming together in my head. "Diana dreamed about Donnie. She told me. She said Donnie was looking at her accusingly." I glanced down at Eric, whose face had lost all color. "You were there," I said. His eyes flickered. Then he looked up at me. I had mentally criticized Simon for badgering Eric at this moment. In a way, since Diana was dead, it seemed pointless as well as heartless. But I knew it was important for me, for Simon, perhaps, someday, for James.

"If it was you who killed Donnie," I said, "why did Diana think she had anything to do with it?"

He closed his eyes and I thought for a moment that he wouldn't or couldn't answer. But then he opened them again.

"She was there when they found Donnie. After that"—he licked his lips—"she had sort of a breakdown. I used to come and see her. I started telling her stopping the elevator was her idea—just a sort of joke to begin with. It was easy, really. She cried and denied it, but she couldn't remember anything—not her trip, nothing—since before she went away. And then one day she said it wasn't really her fault, it was her twin sister's."

"So that's it," Simon said softly. "And when she was well, you repeated her own fantasy about a twin sister back to her, saying it was a rumor."

Eric repeated, "It was easy."

There was a silence. The stain on the front of Eric's vest was now large and there was a slight reddish foam around his mouth.

"But it wasn't any use," Eric said, and sounded almost surprised. "I thought Diana . . . everybody . . . would be different towards me. But they weren't . . ." His voice trailed off.

"What—" I started, but stopped when I heard the siren coming up the hill.

Over in the corner there was an anguished whisper. ". . . Hannibal, Hannibal . . ." James cried.

I looked over. His face in Hannibal's fur, James was sobbing.

330

17

Eric died shortly after he reached the hospital, Hannibal a few hours later.

James had insisted that he go with the vet to the clinic, so he and I had traveled in the station wagon beside the barely conscious, harshly breathing Hannibal.

Dr. Stevens spent a long time in the clinic's operating room trying to mend Hannibal's lacerated internal organs. Then he came out and told us there was nothing else he could do and we would just simply have to wait and see whether or not Hannibal would pull through.

"Can I be with him?" James asked.

Dr. Stevens hesitated. "Let's wait awhile. He should be as quiet as possible. If there's any change I'll let you know right away."

"Why don't we go home, James?" I said. "I know Dr. Stevens would call us if there's any change."

"No," James said. He turned and stared out the window.

I glanced at my watch. It was past four thirty. Outside it was still dark, but I knew that very shortly it would begin to get light.

"You must be tired, James," I said.

He didn't answer. He just went on staring out the window.

After a few minutes I surrendered to the inevitable, sat down in one of the leather chairs in the waiting room, and leaned my head back.

Forty minutes later Simon arrived. He glanced to where James was still staring out the window at the beginning of daylight and said to me in a lowered voice. "Diana died a couple of hours ago."

"Yes. I know."

He frowned. "You knew?"

"Yes." I looked up at his questioning face. "I can't explain how, but I knew. It was in the folly. And then, all of a sudden, she was there."

"Diana once told me that she thought you were psychic."

"She told me that, too. I thought it was a lot of nonsense. . . . But now, I'm not sure. I'm not sure about a lot of things."

Simon said dryly, "I know that state well, I've been in it for some time."

"You mean you've lost your faith, as Diana said?"

"No, *mirabile dictu*. I thought I had, for a while. I became . . . unsure . . . of many things I thought I believed. But when we were saying those prayers, together, in the dark house, and I was scared out of my skin . . . I knew . . . I knew that all I had believed was true, and that I still believed it."

"I'm glad," I said. And was intensely surprised at myself.

He smiled a little. "Coming from your father's daughter . . ."

"Yes. I have decided that my darling father was not right about everything."

"That chasing God is not comparable to searching in a coal cellar at midnight for a black hat that isn't there?"

"No. I think . . . I've come to think . . . there is a hat—of some kind."

Simon glanced at James's unmoving back. "How's Hanni-bal, James?" he said.

"He's going to die." James turned. I could see that he was as white as the wall and had been crying.

332

"Are you sure about that?"

James nodded.

Simon went over and pulled the boy towards him. James rested his head against Simon's sweater.

After a minute James's voice, muffled, said, "I wish I was dead."

Simon lightly rubbed his shoulder. "I don't think you do, really, but I know what you mean."

"I knew when I came over here that everything would die. I knew when we left Walker that Bulzartgay would die. And I was afraid for Hannibal. Mother hated him. And I hated her."

"Your mother's dead, James," Simon said. "She died a few hours ago."

The little boy didn't say anything. For a moment he remained still. Remembering my sense in the folly of her presence and of her warning to me about him, I wanted to tell James that Diana did love him. But I hesitated for a moment, appalled at the prospect of convincing a child whose evidence was entirely to the contrary. But I said it anyway.

"I know you may not believe this, but your mother did love you, James."

He astonished me then. "Yes. I know. It's funny. I thought about her there in the folly, when I had the gun. I wanted to kill Mr. Barrington for kicking Hannibal." His voice quivered. "But that's when I started thinking about her, and I knew I had to give you the gun."

We were all silent. Then James said, "I'm sorry she's dead, but it's not like Hannibal. . . ." And his voice shook again.

"Epitaph for a mother," Simon said. "But who can judge somebody else's hierarchy of love?"

Dr. Stevens came in. "James," he said gently. "I'm not sure whether Hannibal's going to make it. He was pretty torn up inside. And his heart's not that strong." He hesitated, looking intently at the little boy. Then he said, "Would you like to come and sit beside him? I've put a chair near his cage."

"Yes." James ran towards the doctor.

I got up. "Would you like me—"

"No," James said. "I'm going alone." And he and the vet disappeared.

"My God, what a mess!" Simon said. He looked over at me. "Don't cry, darling."

"Why not?" I said. "There's plenty to cry about."

"Yes. There is." He moved towards where I was sitting on the chair and pulled my head towards him much the way he had pulled James to him.

After a while I said, "Do you think Totsie came back for retribution or vengeance? Mrs. Klaveness said that everything that's happened is because the murder—Totsie's murder—had to be paid for. And you said, tonight—only it seems like days ago—you said a price had to be paid and you were not sure it had been. That you didn't think it was over...." I paused. "It was after that, wasn't it, that Diana died? I guess you were right..."

Simon put his fingers on my hair. "It was just a feeling, Candida. Not a theological statement. I think it's a mistake to be too definite about how these things work. As somebody said once, 'we see through a glass darkly.'"

"And Eric died," I said. "I'm sorry about Diana. Really sorry. I came to care for her... but I can't feel much for Eric. Was it really gambling that got him into his financial state? He seemed so superbly respectable I still can't believe what happened in the folly. He was like somebody possessed."

"He was—by the gold, or perhaps, more literally, by his desire for it."

"What did he mean when he said he was watching you watching him?"

Simon put his hands in his pockets and leaned back against the window. "I guess that he knew I was keeping an eye on him and—in his opinion—doing it pretty clumsily."

"But why? I mean, I know now that he was after the gold, but this goes back before that. What made you suspicious of him?"

"Well, the beginnings of this goes back to my days in Intelligence in Germany. When I was working in the army

334

hospital there I became aware that somebody was stealing a lot of drugs from the American supplies. I went to the military police, and they suggested I work as a sort of decoy, since it was easy for me to get my hands on the drugs. That's when the rumors were deliberately put out about me, the ones that Mike heard. Eventually we ran to earth the people who were shipping the drugs to Eastern zone. But in the course of all that I learned that there was another outlet—here in the U.S., in and around the New York area. The FBI and the police were alerted and they tracked down several big buyers, but not, unfortunately, all of them. . . . Anyway, because of that activity, I came to learn a lot of ugly facts about drug dealing here and abroad, mostly about the final target, the kid on the street, and there are hundreds and thousands of them, and not just in the urban ghettos, although the majority are there. So, when I found myself ordained, I decided that I wanted to work in that area. All of which is a long-winded introduction to why I became suspicious of Eric. In Halfway House, Enrico—the kid that James admires so much—used to be a small-time gofer for one of the bigger syndicates. Because he was bright and quick, they promoted him to working in one of their fancier gambling hideouts. Enrico finally got himself busted. I met him when I visited the prison as chaplain. Anyway, he decided to try and straighten out his life, which is why he's in Halfway House. He and I were grocery shopping in the village one day when Eric walked past and stopped to talk. When he finally left and we drove back up the hill Enrico, who'd been very quiet, suddenly came out with the information that he recognized Eric from his days in the gambling establishment, that Eric practically lived there, at least at night, and that according to all the rumors he was in debt to his ears to the syndicate.

"Through some of my old connections I made some investigations and found it was true. For a while there I was afraid that Eric might have recognized Enrico and I'd have to get him out of the house and as far away as possible—fast. But, apparently, he didn't.

"Then when Eric seemed to give his blessing to the con-

335

struction company that Diana wanted to sell Tower Abbey to—and I knew that he had even before Diana said so that night at dinner—I got some of my friends among the city and federal police to dig behind that and—surprise, surprise— well hidden behind several holding companies, there were my old buddies, the syndicate. After that, it wasn't hard to figure out why Eric was so busily pushing their cause. If they were holding all his IOUs, they could pretty well make him do what they wanted. But I didn't have proof of any of that. So I just kept an eye on him, and made sure that he knew I was. It wasn't much in the way of a brake, but I thought that if he knew I suspected him, he'd at least be more careful, and not push Diana quite so hard."

"It still seems funny. By comparison with you and Diana, he was always so staid. In fact, Eric told me he was brought up on the blue-collar work ethic. His father might have been a financial success, but he didn't take on any of the more liberal ways of the upper classes."

"No, he was pretty strict. And Eric towed the line in prac- tically every way. No wild parties, very little drinking, no women to speak of, always at work on time and staying late . . . Just what the old man wanted. Except old mother nature found one loophole for rebellion. Eric developed a taste for gambling and he got in with some very undesirable people. . . . Eventually they came to own most of him."

"Did his wife have anything to do with this?"

"No. I don't think so. I barely remember her, but I seem to recall that she divorced him for neglect, or words to that effect. Whenever she wanted his company he was always somewhere else, playing the horses or the wheel or whatever was going. Women and sex, even when he could have it at home, played a poor second."

"Unlike you," I said, before I could stop myself.

"That's right," he agreed amiably. "Is that going to stand between us?"

"No," I said. "But I can't help hoping that your playboy tendencies are over."

"You can pretty well count on it," he said, and smiled.

After a minute I said, "Do you think Eric was in love with Diana?"

"More, I'd say, with what Diana symbolized for him. She might be in debt and in trouble with alcohol. But to him she was still the princess in the tower. By marrying her he'd become the prince. And I think he had some crazy idea that that would get him out of his difficulty. And, of course, if she sold Tower Abbey to his friends, he'd not only get them—he thought—off his back, she'd have money from the sale. And there was always the treasure. I don't think he ever quite lost sight of that, which is why he went into some kind of overdrive out there in the folly. He'd always thought it was around somewhere and now he—or rather, James—had found where to look. He lost all sense not only of balance, but of his own best interests. And maybe he, too, in some fashion, knew that Diana was going to die."

"Why didn't you want her to go away to someplace where she could maybe dry out, stop drinking?"

"Is that what Eric told you? I did—but not to the places either she or Eric had in mind, where they might take away her alcohol, but substitute even more pills than she was already taking. I even once or twice suggested a place I knew of—a place that would get her off everything and give her therapy to boot. But, as you know, with her mania about her sister and the diary, she wouldn't go anywhere."

"How much do you suppose that treasure is worth? It's awful to be preoccupied with something like that, but out there in the folly, while he was trying to scrape the paint off one of those toy gardening tools, I tried to calculate. What with James and the gun and Diana, I felt guilty even thinking about it. But, nevertheless, I was still figuring . . ."

"Don't feel bad. So was I. And I bet the others were, too. There's always been something magic about gold and its effect on people. Well, what with the tools on the wall and the ones lying around and in the chest—about fifty, I think—at, say, approximately a pound weight per handle—I figured the lot to be about a hundred and twenty-eight thousand dollars, give or take a thousand—not a huge sum for a tycoon's

337

legacy, but that much more than nothing."

"Do you think old Louis left it because he had some premonition that his heirs would run through the money?"

"More for the fun of it, I'd guess. I think the idea of their scrambling around for a treasure that was under their noses with a readymade clue in the family motto pleased him inordinately. No one would seriously call old Louis fanciful. But I bet he imagined himself sitting up there inside the pearly gates cackling his head off."

"Isn't it odd that someone didn't catch on to that sooner—that the toy tools were too heavy?"

"Not really. Everybody was so busy despising the gazebo and everything in it as atrociously bad taste—and that in itself must have given old Louis exquisite pleasure—that they were too arrogant to examine what was under their noses. And then it was locked up for so long."

There was a short pause. Idly, once more, Simon touched my head.

"Simon, I have to ask. . . . That night, ten years ago, at Diana's wedding when I drank the punch and went into a blackout, I could never remember what happened. But I knew something had—to me. Tonight, at dinner, Eric said it was you, that I had led you on and that you had—er—what used to be known as 'taken advantage' of me. I don't think I believed it even then. But I did have a gigantic crush on you, and you did have a reputation."

"But hardly for rape. And you didn't lead me on, you were much too busy being sick. And I've always preferred my women to be willing, and those who were willing, to be women, not children. Besides, damn it, Candida, I may have been the local stud, but I didn't go in for seducing, let alone raping, children. You were sixteen. Any women I had anything to do with were old enough and willing enough and quite aware of what was going on. No, it was the Bigelow boys. First they spiked the punch—you weren't the only one who was done in—and then, after you'd been sick, they somehow got you behind a bush somewhere. They were pretty drunk themselves. Both Eric and I, hearing you yell, arrived on the scene, but not soon enough."

No wonder, I thought, if both Bigelow boys were involved, that I remembered so many tearing hands. Something else occurred to me.

"Then I wonder why my father didn't want me to have anything to do with you after that. I thought it was because it was you who . . . who, you know what I mean."

"He didn't want me to have anything to do with you because on that famous and memorable evening, which turned out to be the bacchanal of all time, I caught him more or less *in flagrante* with one of Diana's friends—that was before he brought the hall bar crashing down—and he thought I'd tell you. He should have known I wouldn't. But he was drinking pretty heavily then, and his thinking wasn't of the straightest."

"Were you in love with Diana? She said you were."

"No, I'm a little ashamed to say."

"Why ashamed? Because she was in love with you? And because of Karin?"

"Yes, I suppose so."

"How did you find out about Karin?"

"She told me. She was in Europe off and on while I was there, and one evening, when she'd had more drinks than she could handle well, she came out with that piece of information. She told me that more to upset me than anything else, and she succeeded."

"Why did she want to upset you?"

Simon paused. "She thought . . . she thought she was in love with me. It's all old history now, Candida. Does it matter?"

"Of course not," I said stiffly, hating myself for asking.

He put his hand under my chin. "I believe you're jealous."

"I am not."

He bent down and kissed me. "Don't say that. Nothing has cheered me so much for ages." Then he kissed me again.

After a while I said, "How did Diana find Mrs. Klaveness?"

"Oh—she was the aunt of the personal maid of one of Diana's European friends, something like that."

"I'm sorry about Karin, Simon."

339

"Yes," he said. "So am I. She didn't have much of a life."

"Do you think it was because of Totsie that she died?"

"Or because she wasn't loved enough, either by Diana or by me. Lots of things have come easily to me, Candida. Too many, maybe. But not loving. I think that was one of the things I realized during my recovery from the accident. I wasn't good at that." He looked down at me. "I learned to love Karin—but too late. And now I love you. Did I tell you that?"

I could feel my heart going thunk, thunk. "No. You didn't actually mention it. I'm glad. Because I love you. The really humiliating part is, I think I always have. Then something usually got in the way."

"Like my charming behavior." He kissed me again. "I'm a little old for you."

"That's all right. I've always had a father complex."

After another while I said, "Will I have to join things like the altar guild?"

"No. The Church today is far more likely to ask you to picket or protest something. Wherever did a little agnostic like you learn about the altar guild?"

"Oh—word trickles down. Simon, with Diana dead, what's going to happen to all that gold?"

"It will be James's now."

"Yes, I suppose so. And the house. Do you think he'll want to sell it?"

"As one of the executors of the will I'll certainly advise it."

"To Catherine Timberlake."

"Yes."

"So it will go back to Totsie's family." Once again I shivered a little. "You know, Agnes Medora had something in the beginning of her diary, something about reaping what you sow. It was a quotation from St. Paul, I think."

"*Be not deceived, God is not mocked. For whatsoever a man soweth, that shall he also reap,*" Simon quoted.

"Yes, but old Louis didn't reap it. Diana did. And Karin. And maybe James."

"That's probably what's meant about the sins of the

340

fathers being passed to the third and fourth generations. Somebody does something to somebody else, who reacts and does something to somebody else, who reacts and does something to somebody else ... and it goes on and on that way. Cause and effect. So the debt that is incurred by one generation is paid by another. Look at slavery."

I digested that. "It's a little like what my friends who've gone into Eastern religions call karma."

"Something like that."

"Then everything could have a religious explanation."

Simon smiled. "When I was thinking about going into the Church, I talked to two people about it, one a mystic and one an atheist, and in different words they said the same thing: that religion encompasses either everything, or nothing. One of them opted for nothing, and one of them for everything."

I decided to think about that later. More comfortable with specifics, I said, "What's going to happen to James?"

"I thought he could live with us. That is, if you're agreeable."

"Yes. Of course. Do you think he'll be in trouble—legal trouble—for shooting Eric? It was an accident, after all."

"No. I'm sure they're aware of that. There certainly were enough witnesses to the fact that he fell and struck his arm." Simon hesitated then said, "But you know I did think ... I was afraid, when he first got hold of the gun that he would shoot him—not as an accident."

"Yes," I said, remembering Diana. "So did I." After a minute I said, "I'm worried about Hannibal."

"I'm afraid he won't make it. Stevens is a good man. I think he was trying to prepare James."

"Oh, poor little boy! What will he do? He adored Hannibal. But it was more than that. He'd built a sort of world around him."

"We'll just have to help him live in a more real one. The fact that you're an animal freak will help, I think."

"No, not right now. Maybe after a while. You see, Hannibal was more than just a cat. He was the ruler of Bulzartgay."

"Bulzartgay—that's what he was singing about to the tune

of 'Here We Go Round the Mulberry Bush.' "

"Yes." That reminded me of something I'd been wanting to ask. "Why did you suspect Eric of killing Donnie? Surely it wasn't just because he didn't like that tune?"

"No, but it seemed to be the final straw of a number of straws pointing towards him. When we—Eric, Diana and I— were very small, Donnie had a habit of grabbing us by the hands and whirling us around in a circle and singing it when she wanted to break up a fight or an argument or distract us. We used to kid her about it and say it was her signature tune. So when you told me yesterday that Eric didn't like it, and when he snapped at James last night in the folly for singing it, various things stirred in my head. I remembered that Eric's father was going to marry Donnie, and I also had a vague recollection that Eric didn't much like her. Like many upper servants to the rich, she was a snob, and she seemed to push Eric's social inferiority complex button. Then there was the fact that Eric's father started out as a master electrician, and Eric used to like to brag to Diana and me about how much he—Eric—knew about currents and wires and fuses. But, curiously, I could never actually remember him bragging about that after Donnie died. Anyway, the possibility that he had something to do with turning off that elevator switch had occurred to me before because, pragmatically speaking, Eric was the only one of us around there when it happened. Diana and her family were away. Eric's father was away. My family was away. The Tower Abbey servants were given holiday. The power plant cut off the house electricity for the summer, but not until the following day. The only person with a connection to Donnie in Tandem was Eric, who was at his family home with a housekeeper. But to think of Eric in that connection always seemed ludicrously farfetched. Then all of a sudden in the folly, with Eric acting like a madman, it didn't seem so farfetched. In fact, in a gruesome way, it all made sense. Which is why I started, rather inhumanely, asking questions when Eric was lying there with a bullet in him. I was pretty sure he wasn't going to pull through and I thought it was important for us to know—and for that matter, for Eric to tell it."

"Confession, in fact."

"In a sense, yes."

"Gruesome is right," I said, thinking about it. "For a not very old house there've been a lot of horrible deaths there. You know it's funny. Diana didn't know that Eric had . . . had killed Donnie, or anything about it. But she said that when she was a child, after Donnie's death, she used to think she could hear her singing that song at night." I shivered. "Do you think, now, that that's all over? That the house will be all right?"

"I hope so. I think so."

"Isn't it a strange coincidence that James should pick that song—'Here We go Round the Mulberry Bush'—for Bulzartgay's national anthem!"

"Not really. Diana probably sang it to him when he was a young child living with her, before he went over to live with Roger. After all, it was in her own memory. By the way, what is Bulzartgay—if that's the way to pronounce it?"

So I told him about Bulzartgay, whose sovereign was Hannibal, whose prime minister was Walker, and whose national scribe was James. And insofar as I could remember them, I told him about the rules and lore and history of the imaginary country. "It was all there on the map," I said.

"What map?"

I sighed. "What a normal, unimaginative, earthbound person like you would call a dirty old Persian prayer rug."

"I see."

"And the reason why Hannibal jumped through the window into the folly, or at least one of the reasons, beyond his knowledge that there were mice there, was the fact that James had made it the headquarters of Bulzartgay. His rug was there and he would go there and sing its anthem and dream up its stories, with Hannibal sitting opposite. . . ." My voice shook as I saw them in my mind again.

"I see. I was about to suggest maybe another cat right away. But I guess that would seem like lèse majesty."

"I'm afraid so, for the moment. I'm going to ask him to

help me with the gerbils and Wisteria and Pandora. And then, if he takes to them, and develops an interest in them, I'll start to work on the idea of another pet."

"So that's why he seemed so intent on dispatching Eric. Eric had done more than kill Hannibal, bad as that was. He had destroyed his inner world."

"Do you think the authorities—whoever they are here and in England—will let us take James? What about his English relations?"

"Well, none of them seemed to come forward when his father died, else you can be sure those careful lawyers would not have permitted him to come back to the care of a mother who had been declared unfit. One of the good things about being Diana's cousin, is that I do have some small family claim."

"So you are. I'd forgotten that. I'm glad. He's going to need an awful lot of loving and understanding to make up for what he's been through."

The door opened and James came slowly out. Simon and I looked at him. There were tear tracks down the thin cheeks. He ignored us and went straight over to the window. After a minute he said, "Hannibal's dead."

"I'm sorry," Simon said.

"Yes, I am, too," I said. "He was a wonderful cat."

"He was a *person*." James's voice quivered.

"He was very much a person," I agreed. It all seemed so inadequate. "I'm especially sorry about it after losing your father and having to leave Walker."

"Would you like me to get in touch with Walker for you?" Simon surprised me by asking. "We could call, or even get him to come over here if you really wanted."

There was a long silence, which I found astonishing. I had warmed to Simon's suggestion and expected the little boy to greet it with enthusiasm. But after a minute he shook his head and said, "Bulzartgay's gone, so there's no point. Not with Hannibal dead." This time his breath shook on a sob.

Simon went over to him and put his hands on his shoulders.

"Maybe you can find another Bulzartgay. Maybe it exists

344

somewhere. When I was in Italy once I felt sometimes as though, if I went around a corner quickly, I'd find the thirteenth century or the fourteenth there, still going on."

James shook his head. "Not without Hannibal," he repeated. He sounded, and looked, as though all the life had gone out of him.

"All right then, why don't you write about it?" I asked. "When you get a little older you can make a novel about it."

When he didn't say anything Simon went on. "Candida and I are going to be married very soon and we thought you might like to come and live with us."

"Yes. All right," James said, without overwhelming enthusiasm. Then he seemed to rouse himself. "That would be nice—nicer than before."

I heard that with a pang, thinking of Diana. But he was right, and in his own terms was realistic and honest.

"When you come and live with us you can help me with my animals," I said, wondering if it was the right thing to say at the moment.

"Yes, I suppose so."

"And you might think about writing it all down," Simon gently insisted. It did seem like a good idea. And any suggestion was worth trying if it would get that terrible look off James's face.

"After all," I put in. "You *are* the national scribe. You told me so. Don't you think you owe it to . . . to King Hannibal and Prime Minister Walker and . . . and the Flatlanders and the Uplanders and"—I scoured my memory "—Omneg and Bootnag to tell their story to the world?"

The defeat seemed to slide a little from his face, leaving the grief still there. Pain and life came into the dark eyes. I knew suddenly and with almost unbearable relief, that he was going to be all right.

"Yes," James said. "You're right. I *am* the national scribe. I'll write it all down properly and tell everyone about Hannibal and his kingdom."

THE END

345

I would like to acknowledge with thanks the hospitality and assistance given me by Mrs. Lilian T. Reinhardt and Mrs. Joseph N. Greene, Jr., of Seven Springs, Mt. Kisco, New York; I am also most grateful to Canon Edward West, Sub-Dean of the Cathedral Church of St. John the Divine, and the Reverend William Walsh, S.J., of the Church of St. Ignatius Loyola for their time and advice and help concerning the rite of exorcism.

I would also like to thank Lloyd Woltz for his helpful comments about metals.